Charles Stross is a full-time writer who was born in Leeds, England in 1964. He studied in London and Bradford, gaining degrees in pharmacy and computer science, and has worked in a variety of jobs, including pharmacist, technical author, software engineer and freelance journalist.

Find out more about Charles Stross at www.antipope.org/charlie/index.html or you can read more about Charles and other Orbit authors by registering for the free monthly newsletter at www.orbitbooks.co.uk

D0522501

By Charles Stross

Singularity Sky
Iron Sunrise

iron
sunrise

CHARLES STROSS

www.orbitbooks.co.uk

ORBIT

First published in Great Britain by Orbit March 2005
This edition published by Orbit August 2005

A CIP catalogue record for this book
is available from the British Library.

ISBN 1 84149 336 8

Printed and bound in Great Britain
by Mackays of Chatham plc

Orbit
An imprint of
Time Warner Book Group UK
Brettenham House
Lancaster Place
London WC2E 7EN

www.orbitbooks.co.uk

For Olivia and Howard

Acknowledgments

Thanks due to: Emmett O'Brien, Caitlin Blasdell, Andrew Wilson, Simon Bisson, Cory Doctorow, Ken MacLeod, and James Nicoll. In particular I'd like to single out Emmett, for going far beyond where any reader might be expected to; Caitlin, my agent, for asking the questions that needed asking; and Geoff Miller, for an inspiring quote.

contents

prologue:
wednesday child

IMPACT: T plus 1392 days, 12 hours, 03 minutes

Wednesday ran through the darkened corridors of the station, her heart pounding. Behind her, unseen yet sensed as a constant menacing presence, ran her relentless pursuer — a dog. The killhound wasn't supposed to be here: neither was she. Old Newfoundland Four was in the process of final evacuation, the last ship supposed to have undocked from bay green fourteen minutes ago — an icon tattooed on the inside of her left eye showed her this, time counting negative — heading out for the nearest flat space-time for the jump to safety. The launch schedule took no notice of tearaway teens, crazed Dresdener captains with secret orders, and gestapo dogs with murder burning in their gunsight eyes. She panted desperately, nerves straining on the edge of panic, lungs burning in the thin, still air. Sixteen years old and counting, and if she didn't find a way to elude the dog and climb back to the docking hub soon—

She didn't want to be there when the wavefront arrived.

Three-point-six light years away, and almost three-point-six years ago, all two hundred million inhabitants of a nondescript McWorld called Moscow had died. Moscow, an introverted if not entirely rural polity, had been in the midst of political upheavals and a nasty trade dispute with New Dresden, something boring to do with biodiversity and free trade, engineering agribusiness and exchange rate controls. Old Newfoundland Four, Portal Station Eleven, was the last remaining sovereign territory of the Federal Republic of Moscow. They'd hauled down the flag in the hub concourse four hours ago, sounded the last retreat with a final blare of brass trumpetry, and marched slowly to the docking hub. Game over, nation dissolved. There'd been a misunderstanding, and Dresdener warships had impounded a freighter from Moscow. Pistol shots fired across a crowded docking hub. Then someone – to this day, the successor Dresdener government hotly denied responsibility, even though they'd executed their predecessors just to be sure – had hit Moscow Prime with a proscribed device.

Wednesday didn't remember Moscow very clearly. Her father was a nitrogen cycle engineer, her mother a protozoan ecology specialist: they'd lived on the station since she was four, part of the team charged with keeping the life-support heart of the huge orbital complex pumping away. But now the heart was still. There was no point in pretending anymore. In less than a day the shock front of Moscow Prime's funeral pyre would slam past, wreaking havoc with any habitat not shielded by a good thirty meters of metal and rock. Old Newfie, drifting in stately orbit around a planet-less brown dwarf, was simply too big and too flimsy to weather a supernova storm at a range of just over a parsec.

Wednesday came to a crossroads. She stopped, panting, and tried to orient herself, biting back a wail of despair.

Left, right, up, or down? Sliding down to the habitat levels of the big wheel had been a mistake. There were elevators and emergency tunnels all the way up to the hub, and all the way down to the heavy zone. The central post office, traffic control, customs, and bioisolation were all located near the maintenance core at the hub. But the top of the pressurized wheel rim was sixty meters above her, then there was another hundred meters of spoke to climb before she could get to the hub, and the dog would sense her if she used the lifts. There was too much centrifugal force down here, dragging at her like real gravity; she could turn her head sharply without feeling dizzy, and her feet felt like lead. Climbing would be painfully slow at first, the Coriolis force a constant tug trying to pull her sideways off the ladder to safety.

Dim lighting panels glowed along the ceiling, turned down to Moonlight Seven. The vines in the small hubgarden at the center of the crossroads drooped, suffering already from eighteen hours of darkness. Everything down here was dead or dying, like the body she'd found in the public toilet two decks up and three segments over. When she realized the dog was still on her tail she'd headed back home to the apartment she'd shared with her parents and younger brother, hoping the scent would confuse the hound while she sneaked away onto one of the other evacuation ships. But now she was trapped down here with it, and what she should really have done was head for the traffic control offices and barricade the doors—

Her training nudged her forward. This sector was given over to administration offices, station police, customs and trade monitors, and the small clump of services that fed them during their work shifts. Darkened office doorways hung open, unattended, dust already gathering on chairs and desks. Very deliberately, she stepped into the police station. Behind the counter a public notice poster scrolled end-lessly, STATION CLOSED. Grunting with effort, she clambered over the chest-high barrier, then rolled down behind it.

The antique leather satchel Herman had told her to take banged against her hip; she cursed it and what it had brought her to. It was half-full of paper: rich, slightly creamy fabric-weave paper, written on with real ink that didn't swim and mutate into different fonts when you stroked the margin. Dumb matter, the sort of medium you used when you really, *really* didn't want some tame infowar worm to unpick your traffic. Nestled at the bottom of the bag was a locked cassette full of molecular storage – records from the station customs post. Records that somebody thought were important enough to kill for.

She twitched a ring, dialing the lights up to Twilight Three, and looked around the cop shop. She'd been there once before, when Constable Barca had given her year a tour of the premises. That had been a pointed adult hint about how to stay out of trouble. Things were different now, the offices and detention areas and waiting rooms all gaping like empty sockets in a skull. The administration thought they knew all about teenagers, but they were wrong. She'd seen the locked cupboard in the ready room and got Pete to front a question about it: sticky foam and pepper gas, breathing masks and handcuffs in case of civil disorder. *In case of riot, break glass.* Old Newfie was mostly peaceful; there'd been just one murder and only a handful of fights in the past thirty years. Admin thought a SWAT team was what you sent to deal with a wasp's nest in a ventilation duct. She paused at the locked cabinet, dumped the satchel, and grabbed something that looked more useful.

Claws rattled on the floor outside the office, and paused.

IMPACT: T plus 1392 days, 12 hours, 10 minutes

'What do you mean, she's missing?' Constable Ito said irritably. 'Can't you keep your children under—'

The tall, stooped man ran his fingers through his thinning hair. 'If you had kids – no, I'm sorry! Look, she's not here. I know she has a shipboard badge because I pinned it on her jacket myself, all right? She's not here, and I'm afraid she might have gone back home or something.'

'Home?' Ito pushed his visor up and stared at the worried father. 'She couldn't be that stupid. Could she?'

'Kids!' It came out like a curse, though it wasn't intended as one. 'No, I don't think she's that stupid. But she's not on the ship, either, or at least she's turned off her implants – Constable Klein sent out a broadcast ping for her an hour ago. And she seemed upset about something this morning.'

'Shit. Implants, huh? I'll put out a notice, all right? Things are insane around here right now. Have you any idea what it's like trying to rehouse fifteen thousand people? She'll probably turn up somewhere she isn't meant to be, crew service areas or something. Or decided to hitch a lift on *Sikorsky's Dream* for the hell of it, before she undocked. She'll turn up, that I promise you. Full ID, please?'

'Victoria Strowger. Age sixteen. ID 3 of that name.'

'Ah, okay.' Ito made an odd series of gestures with the rings on his right hand, tracing runes in copspace. 'Okay, if she's somewhere aboard this pile of junk, that should find her. If not, it'll escalate to a general search in about ten minutes. Now if you'll excuse me until then—'

'Certainly.' Morris Strowger sidled away from the Constable's desk. 'She's probably just dropped her badge down the toilet,' he muttered to himself. Behind him the next in the queue, an elderly woman, was haranguing the Constable about the size of her accommodation module: she refused to believe that her apartment – one human-sized cell in a five-thousand-person honeycomb of refugee pods slung in the cargo bay of the New Dresden freighter *Long March* – was all any of them would get until arrival in the nearest Septagon system. The relocation was paid for, gratis, courtesy of the (new) New Dresden government, and the residual assets of the Republic of Moscow's balance of trade surplus, but the pods weren't exactly the presidential suite of a luxury liner. *I hope Vicki gets tired of hiding soon. Maybe it'll do her some good if the Constabulary find her first and run her in. Teach her not to go looking for trouble in the middle of an emergency* . . .

IMPACT: T plus 1390 days

Take a girl like *that*. Pallid complexion, cropped mop of black hair, pale blue eyes: waif or demon? She was a bit of a loner. Preternaturally smart for her age: her parents planned her, used a sensible modicum of predictive genomics to avoid the more serious pitfalls. Paid for the most expensive interface implants they could buy, imported from Septagon: they wanted only the best for her. She was sixteen and sullen, going through one of those phases. Refusing to wear anything but black, spending her free time poking around in strange service ducts, training an eighteen-million-synapse nerve garden in her bedroom (parents didn't even want to think about what she might be training it to dream of). She grew plants: deadly night-shade, valerian, aconite, hemlock – and what were they going to do with the latter when it reached full height? (Nobody knew. Nobody knows.) She liked listening to depressing music in her room with the door shut. Her anxious parents shoehorned her into the usual healthy outdoor pursuits – climbing lessons, solar sailing, karate – but none of them took a grip on her imagination. Her legal forename was Victoria, but the other teens all called her Wednesday; she hated it, but not as much as she hated her given name.

Wednesday was a misfit. Like misfits from time immemorial, she'd had an invisible friend since she was young: they played together, exploring the espionage envelope. Elevator surfing. Duct diving – with an oxy mask; you could never tell what might be on the other side of a sealed bulkhead. But most kids didn't have invisible friends who talked back via the expensive net implants their parents had shelled out for, much less taught them skills like steganography, traffic analysis, tail spotting, and Dumpster diving. And most kids grew out of having invisible friends, whereas Wednesday didn't. That was because most misfit kids' invisible friends were imaginary. Wednesday's wasn't.

When she was younger she'd told her brother Jeremy about her friend, who was called Herman: but Jerm had blabbed to Mum, and the result was a tense inquisition and trips to the network engineers, then the counselor's office. When she realized what was expected of her she denied everything, of course, but not abruptly; Herman told her how to do it so as to allay their suspicions. *You're never alone with schizophrenia*, he'd joked mordantly, annoying her because she knew that schizophrenia was nothing to do with having multiple personalities, and everything to do with hearing voices in her head. When she'd first learned about it she'd dialed chlorpromazine and flupenthixol up from the kitchen pharm, and staggered around in a haze for days while Herman witheringly explained how she might have poisoned herself: Parkinson's was a not-unknown side effect of primitive neuroleptics. It wasn't a word she'd known before he used it.

Everyone had known evacuation day was coming for months. They'd known about it to the day, to the hour in fact, since a couple of weeks after the Incident. The ships began to arrive a week ahead of zero hour. Normally Old Newfie only received one liner a month, clearing via customs to transfer passengers and cargo to the short-haul local freighters that bounced back and forth across the last parsec. But right now all the docking bays on the hub were extended, piers pressurized like great gray hagfish sucking the guts out of the station.

The surviving in-system freighters had come home for the final time two weeks earlier, rerigged with ferry tanks for the final flight. Everyone huddled together on the one station, thirty thousand souls drifting above the ecliptic of a gloomy red gas giant eight times the mass of Jupiter. They had fuel — that was what Old Newfoundland Four was in the business of selling — six hundred megatons of refined methane ice bunkered in a tank farm streaming kilometers behind the axle of the big wheel. And they were close enough to one of the regular trade routes between Septagon system and the core worlds to pick up passing trade, close enough to act as an interchange for local traffic bound for Moscow. They were still profitable and self-sufficient, had been even since before the disaster. But they couldn't stay there — not with the iron sunrise coming.

The liner *Sikorsky's Dream* nuzzled up to the hub, taking VIPs and the governor and his staff. Behind it hung two freighters from New Dresden, sent in yet another symbolic gesture of reconciliation. They looked like pregnant midwife toads, blistered with bulky refugee pods hanging from their cargo spines, steerage for tens of thousands of passengers on the three-week, forty-light year journey to Septagon for resettlement.

Even Septagon would be uncomfortably close to the shock front, but it was the best relocation center on offer. There was money enough to house and reskill everyone, and a governing polity that actively courted immigration. It would be a chance to draw a line under the incident, to look to the future, and to turn away from the dull despair and the cloud of mourning that had hovered over the station since news of the Zero Incident arrived three and a half years ago. There had been suicides then, and more than one near riot; the station was haunted by a thousand ghosts for every one alive. It was no fit place to raise a child.

Dad and Mum and Jeremy had moved aboard the *Long March* two days ago, dragging Wednesday along in their glassy-eyed optimistic undertow. There were holes in the facade, empty figures in the family photograph. Cousin Jane, Uncle Mark, Grandpa and Grandma weren't coming. At least, not in the living flesh; they were dust now, burned by the godwind that would blow past the station in four days' time.

Harried wardens had shown Wednesday and her family to their deck, corridor, segment, and cell. They had a family space: four sleeping pods and a two-by-three living room with inflatable furniture. It would be home for the voyage. They were to eat in the canteen on Rose Deck, bathe in the communal hygiene unit on Tulip, and count themselves lucky for being alive at all – unlike Mica and her husband, friends and neighbors who'd been home on a month's leave for the first time in five years when the Incident took place.

Within hours, Wednesday had been bored silly. Her plants were dead, her nerve garden shut down for cold storage, and they had been ordered to remain in steerage until after departure, with nothing but the inane prattle of the entertainment net and the ship's lobotomized media repository for company. Some budding genius from New Dresden – a more regimented society than Moscow's – had decided that horror interactives and books were unfit for minors, and slapped a parental control on that section of the database. Her friends – those she counted as friends – were mostly on the other ships. Even Herman had told her he'd be unable to talk after the ship's first jump. It would have been more fun if they'd had cold sleep tankage, but there was no way that the station's facilities could process more than a couple of hundred at a time: so Wednesday was to be a martyr to boredom for the next week.

The only consolation was that she had a whole new world to explore – a starship. She hadn't been on a ship since she was eight, and the itch to put learning into practice was irresistible. Besides, Herman said he knew and could show her the layout of this particular vessel. It was a late-model Backhoe series heavy lifter fabricated in the yards over Burgundy, with life-support superstructure by Thurn und Taxis Pty of New Dresden. It was just a trash hauler – fusion rockets, contrarotating spin wheels – nothing as sophisticated as a momentum transfer unit or grav generators. Its jump module was a sealed unit purchased from someplace where they knew how to make such things; neither Dresden nor Moscow had the level of tech infrastructure necessary to throw naked singularities around. But Herman knew his way around the ship, and Wednesday was bored. So obviously it was time to go exploring; and when she told him, he had some interesting suggestions for where to go.

Wednesday was lousy at staying out of locked rooms. Her second-year tutor had summed it up: 'She's like a cat – takes a shut door as a personal insult.' She took her pick gun and tablet with her as a matter of course, not out of malice or a desire to burgle, but simply because she couldn't abide not knowing what lay on the far side of a door. (The ship had a double-walled hull, and the only doors that breached into vacuum were airlocks. Unless she was stupid enough to pick a door with flashing pressure warning lights, heavy gaskets, and mechanical interlocks, she wasn't running any risks. Or so she thought . . .)

The ship wasn't exactly off-limits to passengers, but she had a feeling her presence would be discouraged if anyone noticed her. So she sneaked up into the central service axis and back down into the crew ring the smart way: sitting on the roof of a powered elevator car, her stiction pads locked to the metal as it swam up the tunnel, decelerating and shedding angular momentum. She rode it up and down twice, searching for ventilation ducts with the aid of a torch, before she made her move. She swam through darkened service shafts, down another tube, hitched a lift on the roof of a passenger car, and surfed all the way into one of the main ventilation bronchi. The maintenance moles in the airflow system left her alone, because she was alive and moving, which was just as well, really. After an hour of hobbiting around in the ducts she was tired and a bit disoriented – and it was then that she came across the filtration hood that Herman had told her to expect.

It sat in the floor of a cramped duct, humming softly to itself, laminar pumps blurring quietly in the twilight. A faint blue glow of ultraviolet lamps shone from the edges. Fascinated, she bent close to inspect it. *Sterilizers aboard a starship?* Only in the life-support system, as a rule. But this was the accommodation deck, so what was it doing here? A quick once-over of the mounting bolts revealed another anomaly – a fine wire leading down through a hole in the floor of the duct. It was obviously an alarm cable. Not the sort of unreliable IR sensor that might be set off by a passing maintenance pig, nor a nerve garden eyeball sensor to be bamboozled by shadows, but an honest old-fashioned burglar alarm! She attacked it with her multitool and the compact maintenance kit she'd acquired a few months ago. Wires were easy—

A minute later she had the filtration hood unbolted and angled up at one side. Dropping an eyeball through was the work of seconds. Her camera-on-a-thread – disguised as a toy spider – swam in dizzy circles, revealing a cramped room, locked inner door, shelves with boxes secured to four of the walls. Purser's office or captain's locker? Wednesday couldn't tell, but it was obviously where they kept the high-value cargo, anything compact that had to be shipped in a safe under lock and key, accessible for inspection during the voyage. Deeds. Share certificates. Papers, orders, DNA samples, cypher keys, the odd rare piece of proprietary software. *'Why don't you go look?'* a familiar voice prodded her. Herman blinked a schematic behind her eyes. *'Observe: according to this original blueprint this room should be part of the Captain's quarters.'*

'Think I'll find any treasure inside?' asked Wednesday, already looking for an attachment point for her rope. The lure of forbidden fruit was more than she'd ever been able to resist.

Locked doors. A teenage girl going through one of those phases. Modifications to a standard lifesystem. Stop all the clocks: a star has died. Blue plastic toy spiders. Confidential orders handwritten on dumb paper. Invisible playmates. Badge dropped down lift shaft. Respiration stops: the universe holds its breath. And . . .

the iron sunrise

IMPACT: T zero

Just outside the expanding light cone of the present a star died, iron-bombed.

Something — some exotic force of unnatural origin — twisted a knot in space, enclosing the heart of a stellar furnace. A huge loop of superstrings twisted askew, expanding and contracting until the core of the star floated adrift in a pocket universe where the timelike dimension was rolled shut on the scale of the Planck length, and another dimension — one of the closed ones, folded shut on themselves, implied by the standard model of physics — replaced it. An enormous span of time reeled past within the pocket universe, while outside a handful of seconds ticked by.

From the perspective of the drifting core, the rest of the universe appeared to recede to infinity, vanishing past an event horizon beyond which it was destined to stay until the zone of expansion collapsed. The blazing ball of gas lit up its own private cosmos, then slowly faded. Time passed, uncountable amounts of time wrapped up in an eyeblink from the perspective of the external universe. The stellar core cooled and contracted, dimming. Eventually a black dwarf hung alone, cooling toward absolute zero. Fusion didn't stop but ran incredibly slowly, mediated by quantum tunneling under conditions of extreme cold. Over a span billions of times greater than that which had elapsed since the big bang in the universe outside, light nuclei merged, tunneling across the high quantum wall of their electron orbitals. Heavier elements disintegrated slowly, fissioning and then decaying down to iron. Mass migrated until, by the end of the process, a billion trillion years down the line, the star was a single crystal of iron crushed down into a sphere a few thousand kilometers in diameter, spinning slowly in a cold vacuum only trillionths of a degree above absolute zero.

Then the external force that had created the pocket universe went into reverse, snapping shut the pocket and dropping the dense spherical crystal into the hole at the core of the star, less than thirty seconds after the bomb had gone off. And the gates of hell opened.

Iron doesn't fuse easily: the process is endothermic, absorbing energy. When the guts were scooped out of the star and replaced with a tiny cannonball of cold degenerate matter, the outer layers of the star, held away from the core by radiation pressure, began to collapse inward across a gap of roughly a quarter million kilometers of cold vacuum. The outer shell rushed in fast, accelerating in the grip of a stellar gravity well. Minutes passed, and from the outside the photosphere of the star appeared to contract slightly as huge vortices of hot turbulent gas swirled and fulminated across it. Then the hammerblow of the implosion front reached the core . . .

There was scant warning for the inhabitants of the planet that had been targeted for murder. For a few minutes, star-watching satellites reported an imminent solar flare, irregularities leading to atmospheric effects, aurorae, and storm warnings for orbital workers and miners in the asteroid belt. Maybe one or two of the satellites had causal channels, limited bandwidth instantaneous communicators, unjammable but expensive and touchy. But there wasn't enough warning to help anyone escape: the satellites simply went off-line one by one as a wave of failure crept outward from the star at the speed of light. In one research institute a meteorologist frowned at her workstation in bemusement, and tried to drill down a diagnostic – she was the only person on the planet who had time to realize something strange was happening. But the satellites she was tracking orbited only three light minutes closer to the star than the planet she lived on, and already she had lost two minutes chatting to a colleague about to go on her lunch break about the price of a house she would never buy now, out on the shore of a bay of lost dreams.

The hammerfall was a spherical shock wave of hydrogen plasma, blazing at a temperature of millions of degrees and compressed until it had many of the properties of metal. A hundred times as massive as the largest gas giant in the star system, by the time it slammed into the crystal of iron at the heart of the murdered star it was traveling at almost 2 percent of lightspeed. When it struck, a tenth of the gravitational potential energy of the star was converted into radiation in a matter of seconds. Fusion restarted, exotic reactions taking place as even the iron core began to soak up nuclei, building heavier and hotter and less stable intermediaries. In less than ten seconds, the star burned through a visible percentage of its fuel, enough to keep the fires banked for a billion years. There wasn't enough mass in the G-type dwarf to exceed the electron degeneracy pressure in its core, collapsing it into a neutron star, but nevertheless a respectable shock front, almost a hundredth as potent as a supernova, rebounded from the core.

A huge pulse of neutrinos erupted outward, carrying away much of the energy from the prompt fusion burn. The neutral particles didn't usually react with matter; the average neutrino could zip through a light year of lead without noticing. But there were so many of them that, as they sluiced through the outer layers of the star, they deposited a good chunk of their energy in the roiling bubble of foggy plasma that had replaced the photosphere. Not far behind them, a tidal wave of hard gamma radiation and neutrons a billion times brighter than the star ripped through the lower layers, blasting them apart. The dying star flashed a brilliant X-ray pulse like a trillion hydrogen bombs detonating in concert: and the neutrino pulse rolled out at the speed of light.

Eight minutes later – about a minute after she noticed the problem with the flare monitors – the meteorologist frowned. A hot, prickling flush seemed to crawl across her skin, itching: her vision was inexplicably streaked by crawling purple meteors. The desk in front of her flickered and died. She inhaled, smelling the sharp stink of ozone, looked round shaking her head to clear the sudden fog, and saw her colleague staring at her and blinking. 'Hey, I feel like somebody just walked on my grave—' The lights flickered and died, but she had no trouble seeing because the air was alive with an eerie glow, and the small skylight window cast razor-sharp shadows on the floor. Then the patch of floor directly illuminated by the window began to smoke, and the meteorologist realized, fuzzily, that she wasn't going to buy that house after all, wasn't going to tell her partner about it, wasn't ever going to see him again, or her parents, or her sister, or anything but that smoking square of brilliance that was slowly growing as the window frame burned away.

She received a small mercy: mere seconds later the upper atmosphere – turned into an anvil of plasma by the passing radiation pulse – reached the tropopause. Half a minute later the first shock wave leveled her building. She didn't die alone; despite the lethal dose they all received from the neutrino pulse, nobody on the planet lived past the iron sunrise for long enough to feel the pangs of radiation sickness.

IMPACT: T plus 1392 days, 12 hours, 16 minutes

Wednesday hid under the desk, heart pounding with terror, clutching a stubby cylinder. She'd seen the body of the customs officer stuffed inside the darkened kitchen; realized he was dead, like the handwritten instructions in the diplomatic pouch said. Now the thing that did it was coming for her, and she wished—

There was a scratching click of claws on polycellulose flooring. I *don't want to be here,* she prayed, fingers slipping around the sweat-lubed cylinder. *This isn't happening to me!* She could see the hellhound outside, imagining it in her mind's eye: jaws like diamond saw blades, wide-set eyes glowing with the overspill from its phased-array lidar. She could see the small, vicious gun implanted in its hollow skull, its brains governed by a set of embedded computers to override its Doberman instincts. Fist-sized overlapping bald patches, psoriatic skin thickening over diamond mesh armor. It could smell her fear. She'd read the papers in the strong room, realized how important they must be, and pushed the door ajar, thinking to leave – yanked it shut barely ahead of the snarl and the leap. Acrid smoke had curled up from the hinges as she scrambled into the duct-work, fled like a black-clad spider into the service axis and through the pressurized cargo tunnel and the shadows of the almost-empty dock, panting and crying as she went. Always hearing a scrabble of diamond-tipped claws on the floor behind her. *I don't exist. You can't smell me!*

Herman – as usual, when she needed him most – wasn't talking.

The dog could smell her – or smell someone. She'd tabbed into a public term and watched the dog, or one of its cousins, stalk across the loading bay like the spectral, elongated shadow of a wolf – something born in frozen forests beneath a midnight sun, evolved to lope across the cyborg-infested tundra of an alien world. It had glanced at the hidden camera with glowing eyes, a glow that spun into static as it locked on and fired. It could sneeze nerve gas and shit land mines, if you believed her kid brother Jerm's cheap third-person scripted arcventures; a product of a more sophisticated technosphere than Moscow's, its muscles didn't run on anything as primitive as actin/myosin contraction, and its bones were built for leverage – a hellhound running at full power hissed like a primitive locomotive, dissipating waste heat as steam hot enough to scald anyone who got too close.

She raised the riot cartridge, fingers tightening on the trigger switch, and pointed it at the doorway. Dim shadow of legs, *too many legs*. They paused, and the shadow swung across the wall, homing in. She squished down on the trigger and the canister kicked back at her hands as a terrible clatter rushed towards her and the air in front turned black. *No, blue: like the dead man's tongue, lying there.* The paper said all but one copy of the data cartridge containing the customs transfer log were to be destroyed, and anyone who knew was to die. A tenuous aerogel foam bubbled and farted, rushing out into a ballooning mass as the dog lunged forward, teeth snapping, making a soft growling sound deep in its throat. It thumped against her feet in a soap-bubble cocoon, the growl turning into a deafening moaning howl of frustration.

Shuddering, Wednesday shuffled backward, pushing the heavy desk over as she stood up. She looked around wildly. The dog's hind legs scrabbled at the floor, driving it after her. She could see a glow of rage in its eyes as it struggled with the sticky antipersonnel foam. 'Good doggie,' she said vacuously, backing away, wondering inanely if she should hit it. But no, if a hellhound thought you had won, it would blow itself up, wouldn't it? They always did that in the arcventures—

Something cold and wet stubbed itself against the back of her neck, and snuffled damply. She sagged, her knees and stomach turning to sacks of ice water; paw-fingers like bone clamped tight on her shoulders, holding her upright. Her eyelid monitor flickered, then died as the lights came up. The hound on the floor seemed to grin up at her – no, *past* her. When he spoke, his voice was surprisingly human, a deep gravelly growl converging from three directions. 'Victoria Strowger, this is emergency police pack four-alpha. By order of Captain Mannheim, superintending evacuation process for Old Newfoundland, we are placing you under arrest. You will return with us to the main hub traffic bay to await uplift. I must caution you that any resistance you offer may be dealt with using weapons of nonlethal intent. Running back aboard this habitat was a senseless waste of police time.' Two of the voices fell silent, but a third continued: 'And while we're about it, why *were* you running away?'

IMPACT: T plus 1392 days, 12 hours, 38 minutes

Twenty-two minutes past departure time and the dogs had rounded up the last stray lamb, herding her into the service lock. Captain Mannheim had other things to worry about this instant, like topping off the number four tank and making sure Misha vented the surplus ullage pressure and kept the flow temperature within good limits. Then he was going to run the launch plan and get the hell out of this ghost system before the storm front blew in, and once clear he'd have it out with the guard dogs. (And why had they let some interfering punk kid sneak around the service core in the first place?) And then . . .

Twenty-two minutes! More than a thousand seconds overdue! There was room for slippage on the critical path – nobody would be insane enough not to make some allowances – but with five thousand passengers, twenty-two minutes meant all of three person-months of consumables gone just like that, virtually in an eyeblink. The refugee pods had an open-loop life-support system, there being no room for recycling tankage on this relief flight, so the whole exercise was running into millions, tens of millions. Some dumb kid had just cost the burghers of New Dresden about, oh, two thousand marks, and Captain Mannheim about two thousand extra gray hairs.

'What's our criticality profile looking like?' he demanded, leaning over to glare at Gertrude's station.

'Ah, all nominal, sir.' Gertrude stared fixedly ahead, refusing to meet his eye.

'Then keep it that way,' he snapped. 'Misha! That tank of yours!'

'Vented and closed out within tolerances.' Misha grinned breezily from across the bridge. 'The load-out is looking sweet. Oh, and for once the toilet plumbing on number two isn't rattling.'

'Good.' Mannheim sniffed. The number two reaction motor's mass-flow plumbing suffered from occasional turbulence, especially when the hydrogen slurry feeding it went over sixteen degrees absolute. The turbulence wasn't particularly serious unless it turned to outright cavitation, with big bubbles of supercooled gases fizzing inside the pipes that fed reaction mass to the fusion rockets. But *that* was potentially catastrophic, and they didn't have any margin for repairs. Not for the first time, Mannheim's thoughts turned enviously to the beautiful, high-tech liner from Novya Romanov that had pulled out six hours ago on an invisible wave of curved space-time, surfing in the grip of an extremal singularity. No messing with balky, mass-guzzling antiquated fusion rockets for *Sikorsky's Dream!* But the *Long March* was as sophisticated a ship as anything the Dresdener merchant syndicate could afford, and he'd do as well with it as was humanly possible. 'Ship! What's our sequence entry status?'

The robotically smooth voice of the autopilot rolled across the bridge. 'Kerberos unit and final passenger boarding notified two minutes ago and counting. Critical path elements in place. Entry status green, no exceptions raised—'

'Then commence launch cycle immediately.'

'Aye. Launch cycle commencing. Station power and utility disconnect proceeding. Station mass transfer disconnect proceeding. Boarding pier disconnect proceeding. Main engine spin-up engaged, station one. Live cargo systems spin-down engaged, station two.'

'I hate live cargo,' Gertrude muttered. 'Live cargo spin-down notification going out.' Fingers tapped invisible cells in the air in front of her face. 'Hub lift interlocks to safe—'

Mannheim stared at the complex web of dependencies that hovered over the blank wall of the bridge, a meter in front of his nose. Slowly, red nodes blinked to green as the huge starship prepared to cast free of the station. It was supposed to be the last ship ever to sail from this port. From time to time, he prodded a station glyph and spoke quietly to whoever's voice answered from the thin air: loadmasters and supercargo and immigration control officers and civil polizei, Jack in the drive damage control center and Rudi in the crow's nest. Once he even talked to Traffic Control. The station's robot minders plodded on imperturbably, unaware that the end of their labor was in sight, coursing toward them on an expanding shock front of radiation-driven plasma. An hour went by. Someone invisible placed a mug of coffee at his right hand, and he drank, carried on talking and watching and occasionally cursing in a quiet voice, and drank again and it was cold.

Finally, the ship was ready to depart.

IMPACT: T plus 8 minutes – 1.5 hours

Moscow system died at the speed of light, death rippling outward on a tsunami of radiation.

First to die were the weather satellites, close in on the star, watching for solar flares and prominences. Buoys built to track breezes were ripped adrift by the tornado blast of the artificially induced nova, not so much disabled as evaporated, adding their stripped nuclei to the boiling fury of the iron sunrise.

Seconds later the radiation pulse melted the huge, flimsy solar collectors that glided in stately orbit half an astronomical unit out, feeding power to antimatter generators a hundred kilometers in diameter. Robot factories unattended by humans passed unmourned and unnoticed. The gamma pulse shed by their tons of stored antihydrogen added a candle glow to the hurricane.

Eight minutes after detonation, the radiation front reached the innermost human habitat in the system: the world called Moscow. The neutrino flux was high enough to deliver a rapidly lethal radiation dose even after traveling right through the planet. The nightside fluoresced, atmosphere glowing dimly against the unbearably bright background. The gamma pulse, close behind it, flashed the dayside atmosphere to plasma and slammed it into the already melting rock. Supersonic tornadoes rippled around the daylight terminator, scouring the surface down to bedrock.

Half an hour into the nova, the process of planetary disintegration was well under way. On the dayside, Moscow's atmospheric pressure dropped drastically, and the primary gaseous constituents were hydrogen and oxygen radicals stripped from the boiling fog that had been the boreal ocean. Cloud top temperatures were already in the thousands of degrees, while Mach waves rippled through the turgid troposphere on the nightside, crushing houses like matchwood kindling to become pyres for the dying bodies of their occupants. The night receded before a ghastly daylight, the sullen glare of an exploding star reflected off the planet's own comet trail of air. To an observer at ground level Moscow Prime would have covered half the sky, a magnesium flare of radiant energy that would still be bright enough to burn out eyeballs tens of trillions of kilometers away. The main shock wave of the explosion was approaching by then, a wave of plasma flash-heated to hundreds of millions of degrees, barely less dense than the dissipated atmosphere and traveling outward at 20 percent of lightspeed. When it arrived, Moscow vanished – swallowed like a watermelon at ground zero in the expanding fireball of an atomic explosion.

Sixty minutes: the radiation pulse ghosted through the rings of Siberia, a huge green ice giant with attendant moons strung around it like lucent pearls. They flashed briefly and sprouted streamers of glowing gas as the rings flared violet, forming a huge glowing disk of light that jetted outward from the star, consuming the mass of a small moon in seconds. Siberia absorbed a huge pulse of energy, sufficient to melt the tundra at its core and spawn gigantic storms. Hurricanes the size of Moscow raced toward the nightside of the giant planet as it, too, sprouted a glowing cometary tail. Unlike the inner bodies, Siberia was too huge to evaporate entirely. Though it glowed white-hot and molten, and its orbital track was distorted by the tremendous shock wave of the stellar explosion, the innermost core of nickel-iron remained – a gravestone marker that would take millions of years to cool in the twilight emptiness of Moscow system.

The first survivor weathered the blast at a range of ninety-eight light minutes.

Sleeping in deep orbit around the outer gas giant Zemlya, a robot beacon blinked awake at the first harsh glare of energy. The beacon carried huge reserves of coolant within its faceted black-armored carapace. Designed to withstand direct hits from a battleship's laser grid, it weathered the storm – although it was sent tumbling, blasted right out of its seventy-year orbit by the surge of heavy charged particles. The beacon was 118 years old, one of 750 in its series. Code-named TALIGENT SPARROW, it was part of the early warning system of the Strategic Retaliation Command of the recently vaporized Moscow Foreign Office.

TALIGENT SPARROW blinked and took stock. The stars

were occluded by glowing gas and debris, some of them its own ablated skin. No matter: it had a task. Deep memory remembered the pattern of the seasons and turned sensors in search of Moscow. It tried vainly to swivel a high-gain antenna that had been reduced to a crumpled mass of molten tissue. Other sensors tried to distinguish the gamma flux of inbound relativistic missiles and failed, overloaded. A primitive expert system plumbed the depths of its decision tree and determined that something unknown had attacked it. Qubits trickled into entropy as TALIGENT SPARROW powered up its causal channel and shrieked murder at the uncaring stars.

Somebody heard.

IMPACT: T plus 1392 days, 13 hours, 02 minutes

The police drone was robotically curt. 'We've found your daughter. Please come to deck G-red, zone two meeting point, and collect her.'

Morris Strowger stood up and glanced at his wife. He smiled. 'I told you they'd find her.' The smile slowly faded.

His wife didn't look up. With her bony fingers thrust together between her knees and her bowed head, Indica Strowger's shoulders shook as if she'd grabbed hold of a live power supply. 'Go away,' she said very quietly, her voice hard and controlled. 'I'll be all right.'

'If you're sure—' Already the police drone was moving off. He glanced back uncertainly at her hunched form, then followed the insect away through crowded, human-smelling partition-runs, runs that were already deteriorating into a high-tech slum patrolled by bees with stun guns. Something about their departure, perhaps the final grim reality of dispossession, had snapped a band of tension that had held everyone together through the dark years just ended, and the solid ground of depression was giving way to a treacherous slurry of despair, hysteria, and uncertainty about the future. Dangerous times.

Wednesday was waiting at the meeting point just as the bee had said. She looked alone and afraid, and Morris, who had been thinking of harsh words, suddenly found himself unable to speak. 'Vicki—'

'Dad!' She buried her chin in his shoulder, sharp-jawed like some young feral predator. She was shaking.

'Where've you been? Your mother's been going crazy!' That wasn't the half of it. He hugged her, firmly, feeling a terrible sense of hollow unease ebb away. His daughter was back, and he was angry as hell at her – and unspeakably relieved.

'I wanted to be alone,' she said very quietly, voice muffled. He tried to step back, but she refused to let go. A pang: she did that when she didn't want to tell him something. She was no good at dissembling, but her sense of privacy was acute. An old woman behind him was raising a fuss at the harassed constable, something about a missing boy – no, her pet dog. Her son, her Sonny. Wednesday looked up at him. 'I needed time to think.' The lie solidified in a crystal moment, and he didn't have the heart to call her on it. There'd be time for that, and to tell her about the official reprimand later: trespassing off-limits on board a ship wasn't the same as exploring the empty quadrants of a station. She didn't know how lucky she was that the Captain was understanding – and that unusual allowances were being made for stressed-out adults, never mind kids leaving home for the first time they could remember.

'Come on.' He turned her away from the desk, rubbed her shoulder. 'Come on. Back to our, uh, cabin. Ship's undocking soon. They'll be widecasting from the bridge. You don't want to miss that?'

She looked up at him, an unreadable, serious expression on her face. 'Oh, no.'

IMPACT: T plus 4 hours, 6 minutes

Two hundred and forty-six minutes after the Zero Incident, the freighter *Taxis Pride* congealed out of empty space, forty-six degrees out of the plane of the ecliptic, six light hours away from its final destination. Brad Mornington, skipper, was on the flight deck, nattering with Mary Haight, the relativistics op. *Taxis Pride* was a three-point shuttle, connecting Moscow to Iceland Seven station, thence to the Septagonese trans-shipment outpost at Blaylock B. Brad had made this zone transfer eighteen times in the past seven years, and it was as routine as the mug of strong, heavily sugared coffee that Alex placed by his elbow before the jump countdown commenced, which was just then cooling down enough to drink.

Brad put out the standard navigation squawk and waited for a detailed flight path. In the meantime he pondered the food situation: the kitchen was getting somewhat monotonous, and the downside ferry would give him a chance to stretch his legs and reacquaint himself with clouds and sky again. *Taxis Pride* was a fast freighter, built to carry time-critical physical mail and perishables. The extremal singularity in her drive core let her accelerate in real space as rapidly as some warships: six light hours was a one-week cruise for her, not the painful odyssey an old hydrogen burner would have to endure. Mary concentrated on a backup star fix – routine, in case the traffic controllers were on strike again, just to keep her professional certification up to date. In her spare moments she was wondering if there'd be time to drop in on an old friend while they were docked for their cargo load cycle.

Then the bridge screamer went off.

'What the – get that!' Brad's coffee went flying as he scrambled for the comm terminal. Mary jolted upright, whey-faced.

'Got it. That's not traffic—'

'Hello, this is flight Echo Gold Nine Zero responding to broadcast squawk from, ah, Delta X-ray Zeus Seven, we have handshake. What's the—'

'Something flaky here, boss—'

Red flashing lights blinked on the conference circuit. There was a thirty-second delay while they waited tensely for a reply.

'Echo Gold Nine Zero this is Delta X-ray Zeus Seven, emergency relay service. Admiralty signal blue four, authentication follows message. This is a systemwide military emergency. Moscow is under quarantine – the whole system is under lockdown, no exceptions. Evacuate immediately. I emphasize, get your kernel spun up and get out of here immediately! Please acknowledge.'

Brad flushed, furious. 'This is some sort of fucking joke!' He waved off the authentication code and punched in the waypoint series for Moscow. 'When I find the asshole—'

'Brad. Come here.' He looked round sharply. Mary was leaning over the repeater from Wang's crow's nest downstairs. She looked sick.

'What is it?'

'Here.' She pointed to a plot that had just shown up. *Taxis Pride* was a fleet auxiliary, liable for mobilization in event of war: it carried near-military-grade passive sensors. 'Gamma plot, classic proton-antiproton curve, about two AUs out. It's redshifting on us. I got a fix on that relay service buoy, Brad: it's at the origin point for that . . . burn.'

'Shit!' The screen swam in front of Brad's eyes. All of a

sudden he remembered what it was like when he was nine, when his father told him his dog had died. '*Shit!*' Positronium was an unstable intermediate created during some matter-antimatter reactions. Redshifted, it was moving away from the reference frame of the observer at some fraction of the speed of light. Out from the star, it could mean only one thing – slower-than-light antimatter rockets, relativistic retaliation bombers cranking up for a kamikaze run on someone's home world. 'They've *launched*. They've fucking launched the deterrent fleet!'

They were a long-practiced team: he didn't have to tell Mary what to do. She was already bringing back up the gravitational potential maps he'd need for the jump. Brad canceled his half-planned course and fed in the return journey jump coordinates. 'Hello Delta X-ray Zeus Seven, this is flight Echo Gold Nine Zero acknowledging. We are preparing to return to Iceland Seven soonest. Can you clarify the situation for us. Other shipping may be in the queue and need warning off. Do you need assistance? Over.' Then he got on the blower to Liz, down in kernel monitoring, explaining to her that, no, this wasn't a joke, and yes, he was going to overrun the drive maintenance cycle, and yes, it was going to put the *Pride* in the dock for a month and there was a good reason for it all—

'Echo Gold Nine Zero, departure cleared. This is Delta X-ray Zeus Seven, relaying through NavServ buoy six-nine-three via causal channel. Situation as follows: inner system exterminated by surprise attack using weapons of mass destruction approximately two-seven-zero minutes ago absolute time. Your range three-six-zero light minutes considered marginal for survival: the star's gone. We're assuming one hundred percent fatalities on Moscow, repeat, *one hundred percent.* V-force has launched, but we've got no idea who did it. As of two hours ago, Moscow

system is under complete interdict. Wait—' for a moment
the steady voice wavered. 'Oh. Oh my! That felt weird.' A
pause. 'Echo Gold Nine Zero, we've just taken a core radiation pulse. Funny, two kilometers of rock shielding
outside us. Ah, shit. Off the scale. Neutrinos, has to be.
Echo Gold Nine Zero, this is Delta X-ray Zeus Seven,
there's – I don't think there's anything you can do for us.
Get the hell out while you still can – warn everybody off.
Signing off now.'

Brad stared at the comm status display without seeing it.
Then he mashed his palm down on the general channel
glyph. 'Crew, captain speaking.' He glanced at Mary and
saw her staring back at him. Waiting. 'We have a situation.
Change of plan.' Glancing down at his panel he blinked and
dragged the urgent course correction into the flight
sequence. 'We're not going home. *Ever.*'

Taxis Pride was the first ship to leave Moscow system
after the explosion. Another two ships made it out, one of
them badly damaged by jumping into the tail of the
shock wave. Word of the explosion filtered out: several
freighters were saved from jumping into a fiery grave by
dint of a massive and well-coordinated emergency alert.
Over the next few weeks, the inhabitants of the Iceland
Seven refinery station – a mere eight light months from
Moscow – were evacuated to Shenjen Principality, and as
the shock wave rolled outward, more vulnerable habitats
were evacuated in turn. The nearest populated planetary
system, Septagon Central, was far enough away to be
saved by the heavy radiation shielding on its orbital
republics. Meanwhile, years would pass before another
starship visited the radiation-scarred corpse of Moscow
system.

IMPACT: T plus 1392 days, 18 hours, 11 minutes

'What's your finding?' demanded the Captain.

The three dogs grinned at him from their positions around his cramped day cabin. One of them bent to lick at a patch of blue foam sticking to its left hind leg. The foam hissed and smoked where saliva ran. 'There is nothing to report on the first incident, the customs officer. We regret to inform you that he must be classed as missing, presumed dead, unless we subsequently learn that he boarded one of the other ships. The second incident was a juvenile delinquent escapade committed by an asocial teenager. No trusted subsystems appear to have been compromised. I have no direct access to the cargo carried in the security zone, but you have assured me yourself that none of the black manifest packages are missing. The recorded history of the delinquent is consistent with this event, as is her subsequent behavior, and a search of the documentation corpus pertaining to socialization of juvenile adults in prewar New Moscow society indicates that territorial escapades of this kind are a not-infrequent response to environmental stress.'

'Why did she get in there in the first place?' Mannheim leaned forward, glaring at the lead hellhound with a mixture of anxiety and distrust. 'I thought you were supposed to be guarding—'

'In my judgment her actions are compatible with typical human adolescent dysfunctional behavior. This search-and-rescue security unit is not authorized to use lethal force to protect bonded cargo, Captain. A secondary consideration was that her absence had been noticed by familial parties and formally reported after she was officially transferred aboard the evacuation ferry. Remanding the delinquent into the care of her parents, with subsequent monitoring and supervision for the duration of the voyage, will prevent repetition and will not invite further attention.'

The dog that had been talking jerked its head pompously. One of its fellows padded over and sniffed at its left ear. Mannheim watched them nervously. Police dogs, incredibly expensive units bought from some out-system high-tech polity, programmed for loyalty to the regime: he'd never even seen any before this voyage, was startled to learn the government owned any, much less that they'd see fit to deploy them on something as mundane as an evacuation run. And then, one of them claimed to be a Foreign Office dog, loaded onto his ship along with orders – sealed orders handwritten on paper for his eyes only – to be turned loose on the ship. Uplifted dogs designed for security and search-and-rescue, a pack hiding one member capable of killing. Exotic sapient weapons.

'Did you carry out your mission?'

Number one dog looked at him. 'What are you talking about?'

'Eh?' Mannheim straightened up. 'Now look here,' he began angrily, 'this is my ship! I'm responsible for everyone and everything on it, and if I need to know something I—'

The dogs stood up simultaneously, and he realized they had him surrounded. Gun-muzzle faces pointed at him, a thousand-yard stare repeated three times over. The FO dog spoke up: the others seemed to be under its control in some way. 'We could tell you, Captain, but then we would have to silence you. Speculation on this matter by parties not authorized by the Ministry of War is deemed to be a hostile act, within the meaning of section two, paragraph four-three-one of the Defense of the Realm Act. Please confirm your understanding of this declaration.'

'I—' Mannheim gulped. 'I understand. No more questions.'

'Good.' The number two dog sat down again, and unconcernedly set about licking the inside of its right hind leg. 'The other units of this pack are not cognizant of these affairs. They're just simple secret police dogs. You are not to trouble them with unpleasant questions. This debriefing is at an end. I believe you have a ship to run?'

IMPACT: T plus 1393 days, 02 hours, 01 minutes

Wednesday watched the end of the world with her parents and half the occupants of the Rose Deck canteen. The tables and benches had been deflated and pushed back against one wall while the ship was under boost. Now a large screen had been drawn across the opposite wall and configured with a view piped down from the hub sensor array. She had wanted to watch on her own personal slate, but her parents had dragged her along to the canteen: it seemed like most people didn't want to be alone for the jump. Not that anybody would know it had happened – contrary to dramatic license, there was absolutely no sensation when a starship tunneled between two equipotent locations across the light years – but there was something symbolic about this one. A milestone they'd never see again.

'Herman?' she subvocalized.

'*I'm here. Not for much longer. You'll be alone after the jump.*'

'I don't understand. Why?' Jeremy was staring at her so she grimaced horribly at him. He jumped back, right into the wall, and his mother glared at him.

'*Causal channels don't work after a jump outside their original light cone: they're instantaneous communicators, but they don't violate causality. Move the entangled quantum dots apart via FTL and you break the quantum entanglement they rely on. As I speak to you through one that is wired into your access implant,*' *and that is how you speak to me, I will be out of contact for some time after you arrive. However, you are in no danger as long as you remain in the evacuation area and do nothing to attract attention.'*

She rolled her eyes. As invisible friends went, Herman could do an unpleasantly good imitation of a pompous youth leader. Dark emptiness sprinkled with the jewel points of stars covered the far wall, a quiet surf of conversation rippling across the beach of heads in front of her. A familiar chill washed through her: too many questions, too little time to ask them. 'Why did they let me go?'

'You were not recognized as a threat. If you were, I would not have asked you to go. Forgive me. There is little time remaining. What you achieved was more important than I can tell you, and I am grateful for it.'

'So what did I accomplish? Was it really worth it for those papers?'

'I cannot tell you yet. The first jump is due in less than two minutes. At that point we lose contact. You will be busy after that: Septagon is not like Old Newfoundland. Take care: I will be in touch when the time is right.'

'Is something wrong, Vicki?' With a start she realized her father was watching her.

'Nothing, Dad.' Instinctive dismissal: *Where did he learn to be so patronizing?* 'What's going to happen?'

Morris Strowger shrugged. 'We, uh, have to make five jumps before we arrive where we're going. The first—' He swallowed. 'Home, uh, the explosion, is off to one side. You know what a conic section is?'

'Don't talk down to me.' She nearly bit her tongue when she saw his expression. 'Yes, Dad. I've done analytic geometry.'

'Okay. The explosion is expanding in a sphere centered on, on, uh, home. We're following a straight line – actually, a zigzag around a straight line between equipotent points in space-time – from the station, which is outside the sphere, to Septagon, which is outside the sphere of the explosion but on the other side. Our first jump takes us within the sphere of the explosion, about three light months inside it. The next jump takes us back out the other side.'

'We're going into the explosion?'

Morris reached out and took her hand. 'Yes, dear. It's—' He looked at the screen again, ducking to see past one of the heads blocking the way. Mum, Indica, was holding Jeremy, facing the screen: she had her hands on his shoulders. 'It's not dangerous,' he added. 'The really bad stuff is all concentrated in the shock front, which is only a couple of light days thick. Our shielding can cope with anything else; otherwise, Captain Mannheim would be taking us around the explosion. But that would take much longer, so—' He fell silent. A heavily accented voice echoed from the screen.

'Attention. This is your captain speaking. In about one minute we will commence jump transit for Septagon Central. We have a series of five jumps at seventy-hour intervals except for the fourth, which will be delayed eighteen hours. Our first jump takes us inside the shock front of the supernova: religionists may wish to attend the multifaith service of remembrance on G deck in three hours' time. Thank you.'

The voice stopped abruptly, as if cut off. A stopwatch appeared in one corner of the wall, counting down the seconds. 'What will we do now?' Wednesday asked quietly.

Her father looked uncomfortable. 'Find somewhere to live. They said they'd help us. Your mother and I will look for work, I suppose. Try to fit in—'

The black-jeweled sky shimmered, rainbow lights casting many-colored shadows across the watchers. A collective sigh went up: the wall-screen view of space was gone, replaced by the most insanely beautiful thing she had ever seen. Great shimmering curtains of green and red and purple light blocked out the stars, gauzy shrouds of fluorescent silk streaming in a wild breeze. At their heart, a brilliant diamond shone in the cosmos, a bloodred dumbbell of light growing from its poles. 'Herman?' she whispered to herself 'Do you see that?' But there was no reply: and suddenly she felt empty, as hollow as the interior of the baby nebula the ship now floated in. 'All gone,' she said aloud, and suddenly there were tears in her eyes: she made no protest when her father gathered her in his arms. He was crying, too, great racking sobs making his shoulders shake: she wondered what he could be missing for a moment, then caught its palest shadow and shuddered.

out of the frying pan

'May I ask what I'm accused of?' Rachel asked for the third time. *Don't let them get to you*, she told herself, forcing her face into a bland smile: *One slip and they'll hang you out to dry*.

The daylight filtering through the window-wall was tinted pale blue by the slab of dumb aerogel, the sky above the distant mountains dimmed to a remote purple. Behind the heads of her inquisitors she focused on the contrail of a commuter plane scratching its way across the glass-smooth stratosphere.

'There are no *charges*,' the leader of the kangaroo court said, smiling right back at her. 'You haven't broken any regulations, have you?' The man next to her cleared his throat. 'Well, none of *ours*,' she added, her exaggeratedly dyed lips curling minutely in distaste. Rachel focused on her hairline. Madam Chairman was dressed in an exaggeratedly femme historical style – perhaps to add a touch of velvet and lace to her S&M management style – but a ringlet of hair had broken free of whatever chemical cosh she used to discipline it, and threatened to flop over one razor-finished eyebrow in a quizzical curl.

'The excursion to Rochard's World was not my initiative, as I pointed out in my report,' Rachel calmly repeated, despite the urge to reach across the table and tweak Madam Chairman's hairdo. *Damn, I'd like to see you manage a field operation gone bad,* she thought. 'George Cho got the runaround from the New Republican government, the idiots had *already* decided to violate the Third Commandment before I arrived on the scene, and if I hadn't been in position, there wouldn't have been *anybody* on the ground when the shit hit the fan. So George sent me. As I think I've already stated, you're not cleared to read the full report. But that's not what this is about, is it?'

She leaned back and took a sip from her water glass, staring at the chief mugger through half-closed eyes. Madam Chairman the honorable Seat Warmer, who evidently rejoiced under the name of Gilda something-or-other, took advantage of the pause to lean sideways and whisper something in Minion Number One's ear. Rachel put her glass down and smiled tightly at Madam Chairman. She had the soul of an auditor and a coterie of gray yes-people; she'd come for Rachel out of nowhere the day before, armed with a remit to audit her and a list of questions as long as her arm, mostly centering on Rachel's last posting outside the terrestrial light cone. It had been clear from the start that she didn't know what the hell Rachel did for the diplomatic service, and didn't care. What she was pissed off about was the fact that Rachel was listed on the budget as an entertainments officer or cultural attaché – a glorified bribe factor for the department of trade – and that this was *her* turf. The fact that Rachel's listing was actually a cover for a very different job clearly didn't mean anything to her.

Rachel fixed Madam Chairman with her best poker face. 'What you're digging for is who it was that authorized George to send me to Rochard's World, and who ordered the budget spend. The long and the short of that is, it's outside your remit. If you think you've got need to know, take it up with Security.'

She smiled thinly. She'd been assigned to Cho's legation to the New Republic on the Ents payroll, but was really there for a black-bag job; she answered to the Black Chamber, and Madam Chairman would run into a brick wall as soon as she tried to pursue the matter there. But the Black Chamber had to maintain Rachel's official cover – the UN had an open hearings policy on audits to reassure its shareholders that their subscriptions were being spent equitably – and she was consequently stuck with going through the motions. Up to and including being fired for misappropriation of funds if some bureaucratic greasy-pole climber decided she was a good back to stab on the way up. It was just one of the risks that went with the job of being a covert arms control inspector.

Gilda's own smile slid imperceptibly into a frown. Her politician-model cosmetic implant didn't know how to interpret such an unprogrammed mood: for a moment, bluish scales hazed into view on her cheeks, and her pupils formed vertical slits. Then the lizard look faded. 'I disagree,' she said airily, waving away the objection. 'It was your job, as officer on-site, to account for expenditure on line items. The UN is *not* made of money, we all have a fiduciary duty to our shareholders to ensure that peacekeeping operations run at a profit, and there is a *small* matter of eighty kilograms of highly enriched – weapons grade – uranium that remains unaccounted for. Uranium, my dear, does not grow on trees. Next, there's your unauthorized assignment of a diplomatic emergency bag, class one, registered to this harebrained scheme of Ambassador Cho's, to support your junket aboard the target's warship. The bag was subsequently expended in making an escape when everything went wrong – as you predicted at the start of the affair, so you should have known better than to go along in the first place. And then there's the matter of you taking aboard *hitchhikers*—'

'Under the terms of the common law of space, I had an *obligation* to rescue any stranded persons I could take on board.' Rachel glared at Minion Number One, who glared right back, then hastily looked away. *Damn, that was a mistake,* she realized. *A palpable hit.* 'I'll also remind you that I have a right under section two of the operational guidelines for field officers to make use of official facilities for rescuing dependents in time of conflict.'

'You weren't married to him at the time,' Madam Chairman cut in icily.

'Are you sure it wasn't a marriage of convenience?' Minion Number Two chirped out, hunting for an opportunistic shot.

'I would say the facts *do* tend to support that assumption,' Minion Number One agreed.

'The facts of the matter are that you appear to have spent *a great deal* of UN *money* without achieving *anything* of any significance,' Madam Chairman trilled in a singsong. She was on a roll: she leaned forward, bosom heaving with emotion and cheeks flushed with triumph as she prepared for the kill. 'We hold you to account for this operation, Junior Attaché Mansour. Not to put too fine a point on it, you wasted more than two million ecus of official funds on a wildcat mission that didn't deliver any measurable benefits you can point to. You're on the personnel roster under *my* oversight, and your screwup makes Entertainments and Culture look bad. Or hadn't you realized the adverse impact your spy fantasies might have on the serious job of market-ing our constituent's products abroad? I can find *some* minor contributions to the bottom line on your part in the distant past, but you're very short on mitigating factors; for that reason, we're going to give you twenty-seven— '

'Twenty-six!' interrupted Minion Number Two.

'—Twenty-six days to submit to a full extradepartmen-tal audit with a remit to prepare a report on the disposition of funds during operation Mike November Charlie Four Seven-slash-Delta, and to evaluate the best practices com-pliance of your quality outcome assurance in the context of preventing that brushfire conflict from turning into a full-scale interstellar war.' Madam Chairman simpered at her own brilliance, fanning herself with a hard copy of Rachel's public-consumption report.

'A full-scale audit?' Rachel burst out: 'You stupid, *stupid*, desk pilot!' She glanced round, fingering the control rings for her personal assist twitchily. A security guard would have gone for the floor at that point, but Rachel managed to restrain herself even though the adrenaline was flowing, and the upgrades installed in her parasympathetic periph-eral nervous system were boosting her toward combat readiness. 'Try to audit me. Just try it!' She crossed her arms tensely. 'You'll hit a brick wall. Who's in your man-agement matrix grid? Do you think we can't reach all of them? Do you really want to annoy the Black Chamber?'

Madam Chairman rose and faced Rachel stiffly, like a cobra ready to spit. 'You, you slimy little minx, you *cowboy*—' she hissed, waving a finger under Rachel's nose – 'I'll see you on the street before you're ever listed under Entertainments and Culture again! I know your game, you scheming little pole-climber, and I'll—'

Rachel was about to reply when her left earlobe buzzed. 'Excuse me a moment,' she said, raising a hand, 'incoming.'

She cupped a hand to her ear. 'Yeah, who is this?'

'Stop that at once! This is *my* audit committee, not a talking shop—'

'*Polis dispatch. Are you Rachel Mansour? SXB active three-zero-two? Can you confirm your identity?*'

Rachel stood up, her pulse pounding, feeling weak with shock. 'Yes, that's me,' she said distantly. 'Here's my fingerprint.' She touched a finger to her forehead, coupling a transdermal ID implant to the phone so that it could vouch for her.

'Someone stop her! Philippe, can't you jam her? This is a disgrace!'

'*Voiceprint confirmed.* I have you authenticated. This is the Fourth Republican Police Corporation, dispatch control for Geneva. You're in the Place du Molard, aren't you? We have an urgent SXB report that's just across the way from you. We've called in the regional squad, but it's our bad luck that something big's going down just outside Brasilia, and the whole team is out there providing backup. They can't get back in less than two hours, and the headcase is threatening us with an excursion in only fifty-four minutes.'

'Oh. Oh, hell!' Situations like this tended to dredge up reflexive blasphemies left over from her upbringing. Rachel turned toward the door, blanking on her surroundings. Sometimes she had nightmares about this sort of thing, nightmares that dragged her awake screaming in the middle of the night, worrying Martin badly. 'Can you have someone pick me up in the concourse? Brief me on the way in. You know I haven't handled one of these in years? I'm on the reserve list.'

'Stop that now!' Madam Chairman was in the way, standing between Rachel and the doorway. She pouted like a fighting fish faced with a mirror, blood-red lips tight with anger and fists balled. 'You can't just walk out of here!'

'What are you going to do, slap me?' Rachel asked, sounding amused.

'I'll bring charges! You arranged this distraction—'

Rachel reached out, picked Madam Chairman up by her elbows, and deposited her on the conference table in a howl of outrage and a flurry of silk skirts. 'Stick to minding your desk,' Rachel said coldly, unable to resist the urge to rub it in. 'The adults have got important work to be getting on with.'

Rachel just about had the shakes under control by the time she reached the main exit. *Stupid, stupid!* she chided herself. Blowing up at Madam Chairman could only make things worse, and with the job ahead she needed desperately to cultivate a calm head. A police transporter was waiting for her in the landscaped courtyard outside the UN office dome, squatting in the shadow of a giant statue of Otto von Bismarck. 'Suspect an unemployed artist and recluse believed to be named Idi Amin Dadaist,' the police dispatcher told her via her bonephone, simultaneously throwing a bunch of images at the inside of her left eyelid. 'No previous record other than minor torts for public arts happenings with no purchase of public disturbance and meme pollution rights, and an outstanding lawsuit from the People's Republic of Midlothian over his claim to the title of Last King of Scotland. He's—'

The next words were drowned out by the warble of alarm sirens. Someone in the headquarters bubble had been told what was going down a few blocks away. 'I haven't even done a training update for one of these in three years!' Rachel shouted into the palm of her hand as she jogged toward the transporter. She climbed in, and it surged away, meters ahead of the human tide streaming out of the building toward the nearest bomb shelters. 'Don't you have anyone who's current?'

'You used to be full-time with SXB, that's why we've still got you flagged as a standby,' said the dispatcher. A worried-looking cop glanced round from the pilot's seat, leaving the driving to the autopilot. 'The regulars, like I said, they're *all* en route from Brasilia by suborbital. We're a peaceful city. This is the first bomb scare we've had in nearly twenty years. You're the only specialist – active or reserve – in town today.'

'Jesus! So it *had* to happen when everyone was away. What can you tell me about the scene?'

'The perp's holed up in a refugee stack in Saint-Leger. Says he's got an improv gadget, and he's going to detonate it in an hour minus eight minutes unless we accede to his demands. We're not sure what kind it is, or what his demands are, but it doesn't really matter – even a pipe bomb loaded with cobalt sixty would make a huge mess of the neighborhood.'

'Right.' Rachel shook her head. ' 'Scuse me, I've just come from a meeting with a bunch of time-wasters, and I'm trying to get my head together. You're saying it's going to be a hands-on job?'

'He's holed up in a cheap apartment tree. He's indoors, well away from windows, vents, doors. Our floor penetrator says he's in the entertainment room with something dense enough to be a gadget. The stack is dusted, but we're having fun replaying the ubiquitous surveillance takes for the past month – seems he started jamming before any-thing else, and his RFID tag trace is much too clean. Someone has to go inside and talk him down or take him out, and you've got more experience of this than any of us. It says here you've done more than twenty of these jobs; that makes you our nearest expert.'

'Hell and deviltry. Who's the underwriter for this block?'

'It's all outsourced by the city government – I think Lloyds has something to do with it. Whatever, *you* bill *us* for any expenses, and we'll sort them out. Anything you need for the job is yours, period.'

'Okay.' She sighed, half-appalled at how easy it was to slip back into old ways of thinking and feeling. Last time, she'd sworn it would be her last job. Last time she'd actually tried to slit her wrists afterward, before she saw sense and realized that there were easier ways out of the profession. Like switching to something even more dangerous, as it turned out. 'One condition: my husband. Get someone to call him, right now. If he's in town tell him to get under cover. And get as many people as possible into bunkers. The older apartments are riddled with the things, aren't they? There is no guarantee that I'm going to be able to pull this off on my own without a support and planning backstop team, and I don't want you to count on miracles. Have you got a disaster kit standing by?'

'We're already evacuating, and there'll be a disaster kit waiting on-site when you arrive,' said the dispatcher. 'Our normal SXB team are on the way home, but they won't be able to take over for an hour and a half, and they'll be into reentry blackout in about ten minutes – I think that means they won't be much help to you.'

'Right.' Rachel nodded, redundantly. She'd dressed for the office, but unlike Madam Chairman, she didn't go in for retrofemme frills and frou-frou: she'd had enough of that in the year she'd spent in the New Republic. *What does the bitch have against me, anyway?* she asked herself, making a mental note to do some data mining later. She dialed her jacket and leggings to sky blue – calming colors – and settled back in the seat, breathing deeply and steadily. 'No point asking for armor, I guess. Do you have any snipers on hand?'

'Three teams are on their way. They'll be set up with crossfire and hard-surface-penetrating sights in about twenty minutes. Inspector MacDougal is supervising.'

'Has he evacuated the apartments yet?'

'It's in progress. She's moving in noisemakers as her people pull the civilians. Orders are to avoid anything that might tip him off that we've got an operation in train.'

'Good. Hmm. You said the perp's an artist.' Rachel paused. 'Does anyone know what *kind* of artist?'

The transporter leaned into the corner with the Boulevard Jacques, then surged down the monorail track. Other pods, their guidance systems overridden, slewed out of its way: two police trucks, bouncing on their pneumatic tires, were coming up fast behind. The buildings thereabouts were old, stone and brick and wood that had gone up back before the Diaspora and gone out of fashion sometime since, lending the old quarter something of the air of a twenty-first-century theme park far gone in ungenteel decay. 'He's an historical reenactor,' said the dispatcher. 'There's something here about colonies. Colonialism. Apparently it's all to do with reenacting the historic process of black liberation before the holocaust.'

'Which holocaust?'

'The African one. Says here he impersonates a pre-holocaust emperor called Idi Amin, uh, Idi Amin Dada. There's a release about reinterpreting the absurdist elements of the Ugandan proletarian reformation dialectic through the refracting lens of neo-Dadaist ideological situationism.'

'Whatever that means. Okay. Next question, where was this guy born? Where did he come from? What does he *do*?'

'He was born somewhere in Paraguay. He's had extensive phenotype surgery to make himself resemble his role model, the Last King of Scotland or President of Uganda or whoever he was. Got a brochure from one of his performances here –

says he tries to act as an emulation platform for the original Idi Amin's soul.'

'And now he's gone crazy, right? Can you dig anything up about the history of the original Mister Amin? Sounds Islamicist to me. Was he an Arab or something?'

The transporter braked, swerved wildly, then hopped off the monorail and nosed in between a whole mass of cops milling around in front of a large, decrepit-looking spiral of modular refugee condominiums hanging off an extruded titanium tree. A steady stream of people flowed out of the block, escorted by rentacops in the direction of the Place de Philosophes. Rachel could already see a queue of lifters coming in, trying to evacuate as many people as possible from the blocks around ground zero. It didn't matter whether or not this particular fuckwit was competent enough to build a working nuke: if the Plutonium Fairy had been generous, he could make his gadget fizzle and contaminate several blocks. Even a lump of plastique coated with stolen high-level waste could be messy. Actinide metal chelation and gene repair therapy for several thousand people was one hell of an expensive way to pay for an artistic tantrum, and if he *did* manage to achieve prompt criticality . . .

The officer in charge – a tall blond woman with a trail of cops surrounding her – was coming over. 'You! Are you the specialist dispatch has been praying for?' she demanded.

'Yeah, that's me.' Rachel shrugged uncomfortably. 'Bad news is, I've had no time to prep for this job, and I haven't done one in three or four years. What have you got for me?'

'A real bampot, it would seem. I'm Inspector Rosa MacDougal, Laughing Joker Enforcement Associates. Please follow me.'

The rentacop site office was the center of a hive of activity, expanding to cover half the grassed-over car park in front of the apartment block. The office itself was painted vomit-green and showed little sign of regular maintenance, or even cleaning. 'I haven't worked with Laughing Joker before,' Rachel admitted. 'First, let me tell you that as with all SXB ops, this is pro bono, but we expect unrestricted donations of equipment and support during the event, and death benefits for next of kin if things go pear-shaped. We do *not* accept liability for failure, on account of the SXB point team usually being too dead to argue the point. We just do our best. Is that clear with you?'

'Crystal.' MacDougal pointed at a chair. 'Sit yourself down. We've got half an hour before it goes critical.'

'Right.' Rachel sat. She made a steeple of her fingers, then sighed. 'How sure are you that this is genuine?'

'The first thing anyone knew about it was when the building's passive neutron sniffer jumped off the wall. At first the block manager thought it was malfing, but it turns out yon Idiot was tickling the dragon's tail. He'd got a cheap-ass assembler blueprint from some anarchist phile vault, and he's been buying beryllium feedstock for his kitchen assembler over the past six months.'

'Shit. Beryllium. And nobody noticed?'

'Hey.' MacDougal spread her hands. 'Nobody *here is* paying us for sparrow-fart coverage. Private enterprise does-n't stretch to ubiquitous hand-holding. We go poking our noses in uninvited, we get sued till we bleed. It's a free market, isn't it?'

'Huh.' Rachel nodded. It was an old, familiar picture. With nine hundred permanent seats on the UN Security SIG, the only miracle was that anything ever got done at all. Still, if anything could stimulate cooperation, it was the lethal combination of household nanofactories and cheap black-market weapons-grade fissiles. The right to self-defense did not, it was generally held, extend as far as mutually assured destruction – at least, not in built-up areas. Hence the SXB volunteers, and her recurring nightmares and subsequent move to the diplomatic corps' covert arms control team. Which was basically the same job on an interstellar scale, with the benefit that governments usually tended to be more rational about the disposition of their strategic interstellar deterrents than bampot street performers with a grudge against society and a home brew nuke.

'Okay. So our target somehow scored twelve kilos of weapons-grade heavy metal *and* tested a subcritical assembly before anybody noticed. What then?'

'The block management 'bot issued an automatic fourteen-day eviction notice for violation of the tenancy agreement. There's a strict zero-tolerance policy for weapons of mass destruction in this town.'

'Oh, sweet Jesus.' Rachel rubbed her forehead.

'It gets better,' Inspector MacDougal added with morbid enthusiasm. 'Our bampot messaged the management 'bot right back, demanding that they recognize him as President of Uganda, King of Scotland, Supreme Planetary Dictator, and Left Hand of the Eschaton. The 'bot told him to fuck right off, which probably wisnae a guid idea: that's when he threatened to nuke 'em.'

'So, basically it's your routine tenant/landlord fracas, with added fallout plume.'

'That's about the size of it.'

'Shit. So what happened next?'

'Well, the management 'bot flagged the threat as being (a) a threat to damage the residential property, and (b) subtype, bomb hoax. So it called up its insurance link, and *our* 'bot sent Officer Schwartz round to have a polite word. And that's when it turned intae the full-dress faeco-ventilatory intersection scene.'

'Is Officer Schwartz available?' asked Rachel.

'Right here,' grunted what Rachel had mistaken for a spare suit of full military plate. It wasn't: it was SWAT-team armor, and it was also occupied. Schwartz turned ponderously toward her. 'I was just up-suiting for to go in.'

'Oh.' Rachel blinked. 'Just what's the situation up there, then?'

'A very large man, he is,' said Schwartz. 'High-melatonin tweak. Also, high-androgenic steroid tweak. Built like the west end of an eastbound panzer. Lives like a pig! Ach.' He grunted. 'He is an *artiste*. This does not, I say, entitle one to live like animal.'

'Tell her what happened,' MacDougal said tiredly, breaking off from fielding a call on her wristplant.

'Oh. This artist demands to be crowned King of Africa or some such. I tell him politely no, he may however he crowned king of the stretch of gutter between numbers 19 and 21 on the Rue Tabazan if he wishes to not leave quietly. I was not armored up at that time, so when *monsieur l'artiste* points a gun at me, I leave quietly instead and thank my fate for I am allowed to do so.'

'What kind of gun?'

'Database says it is a historical replica Kalashnikov mechanism.'

'Did you see any sign of his bomb?' asked Rachel, with a sinking sensation.

'Only the dead man's trigger strapped to his left wrist,' said Officer Schwartz, a glint in his eyes just visible through the thick visor of his helmet. 'But my helmet detected slow neutron flux. He says it is a uranium-gun design, by your leave.'

'Oh *shit!*' Rachel leaned forward, thinking furiously: *Nuclear blackmail. Fail-hard switch. Simple but deadly uranium-gun design. Loon lies bleeding, in the distance the double flash of the X-ray pulse burning the opaque air, plasma shutter flickering to release the heat pulse. Idi Amin Dadaist impersonating a dead dictator to perfection. Fifty-one minutes to detonation, if he has the guts to follow through. The performance artist scorned. What would an artist do?*

'Give him half a chance and an audience, he'll push the button,' she said faintly.

'I'm sorry?'

She looked out of the window at the steady stream of poor evacuees being shepherded away from the site. They were clearly poor; most of them had lopsided or misshapen or otherwise ugly, natural faces – one or two actually looked *aged*. 'He's an artist,' she said calmly. 'I've dealt with the type before, and recently. Like the bad guy said, never give an artist a Browning; they're some of the most dangerous folks you can meet. The Festival fringe – shit! Artists almost always want an audience, the spectacle of destruction. That name – Dadaist. It's a dead giveaway. Expect a senseless act of mass violence, the theater of cruelty. About all I can do is try and keep him talking while you get in position to kill him. And don't give him anything he might mistake for an audience. What kind of profile match do you have?'

'He's a good old-fashioned radge. That is to say, a dangerous fuckwit,' said MacDougal, frowning. She blinked for a moment as if she had something in her eye, then flicked another glyph at Rachel. 'Here. Read it fast, then start talking. I don't think we've got much time for sitting around.'

'Okay.' Rachel's nostrils flared, taking in a malodorous mixture of stale coffee, nervous sweat, the odor of a police mobile incident room sitting on the edge of ground zero. She focused on the notes – not that there was much to read, beyond the usual tired litany of red-lined credit ratings, public trust derivatives, broken promises, exhibitions of petrified fecostalagmites, and an advanced career as an art-school dropout. Idi had tried to get into the army, any army – but not even a second-rate private mercenary garrison force from Wichita would take him. *Nutty as a squirrel cage*, said a telling wikinote from the recruiting sergeant's personal assist. MacDougal's diagnosis was already looking worryingly plausible when Rachel stumbled into the docs covering his lifelong obsession and saw the ancient photographs, and the bills from the cheapjack body shop Idi – his real name of record, now he'd put his dismal family history behind him – spent all his meager insurance handouts on. '*Treponema pallidum* injections – holy shit, he paid to be infected with syphilis?'

'Yeah, and not just any kind – he wanted the fun tertiary version where your bones begin to melt, your face falls off, and you suffer from dementia and wild rages. None of the intervening decades of oozing pus from the genitals for our man Idi.'

'He's mad.' Rachel shook her head.

'I've been telling you that, yes. What I want to know is, can you take him?'

'Hmm.' She took stock. 'He's big. Is he as hard as he looks?'

'No.' This from Schwartz. 'I could myself have easily taken him, without armor. Only he had a gun. He is ill, an autosickie.'

'Well then.' Rachel reached a decision. 'We've got, what? Forty-four minutes? When you've got everybody out, I think I'm going to have to go in and talk to him face-to-face. Keep the guns out of sight but if you can get a shot straight down through the ceiling that—'

'No bullets,' said MacDougal. 'We don't know how he's wired the dead man's handle, and we can't afford to take chances. We've got these, though.' She held up a small case: 'Robowasps loaded with sleepy-juice, remotely guided. One sting, and he'll be turned off in ten seconds. The hairy time is between him realizing he's going down and the lights going out. Someone's got to stop him yelling a detonation command, tripping the dead man's handle, or otherwise making the weasel go pop.'

'Okay.' Rachel nodded thoughtfully, trying to ignore the churning in her gut and the instinctive urge to jump up and run – anywhere, as long as it was away from the diseased loony with the Osama complex and the atom bomb upstairs. 'So you hook into me for a full sensory feed, I go in, I talk, I play it by ear. We'll need two code words. "I'm going to sneeze" means I'm going to try to punch him out myself. And, uh, "That's a funny smell" means I want you to come in with everything you've got. If you can plant a lobotomy shot on him, do it, even if you have to shoot through me. Just try to miss my brain stem if it comes down to it. That's how we play this game. Wasps would be better, though. I'll try not to call you unless I'm sure I can immobilize him, or I'm sure he's about to push the button.' She shivered, feeling a familiar rush of nervous energy.

'Are you about that certain?' Schwartz asked, sounding dubious.

Rachel stared at him. 'This fuckwit is going to maybe kill dozens, maybe hundreds of people if we don't nail him *right now*,' she said. 'What do you think?'

Schwartz swallowed. MacDougal shook her head. 'What is it you do for a living, again?' she asked.

'I reach the parts ordinary disarmament inspectors don't touch.' Rachel grinned, baring her teeth at her own fear. She stood up. 'Let's go sort him out.'

harmless

Earth, seen from orbit in the twenty-fourth century, was a planet harrowed by technological civilization, bearing the scars left by a hatchling transcendence. Nearly 10 percent of its surface had been concreted over at one time or another. Whole swaths of it bore the suture marks of incomplete reterraforming operations. From the jungles of the Sahara to the fragile grassland of the Amazon basin it was hard to find any part of the planetary surface that hadn't been touched by the hand of technology.

Earth's human civilization, originally restricted to a single planet, had spread throughout the solar system. Gas giants in the outer reaches grew strange new industrial rings, while the heights of Kilimanjaro and central Panama sweated threads of diamond wire into geosynchronous orbit. Earth, they had called it once; now it was Old Earth, birth-world of humanity and cradle of civilization. But there was a curious dynamic to this old home world, an uncharacteristically youthful outlook. Old Earth in the twenty-fourth century wasn't home to the oldest human civilizations. Not even close.

For this paradoxical fact, most people blamed the Eschaton. The Eschaton – the strongly superhuman AI product of a technological singularity that rippled through the quantum computing networks of the late twenty-first century – didn't like sharing a planet with ten billion future-shocked primates. When it bootstrapped itself to weakly godlike intelligence it deported most of them to other planets, through wormholes generated by means human scientists still could not fathom even centuries later. Not that they'd had much time to analyze its methods in the immediate aftermath – most people had been too busy trying to survive the rigors of the depopulation-induced economic crash. It wasn't until well over a hundred years later, when the first FTL starships from Earth reached the nearer stars, that they discovered the weirdest aspect of the process. The holes the Eschaton had opened up in space led back in time as well, leading a year into the past for every light year out. And some of the wormhole tunnels went a very great distance indeed. From the moment of the singularity onward, SETI receivers began picking up strong signals; hitherto silent reaches of space echoed with the chatter and hum of human voices.

By the third century after the immense event, the polities of Earth had largely recovered. The fragmented coalitions and defensive microeconomies left behind by the collapsing wake of the twenty-first century's global free-trade empire re-formed as a decentralized network able to support an advanced economy. They even managed to sustain the massive burden of the reterraforming projects. Some industries were booming; Earth was rapidly gaining a reputation as *the* biggest, most open trading hub within a hundred light years. The UN – even more of a deafening echo chamber talking shop than the first organization to bear that name — also included nontribal entities. Restructured to run on profit-making lines, it was amassing a formidable reputation for mercantile diplomacy. Even the most pressing problem of the twenty-second century, the population crash that followed in the wake of the singularity, had been largely averted. Cheap anti-aging hacks and an enlightened emigration policy had stabilized the population at mid-twentieth-century levels, well within the carrying capacity of the planet and in the numbers required to support advanced scientific research again. It was, in short, a time of optimism and expansion: a young, energetic, pluralistic planetary patchwork civilization exploding out into the stellar neighborhood and rediscovering its long-lost children.

None of which made for a bed of roses, as Rachel Mansour — who had been born on this same planet more than a hundred years previously — probably appreciated more than most.

'I'm ready to go in,' she said quietly, leaning against the wall next to the cheap gray aerogel doorslab. She glanced up and down the empty corridor. It smelled damp. The thin carpet was grimy, burdened by more dirt than its self-cleaning system could cope with, and many of the lighting panels were cracked. 'Is everyone in position?'

'We've got some heavy items still assembling. Try not to call a strike for at least the first ten seconds. After that, we'll be ready when you need us.'

'Okay. Here goes.' For some reason she found herself wishing she'd brought Madam Chairman along to see the sort of jobs her diplomatic entertainment account got spent on. Rachel shook herself, took a deep breath, and knocked on the door. Madam Chairman could read all about it in the comfort of her committee room when the freelance media caught on. At the moment, it was Rachel's job, and she needed to keep her attention 101 percent locked on to it.

'Who is that?' boomed a voice from the other side of the partition.

'Police negotiator. You wanted to talk to someone?'

'Why are you waiting then? You better not be armed! Come in and listen to me. Did you bring cameras?'

Uh-oh. 'Schwartz is right,' Rachel muttered to her audio monitor. 'You going to take off now?'

'*Yes. We're with you.*' MacDougal's voice was tinny and hoarse with tension in her left ear.

Rachel took hold of the doorknob and pushed, slowly. The rentacops had applied for the emergency override, and the management had switched off all the locks. The door opened easily. Rachel stood in the doorway in full view of the living room.

'Can I come in?' she asked, betraying no sign of having noticed the whine of insect wings departing her shoulders as the door swung wide.

The apartment was a one-room dwelling: bed, shower tray, and kitchen fab were built to fold down out of opposite walls of the entertainment room. A picture window facing the front door showed a perpetual view of Jupiter as seen from the crust of smoking, yellow Io. It had once been a cheap refugee housing module (single, adult, for the use of), but subsequent occupants had *nested* in it, allowing the basic utility structures to wear out and trashing the furnishings. The folding furniture was over-extended, support struts bent and dysfunctional. The wreckage of a hundred ready-meals spilled across the worn-out carpet. The sickly sweet smell of decaying food was almost masked by the stench of cheap tobacco. The room reeked of cigarette smoke – a foul, contaminated blend, if Rachel was any judge, although she'd given up the habit along with her third pair of lungs, many years ago.

The man sprawled in the recliner in the middle of the room made even the mess around him look like an example of good repair. He was nearly two meters tall and built like a tank, but he was also clearly ill. His hair was streaked with white, his naked belly bulged over the stained waistband of his sweats, and his face was lined. He swiveled his chair toward her and beamed widely. 'Enter my royal palace!' he declared, gesturing with both hands. Rachel saw the dirty bandage wrapped around his left wrist, trailing a shielded cable in the direction of a large crate behind the chair.

'Okay, I'm coming in,' she said as calmly as she could, and stepped inside the room.

A hoarse robot voice burbled from the crate: 'T minus thirty-five minutes and counting. Warning: proximity alert. Unidentified human at three meters. Request permission to accelerate detonation sequence?'

Rachel swallowed. The man in the chair didn't seem to notice. 'Welcome to the presidential palace of the Once and Future Kingdom of Uganda! What's your name, sweetie? Are you a famous journalist? Did you come here to interview me?'

'Um, yes.' Rachel stopped just inside the doorway, two meters away from the sick man and his pet talking nuke. 'I'm Rachel. That's a very nice bomb you've got,' she said carefully.

'Warning: proximity alert. Unidentified human at—'

'Shut the fuck up,' the man said casually, and the bomb stopped in midsentence. 'It *is* a lovely bomb, isn't it?'

'Yes. Did you make it yourself?' Rachel's pulse raced. She blipped her endocrine overrides, forcing the sweat ducts on the palms of her hands to stop pumping and her stomach to cease trying to flip out through the nearest window.

'*Moi?* Do I resemble a weapons scientist? I bought it off the shelf.' He smiled, revealing the glint of a gold tooth – Rachel managed to keep a straight face, but her nostrils flared at the unmistakable odor of dental decay. 'Is it not great?' He held up his wrist. 'If I die, *poof!* All funeral expenses included!'

'How big is it?' she ventured.

'Oh, it's *very* big!' He grinned wider and spread his legs suggestively, rubbing his crotch with one hand. 'The third stage dials all the way to three hundred kilotons.'

Rachel's stomach turned to ice. *This isn't your run-of-the-mill black-market bomb,* she subvocalized, hoping MacDougal would be listening carefully. 'That must have cost you a lot of money,' she said slowly.

'Oh yes.' The grin faded. 'I had to sell everything. I even gave up the treatments.'

'Which treatments?'

Suddenly he was on his feet and ranting. 'The ones that make me Idi Amin! King of Scotland, Victoria Cross, KBE, MBE, Governor of Kiboga and Mayor of Bukake! I am the President! Respect me and fear me! You chickenshit white Europeans have oppressed the people of Africa long enough – it's time for a new world of freedom! I stand for Islamic values, African triumph, and freedom from the oppressors. But you don't give me no respect! Nobody listens when I tell them what to do. It's time for punishment!' Spittle filled the air in front of her. Rachel tried to take a step forward without attracting his attention, but the bomb noticed.

'Alert: close proximity alert! Unidentified human, believed hostile, at—'

'*Don't move,*' MacDougal whispered tinnily in her ear. '*The fucking thing just armed itself. If you get any closer without him telling it you're friendly, it could blow.*'

A bead of sweat trickled down the side of Rachel's face. She forced herself to smile. 'That's really impressive,' she said slowly. Insects whined softly overhead, police wasps circling his head, waiting for an opportunity to strike safely. A thought dug its unwelcome claws into her mind: *Got to get closer! But how?* 'I *like* impressive men,' she cooed. 'And you're really impressive, Mister President.'

I'm going to try to get close enough to immobilize him, she subvocalized. *Tell me exactly what your bugs are loaded with again.*

'Glad you think so, little lady,' said the Last King of Scotland, rubbing his crotch. *Isn't priapism a late-stage symptom?* she subvocalized, staring at his dirty sweats and forcing herself to lick her suddenly dry lips.

'They're loaded with a really strong serotonin antagonist targeted on his reticular activating system. Ten seconds and he'll be in a coma. We just need to stop him telling the bomb to go bang after it goes in and before he nods off. And, uh, yes, it is a symptom.'

'Your little king looks like he wants to hold court.' Rachel smiled invitingly, dry-swallowing and steeling herself for the next step. *First get his confidence, then abuse it . . .* 'What's the protocol for approaching a President, Mister President?'

'You do it naked. Naked folks are my *friends*. Naked people don't have no guns. You hear that, bomb? Naked women are my *friends*. Naked bitches. My special friends.' He seemed to have calmed down a bit, but the set of his jaw was still tense, and he squinted angrily, as if he had a bad sinus headache. 'You going to get *naked*, bitch?'

'If you say so, Mister President.' Rachel locked her jaw muscles in a painful rictus that imitated a smile as she unsealed her jacket and slowly shrugged her way out of it. *Did you hear that?* she subvocalized as she rolled her leggings down around her ankles and stepped out of them. She stood in front of him and held the forced grin, trying to look inviting, willing her endocrine override to give her a flush of subcutaneous blood vessels and a crinkling of nipples. Trying to fake arousal, to do anything to keep the sad bastard distracted from the prospect of wanking his way into nuclear oblivion, taking half a city with him. *Anything* to let her get closer to the trigger—

'You may approach the throne,' declared Field Marshal Professor President Doctor Idi Amin Dadaist, spreading his legs. With a moue of vague disgust he yanked his pants open. His penis was indeed large and stiff: it also bore several weeping sores, like a blighted aubergine. 'Kneel to kiss your emperor!'

Rachel saw his hands raised above his head. His right fingertips brushed against the dead man's wristband as he smiled lazily. She knelt before him, tensing. 'I can do good things with my hands,' she offered as she reached toward his crotch, her skin crawling.

'Then do so,' he said magisterially. 'Remember, as your President I hold the power of life and death over you.'

Rachel nodded and gently stroked his glans. She could see a vein pulsing in it. She leaned closer, trying to judge the distance, swallowing bile. 'May I kiss you, Mister President? You're a very powerful man. Would you like that? I'm your loyal subject. Will you let me kiss you on the mouth?'

The Field Marshal and Professor sat up slightly. 'Certainly,' he said, mustering up a slightly pathetic gravitas: his breath caught as she stroked him.

'Hey, that's a funny smell,' Rachel said quickly. Then she leaned forward and clamped her mouth down onto his lips, tongue questing, fingers busy with his shaft. He tensed slightly, back arching, and she reached up to grab his right arm by the wrist. Something insectoidal flickered past her eyes in a blur of wings as he spasmed and pumped a ropy stream of hot imperial semen across her thigh. His jaws flexed: she stuck her tongue into his mouth as far as she could, squeezing her eyes shut, holding her breath, and prayed that he wouldn't have a seizure as he bucked and jerked against her. The President for Life twitched a couple of times: then his eyes rolled up and he slumped backward in the recliner. His right arm fell sideways as she let go of it. She straightened up, gasping, and managed to turn aside. She spat, trying to get the taste of decaying teeth out of her mouth, then doubled over and vomited noisily across the would-be dictator's feet.

After a few seconds, she felt strong arms around her shoulder. 'Come on,' said MacDougal. 'Let's get you out an' away. It's all under control.'

'Under—' Rachel moved to wipe the tears from her eyes, then realized her hand was sticky. 'Ugh. It's over?'

The room was filling up with naked policewomen toting toolboxes and talking into throat mikes. 'Ordinary bomb team's already here to take over – half of it, anyways. You can come away now.' Without her uniform and body armor, Inspector MacDougal had the most remarkable tattoos Rachel had seen in a long time: angel wings on her shoulder blades, a snake around her narrow waist. She pointed at the four nude women who were leaning over the bomb with instruments and neutron counters. 'That was inspirational, Colonel! "Naked women are my friends."'

Rachel shook her head. An insect buzzed overhead. Not police issue, it was probably the first harbinger of a swarm of journalists. 'I'm not really a colonel, I just play one in the banana republics.' She shuddered. 'I needed to get close enough to gag him and hold his arm out of the way. Whatever it took.'

'Well, if it was up to me, you'd get a medal.' MacDougal

looked hard at the recliner and shook her head. 'Took guts. Some assholes will do *anything* for a handjob.'

'Need water,' Rachel gasped, feeling another wave of nausea coming on.

Someone passed her a bottle. She rinsed and spat, rhythmically, until the bottle was empty, trying to remind herself how much worse it could have been. She could have had her tongue bitten off if he'd gone into a seizure. Or he might have wanted something worse. Another bottle appeared, and she poured half of it over her left hand and thigh. 'I need a shower. Antibiotics. *Lots* of antibiotics. How long does that shot put him out for?'

'How long?' MacDougal sounded puzzled, then spotted the insects: she straightened up, tried to look severe, and went into press-management mode. 'Laughing Joker Security takes WMD incursions extremely seriously. In accordance with our zero tolerance of nuclear sidearms policy, we deployed a destroyer payload targeted on the offender's reticular activating system. He hasn't got one anymore – he'll stay asleep until the rest of his cerebellum fails.' Which, judging from the way she glanced at the erratically snoring figure, would be sooner rather than later. Impromptu art happenings involving nuclear weapons tended to get a bad press even in the laid-back Republique et Canton Genève.

There was a shrill beeping from the pile of discarded clothes near the doorway. Rachel was leaning over it and fumbling for her interface rings before she realized she'd moved. 'Yes?' she said hoarsely.

'You haven't heard the last of this!' Judging from her hectoring tone, Madam Chairman had been following events on multicast, and she was royally pissed off at something – probably the fact that Rachel was still alive. 'I know about you and your cronies in the enforcement branch! Don't think you can get out of the audit hearing the same way!'

'Oh, fuck off!' said Rachel, killing the call. *I'll get you later,* she thought dizzily, leaning against the doorframe. *Find out what your game is and beat you . . .* She tried to get a grip, paranoia running out of control. 'Inspector, can you see I get home? I think I'm about to collapse.' She slid down the wall, laughing and crying at the same time. On the other side of the room a naked lady held up something like a fat shotgun cartridge in both hands, triumphantly. Everyone else seemed to be cheering, but for the life of her Rachel couldn't see why.

magical mystery tour

More than a year earlier, in the middle of a field mission that was rapidly falling apart in all directions simultaneously, Rachel had struck a bargain with the devil. She'd made a deal with something that was indeed perfectly capable of destroying worlds: and much to her disquiet, she discovered afterward that she did not regret it.

In the wake of the singularity, the Eschaton had apparently vanished from the Earth, leaving behind a crippled network, depopulated cities, the general aftermath of planet-shaking disaster — and three commandments engraved on a cube of solid diamond ten meters on a side:

1. I am the Eschaton. I am not your god.
2. I am descended from you and I exist in your future.
3. Thou shalt not violate causality within my historic light cone. Or else.

Some people claimed to understand what this meant,

while others said they were imbeciles or charlatans. The First Reformed Church of Tipler, Astrophysicist, battled it out in the streets with the Reformed Latter-Day Saints. Islam mutated out of recognition, other religions curled up and died. Computer scientists – the few who were left; for some reason the Eschaton seemed to select them preferentially – came out with crazy hypotheses. The Eschaton was a chunk of software that had, by way of who-knew-what algorithm, achieved computational sentience. It had rapidly bootstrapped itself across the Internet, achieving in minutes or hours as much thinking time as a human might attain in a million years. Then it had transcended, achieving a level of intelligence that simply could not be speculated on, an intellect that compared to human thought as a human might compare to a frog. What it did then, it did for motives that no human being was likely to guess, or understand. How it opened macroscopic wormholes in space-time – something human scientists had no clue how to do – remained a mystery.

Bizarre references to the light cone made no sense at all for more than a hundred years, until the first successful construction of a faster-than-light spacecraft. Then it began to fit into a big picture. The universe was seething with human-populated worlds, the dumping grounds where the Eschaton had deposited the nine billion or so people it had abducted in the course of a single frantic day. The wormholes covered immense distances in time as well as space, opening a year back in time for every light year out in distance. Astrophysicists speculated blatantly about the computational implications of causality violation, until silenced in a bizarre jihad by a post-Christian sect from North Africa.

The human consequences of the singularity reverberated endlessly, too. The exiles hadn't simply been dumped on any available world; in almost all cases, they'd been planted in terrain that was not too hostile, showing crude signs of recent terraforming. And the Eschaton had given them gifts: cornucopias, robot factories able to produce any designated goods to order, given enough time, energy, and raw materials. Stocked with a library of standard designs, a cornucopia was a general-purpose tool for planetary colonization. Used wisely, they enabled many of the scattered worlds to achieve a highly automated postindustrial economy within years. Used unwisely, they enabled others to destroy themselves. A civilization that used its cornucopia to produce nuclear missiles instead of nuclear reactors – and more cornucopias – wasn't likely to outlast the first famine, let alone the collapse of civilization that was bound to follow when one faction or another saw the cornucopia as a source of military power and targeted it. But the end result was that, a couple of hundred years after the event, most worlds that had not retreated to barbarism had achieved their own spacegoing capabilities.

Military strategists puzzled endlessly over the consequences of being able to attack an enemy with total surprise, until reminded of the third commandment. One or two of them, it transpired, had tried just that; the typical consequence was that a bizarre accident would befall whoever planned such an attack. Interestingly, even the most secretively prepared attempts to use time travel as a military tactic seemed to be crushed, just before they could actually take place.

Rachel had discovered the hard way just why this was the case. The Eschaton was still a factor in human affairs; reclusive and withdrawn it might be, but it still kept a watchful eye open for trouble. It intervened, too, for its own reasons. Causality violation – time travel – if allowed to flourish without check, offered an immediate threat to its existence; sooner or later somebody would try to grand-father it out of history. Various other technological possibilities also threatened it. AI research might generate a competitor for informational resources; nanotechnology developments might achieve the same results through alternative pathways. Hence the third commandment – and the existence of an army of covert enforcers, saboteurs, and agents of influence working on its behalf.

Two years before, Rachel had met one of those agents. She'd been politically compromised, a witness to his activities: a fifteen-microsecond-induced error in a clock which sealed the fate of a fleet and the interstellar empire that had dispatched it to recapture a planet that hadn't been lost in the first place. She'd stayed quiet about it, tacitly accepting the abhuman intervention in diplomatic affairs. The Eschaton hadn't destroyed a civilization this time; it had simply caused an invasion fleet to arrive at its destination too late to alter history, and in so doing had triggered the collapse of an aggressive militaristic regime. It was the job she'd been sent to do herself, by her controllers in the Black Chamber.

In fact, it had been a very happy coincidence from her point of view, because not only had she met an agent of the Eschaton: she'd married him. And sometimes, on good days, on days when she wasn't being hauled over the coals by bureaucratic harridans or called in to deal with hideous emergencies, she thought that the only thing she was really afraid of was losing him again.

On good days . . .

Rachel had been lying in bed for an hour, showered and bathed to squeaky cleanliness and dosed up with a wide-spectrum phagebot and a very strong sedative, when Martin came home.

'Rachel?' she heard him call, through a blanket of thick, warm, lovely lassitude. She smiled to herself. He was home. *I can come down now,* she thought, *if I want.* The thought didn't seem to mean anything.

'Rachel?' The bedroom door slid open. 'Hey.' She rolled her eyes to watch him, feeling a wave of semisynthetic love. 'Hi,' she mumbled.

'What's—' His gaze settled on the bedside stand. 'Oh.' He dropped his bag. 'I see you've been hitting the hard stuff.' The next moment, he was sitting beside her, a hand on her forehead. 'The polis called,' he said, face clouded with worry. 'What happened?'

Time to come down, she realized reluctantly. Somehow she dredged up the energy to point at the A/D patch sitting by the discarded wrapper. It was the hardest thing she'd ever done, harder than wrapping her fingers around—

'Oh. Yeah.' Nimble digits, far nimbler than hers, unpeeled the backing and smoothed the patch onto the side of her neck. 'Shit, that's strong stuff you're on. Was it really that bad?'

Speech was getting easier. 'You have no idea,' she mumbled. At the edge of her world a tidal wave of despair was gathering, ready to crash down on her as the synthetic endorphin high receded before the antidote patch. Dosing herself up had seemed like a good idea while she was alone and his flight was in plasma blackout on the way down, but now she was coming out from it she wondered how she could have done something so stupid. She reached out and grabbed his wrist. 'Go. Fetch a couple of bottles of wine from the kitchen. Then I'll tell you.'

He was gone a long time – possibly minutes, although it felt like hours – and when he came back he'd shed most of his outerwear, acquired a bottle and two glasses, and his face was pale and drawn. 'Shiva's balls, Rachel, how the fuck did you let yourself get roped into something like that?' Clearly the media had caught up with him in the kitchen. He put the glasses down, sat beside her, and helped her sit up. 'It's all over the multis. That fucking *animal*—'

His arm was round her shoulders. She leaned against him. 'Lunatic squad,' she said hoarsely. 'Once in, never out. I'm a negotiator, remember? There was nobody else here who could do it, so—' She shrugged.

'But they shouldn't have called you— ' His arm tensed.

'You. Listen.' She swallowed. 'Open the bottle.'

'Okay.' Martin, wisely sensing that this wasn't a good place to take the conversation, shut up and poured her a glass of wine. It was a cheap red Merlot, and it hadn't had time to breathe, but she didn't want it for the flavor. 'Was it true you were the only one they could call? I mean—'

'Yes.' She drained the glass, then held it out for more. He poured himself one, then refilled hers. 'And no, I don't think there was anyone else who could do the job. Or any other way. Not with the resources to hand. This is a peaceful 'burg. No WMD team on twenty-four-by-seven standby, just a couple of volunteers. Who were on a training course in Brasilia when the shit hit the fan.'

'It was—' He swallowed. 'There were camera flies all over the place. I saw the feed downstairs.'

'How was Luna?' she asked, changing the subject pointedly.

'Gray and drab, just like always.' He took a sip, but didn't meet her eyes. 'I've . . . Rachel, please don't change the subject.'

'No?' She stared at him until he looked away.

'At least try to give me some warning next time.'

'I tried to get a message to you,' she replied irritably. 'You were in re-entry blackout. It all blew up really fast.' She pulled a face, then sniffed again. 'Jesus, I'm crying,' she said, half-disgusted. 'This isn't like me.'

'Everyone does that sooner or later,' he said. She put the glass down, and Martin stroked the side of her arm, trying to soothe her.

'Asshole thought he could use me as a public convenience,' she said quietly. 'Someone holds a gun to your head and tells you to fuck, most legal codes call that rape, don't they? Even if the gun is actually a bomb, and you get to use your hands instead of your mouth or cunt.' She took a deep breath. 'But I'm not a victim.' She held out her glass. 'Give me a refill. The fucker's sleeping with the donor organs tonight, while *I* shall be getting drunk. All right?' She took another deep breath. Everything was getting easier, now Martin was here, and the alcohol was taking effect. 'Because when I walked through that door I had a good idea what could happen, and I also knew what was at stake, and I did it of my own free will.' Stray drops of wine fell on the comforter, spreading out in a wide stain. 'I've been in worse situations. And in the morning I will be sober, and he'll still be fucking ugly. And dead.' She giggled. 'But y'know what I want right now?'

'Tell me?' he asked, uncertainly.

She sat up, throwing the comforter on the floor. 'I want another bath,' she announced. 'With my favorite bath toy: you. Lots of oil, foam, and stuff. Some good wine this time, not this crap. And I want one of your back rubs. I want to feel your hands all over me. And once I'm relaxed I want to hit up a couple of lines of something to turn me on, and then I want to fuck you until we're both exhausted. And raw.' She sat up, unsteadily, and leaned on Martin as she tried to get out of bed. 'Then tomorrow, or sometime whenever, I'm going to go and piss on the fuckwit's grave. You coming with me?'

Martin nodded, uncertain. 'Promise me you'll try to get your name off the register?' he asked.

'I'll try,' she said, abruptly sober. She shuddered. 'Whether I'll succeed is another matter, though. It's a dirty job, but *someone's* got to do it. And most people are too smart to volunteer in the first place.'

She returned to consciousness slowly, half-aware of a pounding headache and a nauseated stomach, in conjunction with sore leg muscles and crumpled bedding. A feeling that she was far too dirty to have just had two baths preoccupied her for a moment until another thought intruded — where was Martin?

'Ow,' she moaned, opening her eyes. Martin was sitting up on the other side of the bed, watching her with a quizzical expression. He seemed to be listening to something.

'It's George Cho,' he said, sounding puzzled. 'I thought you had your phone blocked?'

'George?' She struggled to sit up. 'What time is it?' An icon blinked into view, hovering in front of the wardrobe. 'Oh shit.' *Three in the morning. What does George want with me at three o'clock?* she wondered. 'Nothing good . . . pass the call?'

'Rachel? No video?'

'We're in *bed*, George,' she said indistinctly. 'It's the middle of the night. What the hell did you think?'

'Oh, I'm sorry.' A picture blinked into view on the flat surface of the wardrobe. George was one of the few mainstream career diplomats senior enough to know what her real job description was. Normally dapper, and cultivating a bizarre facsimile of old age that some of the more primitive polities seemed to mistake for *distinguished*, George currently looked worried and unkempt. 'It's a code red,' he said apologetically.

Rachel sat up as fast as she could. 'Hold on a minute,' she said. 'Where'd you put the hangover juice, Martin?'

'Bathroom, left cupboard, top shelf,' he said.

'Give me a minute,' she told George. 'Okay?'

'Er, yes indeed.' He nodded, looking worriedly at the pickup.

It took her one minute precisely to grab a bathrobe, a glass of water, and the bottle of wakeup juice. 'This had better be good,' she warned George. 'What's the hurry?'

'Can you be ready to move in half an hour?' asked Cho, looking nervous. 'It's a full dress team op. I've been trying to get through to you for hours. You weren't at the office this afternoon – what happened?'

Rachel glared at the camera: 'You were too busy to notice some asshole trying to blow up the whole of Geneva?'

'You were involved in that?' George looked astonished. 'I assure you, I didn't know – but this is far more important.'

'Don't.' She yawned. 'Just spill it.'

'I'll be giving everybody the full briefing en route—'

'*Everybody?* How many people are you bringing in? What do you mean by en route – and how long is this going to take?'

George shrugged uncomfortably. 'I can't tell you that. Just plan for at least a month.'

'A month. Shit.' Rachel frowned at Martin's expression of dismay. 'This would be out-of-system, then?'

'Er, I can't confirm or deny, but that's a good guess.'

'Open-ended.'

'Yes.'

'Diplomatic. Black-bag. Or you wouldn't want me along.'

'I-can-neither-confirm-nor-deny-that. At this time. Obviously.'

'You *bastard*!' she breathed. 'No, not you, George.' She shook her head. 'You realize I'm due about six years' sabbatical, coming up in three months? Do you *also* realize I got married a couple of months ago and we're planning on starting a family? What about my partner?'

George took a deep breath. He looked unhappy. 'What do you want?'

'I want a—'

Rachel stopped dead for a moment. *Code red*, she thought, an icy sense of dread insinuating itself into her tired head. *That's* really *serious, isn't it?* Code red was reserved for war alerts – not necessarily ones that would bring the Security Council into play, but the code didn't get used if shots weren't about to be fired. Which meant . . .

'—I want a double berth,' she snapped. 'I come back from a year-long clusterfuck in the New Republic, get hauled over the coals by some harpy from head office because of the *hospitality* budget, have to deal with the mess when some lunatic is visited by the Plutonium Fairy and tries to landscape downtown Geneva by way of an art happening because he can't get a handjob, and now you want to drag me away from home and hearth on a wild goose chase into the back of nowhere: I figure a double berth is the least you can do for me.'

'Oh.' George held up his right hand. 'Excuse me, just a moment.' His eyes flickered with laser speckle as some urgent news beamed straight onto his retinas. 'You haven't registered a change of status. I didn't realize—'

'Damn right you didn't realize. No long solo postings anymore, George, not for the foreseeable and not without planning.'

'Well.' He looked thoughtful. 'We need you right now. But . . .' He rubbed his chin. 'Look, I'll try to get your husband or wife a diplomatic passport and a ticket out to, er, the embassy destination on the next available transport. But we need *you, now,* no messing.'

Rachel shook her head. 'Not good enough. Martin comes along, or I don't go.'

Across the bedroom, Martin crossed his arms, shrugged, miming incomprehension. Rachel pretended not to see.

'If that's your final word,' George said slowly. He thought for a minute. 'I think I can manage that, but only if your husband consents to sign on as a staff intern. There's a fast courier ship waiting in orbit; this isn't a joyride. Are you willing to do that?'

Rachel glanced sidelong at Martin. 'Are you?'

He raised an eyebrow, then after a moment he nodded. 'It'll do. I've got nothing coming up in the next month, anyway. If you think . . .?'

'I do.' She forced herself to smile at him, then glanced back in-field at George. 'He'll take it.'

'Good,' George said briskly. 'If you can be ready to travel in an hour, that would be good. No need to bring clothing or supplies – there's a budget for that en route. Just bring yourselves. Um, this child – it hasn't been fertilized yet? Neither you nor your husband is pregnant, I hope?'

'No.' Rachel shook her head. 'You want us in one hour? You can't even hint what this is about?'

For a moment Cho looked haggard. 'Not until we're under way,' he said quietly. 'It's a maximum-security issue. But . . . about today. How many lives did you save?'

'Um. Three hundred kilotons would be . . . all of Geneva, if you want to look at it like that. About half a million people. Call it half of them dead, the other half homeless, if our little friend had got his shit together. Why?'

'Because about a thousand times that many people will die if we don't pull this one off,' George said with quiet vehemence. 'And that's just for starters . . .'

another day, another editorial

The Times of London — thundering the news since 1785! Now brought to you by Frank the Nose, sponsored by Consolidated Vultee Interstellar, Mariposa Interstructures, Bank Muamalat al-Failaka, CyberMouse™, and The First Universal Church of Kermit.

LEADER

I want to talk to you about the disaster in New Moscow. Even if you phrase it in the morally bankrupt language of so-called objective journalism, this is a truly sickening mess, the kind of colossal eight-way clusterfuck that exists to keep angels, warbloggers, and every other species of disaster whore as happy as a wino in a whisky barrel. Like most people downline in this venerable organ's light cone, you probably think New Moscow is someone else's headache — a two-cow backwater McWorld populated by sinister sheep-swivers who tried messing around with godbreaker tech and got whacked, hard, by the Eschaton. A bit of hard gamma, a pretty new nebula, and it'll all blow over in a couple more years. A recent flash survey commissioned by this blog found that 69 percent of earthworms had never heard of New Moscow; of those who had, 87 percent were sure that it has nothing to do with Terrestrial politics, and by the way, blow jobs aren't really sexual intercourse, that old pervert Santa Claus comes down your chimney every December 25, and the Earth is flat.

Well, now is the time to peel back the foreskin of misconception and apply the wire brush of enlightenment to this mass of sticky half-truths and lies. The truth hurts, but not as much as the consequences of willful ignorance.

I was on New Moscow nine years ago, doing the usual peripatetic long-haul circuit climb out through the fleshpots of Septagon, the rural sprawl of Two Rivers, and whatever wild overgeneralizations you prefer to pin on places like Al-Assad, Brunei, and Beethoven. New Moscow was – I tell you three times – *not* a bucolic rural backwater. It's kind of hard to be a bucolic rural backwater planet when you've got six continental-scale state governments participating in a planetary federation, cities the size of Memphis, Ajuba, and Tokyo, and an orbital infrastructure capable of building fusion-powered interplanetary freighters.

Insular is a word you might want to try pinning on New Moscow – how cosmopolitan can you be, with only two hundred million citizens and no shipyards capable of manufacturing FTL drive kernels? – but they maintained their core industrial competences better than many postintervention colonies, and they lived pretty well. Just because your ancestors came from Iowa and Kansas and you talk like you're yawning the whole time, it does not follow that you are stupid, primitive, inbred, or a mad imperialist set on galactic conquest. I found the people of New Moscow to be generally as tolerant, friendly, open-minded, outward-looking, energetic, funny and humane as any other people I've known. If you were looking for the stereotypical McWorld, Moscow would be it: settled by unwilling refugees from the twenty-first-century Euro-American mainstream culture, people who took enlightenment values, representative democracy, mutual tolerance, and religious freedom as axioms, and built a civilization on that basis. A McWorld, we call them – bland, comfortable, tolerant, heirs to the Western historical tradition. Another description that fits would be: boring.

Except, someone fucking murdered them.

'Edbot: tweak my scat-profile down to point seven. I think I'm laying it on a bit heavily here.'

Shocked at the bad language? Good: I wanted to get your attention. What happened on New Moscow is shocking because it could have happened anywhere. It could have happened right here, on Earth – where you probably are right now, seeing how 70 percent of you readers are left-behinds – or on Marid's world. It could even have happened to the obnoxious imperialist fuckwits from Orion's Law or the quiet enlightened muslim technocrats of Bohraj. We are *all* vulnerable, because whoever vaped New Moscow has gotten clean away with a monstrous crime, and as long as there's no formal investigation, they're going to think maybe they can do it again. And I'm telling you now, whoever they are they are not a Muscovite.

The Times has managed to secure exclusive access to the Sixfold State Commission's last available internal government budget, passed just under two years before the Zero Incident. (The most recent budget was not publicly released prior to the disaster.) We believe these data to be accurate, and I can assure you that military spending which might have provoked an Eschatological incursion was not even on the radar. A detailed audit [*Edbot: add hyperlinks for supplementary material*] shows that the official military spend was 270 million a year on maintaining the STL deterrent fleet, and another 600 mil on civil defense: mostly against natural disasters. There was not enough slack in the budget to buy more than another 100 mil in black project spend, and New Moscow's shipyards — crucially — lacked the expertise and tooling to build or repair FTL fabrications. No causality-violation warfare here, folks, there's nothing to see, nothing that might have caught the attention of the big E, no infrastructure for developing forbidden weapons or violating Rule Three. Accusing these guys of secretly building a causality-violation weapon just doesn't hold water. On the other hand, they *had* just signed a cooperation and collaboration treaty with their nasty neighbors in Newpeace, which suggests several unpleasant possibilities, but nothing firm enough to print in a newsblog. At least, not yet.

Bottom line, someone did it *to* them. Probably some nasty sneaky human faction with weapons of mass destruction and an axe to grind against Moscow's government, a perceived grudge that drove them to massacre millions of innocents purely to avenge some slight inflicted, no doubt, in complete ignorance of the fact that it *was* a slight. In other words, an act of genocide.

Finally: to the gradgrind scum in the feedback forum who says that the destruction of New Moscow by Act of Weakly Godlike Being means we should withhold funds from the aid and hardship budget to help resettle the refugees, all I can say is fuck off and die. You fill me with contempt. I am so angry that I shouldn't really be writing this; I'm surprised the keyboard isn't melting under my fingertips. I'm appalled that the question ever arose in the first place. You aren't fit to be allowed to read the *Times*, and I'm canceling your subscription forthwith. You are a disgrace to the human species – kindly become extinct.

Ends (*Times* Leader)

Frank stubbed out his cigar angrily, grinding what was left of it into the ashtray with his thumb. 'Fuck 'em,' he grumbled to himself 'Fuck 'em.' He took a deep breath, sucking in the blue soup that passed for air in his cramped stateroom. Sooner or later he'd have to turn the ventilation back on and pull down the plastic film he'd spread all over the smoke detector – otherwise, the life-support stewards would come round and give him their usual patronizing-but-polite lecture on shipboard life-support systems – but for now he took an obscure comfort in his ability to inhale the smog of his choice. Everything else about this ship was out of his grasp, locked down like a mobile theme park, and as a compulsive control-twiddler, Frank was pathologically uncomfortable with any environment he couldn't mess up to his heart's content.

Frank was pissed. He was so angry he had to get up and walk, before he gave in to the temptation to start banging his head on the bulkhead. It was one of his biggest problems, he admitted: he had an appalling capacity to feel other people's pain. If he'd been able to have it surgically removed, he'd have done so – maybe he'd then have been able to make a career for himself in politics. But as it was, given his vocation, it just gave him violent conscience-aches. Especially when, as on this cruise, he was going to have to exorcise some of his own ghosts. So he blinked away the workflow and copy windows, folded up his keyboard and dropped it in a pocket, stood up, took a final deep breath of the blue toxic waste cloud – then opened the door for the first time in nearly twenty-four hours.

Somewhere in the crew quarters of the *Romanov* an alarm siren was probably whooping: 'Danger! The troll in suite B312 has emerged! Send deodorant spray and prepare to decontaminate corridor B3! Danger! Danger! Chemical warfare alert!' He sniffed the unnaturally pure air, nostrils flaring. A big man, with a beetling brow and an expressive nose, one of his ex-lovers had described him as resembling a male silverback gorilla, a resemblance that his silver-and-black close-cropped hair only emphasized. Right then his skin glowed with youthful vigor, and he was almost vibrating with energy: he'd had his first telomere reset and aging fix only six months before, and was filled with a restless teenage exuberance that he'd almost forgotten existed. It was overflowing into his work by way of pugnacious editorials and take-no-prisoners prose, and after a few hours of writing it nearly had him bouncing off the ceiling.

The corridor was lined with doorways and walled with plush beige carpet, recessed handholds, and safety nets ready to turn it into a series of safety cubes in event of off-axis acceleration. Here and there, recessed false windows looked out onto scenes of bucolic harmony, desert sunsets and sandy beaches, vying with lush tropical rain forests and breathtaking starscapes. Indirect lighting turned it into a shadowless tube, bland as a business hotel and twice as boring. And it smelled of synthetic pine.

Frank snorted as he ambled along the corridor. He detested and despised this aspect of interstellar travel. What was the point of embarking on a perilous journey to far-off worlds if the experience was much like checking into one of those expensively manicured racks of self-contained service apartments designed to appeal to the lowest-common-denominator shit-for-brains salesdrone? Hotels with carefully bland hand-painted artwork on the walls, a cupboard where the ready-meal of your choice would appear in a prepack ready to eat, and the ceiling above the emperor-sized bed was ready to screen a hundred thousand crap movies or play a million shit immersives.

Well, fuck 'em! Fuck the complacent assholes, and their trade-mission-to-the-stars quick buck mentality. Inward-looking, pampered, greedy, and unwilling to look at anything beyond the end of their noses that doesn't come with a reassuringly expensive price tag attached. Fuck 'em and their consumer demand for bland, boring flying hotels with supercilious or patronizing hired help, and absolutely nothing that might give them any sign they weren't in Kansas anymore, Toto, that they might actually be aboard a million tons of smart matter wrapped around a quantum black hole slipping across the event horizon of the observable universe on a wave of curved space-time. Gosh, if they realized what was happening, they might be *disturbed, frightened,* even! And that might make them less inclined to buy a ticket with WhiteStar in future, thus impacting the corporate bottom line, so . . .

Frank had traveled by oxcart. He'd traveled on antiquated tramp freighters that had to spin their crew quarters like a wheel to provide a semblance of gravity. He'd spent one memorable night huddling with other survivors on the back of an armored personnel carrier thundering across desert sands, neck itching in the edgily imagined sights of the victor's gunships, and he'd spent a whole week huddled in the bottom of a motorized vaporetto in a swampy river delta near the town of Memphis, on Octavio. Compared to any of those experiences this was the lap of luxury. It was also puerile, bland, and – worst of all – characterless.

At the end of the gently curving corridor Frank pushed through a loose curtain that secured access onto a landing that curved around the diamond-walled helix of a grand staircase, spacecraft-style. The staircase itself was organic, grown painstakingly from a single modified mahogany tree that had been coaxed into a spiral inside its protective tube, warped into a half-moon cross-section, then brutally slain and partially dissected by a team of expert carpenters. It led up through the eleven passenger decks of the ship, all the way to the stellarium with its diamond-phase optically clean dome – covered, now, because the aberration of starlight from the ship's pilot wave had dimmed everything except gamma-ray bursters to invisibility. He glanced around, puzzled by the lack of passengers or white-suited human stewards, then did a double take as he checked his watch. 'Four in the morning?' he grunted at nobody in particular. 'Huh.' Not that the hour meant much to him, but most people lived by the ship's clocks, trying to keep a grip on the empire time standard that bound the interstellar trading circuits together, which meant they'd be asleep, and most of the public areas would be shut for maintenance.

The night bar on F deck was still open, and Frank was only slightly breathless from hauling himself round fifteen hundred degrees of corkscrewing staircase when he arrived, pushed through the gilt-and-crystal doors, and looked around.

A handful of night owls hung out in the bar even at this late hour: one or two lone drinkers grimly tucked away the hard stuff, and a circle of half a dozen chattering friends clustered around a table in the corner. It was often hard to judge people's age, but there was something that looked young about their social interaction. Maybe they were students on the Grand Tour, or a troupe of workers caught up in one of those unusual vortices of labor market liquidity that made it cheaper to take the workers where the work was rather than vice versa. Frank had seen *that* before – he'd been on the receiving end himself once, back when he was young and clueless. He snorted to himself and slouched onto one of the barstools. 'I'll have a Wray and Nephew on ice, no mixer,' he grunted at the bartender, who nodded silently, realized that Frank didn't want a whole lot of chatter with his drink, and turned away to serve it up.

'Good voyage so far, eh, what-what?' chirped a voice from somewhere by his left shoulder.

Frank glanced round. 'Good for some,' he said, biting back his first impulsive comment. You never could tell who you'd run across in a bar at four in the morning, as at least one senior government bureaucrat had discovered after being mugged by the *Times* and left for dead in the Appointments pages. Frank had no intention of giving anything away, even to an obvious weirdo. Which this guerrilla conversationalist clearly was, from the tips of his ankle boots – one of which was red, and the other green – to the top of his pointy plush skull cap (which was electric blue with a dusting of holographic stars). Soulfully deep brown eyes and crimson moustache notwithstanding, he looked like an escapee from a reeducation camp for fashion criminals. 'You'll pardon me for saying this, but I didn't come down here for a co-therapy session,' Frank rumbled. The bartender punctuated his observation with a clink of crystal on teak; Frank picked up his shot glass and sniffed the colorless liquid.

'That's all right, I didn't come here for a good laugh, either.' The colorful squirt nodded in exaggerated approval then snapped his fingers at the bartender. 'I'll have one of whatever he's having,' he piped.

Frank stifled a sigh and glanced at the gaggle of youths. They had a depressingly clean-cut, short-haired, brutally scrubbed look: there was not a single piercing, chromatophore, braid, or brand among the whole lot. It reminded him of something disturbing he'd seen somewhere, but in thirty-odd years of traveling around the settled worlds he'd seen enough that the specifics were vague. They seemed suspiciously healthy in a red-cheeked outdoors kind of way. Probably Dresdener students, children of the hereditary managementariat, off on their state-funded *wanderjahr* between high gymnasium studies and entry into the government bureaucracy. They all wore baggy brown trousers and gray sweaters, as identically cut as a uniform, or maybe they just came from a world where fashion victims were run out of town on a rail. There was just enough variation to suggest that they'd actually chosen to dress for conformity rather than having it thrust upon them. He glanced back at the technicolor squirt. 'It's cask-strength,' he warned, unsure why he was giving even that much away.

'That's okay.' The squirt took a brief sniff, then threw back half the glass. 'Whee! Hey, I'll have another of these. What did you say it was called?'

'Wray and Nephew,' Frank said wearily. 'It's an old and horribly expensive rum imported direct from Old Earth, and you are going to regret it tomorrow morning. Um, evening. Or whenever you get the bill.'

'So?' The paint factory explosion picked up his glass,

twirled it around, and threw the contents at the back of his throat. 'Wow. I needed that. *Thank you* for the introduction. I can *tell* we're going to have a long and fruitful relationship. *Me* and the bottle, I mean.'

'Well, so long as you don't blame me for the hangover . . .' Frank took a sip and glanced around the bar, but with the exception of the Germanic diaspora clones there didn't seem to be any prospect of rescue.

'So where are you going, what-what?' asked the squirt, as the bartender planted a second glass in front of him.

'Septagon, next.' Frank surrendered to the inevitable. 'Then probably on to New Dresden, then over to Vienna – I hear they've taken in some refugees from Moscow. Would you know anything about that? I'm skipping Newpeace.' He shuddered briefly. 'Then when the ship closes the loop back to New Dresden, I'm coming aboard again for the run back to Septagon and Earth, or wherever else work takes me.'

'Ah! Hmm.' A thoughtful look creased the short guy's face. 'You a journalist, then?'

'No, I'm a warblogger,' Frank admitted, unsure whether to be irritated or flattered. 'What are you here for?'

'I'm a clown, and my stage name's Svengali. Only I'm off duty right now, and if you ask me to crack a joke, I'll have to make inquiries as to whether your home culture permits dueling.'

'Erm.' Frank focused on the short man properly, and somewhere in his mind a metaphorical gear train revolved and locked into place with a *clunk*. He took a big sip of rum, rolled it around his mouth, and swallowed. 'So. Who are you *really?* Uh, I'm not recording this – I'm off duty too.'

'A man after my own heart.' Svengali grinned humorlessly. 'There's nothing funny about being a clown, at least not after the first six thousand repetitions. I can't even remember my own name. I'm working my way around the fucking galaxy entertaining morons who live in shitholes and stashing away all the *blat* I can manage. People who don't live in shitholes I don't perform for because I might want to retire to a non-shithole one of these days.'

'Oh. So you're working for WhiteStar?'

'Yes, but strictly contract. I don't hold with industrial serfdom.'

'Oh. So is there much call for clowns on a liner?'

Svengali took another sip of rum before replying in a bored monotone: 'The WhiteStar liner *Romanov* carries 2,318 passengers, 642 cabin crew, and 76 engineering and flight crew. By our next port of call, in eleven days' time, that number will have increased by one – two births and, according to the actuaries, there's a 70 percent probability of at least one death on this voyage, although there hasn't been one yet. There are thirty-one assorted relatives and hangers-on of crew members aboard, too. Now, most of this mob are well into their extended adulthood, but of the total, 118 are prepubertal horrors suffering from too much adult attention – they're mostly single children, or have siblings more than twenty years older than them, which makes for much the same species of spoiled brat. Someone has to keep the yard apes entertained, and they're far more demanding than adults: cheap passives and interactives only go so far. In fact' – Svengali raised his glass and tipped the bartender a wink – 'they're exhausting. And that's before you get me started on the so-called adults.'

Frank put his glass down. 'The revue,' he said. 'That damn cabaret act that keeps spamming me with invitations. Is that anything to do with you?'

Svengali looked disturbed. 'Don't blame me,' he said. 'It's official company Ents policy to rape the nostalgia market for all it's worth. Consider yourself, a business traveler who can use his time productively on the journey: you're an exception to the general rule, which is that most travelers are bored silly and can't do anything about it. People travel to arrive at a destination. So, why would they want to stay awake through weeks of boredom, eating their heads off in an expensive stateroom when they could be tucked up in a vitrification pod in the cargo bay? Deadheads in steerage consume no oxygen, don't get bored, and buy no expensive meals or entertainments en route. So the company has to lay on *diversions* and *novelties* if they are to extract the maximum revenue from their passengers. Do you realize that the Ents manager on this ship outranks the chief engineer? Or that there's an unofficial revenue enhancement target of 50 percent over the bare room and board tariff per waking passenger?' He nodded slyly at Frank's refilled glass of rum. 'For all you know, I could be a revenue protection officer and this glass of mine is drinking water. I'm here to keep you drinking in this bar until you collapse under the table, to the greater glory of WhiteStar's bottom line.'

'You wouldn't do that,' Frank said with a degree of magisterial assurance that came from three shots of cask-strength rum and a finely tuned bullshit detector. 'You're a fucking anarchist, and your next drink's on me, right?'

'Um.' Svengali sighed. 'You're making presumptions on my honesty, and I've only known you for five minutes, but I thank you from the bottom of my bitter and twisted little ventricles. What kind of blogger *are* you, to be giving precious alcohol away?'

'One who wants to get drunk as a skunk, in company. Hard fucking editorial, the copy fought back, and there are no politicians to go beat up on until we get wherever it is that we're going. My momma always told me that drinking on your own was bad, so I'm doing my best to live up to her advice. Really, you won't like me anymore when you get to know me; I'm heartless when I'm sober.'

'Hmm, I may be able to help you. I've got the heart of an eight-year-old boy; I keep it in a jar of formaldehyde in my luggage. Er, please excuse me – if that's funny I'm supposed to bill you.'

'Don't worry, it was dead on arrival.'

'That's all right then.'

'Make mine a Talisker,' said Frank, turning to the bartender. 'What cigars have you got?'

'Cigars, you say?' asked Svengali: 'I'm fresh out of bangers.'

'Yeah, cigars.' In the far corner the clean-living crew began singing something outdoors-ish and rhythmic in what sounded to Frank's ear to be a dialect descended from German. Much thumping of beer glasses ensued. Svengali winced and took two fat Havanas from the offered humidor, then passed one to Frank. 'Hey, you got a light?' Svengali shrugged and snapped his fingers. Flame blossomed.

'Thanks.' Frank took an experimental puff, winced slightly, and took another. 'That's better. Whisky and cigars, what else is there to life?'

'Good sex, money, and the death of enemies,' said Svengali. 'Not right now, I hasten to add: experience and honesty compels me to admit that mixing shipboard life with sex, money, and murder is generally a bad idea. But once I get off at New Dresden – end of this circuit, for now, for me – I confess I might just indulge in one or the other preoccupation.'

'Not murder, I hope.'

Svengali grinned humorlessly. 'And what would a simple clown have to do with that? The only things I murder are straight lines.'

'I'm glad to hear it.' Frank took another puff from his cigar and let the smoke trickle out in a thick blue stream. He pretended not to notice the bartender surreptitiously inserting a pair of nose plugs. 'Did you ever run into any refugees from Moscow?'

'Hmm, that would be about, what, four years ago indeed?'

'About that,' Frank agreed. 'The event itself happened' – he paused to check his watch – 'about four years and nine months ago, normalized empire time.'

'Hmm.' Svengali nodded. 'Yes, there were outlying stations weren't there? I remember that.' He put his cigar down for a moment. 'It really bit the flight schedules hereabouts. Every ship had to stand to arms for rescue missions! Indeed it did. However, I was working for a most malignant circus impresario at the time, groundside on Morgaine – a woman by the name of Eleanor Ringling. She had this strange idea that clowning was in the nature of unskilled labor, and used us harder than the animals. In the end I actually had to *escape* from that one, false papers and cash down for a freezer ticket off planet because she was trying to tie me up in court over an alleged bond of indenture she'd faked my spittle on.' He snorted. 'Think I'll stay on the rum, what?'

'Be my guest.' Frank puffed on his cigar, which, while not on a par with his private supply, was well within the remit of various arms control committees and definitely suitable for a public drinking establishment. 'Hmm. Ringling. Name rings a bell, I think. Didn't she turn up dead under peculiar circumstances a couple of years ago? Caused a scandal or something.'

'I couldn't possibly comment. But it wouldn't surprise me if an elephant sat on her – the woman had a way of making enemies. If I'm ever on the same continent, I think

I'll make a point of visiting her grave. Just to make sure she's dead, you understand.'

'You must have got on like a house on fire.'

'Oh we did, we did,' Svengali said fervently. 'She was the arsonist and I was the accelerant: her predilection for being tied up and sat on a butt plug while being beaten with sausages by a man wearing a rubber nose was the ignition source. We—' He stopped, looking at something behind Frank.

'What is' – Frank turned round – 'it?' he finished, looking up, and up again, at the silent and disapproving face of one of the youths from the other table. He was blond, lantern-jawed, and built like a nuclear missile bunker. He was so tall that he even succeeded in looking over Frank.

'You are poisoning the air,' he said, icily polite. 'Please cease and desist at once.'

'Really?' Frank switched on his shit-eating grin: *There's going to be trouble.* 'How strange, I hadn't noticed. This is a public bar, isn't it?'

'Yes. The matter stands. I do not intend to inhale your vile stench any further.' The kid's nostrils flared.

Frank took a full mouthful of smoke and allowed it to dribble out of his nostrils. 'Hey, bartender. Would you care to fill laughing boy here in on shipboard fire safety?'

'Certainly.' It was the first thing he'd heard the bartender say since he arrived. She looked like the strong, silent type, another young woman working her way around the worlds to broaden her horizons on a budget. One side of her head was shaven to reveal an inset intaglio of golden wires; her shoulder muscles bulged slightly under her historically inauthentic tank top and bow tie. 'Sir, this is a general intoxicants bar. For passengers who wish to smoke, drink, and inject. It's the only part of this ship they're allowed to do that in, on this deck.'

'So.' Frank glared at the fellow. 'What part of that don't you understand? This is the smoking bar, and if you'd like to avoid the smell, I suggest you find a nonsmoking bar — or take it up with the Captain.'

'I don't think so.' For a moment square-jaw looked mildly annoyed, as if a mosquito was buzzing around his ears, then an instant later Frank felt a hand like an industrial robot's grab him by the throat.

'Hans! No!' It was one of the women from the table, rising to her feet. 'I forbid it!' Her voice rang with the unmistakable sound of self-assured authority.

Hans let go instantly and took a step back from Frank, who coughed and glared at him, too startled to even raise a fist. 'Hey, asshole! You looking for a—'

A hand landed on his shoulder from behind. 'Don't,' whispered Svengali. 'Just *don't*.'

'Hans. Apologize to the man,' said the blonde. 'At *once*.'

Hans froze, his face like stone. 'I am sorry,' he said tonelessly. 'I did not intend to lay hands on you. I must atone now. Mathilde?'

'Go — I think you should go to your room,' said the woman, moderating her tone. Hans turned on his heel and marched toward the door. Frank stared at his back in gathering fury, but by the time he glanced back at the table the strength-through-joy types were all studiously avoiding looking in his direction.

'What the fuck was that about?' he demanded.

'I can call the purser's office if you'd like an escort back to your room,' the bartender suggested. She finally brought both hands out from below the bar. 'That guy was *fast*.'

'Fast?' Frank blinked. 'Yeah, I'd say. He was like some kind of martial arts—' He stopped, rubbed his throat, glanced down at the ashtray. His cigar lay, half-burned, mashed flat as a pancake. 'Oh fuck. *That* kind of fast.

Did you see that?' he asked, beginning to tremble.

'Yeah,' Svengali said quietly. 'Military-grade implants. I think my friend here could do with that escort,' he told the bartender. 'Don't turn your back on that guy if you see him again,' he added in a low conversational tone, pitched to avoid the other side of the room.

'I don't understand—'

'This drink's on me. One for you, too,' Svengali told the bartender.

'Thanks.' She poured them both a shot of rum, then pulled out a bottle of some kind of smart drink. 'Sven, did my eyes fool me, or did you have some sort of gadget in your hand?'

'I couldn't possibly comment, Eloise.' The clown shrugged, then knocked back half the glass in one go. 'Hmm. That must be my fifth shot this evening. Better crank up my liver.'

'What *was* that about—'

'We get all types through here,' said Eloise the bartender. She leaned forward on the bar. 'Don't mess with these folks,' she whispered.

'Anything special?' asked Svengali.

'Just a feeling.' She put the bottle down. 'They're flakes.'

'Flakes? I've done flakes.' Svengali shrugged. 'We've got fucking Peter Pans and Lolitas on the manifest. Flakes don't go crazy over a little cigar smoke in a red-eye bar.'

'They're not *normal* flakes,' she insisted.

'I think he'd have killed me if she hadn't stopped him,' Frank managed to say. His hand holding the glass was shaking, rattling quietly on the bar top.

'Probably not.' Svengali finished his shot glass. 'Just rendered you unconscious until the cleanup team got here.' He raised an eyebrow at Eloise. 'Is there a panic button under the bar, or were you just masturbating furiously?'

'Panic button, putz.' She paused. 'Say, nobody told me about any ersatz juvies. How do I tell if they come in my bar?'

'Go by the room tag manifest for their ages. Don't assume kids are as young as they look. Or old folks, for that matter. You come from somewhere that restricts life extension rights, don't you?' Svengali shrugged. 'At least most of the Lolitas have a handle on how to behave in public, unlike dumb-as-a-plank there. Damn good thing, that, it can be really embarrassing when the eight-year-old you're trying to distract with a string of brightly dyed handkerchiefs turns out to have designed the weaving machine that made them. Anyway, who *are* those people?'

'One minute.' Eloise turned away and did something with the bar slate. 'That's funny,' she said. 'They're all from someplace called Tonto. En route to Newpeace. Either of you ever heard of it?'

There was a dull *clank* as Frank dropped his glass on the floor.

'Oh shit,' he said.

Svengali stared at him. 'You dropped your drink. Funny, I had you pegged for a man with bottle. You going to tell me what's bugging you, big boy?'

'I've met people from there before.' He glanced at the mirror behind the bar, taking in the table, the five clean-cut types playing cards and studiously ignoring him, their quasi-uniform appearance and robust backwoods build. 'Them. Here. Oh *shit*. I thought the *Romanov* was only making a refueling stop, but it must be a real port of call.'

An elbow prodded him in the ribs; he found Svengali staring up at him, speculation writ large on the off-duty clown's face. 'Come on, back to my room. I've got a bottle stashed in my trunk; you can tell me all about it. Eloise, room party after your shift?'

'I'm off in ten minutes, or whenever Lucid relieves me,' she said. Glancing at him, interestedly: 'Is it a good story?'

'A story?' Frank echoed. 'You could say.' He glanced at the table. A flashback to icy terror prickled across his skin, turned his guts to water. 'We'd better leave quietly.' The woman, Mathilde, the one in charge, was watching him in one of the gilt-framed mirrors. Her expression wasn't so much unfriendly as disinterested, like a woman trying to make up her mind whether or not to swat a buzzing insect. 'Before they really notice us.'

'Now?' Svengali hopped down off his stool and got an arm under Frank's shoulder. He'd had rather a lot to drink, but for some reason Svengali seemed almost sober. Frank, for his part, wasn't sober so much as so frightened that it felt like it. He let Svengali lead him through the door, toward a lift cube, then from it down a narrow uncarpeted corridor to a small, cramped crew stateroom. 'Come on. Not much farther,' said Svengali. 'You want that drink?'

'I want—' Frank shivered. 'Yeah,' he said. 'Preferably somewhere where they don't know it's my room.'

'Somewhere.' Svengali keyed the door open, waved Frank down at one end of the narrow bunk, and shut the door. He rummaged in one of the overhead lockers and pulled out a metal flask and a pair of collapsible shot glasses. 'So how come you know those guys?'

'I'm not sure.' Frank grimaced. 'But they're from Tonto, and going to Newpeace. I had a really bad time on Newpeace once . . .'

the bullet season

Newpeace, 36 years earlier

Frank and Alice watched the beginnings of the demonstration from the top of the Demosthenes Hotel in downtown Samara. The top of the hotel was a flat synrock expanse carpeted in well-manicured grass, now browning at the edges. The swimming pool and bar in the center of the lawn was drained, water long since diverted for emergency irrigation. In fact, most of the hotel staff had gone – conscripted into the Peace Enforcement Organization, fled to the hills, joined the rebels, who knew what.

It wasn't quite Frank's first field job, but it was close enough that Alice, a tanned, blond, hard-as-nails veteran of many botched campaigns, had taken him under her wing and given him a clear-cut – some would say micromanaged – set of instructions for how to run the shop in her absence. Then she'd taken off into the heart of darkness in search of the real story, leaving Frank to cool his heels on

the roof of the hotel. She'd returned from her latest expedition three days earlier, riding the back of a requisitioned
militia truck with a crateful of camera drones and a magic
box that took in water at one end and emitted something
not entirely unlike cheap beer at the other – as long as the
concentrate cans held out. Frank welcomed her back with
mixed emotions. On the one hand, her tendency to use him
as a gofer rankled slightly; on the other, he was slowly
going out of his skull with a mixture of boredom and paranoia, minding the shop on his own and hoping like hell
that nothing happened while the boss was away.

To get the hotel roof (right on the edge of City Square,
empty and untended in the absence of foreign business travelers and visiting out-of-town politicos) they'd had to pay
off the owner, a twitchy-eyelidded off-world entrepreneur
called Vadim Trofenko, with untraceable slugs of buttery,
high-purity gold. Nothing else would do in these troubled
times, it seemed. Getting hold of the stuff had been a royal
pain in the ass, and had entailed Alice going on a week-long
trip up to orbit, leaving Frank to mind the bureau all on his
lonesome. But at least the agency's money was buying them
the penthouse suite, however neglected it was. Most of the
other hacks who'd descended like flies on the injured flank
of the city of Samara to watch the much-ballyhooed descent
into civil war at firsthand had discovered that they could
find accommodation for neither love nor money.

Frank had hung in while his boss was away, hammering
out hangovers and human-angle commentaries by day, and
descending like some kind of pain-feeding vampire from his
rooftop every night to walk the streets and talk to people in
the cafes and bars and on boulevard corners, soaking up
the local color and nodding earnestly at their grievances.
Lately he'd taken to hanging out in the square with a
recorder, where the students and unemployed gathered to

chant their slogans at the uncaring ranks of police and the blank facade of the provincial assembly buildings. He did this long into the night, before staggering back to the big empty hotel bed to crash out. But not this morning.

'I've got a bad feeling, kid,' Alice had told him. She stared pensively out at the square. 'A *really* bad feeling. Look to the back door; you wouldn't want to catch your ass in it when they slam it shut. Somebody's going to blink, and when the shit hits the fan . . .' She gestured at the window, out at the huge poster that covered most of the opposite wall of the square. 'It's the tension, mostly. It seems to be slackening. And that's always a bad sign.'

Big Bill's avuncular face beamed down, jovial and friendly as anyone's favorite uncle, guarded from the protesters by a squad of riot police, day and night. Despite the sentries, someone had managed to fly a handheld drone into the dead politician's right eye, splashing a red paint spot across his iris in a grisly reminder of what had happened to the last elected President.

'I didn't exactly think things were getting better,' Frank equivocated. 'But isn't it just political chicken? Same old same old – they'll devalue the dollaro and get a public works program going, someone will go out into the outback and haggle with Commandante Alpha, and things'll begin working again. Won't they?'

Alice snorted. 'You wish. It only seems to be lightening up because the jokers are getting ready to pull something serious.'

Up top wasn't much different. 'It's gonna burn,' said Thelma, a short, deeply tanned woman who was related to one of the public bizintel agencies out around Turku in some obscurely mercenary way, and who'd weaseled her way into Alice's confidence by sharing her stash of fuel cells with her. She was working over one of Alice's tripod-mounted bug launchers when Frank came up onto the roof. The air still held the last of the night's chill, but the vast glazed dome of the sky promised another skull baker of a day. 'Did you hear about the mess down Cardinal's Way yesterday?'

'Nope. What happened?' Frank held a chipped coffee mug bearing the hotel's crest under the nozzle of Alice's fizzbeer contraption and pushed the button. It gurgled creakily and dribbled a stream of piss-colored fluid, propelled by whatever was left of the hotel's water tankage. The Peace Enforcement had turned off the water supply to the hotels in the business district two days before, officially in case they fell into the hands of subversive elements. In practice, it was a not-so-subtle 'Fuck off, we've got business in hand' signal to the warblogger corps.

'Over by the homeless aid center on West Circular Four. Another car bomb. Anyway, the polis cordoned off the area afterward and arrested *everyone*. Thing is, the car that went bang was an unmarked polis car: one they used for disappearances until a resistance camera tagged it a week ago. The only people who got hurt were doalies queuing for their maintenance. I was on my way there to meet Ish – a source – and word is that before it went up, a couple of cops parked it, then walked away.'

'Uh-huh.' Frank passed her the mug of lukewarm fizzbeer. 'Have you had any luck messaging off planet today?'

'Funny you should ask that.' It was Alice, arriving on deck without warning. 'Someone's been running all the outgoing imagery I sent via the post office through a steg-scrubber, fuzzing the voxels.' She cast Frank a sharp look. 'What makes you ask?'

'Well, I haven't had as much mail as usual . . .' he trailed off. 'How do you know it's being tampered with?' he asked, curiosity winning out.

'How the fuck do you think Eric gets his request messages to me without the Peace Enforcement bugging the call? It's our little back channel.' (Eric was their desk editor back home.)

'That makes sense.' Frank was silent for a moment. 'What's he saying?'

'Time to check our return tickets.' Alice gave a tight little smile.

'Will you guys stop talking in code and tell me what you think's going on?' demanded Thelma.

'The cops are getting ready to break skulls, wholesale,' said Alice, pointing at the far side of the square. 'They've been piling on the pressure for weeks. Now they're lifting off, to let the protesters think they've got a bit of slack. They'll come out to complain, and the cops get to round them all up. If that's the right way to describe what's coming.'

The situation on Newpeace – or, more accurately, in the provincial capitals of Redstone and Samara and Old Venice Beach – had been deteriorating for about three years, ever since the last elections. Newpeace had been settled by (or, it was more accurate to say, the Eschaton had dumped on the planet) four different groups in dispersed areas – confused Brazilian urbanites from Rio; ferocious, insular, and ill-educated hill villagers from Borneo; yet more confused middle-class urban stay-at-homes from Hamburg, Germany; and the contents of a sleepy little seaside town in California. Each colony had been plonked down in a different corner of the planet's one major continent – a long, narrow, skinny thing the shape of Cuba but nearly six thousand kilometers long – along with a bunch of self-replicating robot colony factories, manuals and design libraries sufficient to build and maintain a roughly late-twentieth-century tech level McCivilization, and a ten-meter-tall diamond slab with the

Three Commandments of the Eschaton engraved on it in ruby letters that caught the light of the rising sun.

Leave a planet like that to mature and ferment for three centuries: the result was a vaguely federal system with six major provinces, three languages, a sizable Catholic community, and an equally sizable bunch of Eschaton-worshiping nutbars from the highlands who spent their surplus income building ten-meter-tall cargo cult diamond monoliths. It hadn't been entirely tranquil, but they hadn't fought a major war for nearly two hundred years – until now.

'But isn't most of the resistance out in the hills?' asked Frank. 'I mean, they're not going to come down hard in the towns, are they?'

'They've got to do it, and do it soon,' Alice said irritably. 'Running around the hills is hard work; at least in the city the protesters are easy to find. That's why I say they're going to do it here, and do it soon. You seen the latest on the general strike?'

'Is it going ahead?' Frank raised an eyebrow.

Thelma spat. 'Not if the Peace Enforcement Organization scum get their way.

'Wrong.' Alice looked grimly satisfied. 'The latest I've got from the Transport Workers' collective, last time I spoke to them – Emilio was clear on it being a negotiating gambit. They don't expect actually to have to play that card: it would hurt them far more than it would hurt the federales. But the feds can act as if it's a genuine threat. The collective are playing into their hands. Watch my lips: there's going to be a crackdown. Ever since Friedrich Gotha bought the election after Wilhelm he's been creaming himself looking for an excuse to fuck the rebels hard. Did you hear about Commandante Alpha being in the area? That'd be a bad sign, you ask me. I've been trying to arrange an interview but—'

'Commandante Alpha does not exist,' a woman's voice called from the staircase. Frank turned and squinted against the rising sun. Whoever she was, she'd come up the service stairs: despite the sun in his eyes he had a vague impression of a slightly plump ice blonde, dressed for knocking around the outback like all the other journalists and war whores thronging the city and waiting for the storm to break. Something about her nagged at him for a moment before he realized what it was; her bush jacket and trousers looked as if they'd been laundered less than five minutes earlier. They were crisp, video anchor crisp, militarily precise. *Whoever's paying for the live video bandwidth better have deep pockets*, he thought vaguely as she continued. 'He's a psywar fabrication. Doesn't exist, you see. He's just a totem designed to inspire support and loyalty to the resistance movement among confused villagers.'

'Does it make any difference?' asked Alice. She was busy unpacking another drone as she talked. 'I mean, the thing about a mass movement is, once it gets going it's hard to stop it. Even if you take down a charismatic leader, as long as the roots of the grievance remain, another fucking stupid hero will come along and pick up the flag. Leaders generate themselves. Once you get a cycle of revenge and retribution going . . .'

'Exactly.' The new arrival nodded approvingly. 'That's what's so interesting about it. Commandante Alpha is an idea. To dispose of him the PEO will have to do more than simply point out that he does not exist.'

'Huh?' Frank heard a distant noise like the tide coming in; an impossibility, for they were more than three hundred kilometers from the sea, and besides, Newpeace had no moons large enough to raise tides. He pulled out his keyboard and tapped out a quick note to himself. 'Who did you say you were?'

'I didn't.' The woman stared at him. It was not a friendly expression. 'You are Frank the Nose Johnson, correct?'

Something about her manner made him tense. 'Who's asking?'

She ignored the question. 'And *you* are Alice Spencer, so *you* must be Thelma Couper. Three little piggies, warbloggers united. It's your good luck that you're all very lazy little piggies, up here on the roof this historic morning rather than down on the streets with the unsuspecting mob. If you're *smart* little piggies, you'll stay here and not try to leave the building. Relax, watch the fireworks, drink your beer, and don't bother trying to get an outside line. I'll come for you later.'

Alice grabbed hold of Frank's arm, painfully hard. He hadn't even noticed that he'd begun to move toward the stranger. 'Who the fuck are you?' he demanded.

The woman ignored him, instead turning back to the staircase. 'See you around,' she called over her shoulder, a mocking smile on her face. Alice loosened her grip on Frank's elbow. She took two steps toward the stairwell, then froze. She slowly spread her arms and stepped backwards, away from the steps.

'What—'

'Don't,' Alice said tightly. 'Just don't. I think we're under house arrest.'

Frank looked round the open doorway leading down to the penthouse.

'Hey, freak! Get back! Didn't you hear the boss-woman?'

Frank got. 'Shit!'

'My thoughts exactly.' Alice nodded. 'Y'know what? I think they *want* witnesses. Just far away enough not to smell the tear gas.'

Frank found that his hands were shaking. 'That cop—'

'Smart guy.' It was Thelma; she sounded mocking, but

maybe it was simply nerves – his or hers, didn't matter. 'How's he armed?'

Alice seemed mostly unaffected. 'He's got body armor. Some kind of riot gun.' She paused. 'Shit! He's in blue. Did you see that, Frank?'

Frank nodded. 'So?'

'So, cops hereabouts wear black. Blue means army.'

'Oh. *Oh!*'

The noise outside was getting louder.

'Does that sound like a demonstration to you?' asked Thelma.

'Could be the big one, for the land protesters they locked up last week.' Alice started dictating names to her chunky plastic disposaphone – she'd had it for only three weeks, since she arrived on Newpeace, but the digits were already peeling off the buttons on its fascia – then frowned. 'It keeps saying "network congested." Fuck it. You guys? Can you get through to anyone?'

'I can't be arsed trying,' Thelma said disgustedly. 'It's a setup. Leastways we're supposed to survive this one long enough to file our reports and get out. I think.'

Frank looked at his own phone: it blinked its display at him in electronic perplexity, locked out of the network. He shook his head, unsure what to believe. Then there was a thud from behind him. He turned and saw that someone had come out of the stairwell and fallen over, right at the top. There was blood, bright on the concrete. It was Phibul, the small guy from Siam who was booked in one floor down. Frank knelt beside him. Phibul was breathing fast, bleeding messily from his head. 'You!' Frank looked up and found himself staring up the barrel of a gun. He froze. 'Get this sack of shit outa my face. You show your head, you bettah pray I don' think you doalie.'

Frank licked his lips; they felt like parchment. 'Okay,' he

said, very quietly. Phibul groaned. The guard took a step back, servos whining at knee and ankle. The gun barrel was flecked with red.

'Nothing happen' here,' said the guard. 'You unnerstand?'

'I – I understand.' Frank blinked, humiliated and angry, but mostly just frightened. The guard took another step back, down the stairs, then another. Frank didn't move until he was out of sight at the bottom. Phibul groaned again and he looked down, then began fumbling in his pockets for his first-aid kit.

The surf-on-a-beach noise was joined by a distant hammering drone: the sound of drums and pipe, marching with the people.

'Let me help, dammit!' Frank looked up as Thelma knelt beside him. 'Shit.' She gently peeled back one of Phibul's eyelids, then the other. 'Pupillary reflex is there, but he's gonna have some concussion.'

'Fucker whacked him over the head with his gun barrel.'

'Could be worse,' she said tersely. 'C'mon. Let's get him over to the sun lounger.'

A couple of pops and whines came from the edge of the roof – Alice was sending bird-sized drones spinning through the air to orbit overhead, circling for perspective shots taking in the entire square. Frank took a deep breath, smelling hot blood, Thelma's sweat – surprisingly rank – and the stink of his own fear. A hot tangy undernote of dust rose from the soon-to-be-baking surface of the plaza. 'I've got an open channel,' Alice called over her shoulder. 'One of the local streams is relaying some kind of federal announcement. Do me a favor, Frank, get it out of my face. Transcribe and summarize.'

'Okay.' Frank accepted the virtual pipe, let it stream through the corner of his left eye as he watched Thelma efficiently cut up a wound dressing and gum it down on the mess of blood and thin hair atop Phibul's head. Despite the fear he was glad they were facing this together – not alone and frightened, locked in their rooms or in a police cell. The distant surf had become an approaching roar of voices. Alice threw some output at him from two of her birds, and he shuffled them round until he could see the back of his own head, kneeling alongside the drained swimming pool next to an injured reporter and a busy woman. 'This is – hey, everybody!'

He tweaked the stream over onto one of Alice's repeater screens. There was a background of martial music (which hereabouts sounded like classical heavy metal) and a pompous guy in midnight blue, lots of technicolor salad on his chest, sitting uneasily behind a desk. 'In view of the state of emergency, the Peace Commission has instructed all loyal citizens to stay indoors wherever possible. In the affected cities of Samara and Redstone, a curfew came into effect as of 2600 hours yesterday. Anyone outdoors in the region of Greater Samara and Metropolitan Redstone must seek shelter immediately. Assembly in groups of more than four individuals is forbidden and, in accordance with the Suppression of Terrorism Regulations, Peace Enforcement units will use lethal force if they consider themselves to be under threat—'

Thelma stood up. 'I've got to get a channel off-world,' she said tensely. 'You guys up to helping me?'

'How do you propose to do that?' Alice asked mildly, turning round. She was wearing repeater glasses rather than using optic implants – a stupid retro affectation, in Frank's view – and they cast a crazy quilt of colored light across her eyes. 'Didn't you hear? We're being routed around. If you try to crack their security, they'll probably point some of their infowar assets your way—'

'I've got a causal channel in my luggage,' Thelma confessed, looking scared but determined. 'It's on the second floor. If we could get past laughing boy downstairs—'

'You've got your own causal channel?' Frank asked, hope vying with disbelief

'Yeah, one that goes straight home to Turku via a one-hop relay in Septagon. No worries.' She turned her hands palms up. 'Ask me no questions, I'll tell you no lies. But if I can't get a secure handshake with it, it's not a lot of use, is it?'

'What do you need?' Alice asked, suddenly intent. Frank focused on her expression in a sudden moment of scrutiny: eyes widening, cheekbones sharp under dark skin, breath speeding—

'I need the thing physically up here, so I can handshake with it. I didn't know we were going to be bottled up here when—' She shook her head in the direction of the stair-well.

'How big is it?' Alice demanded.

'Tiny – it's the second memory card in my camera.' She held her thumb and forefinger apart. 'Looks just like a normal solid-state plug. Blue packaging.'

'Your camera doesn't do real time?' Frank asked.

'I've seen it and it does; it's got local memory backup against network outages,' Alice said tersely. 'Let me guess. You've got the channel in your camera so you can bypass local censorship, shoot in real time, and have the outtake saved straight to your editor's desk? That's got to be costing someone an arm and a leg. All right, this camera is where, exactly?'

'Room hundred and seventeen, floor two. Corner window with a balcony.'

'Hmm. Did you leave the balcony door open?'

'I think so – why?'

Alice looked over the waist-high safety wall, then backed away from the edge. 'I'm not climbing down there. But a bird – hmm. Think I've got a sampler head left. If it can eject the card . . . you want me to have a go? Willing to stake half your bandwidth to me if I can liberate it?'

'Guess so. It's got about six terabits left. Fifty-fifty split.' Thelma nodded. 'How about it?'

'Six terabits—' Frank shook his head in surprise. He hated to think how much it must have cost to haul those milligrams of entangled quantum dots across the endless light years between here and Turku by slower-than-light starwisp. Once used they were gone for good, coherence destroyed by the process that allowed them to teleport the state of a single bit between points in causally connected space-time. STL shipping prices started at a million dollaros per kilogram-parsec; it was many orders of magnitude more expensive than FTL, and literally took decades or centuries of advance planning to set up. But if it could get them a secure, instantaneous link out onto the interstellar backbone nets . . .

'Yeah, let's try it,' said Alice. The noise from beyond the balcony was getting louder.

Frank saw that Alice was already rooting through her bag of tricks. She surfaced with a translucent disc the size of her hand, trailing short tentacles that disquietingly resembled those of a box jellyfish. 'I think this should do the trick.'

'Is it strong enough?' Thelma asked edgily. 'If that thing drops it, we'll never—'

'It'll do,' Alice called. She flipped it upside down and coupled it to its small propane tank. 'With you in a minute, just as soon as I've gassed it up.'

'Okay.' Phibul groaned again, then groaned louder; Frank turned and knelt by him. 'Easy, man. Easy. You're going to be all right. Phibul?'

'My—' Phibul tried to raise one hand. Frank caught it, torn between sympathy and a strong urge to go and take a look over the parapet at the plaza. The crowd noise was enormous. Alice had stopped tracking her airborne birds, and they'd wandered off-station; Frank had a dizzying, unstable view down side streets, watching a sea of heads flowing down the Unity Boulevard, then across the roofline of a bank to another road, where boxy gray vehicles were moving purposefully—

'Alice!' he shouted, sitting up: 'Don't launch it!'

Alice looked at him abstractedly as she flipped the trigger on her tripod and sent the discus spinning into the air above the rooftop. 'What did you say?' she called, and for a desperate moment Frank thought it meant that everything would be all right, that the gray-painted vehicles and the brightly spinning disc and the sunburst flashes in the corner of his eye didn't mean anything. But the window in his left eye disappeared, all the same. The laser beam sky-bounced from the antimissile battery to the fighting mirror above the bank building was invisible to the naked eye, and the fighting mirror sure didn't care about journalistic credentials or, indeed, who owned the recce drones floating high above the city. All it knew about was friend, enemy, and counterbattery fire. 'Take cover!' Frank yelled, just as the top of Alice's head vanished in a spray of red mist with a horrible popping sound, like an egg exploding in a microwave oven.

For a minute or so Frank blanked. There was a horrible noise, a screeching roar in his ears – blood on his hands, blood on his knees, blood everywhere, an ocean to Phibul's dried-up creek. He was dizzy and cold and the hand holding his didn't seem to help. It seemed to want to let go. Alice in the bar downstairs. Alice explaining the facts of life to him after bribing a government official, joking about the honeymoon suite when they moved in. Alice flying drones over the cityscape far below, spotting traffic, spotting likely hot spots with a look on her face like—

There was shouting beyond the balcony. Shouting, and a grinding metallic squeal he'd heard before, down below. Alice was dead and he was stranded with a dried-up swimming pool, a stranger from Turku, and no way to make the fuckers pay. No real-time link.

'You can't do anything for her.' There was a hand on his shoulder, small and hard – he shook it loose, then pushed himself to his knees dizzily.

'I know,' he heard someone else say. 'I wish—' His voice cracked. He didn't really know what that person wished anymore: it wasn't really relevant, was it? He hadn't been in love with Alice, but he'd *trusted* her; she was the brains of the operation, the wise older head who knew what the hell to do. This wasn't supposed to happen. The head of mission wasn't supposed to die in the field, brains splattered all over the roof by—

'Keep *down*,' Thelma whispered. 'I think they're going to start now.'

'Start?' he asked, shivering.

A hush fell across the square, then the noise of the crowd redoubled. And there was another sound; a pattering, like rain falling onto concrete from a clear blue sky, accompanied by a crackling roar. Then the screams. 'Alice was right,' said Thelma, shuddering and crouching down below the parapet. Sweating and whey-faced, she looked the way Frank felt. 'It's the season for bullets.'

Below them, in the packed dusty square before the government buildings, the storm drains began to fill with blood.

Svengali had drunk half a bottle of single malt by the

time Frank reached the massacre. His throat was hoarse, but he hadn't stopped for long enough to ask for a refill. It hurt too much to pause. Now he held his glass out. 'I don't know how your liver copes with that.'

'He's got the guts of a rat,' slurred Eloise: 'hepatic alcohol dehydrogenase pathway and all.' She stood up, wobbling slightly. 'Scuse me, guys, but this isn't my night for partying after all. Nice of you to invite me and maybe some other time and all, but I think I'm going to be having nightmares tonight.' She hit the release button on the doorframe and was gone into the twilight of the ship's crew accommodation deck.

Svengali shook his head as he pulled the door shut. 'And here I was, hoping for a threesome,' he said. He tipped a generous measure into Frank's glass, then put the rapidly emptying bottle down. 'So, the troops massacred the demonstrators. What has this got to do with those guys, whoever they are?'

'The—' Frank swallowed bile. 'Remember the spook woman? She came back, after the massacre, with soldiers. And Thelma's camera. She let Thelma scan the courtyard, then the guards sat her down with a gun at her head and the spook dictated my copy to me. Which I signed and submitted under my own name.'

'You—' Svengali's eyes narrowed. 'Isn't that unethical?'

'So is threatening to execute hostages. What would you do in my shoes?'

'Hmm.' The clown topped off his own glass and took a full mouthful. 'So you sent it, in order to . . .'

'Yeah. But it didn't work.' He fell silent. Nothing was going to make him go into the next bit, the way they'd cuffed him, stuck needles full of interface busters in his arm to kill off his implants, and flipped him on his stomach to convulse, unable to look away or even close his eyes while they gut-shot Phibul and left him to bleed out, while two of the soldiers raped Thelma, then cut off her screams and then her breasts with their bayonets. Of the three of them, only Frank's agency had bought him a full war correspondent's insurance policy.

It had been the beginning of a living nightmare for Frank, a voyage through the sewers of the New Settlement's concentration camps that only ended nine months later, when the bastards concluded that ensuring his silence was unnecessary and the ransom from his insurers was a bigger asset than his death through destructive labor. 'I think they thought I was sleeping with her,' he said fuzzily.

'So you got away? They released you?'

'No: I ended up in the camps. They didn't realize at first, the Newpeace folk who supported the Peace Enforcement, that those camps were meant for everyone, not just the fractious unemployed and the right-to-land agitators. But sooner or later everyone ended up there – everyone except the security apparat and the off-planet mercenaries the provisional government hired to run the machine. Who were all smartly turned-out, humorless, efficient, fast – like those kids in the bar. *Just* like them. And then there were the necklaces.'

'Necklaces?' Svengali squinted. 'Are you shitting me?'

'No.' Frank shuddered and took a mouthful of whisky. 'Try to pull it off, try to go somewhere you're not supposed to, or just look at a guard wrong, and it'll take your head off.' He rubbed the base of his throat, unconsciously. *And then there was Processing Site Administrator Voss, but let's* not *go there.* 'They killed three thousand people in the square, you know that? But they killed another two million in those camps over the next three years. And the fuckers *got away with it.* Because anyone who knows about them is too shit-scared to do anything. And it all happened a long time ago and a long way away. The first thing they did was pin down all the causal channels, take control of any incoming STL freighters, and subject all real-time communications in and out of the system to censorship. You can emigrate – they don't mind that – but only via slower-than-light. Emigrants talk, but most people don't pay attention to decades-old news. It's just not *current* anymore,' he added bitterly. 'When they decided to cash in my insurance policy they deported me via slower-than-light freighter. I spent twenty years in cold sleep: by the time I arrived nobody wanted to know what I'd been through.'

And it had been a long time before he'd been ready to seek the media out for himself: he'd spent six months in a hospital relearning that if a door was open, it meant he could go through it if he wanted, instead of waiting for a guard to lock it again. Six months of pain, learning again how to make decisions for himself. Six months of remembering what it was to be an autonomous human being and not a robot made out of meat, trapped in the obedient machinery of his own body.

'Okay. So they . . . what? Go around conquering worlds? That sounds insane. Pardon me for casting aspersions on your good self's character, but it is absolutely ridiculous to believe anyone could do such a thing. Destroy a world, yes, easily – but conquer one?'

'They don't.' Frank leaned back against the partition. 'I'm not sure *what* they do. Rumor in the camps was, they call themselves the ReMastered. But just what that means . . . Hell, there are rumors about everything from brainwashing to a genetically engineered master race. But the first rule of journalism is you can't trust unsubstantiated rumors. All I know is, this ship is going to Newpeace, which they turned into a hellhole. And those guys are from somewhere called Tonto. What the fuck is going on?'

'You're the blogger.' Svengali put the bottle down, a trifle unsteadily. He frowned. 'Are you going to try to find out? I'm sure there's a story in it . . .'

interlude: 1

In a stately home by the banks of a dried-up river on a world with two small moons, a woman with sea-green eyes and crew-cut black hair sat behind a desk, reading reports. The house was enormous and ancient, walls of stone supported by ancient oak timber beams, and the French windows were thrown wide open to admit a breeze from the terrace before the house. The woman, engrossed in her reading, didn't notice the breeze or even the smell of rose blossom wafting in on it. She was too busy paging through memoranda on her tablet, signing warrants, changing lives.

The door made a throat-clearing sound. 'Ma'am, you have a visitor.'

'Who is it, Frank?' She glanced at the brass terminal plaque that had been hacked into the woodwork by an over-enthusiastic former resident.

'S. Georg Frazier Bayreuth. He says he has some sort of personal report for you.'

'Personal,' she muttered. 'All right. Show him in.' She

pushed her chair back, brushing imaginary lint from the shoulder of her tunic, and thumbed her tablet to a security-conscious screen saver.

The door clicked, and she rose as it opened. Holding out a hand: 'Frazier.'

'Ma'am.' There was no click of heels – he wore no boots – but he bowed stiffly, from the neck.

'Sit down, sit down. You've been spending too much time in the New Republic.'

S. Frazier Bayreuth sank into the indicated chair, opposite her desk, and nodded wearily. 'They rub off on you.'

'Hah.' It came out as a grim cough. 'How are the compatibility metrics looking?'

'Better than they were a year ago, better than anybody dared hope, but they won't be mature enough for integration for a long time yet. Reactionary buffoons, if you ask me. But that's not why I'm here. Um. May I ask how busy you are?'

The woman behind the desk stared at him, head slightly askew. 'I can give you half an hour right now,' she said slowly. 'If this is urgent.'

Bayreuth's cheek twitched. A wiry, brown-haired man who looked as if he was made of dried leather, he wore blue-gray seamless fatigues; battle dress in neutral, chromatophores and impact diffusers switched off, as if he'd come straight from a police action, only pausing to remove his armor and equipment webbing. 'It's urgent all right.' He glanced at the open window. 'Are we clear?'

She nodded. 'Nobody who overhears us will understand anything,' she said, unsmiling, and he shivered slightly. In a ubiquitous surveillance society, any such bare-faced assertion of privacy clearly carried certain implications.

'All right, then. It's about the Environmental Service cleanup report on Moscow.'

'The cleanup.' She gritted her teeth. 'What is it this time?'

'Arbeiter Neurath begs to report that he has identified auditable anomalies in the immigration trace left by the scram team as they cleaned up and departed. On at least three occasions over the three years leading up to the Zero Incident and the five years since then, personnel working in the Environmental Operations Team under U. Vannevar Scott failed to behave consistently in accordance with best practice guidelines for exfiltrating feral territory. *That*, in itself, I would not need to bring to your attention, my lady. The guilty parties have been reprocessed and their errors added to the documentation corpus *pour encourager les autres*.' He cleared his throat. 'But . . .'

The woman stared at him, her expression relaxed: Bayreuth tensed. When U. Portia Hoechst looked most relaxed she was at her most dangerous – if not to him, then to someone else, some designated enemy of the mission, roadkill on the highway to destiny. She might be thirty, or ninety – it was hard to tell with ReMastered, before the sudden unraveling of the genome that brought their long lives to an abrupt but peaceful close – but if asked to gamble Bayreuth would have placed his money at the higher end of the scale. Peaceful eyes, relaxed eyes, eyes that had seen too many horrors to tense and flicker at a death warrant.

'Continue,' she said in a neutral tone of voice.

'Neurath took it upon herself to examine the detailed findings of U. Scott's team. She discovered further anomalies and brought them to my attention. I confirmed her observations and realized the issue must be escalated. In addition to the breakdown of operational discipline in the Moscow away team, there is some evidence that Scott has been, ah, relocating skeletons from the family closet into the oubliette, if you follow me.'

'You have evidence.'

'Indeed.' Bayreuth suppressed an urge to shuffle. Hoechst made him nervous; she was far from the worst mistress he'd served – quite the contrary – but he'd never yet seen her *smile*. He had a horrible feeling that he was about to, and the consequences made him increasingly uneasy. Her dislike of U. Vannevar Scott needed no explanation – they were of different clades, and in no way compatible other than their service to the ultimate – but it was to be devoutly hoped that none of it rubbed off on him. The wars of the bosses at over-staffsupervisor level and above were best avoided if you wanted to keep your head, much less aspire to those heights yourself one day.

'Disclose it.'

Bayreuth took a deep breath. *You can't back out now*. 'A major weak link has come to light. It turns out that Scott's team established an MO by which all traffic to and from Moscow went through a single choke point. The theory was that in event of a leak, only the one location would require sanitizing. Leaving aside the question of backup routing and fail-over capacity, this means that the immigration desk at this one location held a complete audit trail of all our agents' movements in and out of the system.'

U. Portia Hoechst frowned very slightly. 'I do not follow your argument. Surely this would have been destroyed by the Zero Incident . . . ?'

Bayreuth shook his head slowly and watched her eyes widen. 'The bottleneck they picked was an isolated fuel dump and immigration post about a parsec from Moscow. It was evacuated some time ago, before the shock wave hit. U. Scott sent a proxy squad to tidy up any loose ends on the station, trash the immigration records, liquidate any witnesses, that sort of thing. Doubtless if it had worked properly it would have been an elegant and sufficient solution to the problem, but it would appear that a number of unexplained incidents occurred during the evacuation. Such as his *written instructions* to the agent on-site *going missing*, such as the failure to return all copies of the backup dumps from the sealed immigration desk, and possibly more. There is some question over a classified log of the experimental protocols that were then in progress, which appears to have been misplaced during the evacuation. The agent sent *dogs*, boss. State security dogs borrowed from the Dresdener Foreign Office. He seemed to think that sending a proper sterilization team to do the job by the book was unnecessary. All swept under the rug, of course, the evidence securely encrypted – that's why it's taken so long to come to light.'

'Oh dear.' Hoechst grinned at him. 'Is that *all*?' she asked warmly, and Bayreuth shivered. From being cold as ice, suddenly Hoechst had warmed to him. 'And he failed to report this?'

Bayreuth nodded. He didn't trust himself to speak right then.

'And your channel into Scott's department . . .' She raised an eyebrow.

'The channel is a *very personal* friend of Otto Neurath,' he emphasized. 'However you decide to act on this information, I would ask you to behave leniently in her case. I believe Otto shows a lot of potential for intelligent action in support of his superior's goals, and an indelicate response to his special friend might, ah, compromise his future utility. Parenthetically speaking.'

'Oh, Georg. What kind of monster do you take me for?' The terrible smile disappeared. 'I'm not stupid, you know. Or bloodthirsty. At least, not needlessly.' She snorted. 'Otto can keep his toy, once her loyalties have been retargeted on our team. I won't break her for him.' Bayreuth nodded, relieved. Her restraint, for which he could claim responsibility, would only serve to bind Otto tighter to his rising faction. 'As for you—' the terrifying grin was back – 'how would you like to open discussions with Scott's department, about our forthcoming merger?'

'Me?' He blinked, shocked.

'Yes, you.' She nodded. 'I've been thinking you deserved the added opportunities that come with an elevated degree of responsibility for some time now, Georg. What was that phrase? A lot of potential for intelligent action in support of his superior's goals, I think you said.'

'Why, I'm deeply grateful, but—'

'Don't be. Not yet.' She gestured out through the window, at the terrace of rosebushes and the garden beyond the ha-ha, the walls and trees and the avenue leading uphill to the stately home. 'If what you're telling me is correct, we have a serious leak to fix. And I think I may need to fix it on-site. I've been weaving destinies from behind a desk for too long, Georg. Scott's mistake is typical of what happens when you stay out of the field and lose touch with reality.'

'Are you going to travel in person, then? What about your estates and committees—'

'They'll look after themselves. They'd better – they'll know I'll be back.' Another smile, this time almost coy; if he hadn't known better, he'd have sworn she was *flirting* with him. 'But seriously. I can combine the trip with a tour of the new candidates, consolidate my control over Scott's puppets in the field, and get back in touch with what it's really about. The great program, Georg. Fancy that!' She tapped her tablet. 'Get me a full briefing. Then I'll arrange a session with Overdepartmentsecretary Blumlein, and obtain permission before issuing the formal denunciation by way of the Committee of Inquiry. After which we'll discuss how you're going to mind the shop for me while I'm gone.'

He caught her eye. 'Me? The whole thing?'

She didn't blink. 'Did you have any other plans for tonight? No? Good, then I assume I can safely invite you to dine with me. We have a lot of things to discuss, Georg. Including how to ensure that you don't disappoint me the way U. Scott has . . .'

The action went down hard and fast, once Hoechst had drawn certain facts to the elevated attention of Overdepartmentsecretary Blumlein. Blumlein had stared at her with those icy blue eyes, set just too close together: 'Do it,' he'd said, and that was all. Leaving her enough rope to hang herself with if it turned out she was wrong and U. Vannevar Scott's Subdepartment of External Environmental Control was, in fact, clean.

Walking in through the smashed glass doors of the office building in Samara, Hoechst nodded and smiled at the troops holding the front desk. *Show the flag*, as her creche-leader Fergus had exhorted her. One or two walking wounded waited stoically for the medevac truck to show up. A pile of pithed and drained bodies lay stacked like cordwood on the polished granite tiles at one side of the foyer, leaking blood from their ears and eyes, their minds already taken by the Propagators. Hoechst ignored them, concentrated on shaking hands and exchanging congratulations with her staff. *First things first*. Blood on the soles of her boots. She'd get to Scott in due course: *Damn him for forcing me to this!*

Of course, Scott's headquarters wasn't the only target of the action. Nodes had gone down all over the planetary net, branch offices off-lined and isolated during the mop-up. Out in the country, Peace Enforcement troops had punched in the doors of his harem, taken the puppets by the brain stem and turned them in for processing – those that weren't put down immediately as a poor cost/benefit risk for reclamation. It was all part and parcel of the messy business of taking down a ranking ubermensch who had been accused of malfeasance, and Hoechst hated him for it, hated him for forcing her to publicly expose a ReMastered who was less than adequate at his assigned role. But she had no real alternative. A failure to act right then might only encourage him, or worse, expose her own people to accusations of inadequacy; and in the long run it risked undermining the destiny of the people.

Troops in cream-and-beige office camouflage wedged fire and blast doors open for her as she walked through the administrative castle toward the executive service core. Her bodyguards kept pace with her, anonymous behind their masks. Staff officers followed in their wake, apprehensive and eager to serve her. There were few signs of damage, and little violence, for U. Scott's castle had been taken by stealth in the first instance. A scheduled movement of internal security troops had been replaced by Hoechst's own storm groups, welcomed with open arms by slack defenders who never suspected that their death warrant had been ordered by the planetary overdepartmentsecretary with a curt two-word phrase.

At the core of the building stood a secure zone, doors locked open by a treacherous override. Hoechst climbed the staircase, her mood bleak. At the top, a mezzanine floor looked out across Scott's control hub. He was one of those who seemed to thrive on oversight, she noted, as if he couldn't trust anything that happened outside the reach of his own senses. The doorway onto the mezzanine was splattered with drying clots of blood, brown and sharp-smelling beneath the emergency lights. Her guards waited at either corner. In the middle of the floor a curious triumvirate waited for her. In the big chair, U. Vannevar Scott himself, pithed and locked down, his limbs limp and his face an accusatory mask. Behind it, to either side, stood S. Frazier Bayreuth and another person, a woman in the robe and veil of the Propagators' Order.

'Vannevar, my dear. A shame we had to run into each other again under such distressing circumstances.' Hoechst smiled at the man in the chair. His eyes tracked her slowly, barely able to move. 'And yourself, Bayreuth. And to whom else do I have the pleasure?'

The strange woman inclined her head: 'U. Doranna Mengele, your excellency. Here by order of the overdepartmentsecretary to pay witness to the proceedings and ensure that all is conducted in accordance with the best practices and customs of the enlightenment.'

The body in the chair seemed to be agitated. Hoechst leaned close: 'You should relax, Van. Struggling won't help. Those nerves won't grow back, you know.' It was necessary for her image; inside, something was screaming, *You stupid unplanned* bastard! *What in the dead god's name did you think you were doing?* 'We were given a warrant and we have executed it.'

She glanced at Bayreuth. 'Do you have an activation key?'

He turned and beckoned a guard over. 'Switch this one back on for the supervisor,' he said tersely. The Propagator cocked her head to one side and watched, silently. Hoechst tried not to pay any attention to her. There was no avoiding it. With a Propagator to witness everything, spooling the uploaded sensory take straight into the distributed network of her order, any attempt at dissembling – or mercy – would be exposed instantly.

The guard touched his wand to the back of U. Scott's neck, and some expression returned to the man's face. A finger twitched. He slurred something, fighting for control: 'Portia. How could you?'

'Certain facts were drawn to my attention,' she said drily, half-noticing the way Bayreuth had turned pale behind the chair. *Facts I could not ignore once they were on the record*, she added to herself, expanding the eulogy. 'Sloppy procedures. Failure to abide by best practice and custom. Potential treason.'

He closed his eyes. 'I would never commit treason.'

'Not through commission,' she said, then damned herself for her weakness in conceding even that much in front of the Propagator's eyecams. 'Nevertheless. A risk of exposure was noted – and more importantly, swept under the rug.' She leaned over him, rested a fine-boned hand on one immobile shoulder. 'We couldn't ignore that,' she said quietly.

'I was in the process of cleaning up.' He sounded infinitely tired already; the upload bush would have digested his cerebellum, already be eating away at his thalamus, preserving him for posterity and the glory of the unborn god. Without the activator he'd soon be dead, not simply immobilized. Although he'd die soon enough, when the Propagator took his mind. 'Didn't you know, Portia? I thought, you . . . you . . .'

'Booster.' She snapped her fingers, fuming angrily. *Don't ghost out on me now!* His shoulder felt like a joint of uncooked meat, solid and immobile. There was a nasty stench in the air – if he'd lost bowel control already, that meant he was farther along than she'd wanted. 'Witness for the Propagation, I request access to this one's lineage. While the instance vector has proven unreliable, I believe with suitable guidance the phenotype may prove stable and effective.'

Bayreuth was blinking at her in surprise. The Propagator nodded. 'Your request has been received,' she said distantly. 'A reproductive license is under consideration. Or were you thinking of a clone?'

'No, recombination only.' Hoechst leaned closer, staring into U. Vannevar Scott's eyes, remembering earlier days, more innocent, both of them interns on the staff of an ubermensch — stolen nights, sleepless days, the guilt-free pleasure before responsibility became a curse. Politics. *What, thirty years? Thirty-seven years?* She could barely remember his body; some lovers were like that. Well, others you remembered for life. Scott . . . Scott was history, in more than one way. 'It will be something to recall him by.'

'Your request will be considered by the Race Genome Improvement Committee,' said the Propagator, placidly straightening her wimple. 'Is there anything else?'

'Termination witness.' She kept her hand on his shoulder while the guard administered the coup, switching the tree into uncontrolled dendritic mapping. His sightless eyes closed; presently a pale fluid began to leak from the back of his skull. The touch of dead meat; once she'd hated that . . . now it just left her feeling glad it wasn't her turn. She smoothed his hair down, straightened up, and caught Georg Bayreuth's eye. 'Have this taken away for recycling.' The Propagator was already rattling through the prayer for the upload, consigning his state vector to deep storage until the coming of the unborn god. 'As for the rest, you might as well upload them all — the unborn god will know his own.' She sighed. 'Now. Have we found where he kept his master list of puppets?'

'Well. Portia. That brings me to the next question. How *is* your pet project going?'

Hoechst leaned back in the overstuffed velvet-lined recliner, and stared at the gold leaf intaglio on the ceiling. She took her time answering: it was all a little overpowering. Truth be told, she was unused to having the confidence of the Overdepartmentsecretariat, and U. Blumlein's avuncular tone put her on a defensive edge. It reminded her of one of her teachers, from the hazy years back in the creche, a fellow whose temperament alternated between confiding warmth and screaming tantrums – contrived, she later discovered while reading the creche's policy mandate, to teach the youngsters the benefits of close-lipped circumspection. She'd been a good pupil, perhaps too good, and it was unnerving to find that the kindly professor's object lesson in pain had such direct applicability to the upper reaches of the clade. It just went to show that *that which does not kill us makes us stronger* was more than just an empty platitude.

'I asked a question,' her superior reminded her.

'I believe I have the basic issues under control,' she said confidently, raising her glass and taking a cautious sip of almond liqueur to cover her moment of hesitation.

'The basic issues,' Blumlein echoed, and smiled. He held out his glass and a moppet hastened to refill it. Hoechst shuffled slightly in her chair and ran a finger under the shoulder of her gown. She smiled back at him, although she was anything but relaxed.

An invitation into her superior's parlor for an evening's entertainment was normally public recognition, a sign of favored status within the clade. But a *private* invitation, to dinner for two, was something else again. The only people who'd see her were their bodyguards, private secretaries, and the service moppets, all of whom – apart from the secretaries – were disposables who counted as nothing in the sparse social networks of the ReMastered. What could he have in mind? Special orders? It certainly wasn't a seduction attempt – his tastes lay notoriously in other directions – and she couldn't see herself being important enough to cultivate for other reasons. One thing every ReMastered acquired early was a sensitive nose for relative status, and this discreet assignation simply didn't make sense from any angle she could think of. Unless he had, for some inexplicable reason, decided to assess her for the role of his public partner, a remarkable if knife-edged honor.

'I'd like you to recap the basic issues, Portia. In your own words and in your own time, if you please.'

'Oh. Well.' Portia shook herself. *Idiot!* She cursed. *What else could it be about?* 'Scott failed miserably on Moscow. Or rather, he succeeded inappropriately. The result was, well, not what we anticipated. Sixteen ubermenschen dead, not to mention the loss of an entire client world that was less than eighteen months from open phase-two restabilization – that was a major setback in its own right. Worse, the weapons tests – the causality-violation devices his puppets were testing – have probably attracted the attention of the Enemy. Bluntly, he failed on *two* levels; his treason against his own kind failed, and worse, the weapons tests also failed catastrophically, leading to the loss of the system. It was, all told, a disaster, and Scott knew he would attract unwelcome attention if he could not provide a compensatory positive outcome.'

'Hmmph.' Blumlein grunted, something approximating a twinkle of amusement in his eyes. On the stage behind her, three or four moppets were performing some sort of erotic dance: Portia angled her chair so that she could watch sidelong, while keeping her attention on the planetary overdepartmentsecretary. 'Juggling on the tightrope over the abyss is a long and honorable tradition, I suppose.' He smiled, not unkindly. 'What long-term plans did U. Scott intend to pursue?'

'I think he was going to take over New Dresden, but he didn't leave any written records.' Portia sniffed. 'Not surprising.' His attitude encouraged her to return the smile as a peer – a gamble, but one that might bring serious advancement if it paid off.

'Absolutely.' Blumlein's expression turned chilly. 'How could he possibly have been so stupid?'

She shrugged, dismissively. 'Scott has — well — never lacked for self-confident ambition.' *You can say that again.* A brief flashback: lying in bed listening to him rant, plans to create his own clade, bring about the unborn god, steal whole worlds from the flock. 'I worked closely with him for several years, when we were younger. It's probably a good thing time ran out on him; he wasn't keeping his eye on the fine detail, and if he'd gotten his plan past the second stage, the consequences could have been even worse than the slow-motion disaster he's left us with.'

Blumlein put his glass down, leaned closer, his pupils dilating slightly. Portia mirrored his gestures, becoming the confidante. 'Tell me what Scott was working on in that sector,' he said quietly. 'And what you think you might have done with it in his stead.'

'The—' Her eyes swiveled sideways.

The overdepartmentsecretary caught her glance and nodded. 'They won't remember any of this tomorrow,' he said.

'Good. I'd hate to be responsible for spoiling such well-trained dancers.'

'I thank you for your attentiveness to my estate, but would you mind returning to the matter in hand? We don't have all evening.' There was an edge to his voice that hadn't been there a moment before, and Portia cursed silently, nodding.

'Very well. Scott's official task was to take over Moscow and divert it to serve the purposes of the Defense Directorate by developing munitions types forbidden to us by the Enemy. Then he was to prepare Moscow for assimilation. His agents infiltrated the government of Moscow quite effectively using only routine puppetry and a modicum of bribes. But in addition to the official project plan he paid special attention to their Defense Ministry. This paid off with the entire attack plan for the system's deterrent force, at which point Scott started getting ambitious. He got the lot – go codes, stop codes, waypoints, and insertion vectors for every possible target – and when the Zero Incident occurred that data was safely filed away in his office.'

'Ah.' Blumlein nodded and smiled, his expression thawing. 'And now.'

'Well.' She considered her next words with care. 'I trust the copies of the go codes and stop codes arrived at your office satisfactorily. And Moscow itself is a nonissue, thanks to the failure of certain technological initiatives. But there's still the issue of how to clean up after Scott's little adventure. Not to mention the issue of how you want to deal with the leverage this situation places in your hands with respect to the neighbors.'

Blumlein nodded carefully. 'In your assessment, how good was Scott's final plan?'

'The general theory is audacious – nobody has ever done anything quite like it before – but the substance I wouldn't touch with a pointy stick.' The words came out automatically. 'He got sloppy with Moscow, sloppy enough that he left loose ends dangling. Exfiltration witnesses, basically, but it could all unravel from there if somebody with enough time and resources got their hands on the details and backtracked to find out where the bodies were coming from, or going to.'

She took a breath. 'And while the basic scheme was interesting, his secondstage scheme relied too much on synchronicity – and took enormous risks. What makes it worse for us is that he'd actually begun to implement it. The moves against the Muscovite diplomatic team, for example – they're already in progress, if not completed. We can't tell until the telegrams come in, but my guess is that they'll succeed, and they'll make every chancellery within a hundred light years shit themselves. Not to mention what will happen when the High Directorate finds out. To take a whole planet for himself, then use its weapons of mass destruction to set himself up as an interplanetary emperor – it's insanely audacious, I'll grant you that. But his plan relied on the bystanders believing that a bunch of *democrats* would willingly do what he wanted. And I think it was only wishful thinking that made him contemplate such a dependency.'

'Then that brings me to my next question.' Blumlein paused for a moment, looking thoughtful, then snapped his fingers; a moppet minced forward, knelt to present a small silver box atop a velvet cushion. He took the box, flipped the lid open, and removed the inhaler within: 'Dose?'

'Thank you kindly, no.'

He nodded, then bent over it for a few seconds. 'Ah, that's better.' Cold blue eyes, pinprick pupils. 'The core of the matter. In the hypothetical case that I was to charge you with implementing U. Scott's plan and carrying it to completion, for the greater good of the clade—' he sent a flickering glance in the direction of the stage, and at that moment Hoechst realized that despite every protestation of privacy, he believed the Propagators or the Arm might be watching, might have corrupted his own puppet master – 'how would you go about it?'

Oh. Oh. Portia shivered, appalled by the vista of opportunities before her. This could mean her elevation to parity with Blumlein, to board level for an entire planet if she played her hand successfully. An almost sexual thrill: *Then nobody could touch me!* To be in control of the mechanics – she clamped down on the thought immediately, before it could form. *First things first.* The cost would be high, the temptation to Blumlein to have her executed before she could become a threat would be enormous . . .

Composing herself, she nodded slightly and picked up her glass. 'I would first have to assure myself that I had the approval of the Directorate,' she began, not glancing at the stage. 'Then, once I had that, I'd pursue U. Scott's general plan, but directing events on-site in person rather than entrusting control to an extra layer of subordination. I don't believe you can have a sufficiently tight grasp on an action if you try to exercise remote control; every level of authority you delegate adds delay and an additional risk of failure, and the plan has too many contingencies to entrust command to a junior puppeteer who lacks the big picture. And I'd divert the target of his enterprise to a, ah, more acceptable one . . .'

party girl

Centris Magna was a boringly average asteroid colony, built to a classic design that didn't rely on gravity generators: a diamond tube fifty kilometers along the main axis and eight kilometers in diameter, spinning within the hollowed-out husk of a carbonaceous chondrite somewhere in Septagon Four's inner debris belt. The inner core consisted of service facilities while the outer, high-gee levels were mostly zoned as parklands or recreational zones: the occupants lived in multilevel tenements in the mid-gee cylinders. It was a pattern repeated endlessly throughout the Septagon systems, among the hundreds of worldlets that made up the polity that had taken in most of the refugees from Moscow. And three years after her arrival, Wednesday had learned to hate it, and the grinding poverty it rubbed her nose in every minute of every day.

'Wednesday?' Her father's voice was attenuated by her barely open bedroom door: if she pulled it shut, she could block him out completely. But if she pulled it shut—

'Wednesday. Where are you?'

Biting her tongue in concentration she finished tying her bootlaces, getting them perfect. *There.* She stood up. Boots, new boots, nearly knee high, gleaming like black mirrors over her skintight cloned pantherskin leggings. 'Here, Dad.' Let him find her. A last look in the window, set to mirror-mode, confirmed that her chromatophores were toned in: blood-red lips, dead white skin, straight black hair. She picked up her jacket and stroked it awake, then held out her arms and waited for it to crawl into place and grip her tightly at elbows and shoulders. *Nearly ready—*

'Wednesday! Come here.'

She sighed. 'Coming,' she called. Quietly, to herself: 'Bye, room.'

'Goodbye,' said her bedroom, dimming the lights as she opened the door, feeling tall and slightly unbalanced in her new boots and headed through to the living room, where Dad would probably be waiting.

Morris was, as she'd expected, in the main room of the apartment. It was a big open space, a mezzanine floor upstairs on top of the dining room providing him with an office from which he could look down on the disordered chairs and multiforms of the communal area. Jeremy had been trying to undo amah's housekeeping again, building an intricate dust trap of brightly colored phototropic snowflakes in the middle of the antique dining table that Dad periodically insisted they sit around for formal meals. The dust trap writhed toward her when she opened the door. Her father had been watching a passive on the wall; it froze as he looked round at her, ancient avatars looking impossibly smooth and shiny in the perspective-bending depths. 'What's *that* you're wearing?' he asked wearily.

'Sammy's throwing a party tonight,' she said, annoyed. (She almost added, *How come you never go out?* – but thought better of it at the last minute.) 'I'm going with Alys and Mira.' Which was a white lie – she wasn't talking to Mira, and Alys wasn't talking to her – but they'd both be there, and anyway did it really matter who she went with when it would only take ten minutes and she'd be out all night? 'First time out for my new boots!'

Dad sighed. He looked unwell, his skin pasty and bags under his eyes. Too much studying. Study, study, *study* – it was all he ever seemed to do, roosting up on top of the kitchen roof like a demented owl-bird. Smart drugs didn't seem to help; he was having real difficulties assimilating it all. 'I was hoping to have some time to talk with you,' he said tiredly. 'Are you going to be out late?'

'All night,' she said. A frisson of anticipation made her tap her toes, scuff the floor: they were remarkably fine boots, shiny, black, high-heeled and high-laced, with silver trim. She'd found the design in a historical costuming archive she'd Dumpstered, and spent most of a day turning them into a program for the kitchen fab. She wasn't going to tell him what the material had cost, real vat-grown leather like off a dead cow's skin made some people go 'ick' when you told them what you were wearing. 'I like dancing,' she said, which was another little white lie, but Dad still seemed to harbor delusions of control, and she didn't want him to get any ideas about grounding her, so making innocent noises was a good idea.

'Um.' Morris glanced away, worried, then stood up. 'Can't wait,' he mumbled. 'Your mother and I are going to be away all day tomorrow. Sit down?'

'All right.' Wednesday pulled out one of the dining table chairs and dropped onto it back to front, arms crossed across the back. 'What is it?'

'We're – your mother and I, that is, uh—' Flustered, he ground to a halt. 'Um. We worry about you.'

'Oh, is that so?' Wednesday pulled a face at him. 'I can look after myself.'

'But can you—' He caught himself, visibly struggling to keep something in. 'Your school report,' he finally said.

'Yeah?' Her face froze in anticipation.

'You're not getting on well with the other children, according to Master Talleyrand. He, they, uh, the school social board, are worried about your, um, they call it "acculturation".'

'Oh, great!' she snapped. 'I've—' She stopped. 'I'm going out,' she said rapidly, her voice wobbling, and stood up before he could say anything.

'We'll have to talk about this sometime,' he called after her, making no move to follow. 'You can't run away from it forever!'

Yes I can: watch me. Three steps took her past the kitchen door, another hop and a skip – risking a twisted ankle in the new boots – took her to the pressure portal. Pulse hammering, she thumped the release plate and swung it open manually, then dived through into the public right-of-way with its faded green carpet and turquoise walls. It was dim in the hallway, the main lights dialed down to signify twilight, and apart from a couple of small maintenance 'bots she had the passage to herself. She began to walk, a black haze of frustration and anger wrapped tightly around her like a cloak. Most of the front doors to either side were sealed, opening onto empty – sometimes depressurized – apartments; this sub-level was cheap to live in, but only poor refugees would want to do so. A dead end, like her prospects. *Prospects* – what prospects? From being comfortably middle-class her family had sunk to the status of dirt-poor immigrants, lacking opportunities, looked down on for everything from their rural background to things like Wednesday's and Jerm's implants – which had cost Morris and Indica half a year's income back on Old Newfie, only to be exposed as obsolete junk when they arrived here. 'Fucking social board,' she muttered to herself. 'Fucking thought police.'

Centris Magna had been good in some ways: they had a much bigger apartment than back home, and there was lots of stuff happening. Lots of people her age, too. But there were bad things, and if anyone had asked Wednesday, she'd have told them that they outweighed the good by an order of magnitude. Not that anyone *had* actually asked her if she wanted to be subjected to the bizarre cultural ritual known as 'schooling,' locked up for half her waking hours in an institution populated by imbeciles, sadistic sociopaths, bullies, and howling maniacs, with another three years to go before the Authorities would let her out. Especially because at fifteen in Moscow system she'd been within two years of adulthood – but in Septagon, you didn't even get out of high school until you were twenty-two.

Centris Magna was part of the Septagon system, a loosely coupled cluster of brown dwarf stars with no habitable planets, settled centuries ago. It was probably the Eschaton's heavy-handed idea of a joke: a group called the space settlers' society had found themselves the sole pro-prietors of a frigid, barely terraformed asteroid, with a year's supply of oxygen and some heavy engineering equipment for company. After about a century of bloodshed and the eventual suppression of the last libertarian fanatics, the Septagon orbitals had gravitated toward the free-est form of civilization that was possible in such a hostile environment: which meant intensive schooling, conscript service in the environmental maintenance crews, and zero tolerance for anyone who thought that hanging separately was better than hanging together. Wednesday, who had been one of the very few children growing up on a peripheral station supported by a planet with a stable biosphere, was not used to school, or defending the atmospheric commons, or to being expected to fit in. Especially because the education authorities had taken one look at her, pigeonholed her as a refugee from a foreign and presumably backward polity, and plugged her straight into a remedial school.

Nobody had inquired in her first year as to whether she was *happy*. Happy, with most of the people she knew light minutes away, scattered across an entire solar system? Happy, with the Bone Sisters ready to take any opportunity to commit surreptitious acts of physical violence against her? Happy when the first person she'd confided in had spread her private life around the commons like a ripped laundry bag? Happy fitting in like a cross-threaded screw, her dialect an object of mockery and her lost home a subject of dead yokel jokes? Happy to sit through endless boring lectures on subjects she'd taken a look at and given up on years ago, and through more boring lectures on subjects she was good at by teachers who didn't have a clue and frequently got things wrong? *Happy?*

Happy was discovering that the school surveillance net had been brainwashed to ignore people wearing a specific shade of chromakey green, and to track people wearing black. Happy was discovering that Ellis could be counted on to have a stash of bootleg happy pills and would trade them for help with the biochemistry courseware, which at age nineteen was still about three years behind where she'd got to on her own at age fifteen. Happy was finding a couple of fellow misfits who didn't have bad breath and boast about getting their ashes hauled the morning after. Happy was learning how not to get beaten up in camera blind spots by invisible assailants, and accused of confabulation and self-mutilation when she cried for help.

She didn't dare think about the kind of happy that

might come from Mom or Dad finally reskilling to the point where they could land themselves some paid work, or being able to move out of this shithole of a slum tenement, or even able to emigrate to a richer, bigger hab. About not having to look forward to the prospect of being treated like a baby for more than two-thirds of her current life span, until she hit thirty – the age of majority in Septagon. Or about—

Oops, she thought, glancing around. *That wasn't very smart, was it?*

Introspection had distracted Wednesday as she left home. Which wasn't particularly bad, normally: even the sparsely inhabited subsidized apartment corridors had surveillance coverage and environmental support. But she'd turned two corners, taken a shortcut through a disused corporate warren with overrideforced doors, and been heading farther toward the distal pole where the party supposedly was. Sammy and her gang (who were not the school bullies, but the arbiters of fashion and cool, and never let Wednesday forget how lucky she was to be invited) had done this before, taken over an abandoned apartment or office zone, or even a manufacturing cube, gutted it, brought in temporary infrastructure and bootleg liquor, and cranked up the music. Moving out into the distal zone was daring: the sub-basement there was some of the oldest housing in the colony, long abandoned and scheduled for restructuring and development some time in the next ten years or so.

Wednesday had been blindly running the inertial route map Johnny deWitt had nervously beamed her the day before, saved to her cache: a flashing ring on her index finger pointed the path out to her. In her self-absorbed haze she hadn't noticed how very deep the shadows were getting, nor how sparse the pedestrian traffic was, nor how many of the corridor lighting strips were smashed. Now she was alone, with nobody else in sight. There was detritus under foot, broken roofing panels, a stack of dusty utility hoses, missing doors gaping like rotten teeth in the walls – this whole sector looked unsafe, *leaky*. And now it occurred to her to start thinking. 'Why Johnny?' she asked quietly. 'Johnny?' Short, spotty, and ungifted with any sense of fashion, he'd have been the class nerd if he'd been smarter: as it was, he was simply a victim. And he hadn't beamed her the ticket with any obvious ulterior motive, no stammering invitation to hole up in a soft space for an hour – just plain nervous, staring over his shoulder all the time. *I could phone him and ask, but then I'd look like a fool.* Weak. But . . . *if I don't phone him, I'll be a fool.*

'Dial Johnny the Sweat,' she subvocalized. *Connecting . . . no signal.* She blinked in disbelief. Surely there should be bandwidth down here? It was even more fundamental than oxygen. With bandwidth you could get rescue services or air, or find your way out of trouble. Without it, *anything* could happen.

There were rumors about these abandoned hab sectors. Dismembered bodies buried in the cable ducts, surveillance cams that would *look away* if you knew the secret gesture to bypass their programming, invitingly abandoned houses where one of the rooms was just a doorknob away from hard vacuum. But she'd never heard rumors of entire segments that were blacked out, where you couldn't call someone or talk to your agents or notepad, where maintenance 'bots feared to crawl. That was beyond neglect; it was actively dangerous.

She walked through a wide, low-ceilinged hall. From the rails along one side and the lack of decoration it looked to have been some kind of utility tunnel, back when people lived and worked there. Empty doorways gaped to either side, some of them fronted with rubble – crushed dumb aerogel and regolith bricks, twisted frameworks. Most of the lights were dead, except for a strip along the middle of the ceiling that flickered intermittently. The air was stale and smelled musty, as if nothing much stirred it. For the first time Wednesday was glad of her survival sensor, which would scream if she was in danger of wandering into an anoxic gas trap.

'This can't be right,' she muttered to herself. With a twitch of her rings she brought up a full route map, zoomed to scale so that this corner of the colony's public spaces was on the display. (The rings were another thing that rubbed it in; back in Moscow's system they'd have been a bulky, boxy personal digital assistant, not a set of hand jewels connected to her nervous system by subtle implants.) The whole segment was grayed out, condemned, off-limits. Somewhere on the way she'd gone blundering through a doorway that was down on the map as a blank wall. 'Bother.' The party – she dumped her follow-me tag into the map – lay roughly a hundred meters outside the shield wall of the pressure cylinder. 'Shit,' she added, this time with feeling. Someone had put Johnny up to it, spiking her with a falsie – or, more subtly, run a middleman spoof on his hacked ring. She could see it in her mind's eye: a bunch of mocking in-things joking about how they'd send the little foreign bitch on a climb down into the dirty underbelly of the world. Something rattled in the rubbish at one side of the hall, rats or—

She glanced round, hastily. There didn't seem to be any cams down there, just hollow eye sockets gaping in the ceiling. Ahead, a dead zone sucked up the light: a big hall, ceiling so high it was out of sight, opened like a cavern off the end of the service tunnel. And she heard the noise again. The unmistakable sound of boots scuffing against concrete.

What do I – Old reflexes died hard: it took Wednesday a split second to realize that it was no good asking Herman for advice. She glanced around for somewhere to hide. If someone was stalking her, some crazy – more likely, a couple of Bone Sisters who'd lured her down there to whack her bad for wearing team invisicolors and carrying a cutter on their loop – she wanted to be way out of sight before they eyeballed her. The big cavern ahead looked like a good bet, but it was dark, too dark to see into, and if it was a dead end, she'd be bottled in. But the doorways off to the left looked promising; lots of housing modules, jerked airlocks gaping like eye sockets.

Wednesday darted sideways, trying to muffle her bootheels. The nearest door gaped wide, floor underlayers ruptured like decompressed intestines, revealing a maze of ducts and cables. She stepped over them delicately, stopped, leaned against the wall and forced herself to close her eyes for ten seconds. The wall was freezing cold, and the house smelled musty, as if something had rotted in there long ago. When she uncovered her eyes again, she could see some way into the gloom. The floor paneling resumed a meter inside the threshold, and a corridor split in two directions. She took the left fork hesitantly, tiptoeing quietly and breathing lightly, listening for the sound of pursuit. When it got too dark to see she fumbled her tracker ring round, and whispered, 'I need a torch.' The thin blue diode glow wasn't much, but it was enough to outline the room ahead of her – a big open space like her family's own living room, gutted and abandoned.

She looked around the room. A broken fab bulked in one corner next to an exposed access crawlway. A sofa, seat rotted through with age and damp, occupied the opposite wall. Holding her breath, she forced herself not to sneeze. Words came to her, unbidden, on the breeze: '—fuck da bitch go?'

'One o' these. Youse take starboard, I taken the port.'

Male voices, with a really *strange* accent, harsh-sounding and determined. Wednesday shuddered convulsively. *Not the Sisters!* Bone Sisters were bad – you crossed them, they crossed you and you needed surgery – but the white sorority didn't hang out with—

Crunch. Cursing. Someone had stuck a foot in the open cable channel. Teetering on the edge of blind panic, Wednesday scurried toward the half-meter-high crawlway and scrambled along it on hands and knees, headfirst into a tube of twilight that stretched barely farther than arm's length. The tube kinked sharply upward, pipes bundled together against a carrier surface. She paused, forced herself to relax, and rolled over onto her back so that she could see round the bend. *Can I . . . ?* Push from the knees, begin to sit up, stick boot toes into gaps in the carrier trunking, *push . . .*

Panting with effort, she levered herself up and out of view of the room. *Please don't have infrared trackers or dogs.* The thought of the dogs still woke her up in a cold, shivering sweat, some nights. *Please just be muggers.* Knowing her luck, she'd crossed paths with a couple of serial fuckmonsters, transgressive nonconsensuals looking for a meat puppet. And she didn't have a backup: that cost real money, the kind that Mom and Dad didn't have. She shuddered, forcing back panic, braced her elbows against the walls of the duct, and flicked her rings to shutdown. She switched off her implants – backup brain, retinal projectors, the lot. Completely *off*. She could die there and nobody would find the body until they tore down the walls. There could be a gas trap, and she'd never know. But then again, the hunters might be following her by tracking her emissions.

'She come 'ere? I not am 'inking dis.' Scuffling and voices and, frighteningly, a faint overspill of light from a hand torch. A second voice, swearing. 'Search'e floor! Have youse taken beneath dat?'

'I have. Tracer an' be saying she – shitting vanish. Tracer be losing she. Signal strong al'way from she's home. Prey be wise to sigint 'striction.'

Not some girl gang shit: they were stalking her, had followed her all the way from home. Forget muggers, forget ordinary sickheads. Wednesday stifled a squeak of pure cold terror.

'I an' be checking over the way. You be clearing dis side an' if-neg we-all be waiting mid-way. If she be hiding, she-an be come out.'

'An' we be dumping nitro down here? Bath she in unbreathable?'

The second one replied, contemptuous: 'You-an' be finding rotten meat after, you be dumping de breathing mix. Contractees, t'ey wanting authentication.' Footsteps clattered over the grating, stopped.

They're going to wait me out in the corridor? At least they weren't going to flood the entire sector with nitrogen, but even hearing them talking about it was frightening her. *Rotten meat. They want to* know *I'm dead,* she realized, and the dizzying sense of loss made her stomach heave. *How do I get out of this?*

Just asking the question helped; from somewhere she dredged up a memory of her invisible friend lecturing her, an elevator-surfing run during happier days back home. *The first step in evading a pursuit is to identify and locate the pursuers. Then work out what sort of map they're using and try to locate their blind spots.* Not to take the stairs or the elevator, but to go through a service hatch, carefully step onto the roof of a car, and ride it to safety – or as a training game, all the way to Docking Control and back down again without showing up anywhere on Old Newfie's security map. She'd learned to ghost through walls, disappear from tracking nets, dissolve in a crowd. Ruefully, Wednesday recalled Herman's first lesson: *When threatened, do not let yourself panic. Panic is the most likely thing to kill you.* At the time, it had been fun.

It still is *a game,* she realized suddenly. *A game for* them. *Whoever they are. But I don't have to play by their rules.* With that realization, she managed to recapture a tenuous sense of self-confidence. *Now where?*

The duct was pitch-black, but she vaguely recalled it leading upward before she'd switched her gear off. It looked like it had been a house once, a slum tenement for cheap labor – so cheap it didn't even have en suite bathrooms and automated amahs to do the cleaning. Apartments there were prefab assemblies: a bunch of sealed, airtight modules connected by pressure-tight doors, bolted together in a big empty space and linked to the pressurized support mains by service tunnels like this one. This duct had to run somewhere pressurized. The only question was whether there was room for her to follow it all the way.

Wednesday braced herself against the back of the tube and began to lever herself up. The pipes and cables with their regular ties and their support grid were nearly as good as a ladder, and their insulation was soft and friable with age, forming spongy handholds for her questing fingers. She paused every half meter to feel above her with one hand and tried not to think about her clothing: the boots were a miserable pain for climbing in, but she couldn't take them off, and as for what the duct was doing to her jacket . . .

Her questing hand found empty space. Gasping quietly she reached up, then felt the cables bend over in a curve onto what had to be the top of the rooms' outer gas containment membrane. A final convulsive heave brought her up and over, and left her doubled over across the cable support, panting for breath, her legs still dangling over three meters of air space. Now she risked turning on her locater ring for a moment, still dialed to provide a light glow. Glancing around, she felt an edgy bite of claustrophobia. The crawl space widened to almost a meter, but was still only half a meter high. Ahead, there was a darkness that might be a branch off to one side, in the direction of the front door *if* she hadn't lost her bearings. Wednesday pulled her legs up and crawled toward it.

She came to a branch point, an intersection with a duct that had been built with humans in mind. The ceiling rose to a meter, and another quick flash of the ring revealed lighting panels (dead and dusty) and a flat, clear crawlway. She worked her way round into it, and shuffled along on hands and knees as fast as she could go. After about six meters she came to a large inspection hatch and paused. *I'm over the road, aren't I?* She put her ear to the hatch and listened, trying to ignore the thudding of her pulse.

'—be not seeing anyt'ing.' The voice was faint and tinny, but distinct.

'But she not being 'ere!' Protest, muted by metal. ' 'An being gone. Considered an' we tracer 'coy with 'an wall ghost? Be telling you not she'an 'ere.'

'Tell you th'man she not being not here? I an' you wait.'

Wednesday crept forward, taking shallow breaths and forcing herself not to move too fast. On the other side of the road there'd be another apartment module, and maybe a utility hub or a tunnel up to the next level, where she could get away from these freaks, whoever they were, with their weird dialect and frightening intent. She was still sick with fear, but now there was a hot ember of anger to go with it. *Who do they think they are?* Hunting her like dogs through the abandoned underbelly of the cylindrical city – the years fell away, bringing back the same stomach-churning fear and resentment.

Another node, another risky flash of light revealing another tunnel. This time she took the branch that headed toward the big empty cavern at the end of the passage. It ran straight for ten meters, then she flashed her ring again and saw a jagged edge ahead, dust and debris on the floor, what looked like the mummified turds of some tunnel-running animal and a pile of blown-out wall insulation. Beyond the ledge her light was swallowed by darkness and a distant dripping noise.

Shit. She knelt on the cold metal floor and glanced back. Below and behind her, two strange men were stalking her network shadow. Here in meatspace, though, she was blocked. Wasn't she? She crawled forward slowly and looked out into the cavern. There could be anything here: a gas trap full of carbon dioxide, or a cryogenic leak, insulation ripped and walls so cold you'd freeze to them on contact. She sniffed the air, edging close to panic again. *Herman would know . . .* But Herman wasn't there. Herman hadn't followed her from Old Newfie. He'd told her at the time: causal channels broke when you tried to move an end point faster than light, and the one his agent had planted on her – a pediatrician who'd spent an internship on the hab when she was twelve – was now corrupt. She'd have to figure it out for herself if she wanted to get to Sammy's party. Or anywhere. Home, even.

'An' chasing ghost.' The voice was muffled, distant, echoing up the corridor below her. 'If she here, how an' finding she? Dustrial yard my son, dustrial. An' ghost I telling.' A light flickered across shadows in the gloom on the floor of the cavern and Wednesday held her breath.

'Terascan—'

'—Show none. See, titan alloy walls, you be seeing? She ghost decoy, an' I telling you.'

'Yurg, he an' being not happy.'

Titanium walls? She looked down. Metal ductwork. If they had a terahertz scanner, they'd find her in a flash – except these old dumb metal ducts, fabbed from junk metal ore left over from the quarrying of the asteroid, made an excellent Faraday cage. *No signal.* Her shoulders shook as she heard bootheels below her, stomp and turn.

'Me an' you, we be going back uplight her patch. Wait there an' she.'

Stomp. Stomp. Angry footsteps, moving away down the corridor. Wednesday took a deep breath. *Can't hurt?* She twitched her rings back on for ten seconds and waited, then off again. The footsteps didn't return, nor the angry searching voices, but it was several minutes before she trusted herself to turn them back on again, and this time leave them glowing at her knuckles.

'Fuckmonsters,' she mumbled. Not that Centris Magna was exactly overflowing with sex criminals, but it was easier to believe than—

Her phone squeaked for attention.

'Yes?' she demanded.

'Wednesday. This is Herman. Do you understand?'

'What—' Her head was reeling with coincidence. 'It's been a long time!'

'Yes. Please pay attention. Your life is in danger. I am transferring funds to your purse for later retrieval. Keep your implants turned off: if you do that, I will be able to make it difficult for your pursuers to locate you. There is a ladder to one side of your current location; climb one floor, take the second exit on the left, first right, and keep going until you enter a densely populated area. Mingle with a crowd if you can find one. Do *not* go home, or you will endanger your family. I will contact you again shortly and provide directions. Do you understand?'

'Yes, but—' She was talking to herself.

'Fuckmonster,' she snapped, trying to sound as if she meant it. *Herman?* After three years of silence she felt weak at the knees. *Did I imagine it?* She turned up the light on her finger, saw the piles of debris and the scuff marks on her oh-so-labor-intensive boots. 'No.' Saw the ladder running down to floor level and up to the next corridor; beside the platform. 'Yes!'

the damned don't die

For this party Sam had repoed a dead light industrial unit on the edge of the reclaim zone. Wednesday didn't go there immediately; she headed uplight a couple of levels to a boringly bourgeois housing arc, found a public fresher, and used the facilities. Besides getting the muck off her boots and leggings and telling her jacket to clean itself over the toilet, her hair was a mess and her temper was vile. *How dare those scumbags follow me?* She dialed her lips to blue and the skin around her eyes to angry black, got her hair back into a semblance of order, then paused. 'Angry. *Angry!*'

She shook her head; the face in the mirror shook right back, then winked at her. 'Can I recommend something, dear?' asked the mirror.

In the end she let it talk her into ordering up a wispy, colorful sarong, a transparent flash of silky rainbows to wrap around her waist. It didn't fit with her mood, but she had to admit it was a good idea – her jacket, picking up on her temper, had spiked up across her shoulders until she resembled an angry hedgehog, and without the softening touch she'd have people avoiding her all evening. *Then* she used the mirror to call Sam's receptionist and, swallowing her pride, asked for directions. The party was impromptu and semirandom; as good a place to hide out as anywhere, just as long as nobody tailed her there. And she had no intention of letting herself be tagged and followed twice in one night shift.

Sam had taken over an empty industrial module a couple of levels below the basement slums, spray-bombed it black, and moved in a bunch of rogue domestic appliances. Light pipes nailgunned to rubbery green foam flared erratically at each corner of the room. The seating was dead, exotic knot-works of malformed calcium teratomas harvested from a biocoral tank, all ribs and jawbones. Loud waltz music shotgunned into screeching feedback by a buggy DJ-AI attacked her eardrums. There was a bar full of dumb and dumber, the robot waiter vomiting alcoholic drinks, and passing out joints and pink noise generators. Sameena knew how to run a party, Wednesday grudgingly acknowledged. Decriminalization lite, prosperity-bound urban youth experimenting with the modicum of risk that their subtly regimented society allowed them. A cat lay on top of a dead solvent tank, one foreleg hanging down, staring at everyone who entered. She grinned up at it. It lashed its tail angrily and looked away.

'Wednesday!' A plump boy, mirrored contact lenses, sweat gleaming red in the pit lights: Pig. He clutched a half-empty glass of something that might be beer.

'Pig.' She looked around. Pig was wired. Pig was always wired, boringly religious about his heterocyclic chemistry: a bioresearch geek. Ten kilos of brown adipose cells full of the weirdest organic chemistry you could imagine boiled away beneath his skin. He kept trying to breed a better liposome for his gunge-phase experiments. Said it kept him warm: one of these days someone was going to light his joint, and he'd go off like one of those old-time suicide bombers. 'Have you seen Fi?'

'Fi? Don't want hang round Fiona! She boring.'

Wednesday focused on Pig for the first time. His pupils were pinpricks, and he was breathing hard. 'What are you on?'

'Dumbers. Ran up a nice little hydroxylated triterpenoid to crank down the old ethanol dehydrogenase. Teaching m'self about beer 'n' hangovers. What did you bring?' He made as if to paw at her sleeve. She ducked round him gracefully.

'Myself,' she said, evaluating and assessing. Pig, sober, would just about fill her needs. Pig, drunk, wasn't even on the cards. 'Just my wonderful self, fat boy. Where's Fi?'

Pig grunted and took a big swig from his glass. Swaying, he spilled some of it down his chin. 'Next cell over.' Grunt. 'Had bad day thinking too hard this-morn. 'M'I dumb yet?'

She stared at him. 'What's the cube root of 2,362?'

'Mmm . . . six-point-nine . . . point-nine-seven . . . point-nine-seven-one . . .'

She left Pig slowly factoring his way out of her trap in a haze of Newtonian approximation and drifted on into the night, a pale-skinned ghost dressed in artful black tatters. Fancy dress, forgotten youthful death cults. She allowed herself to feel a bit more mellow toward Pig, even condescending to think fondly of him. Pig's wallowing self-abasement made her own withdrawn lack of socialization feel a bit less retarded. The world was full of nerds and exiles. The hothouse of forced brilliance the Septagon system produced also generated a lot of smart misfits, and even if none of them fit in individually, together they made an interesting mosaic.

There were people dancing in the next manufactory cell, accelerated bagpipes, feedback howls, a zek who'd hacked himself into a drum-machine trance whacking on a sensor grid to provide a hammering beat. It was an older crowd, late teens/early twenties, the tail end of high school. There were fewer fashion victims than you'd see at a normal high school hop, but wilder extremes; most people dressed – or didn't – as if they picked up whatever was nearest to their bed that morning, plus one or two exaggeratedly bizarre ego statements. A naked, hairless boy with a clanking crotch full of chromed chain links, dancing cheek to cheek with another boy, long-haired, wearing a swirling red gown that left his pierced and swollen nipples visible. A teenage girl in extreme fetish gear hobbled past; her wasp-waist corsetry, leather ball gag, wrist and ankle chains were all visible beneath a transparent, floor-sweeping dress. Wednesday ignored the exhibitionist extremals: they were fundamentally boring, attention-craving types who needed to be needed and were far too demanding to make good fuckfriends.

She headed for the back of the unit, hunting real company. Fiona was sitting on top of a dead cornucopia box, wearing black leggings and a T-shirt locked to the output from an entropy pool. She was chatting to a boy wearing a pressure suit liner with artfully slashed knees. The spod clutched a nebulizer, and was gesticulating dreamily. Fi looked up and called, 'Wednesday!'

'Fi!' Wednesday leaned forward and hugged her. Fiona's breath was smoky. 'What is this, downer city?'

Fi shrugged. 'Sammy said make it dumb, but not everyone got it.' (On the dance floor Miss Ball Gag was having difficulty communicating with some boy in a black rubber body-stocking who wanted to dance: their sign language protocols were incompatible.) Fi smiled. 'Vinnie, meet Wednesday. You want a drink, Wednesday?'

'Yeah, whatever.'

Fi snapped her fingers and Vinnie blinked slowly, then shambled off in the direction of the bar. 'Nice guy, I think, under the dumb layer. I dunno. I didn't want to get wasted before everybody else, know what I mean?'

Wednesday hitched up her sarong and jumped up on the box beside Fi. 'Ack. No uppers? No inverse-agonists?'

Fiona shook her head. 'House rules. You want to come in, you check your IQ at the door. Hear the jammers?'

'No.' When she said it, Wednesday suddenly realized that she could: the pink noise field was like tinnitus, scratching away at the edges of her implant perceptions. *Does Herman talk to Sam?* she wondered. 'So that's what's got to Pig.'

'Yeah. He's cute when he's thick, isn't he?' Fi giggled a bit and Wednesday smiled – sepulchrally, she hoped, because she didn't really know how Fi expected her to respond. ' 'Sa good excuse. Get dumb, get dumber, stop thinking, relax.'

'You been at it already?' Wednesday kept her voice down.

'Yeah. Just a bit.'

'Too bad. Was hoping to talk about—'

'Shh.' Fi leaned against her. 'I am going to get in Vinnie's pants tonight, see if I don't!' She pointed at the spod who was swaying back and forth, and working his way toward them. 'Ass so tight you could drop him and he'd bounce.'

The music was doing things to him and to Fi that sent a stab of jealousy all the way from Wednesday's amygdala to her crotch. She smoothed her skirt down. 'What do you expect to find in his pants? A catfish?'

Fi giggled again. 'Listen, just this once! Relax. Let go, ducky. Stop thinking, fuck like a bunny, learn the joy of grunt. Can't you switch off?'

Wednesday sighed. 'I'll try.' Vinnie was back. Wordlessly he held out a can of grinning neural death. She took it, hoisted a toast to higher cerebral shutdown, tried to chug it – ended up coughing. The night was young, the air full of augmentation jammers and neuroleptics and alcohol, and the party was just beginning to mix down to the right level of trancelike zombie heaven that highpressure synthetic geniuses needed to switch off and groove.

A long way down to the unthinking depths. She briefly wondered if she'd meet Pig down there and find him attractive.

In the end it wasn't Pig; it was a boy called Blow, green skin and webbing between his fingers and toes – but not his cock and balls – and she ended up on his arm giggling at a string of inane puns. He'd slipped a hand into the slit in her skirt but politely gone no farther and left it to her to pop the question, which she did for reasons that escaped her in the morning except that he'd been clean and well-mannered, and none of her usual fuckfriends were around and free, and she felt so *tense* . . .

. . . and the poor lad had ended up staying with her half the night just to give her a back rub, after she'd finished screaming and clawing his buttocks in one of the anti-sound-curtained alcoves at the sides of the dance floor.

'You're *really* tight,' he said in amazement, kneading away at one shoulder.

'Oh, you bet.' Her jacket had crawled into one corner and curled protectively around the rest of her gear. She lay facedown on the pad, damp and sweaty and postorgasmic and a bit stoned, trying to let go and relax, as he worked on her upper back. 'Aaah.'

He paused. 'Want to talk about it?' he asked.

'Not really,' she mumbled.

After a moment he went back to prodding at the sore patch on her left shoulder blade. 'You should relax.' *Rub*. 'It's a party. Was it someone here? Or someone else?'

'I said I don't want to talk about it,' she said, and he broke off from trying to get her back to relax.

'If you don't want to talk about it, what do you want?' he asked, beginning to sound annoyed. 'I could be out there.' He didn't sound as if he believed it.

'Then go.' She reached backward and grabbed his thigh blindly, contradicting herself. 'Stay. I'm not sure.' She was always bad at handling this, the difficult morning-after socializing that went with a one-off fuck with someone who she didn't know. 'Why do you have to talk?'

'Because you're interesting.' He sounded serious, which was a bad sign. 'I haven't met you before. And I think I like you.'

'Oh.' She glanced over at the dance floor, legs moving in irregular strobing flashes of light only a meter or two from their sweaty nest. He smelled of some kind of musk, and the faint tang of semen. She rolled over on her back, fetching up against the padded back of the recess, and looked at him. 'You got something else in mind?'

He stared at her sleepily. 'If you want to swap links, maybe we could meet up some other time?'

I'm being propositioned! she realized, startled. Not just sex. 'Maybe later.' She looked him up and down, mentally dressing him, wondering what it would be like. *A boyfriend?* Tension clawed at her, an unscratchable itch. She glanced at her hand. 'My phone's turned off, and I can't switch it back on.'

'If that's—'

'No!' She grabbed his hand: 'I'm really, not, uh, being—' She pulled him towards her. 'Oh.' *That wasn't the right answer, was it?* she thought, as the slide of hot skin against her – and the interesting drugs they'd been taking – made the breath catch in her throat and brought a twitch of life to his groin. She reached out and caught him in her hands. 'No swapping links. Just tonight. Make it like it's your last, best time.' Cunning fingers found a nipple. 'Oh, that's too easy.' And it was back into the unthinking depths, with a frogman called Blow to be her skin pilot and a nagging tension at the back of her skull, banished for the moment by an exchange of lust.

Wednesday came awake suddenly, naked and sticky and alone on the foam pad. It still smelled of Blow. The dance floor action was going, but more slowly, the music ratcheting toward a false dawn shutdown. She felt alone for a moment, then cold. *Damn,* she thought hazily. *He was good. Should have swapped—*

There was a set of rings on the pad next to her. And a self-heating coffee can set solicitously close to them.

'What the fuck?' She shook her head, taking stock. *What a guy.* She felt a momentary stab of loss: someone who'd take time out from a party to give her a back rub *after* making skinny, even if she hadn't wanted to talk . . . that was worth knowing. But he'd left a set of rings. She picked them up, puzzling. They looked to be about the right size. Still puzzled, she flipped the heater tab on the coffee and slid her own rings off, pulled the new set on, and twitched them alive. Instead of the half-expected authentication error, there was a tuneful chord and a smell of rose blossom as they glommed on to her implants and registered her as their rightful owner. Fully authenticated, with access to a whole bunch of stuff that was now instantiating itself in her implants from off a public server somewhere: 'Wow! Hey, voice mail. Any word from Herman?' she asked.

'Retrieving. You have a noninteractive message. Hello, Wednesday. This is Herman. Your instructions are as follows. Do not go home. Go to Transit Terminal B. There is a ticket waiting for you there, booked under the authority of professor-gymnast David Larsen, for your participation in a student work placement project. Collect the ticket and leave this hab immediately. Retain these rings, they're keyed to a new identity and set up to route packets to you via a deep market anonymizer. You cannot be traced through them. I will contact you in due course. Let me emphasize that you should not, under any circumstances, go home.' *Click.*

She stared at her rings in astonishment. 'Herman?' she asked, biting her lower lip. 'Herman?' *Don't go home.* A cold chill brought up the gooseflesh on her back. *Oh shit.* She began fumbling with her pile of clothes. '*Herman . . .*'

Her invisible agents, the software ghosts behind the control rings and her implants and the whole complex of mechanized identity that was Wednesday's persona within the Septagon network, didn't reply. She dragged her leggings and boots on, shrugged into the spidersilk camisole, and held out her arms for the jacket; the sarong she stuffed in a temporary pocket. Jittery and nervous with worry, mouth ashy with the taste of overstewed Blue Mountain, she lurched out of the privacy niche and around the edge of the dance floor. Miss Ball Gag was gagged no longer, straddling the lap of Mister Latex, taking it hard and fast and letting the audience know about it with both lungs. *Exhibitionists.* Wednesday spared her a second's snort as she slid past the bar and round the corner and out along a corridor – then up the first elevator she came to. She had a bad feeling, and the sense of unease grew worse the farther she went. She felt dirty and tired and she ached, and a gnawing edge of guilt bit into her. Shouldn't she have called home, warned someone? Who? Mom or Dad? Wouldn't they think she—

'Holy shit.'

She stopped dead and abruptly turned away from the through-route, heart hammering and palms sticky.

The corridor that led to her home run was blocked dead, the eery blue ghost glow of polis membrane slashed across it like a scar. Cops in full vacuum gear stood beside a low-loader with green-and-orange flashing spurs, pushing a mobile airlock toward the pressure barrier.

'Oh shit oh shit oh shit . . .' The seconds spurted through her fingers like grease. She ducked around another corner, opened her eyes, and began looking for a dead zone. *Fucking Bone Sisters* . . . well no, this wasn't their doing, was it? Dom games require a sub witness, a survivor. This was *Yurg, he an being not happy* and strangers' boot steps clicking in the cold, wet darkness behind her. And Herman on the phone for the first time in years. She found a corner, stopped, and massaged the pressure points in her jacket, the ones she'd spent so much time building into it. It clamped together around her ribs like a corset, then she reached over and pulled the hood over her head. The leggings were part of the same outfit; she rucked them up, then stretched the almost-liquid hem right over the outside of her boots, her beautiful dumb-matter platform-heeled lace-up air-leaking boots. 'Pressurize,' she said, then a moment later: 'Fade.' The jacket rubbed between her shoulder blades, letting her know it was active, and the opaque hood over her face flickered into transparency. Only the hissing of her breath reminded her that from then on in she was impregnable, hermetically sealed, and invisible so long as she danced through the Bone Sisters' blind spots.

There was a service passage one level up and two over, and she ghosted past the slave trolleys, trying to make no noise on the hard metal floor as she counted her way toward the door leading to—

'Shit and corruption.' The door handle was sealed with the imperious flashing blue of a police warning. Below the handle, the indicator light glowed steady red, a gas trap alert. Panicky claustrophobia seized her. 'Where the fuck is my family?' She brought up her rings and called up the home network. 'Dad? Mom? Are you there?'

A stranger's voice answered her: 'Who is this?'

She cut the link instantly and leaned against the wall. 'Damn. *Damn!*' She wanted to cry. *Where are you?* She was afraid she knew. 'Headlines, rings.' *Anoxic sink hits residential street in sector green, level 1.24, six dead, eight injured.* 'No!' The walls in front of her blurred; she sniffed, then rubbed her eyes through the smart fabric of her hood.

The door was sealed, but the bottom panel bulged about ten centimeters out of it – an emergency lock. She knelt and yanked the red handle, stood back as it inflated and unfolded from the door and bulged out, until it occupied half the corridor. Fumbling at the half-familiar lock tags with her gloves, she unzipped it halfway and scrambled in. She was beyond panic, by then, just a high voice at the back of her head crying *NoNoNoNoNo* continuously, weeping for her while she got on with the job. Rolling on her back and zipping the entrance panel shut, she kicked her way forward into the lock segment on the other side of the door and poked at the display on the other tag. 'This can't be happening,' someone said. The pressure outside was reading fifty millibars – not vacuum, but as close as made no difference. Even pure oxy wouldn't keep you alive at that. 'If they're in there and running on house gas, they'll be safe until the cops reach them,' the voice calmly told her, 'but if the bad guys hacked the house gas reserve, then dumped pressure overnight, they're dead. Either way, you can't help them. And the bad guys were going to wait there for you.' *ButButBut.*

Her fingers were buzzing, her rings calling. She held them to the side of her head. 'I told you not to go home.' It was Herman. 'The police have noticed an airlock trip. You have three minutes at most to clear the area. They'll think you did it.' *Silence.*

Wednesday could hear her heartbeat, the swish of blood in her ears. An impossible sense of loss filled her, like a river bursting its banks to sweep her away. 'But Dad—'

The next thing she knew she was standing in the corridor beside a slowly deflating emergency airlock, walking round a bend back toward human territory, away from the blue-lit recesses of the service tunnel. 'Jacket, back to normal.' The hood dropped loose and she pushed it back, forming a snood; the leggings could wait. She walked away jerkily, tugging her gloves off and shoving them into a pocket, half-blind, almost walking into a support pillar. *Oh shit oh shit oh shit.* She slid back into the aimless stroll of a teen out for a walk, slowly reached up with a shaking hand to unfasten her jacket. It relaxed quickly, blousing out loosely around her. *Oh shit.*

Possessed by a ghastly sense of loss, Wednesday headed toward Transit Terminal B.

Centris Magna was a small hab; its shuttle port wasn't designed to handle long-haul craft, or indeed anything except small passenger shuttles. Bulk freight traveled by way of a flinger able to impart up to ten klicks of delta-vee to payloads of a thousand tons or so – but it would be a very slow drift to the nearest ports of call. Only people traveled by fast mover. Consequently, the terminal was no bigger than the hub of Old Newfie, its decor dingy and heavily influenced by the rustic fad of a decade or so earlier.

Wednesday felt a flicker of homesickness as she walked into the departure lounge, almost a relief after the sick dread and guilt that had dogged her way there.

She zeroed in on the first available ticket console. 'Travel ticketing, please.'

The console blinked sleepy semihuman eyes at her: 'Please state your destination and your full name?'

'Vicky Strowger. Um, I have a travel itinerary on file with you for educational purposes? Reference, uh, David Larsen's public schedule.'

'Is that Vocational Educator Larsen, or the David Larsen who paints handmade inorganic toys and designs gastrointestinal recycling worms for export to Manichean survivalists?'

'The former.' Wednesday glanced around nervously, half-expecting blankfaced fuckmonsters with knives and manglers to lurch out at her from behind the soft furnishings. The wide hall was almost empty; grass, service trees, gently curling floor (it was so close to the axial end cap that the curvature was noticeable and the gravity barely a quarter of normal) – it was too big, positively threatening to someone who'd spent her youth on a cramped station.

'Paging. Yes, you have a travel itinerary. Payment is debited to the Outbound Project on—'

It's now or never. 'I'd like to upgrade, please.'

'Query?'

'Sybarite class, please, or the nearest thing to it you can find for me.' She'd checked her credit balance and she was damned if she was going to hunch restlessly in a cattle class seat for the duration of the transfer flight.

The terminal mumbled to itself for a while. 'Acknowledged. Annealing to determine how we can accommodate your wishes – confirmed. Departure from bay sixteen in two hours and four minutes, local shuttle to

Centris Noctis orbital for transfer to luxury liner WSL *Romanov* for cycle to Minima Four. Your connection will be in twenty-eight hours. Which option would you like and how would you like to pay?'

'Whichever.'

The terminal cleared its throat: 'I'm sorry, I was unable to understand that. What economic system would you like to pay in? We accept money, approved modal barter, agalmic kudos metrics, temporal futures, and—'

'Check my purse, dammit!'

The terminal abruptly closed its eyes and opened its mouth. A small blue six-legged mouse poked its head out. 'Hello!' it piped. 'I am your travel voucher! Please allow me to welcome you to TransVirtual TravelWays on behalf of all our entities and symbionts! We hope your journey with us will be enjoyable and your business will be fruitful! Please keep your travel voucher in your possession at all times, and – *squeep*—'

Wednesday caught it.

'Shut the fuck up,' she snarled. 'I am not in the fucking *mood*. Just show me to my cabin and fuck off.'

'—Please note that there is a security deposit for damage to TransVirtual TravelWays property, including fittings, fixtures, and emotivationally enhanced passenger liaison systems! We hope you have a pleasant voyage and a succulent profession! Please ensure your luggage remains under your control at all times, and proceed now to the green walkway under the cherry tree for transit to departure bay sixteen, where the VIP suite is awaiting your excellency's attention.'

The mouse-ticket shut up once Wednesday transferred it to a pocket that didn't contain any power tools or high-density energy storage devices. The path winked green in front of her feet, red behind her, as it guided her round a couple of strategically placed cherry trees and into a blessedly spartan metal-walled walkway that curved up and over the departure hall like a socialist-realist rendering of a yellow brick road.

Three hours to go. What am I going to do? Wednesday wondered nervously. *Wait for Herman to phone?* If he could be bothered talking to her – for some reason he didn't seem to want to stay close. A twinge of loneliness made her clench her jaw. *What am I letting myself in for?* And then a stab of guilt so sharp she nearly doubled over fighting back the urge to vomit. *Mom! Dad!*

The VIP lounge was privacy-spoofed, a huge acreage of black synthskin and gleaming ivory patrolled by silent gray partition walls that flickered from place to place while her back was turned, ensuring that she could wander freely without seeing – or being seen by – the other transit passengers. A dumb waiter followed her around, all bright gleaming brass and scrollwork, eager to fulfill her every desire. 'When do we board?' she asked.

'Ahem. If madam would follow me, her personal transshipment capsule is being readied now. If there are any special dietary or social or religious requirements—'

'Everything is just fine,' Wednesday said automatically, her voice flat. 'Just find me a sofa or something to sit on. Uh, maximum privacy.'

'Madam will find one just behind her.' Wednesday sat. The walls moved around her. A few meters away the floor was moving, too. It all happened too smoothly to notice by accident. Something in one of her pockets twitched, then began to recite brightly: 'We provide a wide range of business services, including metamagical consultancy, stock trading and derivatives analysis systems, and a full range of communications and disinformation tools for the discerning corporate space warrior. If you would like to take advantage of our horizontally scalable—'

Wednesday reached into her pocket and picked up her travel voucher by the loose skin at the scruff of its neck. 'Just shut up.' It fell silent and drew its tail up, clutching it with all six paws. 'I want a half hour call before boarding. Between now and then, I want total privacy – so private I could die and you wouldn't notice. No ears, no eyes, no breathing gas mixture analysis, nobody disturbs me. Got it?'

The voucher blinked its wide, dark, excessively cute eyes at her. 'Good.' She dropped it back in her pocket and stretched out on the huge expanse of padded cushions behind her. For a moment she wondered if she should have asked the voucher to leave her a bottle of something drinkable, then dismissed the thought. Privacy was more important just then, and besides, if there was something to drink, the way her luck was running right now she'd probably drink herself into a sodden stupor and choke on her own vomit. She held her hand to her face. 'Get me Herman.'

'I'm here.' The voice was anonymous, bland.

'You corpsefucker,' she hissed.

'I can tell you what is happening,' said Herman.

After a moment, she made a noise.

'On Old Newfoundland, before the evacuation. I made a mistake, Wednesday.'

'No shit.'

'Like the mistake you made in attempting to return home. There were skin particles on the outside of your jacket, Wednesday. Both you and your friend. It will take at least four hours for the police forensics to identify your genome, but then you may be suspected of vandalism at best, conspiracy to commit murder at worst. Your friend will be eliminated from the investigation rapidly, but you may be unable to return home until the situation is resolved. Did you want that to happen to you?'

She couldn't see anything. Her rings, biting into the palm of her hand, were her only contact with reality.

'What did you say?'

'I said.' She took a deep breath and tried to remember. 'Meant to say. What makes you think this is home?'

'You live here.'

'That's not good enough.' She fell silent. Herman, too, fell silent for a few seconds. 'I would have protected your family if I could.'

'What do you mean, *if*?'

'I thought there were only two or three hunters. I was wrong. Earlier, I thought events were of no significance that were highly significant. I should not have left you alone here. I should not have let your family stay here, so close to the resettlement hub. I should not have let you settle in Septagon at all.'

'What do you *want*?' Her voice rose to a squeak that she hated.

'I want you to be my helper again.' Pause. 'I want you to go on a voyage for me. You will be provided with money. There will be an errand. Then you can let go. It will take less than two hundred days, no longer.'

'I want my family back. I want . . .' She couldn't go on.

'I cannot give you your parents.' Herman sounded infinitely remote, flat, abhuman. 'But if you work for me, the hunters who took them will suffer a setback. And they will never trouble you again.'

murder by numbers

Forty light years from Earth, the yacht *Gloriana* congealed out of the cold emptiness between stars, emitting an electric blue flare of Cerenkov radiation. If it drifted at the residual velocity carried over from its last reference frame shift, it would take nearly two hundred years to cover the distance separating it from the star system it was heading for, but drifting wasn't the name of the game. After only a few minutes the ship's inertial transfer unit came online. Lidar probed the space ahead for obstacles as the yacht came under acceleration.

The *Gloriana* had started life as a billionaire's toy, but these days almost half the passenger volume was filled by the extensive diplomatic function spaces of a mobile embassy. The ship – and its three sisters – existed because it was cheaper for the UN to swallow the extra costs of running a starship than maintaining consulates on the couple of hundred planets that received visitors from Earth more than once in a decade but less than a thousand times a year.

Now running between jump zones at full acceleration, *Gloriana* had been under way for a week; over the course of which time Rachel Mansour had become increasingly annoyed and worried by George Cho's refusal to disclose the purpose or destination of the mission.

Finally, however, it looked as if she was about to get some answers.

The conference room was walled in a false woodgrain veneer that hardly sufficed to cover the smart skin guts of the ship. Tricked out in natural surfaces, the whole thing was as artificial as a cyborg smile. Maybe the big boardroom table (carved in the ornate intricacies of the neo-retrogothic fad of a century earlier) was made of wood, but Rachel wasn't betting on it. She glanced round the occupied chairs as she sat down, recognizing Pritkin, Jane Hill, Chi Tranh, and Gail Jordan. *George's little munchkins are out in force,* she noted ironically. She'd worked with most of them in the past; the lack of new faces told its own story.

'I take it nothing's running to schedule, is it?'

'The best-laid plans of mice and men,' Cho commented apologetically. 'You can lock the door now,' he told Pritkin. 'I've got some papers for you, dumb hard copy only, and they do *not* leave this room.' He reached under the desk and retrieved six fat files, their covers banded with red and yellow stripes, then tapped a virtual button on his pad. There was a faint hissing sound from the air conditioning. 'We're now firewalled from the rest of the ship. No bandwidth, bottled air, and the ship itself isn't within hailing distance of anything else . . . you can't be too careful with this stuff.'

Rachel's skin crawled. Last time she'd seen George put on the full-dress, loose-lips-sink-ships song and dance it had been the run in to the mess on Rochard's World. Which had involved dirty-tricks black ops that could have backfired to the extent of starting an interstellar war. 'How does this rate with the last, uh, mission?' she asked.

'Messier. All turn to page 114.' There was a rustle of dumb paper as everybody opened their files simultaneously. Someone whistled tunelessly, and Rachel glanced up in time to see Gail looking startled as she studied the page. Rachel began to read just in time for George to derail her concentration by talking. 'Moscow. Named after the imperial capital of Idaho rather than the place in Europe, except Idaho didn't have an empire back when the Eschaton grabbed a million confused Midwesterners from the first republic and stuffed them through a wormhole leading to the planetary surface.'

The words on the page swam before Rachel's eyes: *Bill of indictment in re: signatories of the Geneva Conventions on Causality Violation versus Persons Unknown responsible for the murder of—*

'Moscow was, bluntly, another boring McWorld. And a bit backward, even by those standards. But it had a single – and fairly enlightened – federal government, a single language, and no history of genocide, nuclear war, cannibalism, slavery, or anything else very unpleasant to explain it. It wasn't utopia, but neither was it hell. In fact, I'd have said the Muscovites were rather *nice*. Easygoing, friendly, laid-back, a little sleepy. Unlike whoever murdered them.'

Rachel leaned back in her chair and watched George. Cho was a diplomat, and a polished and experienced gambler who liked nothing better than a game of three-stud poker – so the experience of seeing him actually looking angry and upset about something was a novelty in its own right. The wall behind him showed supporting evidence. Rippling fields of grain as far as the eyes could see, a city rising – if that was the word for an urban sprawl where only city hall was more than three stories high – from the feet of blue-tinted mountains, white-painted houses, huge automated factory complexes, wide empty roads stretching forever under a sky the color of bluebells.

'Not everyone on Moscow was totally laid-back,' George continued, after taking a sip from his water glass. 'They had a small military, mostly equipped for disaster relief work – and a deterrent. Antimatter-fueled, ramscoop-assisted bombers, hanging out in the Oort cloud, about twelve light hours out.'

The wall dissolved into icy interstellar darkness and a close-up of a starship – not an elegant FTL yacht like this one, with the spherical bump of its drive kernel squatting beneath a tower of accommodation and cargo decks, but the evil angular lines of a planet-buster. Most of the slower-than-light bomber consisted of fuel containment vessels, and the huge inverted funnel of the ram field generator. Scooping up interstellar hydrogen for reaction mass, using antimatter to energize it, the warship could boost itself to more than 80 percent of lightspeed in a matter of weeks. Steering toward a target, it would then drift until it was time for terminal approach. Then, instead of decelerating, the crew and the ramscoop would separate and make their own way – leaving the remains of the ship to slam into the target planet.

'This is a reconstruction of a Muscovite Vindicator-class second-strike STL bomber. Our best intelligence gives it a maximum tau factor of point two and a dry rest mass of three kilotons – extremely high for the product of a relatively backward world – with an aggregate kinetic yield of 120 million megatons. It's probably designed to prefragment prior to impact, and coming in at 80 percent of lightspeed with several hundred penetration aids and a wake shield against ablator clouds, it would be able to saturate any reasonable planetary ballistic defense system. It would deliver about 20 percent more energy than the Chicxulub impactor that hit Earth 65 million years ago, enough to devastate a continent and trigger a dinosaur winter. In other words, it's a pretty typical second-strike slower-than-light deterrent for a planet that didn't have any enemies or major foreign policy engagements; an insurance policy against invaders.

'Moscow had four of these monsters, and we know for sure that the early warning system alerted them before the stellar shock front reached their firebases; we know at least three of them came under acceleration. What happened to the fourth ship is unclear at this time. They probably took some serious damage from the nova, but we have to assume that those four ships are engaged on a strike mission.'

George sat down again and refilled his water glass. Rachel shivered slightly. *They launched? But where to?* The idea was disquieting, even revolting: 'Has anyone ever actually launched an STL deterrent before, that you know of? I don't think I've ever heard of one being used . . .'

'May I?' It was Chi Tranh, lean-featured and quiet, the expert on weapons of mass destruction and, sometimes, her back-office researcher. Not a field agent, but George had evidently included him in the operation from the start, judging by the way he nodded along. 'The answer is no,' said Tranh. 'We have *never* seen one of these weapons systems used in anger. Nobody can start a war using STL ships – it would give years for a pre-emptive retaliatory strike. The idea is simply to have a deterrent – a club up your sleeve that makes the cost of invading and occupying your world too expensive for an aggressor to bear. This is a first, at least within our light cone.' He sat back and nodded at George.

'Who were they directed at?' Gail asked tentatively.

'I mean, who would do such a thing? How are they controlled? Have they—' She looked bewildered, which gave Rachel little satisfaction: the easily flustered protocol officer wasn't her first choice of someone to bring into the inner circle. *What was George thinking?* she wondered.

'Peace.' George made soothing gestures with his left hand. 'We, um . . . at the time of the event, Moscow was engaged in heated and unpleasant trade discussions with New Dresden. That's in your briefing documents, too, by the way. A previous trade deal cemented between a Muscovite delegation and the central committee of the Balearic Federation collapsed when the, um, Balearics were finally forced to sue for peace with the provisional government of Novy Srebrenicza. Prior to the peace of '62, the Balearics controlled the planet's sole surviving skyhook, which gave them a chokehold on the surface-to-orbit bulk freight trade. But after '62, the Patriotic Homeland Front was running the show. They decided to renegotiate several of their local bilateral trade arrangements – in their favor, of course – to help with the reconstruction. Things got extremely heated when they impounded a Muscovite starship and confiscated its cargo: differential levels of engineering support orbit-side in both systems meant that, although New Dresden had more turmoil and a war to recover from, heavy shipping was a proportionately much more expensive item on Moscow, which didn't have the tech base to fabricate drive kernels. The Muscovites' consulate was downsized to a negotiating core, and a large chunk of the Dresdener embassy was expelled a couple of weeks before the, ah, event.'

'So the bombers launched, on New Dresden,' Rachel concluded with a sinking feeling.

'We, um, think so,' said George. 'We're not sure. Tranh?'

'We can't track RAIR bombers once they go ballistic,'

said Tranh. 'It's standard procedure to launch in a random direction at high delta-vee, crank up to about point one light, then shut down and drift for a bit before lining up on the real target and boosting steadily to cruise speed. The drive torch is highly directional, and if nobody is in line behind it to see the gamma signature, it's easy to miss. Especially as the bombers launch from out in the Oort cloud and aim their exhausts to miss the inner system completely during the initial boost phase. Once they're under way the crew, usually four or six of them, enter suspended animation for a month or more, then the Captain wakes up and uses the bomber's causal channel to establish contact with one of the remaining consulates or embassies. He or she also opens any sealed orders. In this case, we've been informed – through confidential channels, initially by the Muscovite embassy on Earth – that a week before Moscow was hit, the Governor-General's office updated the default fire plan for the V-force to target New Dresden. We don't know *why* she did that, but the trade dispute . . .' Tranh trailed off.

'That's the situation.' George shook his head. 'Doubtless the Muscovite government didn't expect to be attacked by New Dresden – but as a precaution they selected New Dresden as a default target, leaving the fallout for the diplomatic corps to deal with. New Dresden is thirty-six light years from Moscow, so at full bore the bombers can be there in forty years. Thirty-five now, and counting. New Dresden has a population of over eight hundred million. There is no way, even if we install extra skyhooks and obtain maximum cooperation from the neighbors, that we can evacuate nearly a billion people – the required cubage, over thirty million seats a year, exceeds the entire terrestrial registered merchant fleet's capacity. Never mind the refugee problem – who'd take them in?'

'I don't believe they could be so stupid!' Gail said vehemently. Rachel watched her cautiously. Gail might be good at organizing the diplomatic niceties, but in some respects she was very naive. 'How could they? Is there a recall signal?'

'Yes, there's a recall code,' George admitted. 'The problem is getting the surviving members of the Muscovite diplomatic corps to send it.'

Rachel flipped through the pages of her briefing document rapidly. *Ah, yes, I was* afraid *it would be something like this.* Background: the bombers communicated with the remaining embassies via causal channel. In the absence of a recall code, the bombers would proceed on a strike mission to the designated target, their crews in cold sleep for most of the voyage. After conducting the attack, the crew – with their ramscoops and life-support modules – could decelerate or cruise on to another system at near lightspeed. If a recall code was received first, standard procedure was for the crew to burn their remaining fuel, braking to a halt in deep space, and for the embassy to lay on a rescue ship to remove the crew, laying scuttling charges to decommission the bombers *in situ*.

'How is a recall code sent?' Rachel inquired.

'Via causal channel from one of the embassies,' said Tranh. 'Because the bombers are strictly STL, they maintain contact with the government-in-exile. The ambassadors possess authentication tokens that the bomber crews can use to confirm their identity. Having authenticated themselves, they have a vote code system – if two or more of them send a recall code, the bomber crews are required to stand down and disclose their position and vector for a decommissioning flight. But – and this is a *big* but – there's also a coercion code. It is known only to the ambassadors, like the recall code, and if three or more ambassadors send the coercion code, the bomber crews are required to destroy their causal channel and proceed to the target. The coercion code overrides the recall code; the theory is that it will only be used if an aggressor has somehow managed to lay his or her hands on an ambassador and is holding a gun to their head. The ambassadors can tell the black hats the wrong code and, if three or more of them are under duress, ensure that the strike mission goes forward.'

'Oh. Oh.' Gail shook her head. 'Those poor people! How many ambassadors do we have to work on? With?'

George tapped the tabletop. 'It's in your dossier. There were twelve full-dress embassies from Moscow in residence at the time of the disaster. Unfortunately, two of the ambassadors had been recalled for consultation immediately before the incident, and they are presumed dead. Of the remaining ten, one committed suicide immediately, one died in a vehicular accident six months later – it was ruled an accident; he seems to have fallen in front of a train – and, well, this is where it gets *interesting*. I hope you all have strong stomachs . . .'

After the meeting she caught up with Martin. He was idling on the promenade deck, playing with the image enhancement widgets on the main viewing window.

'How did it go?' he asked, glancing up at her from the chaise longue. He seemed to be treating the journey as an enforced vacation, she noticed; dressing casually, lounging around, catching up on his reading and viewing, spending his surplus energy in the gym. But he looked worried now, as if she'd brought a storm cloud of depression in with her.

'It's a lot to swallow. Budge over.' He made some space for her to sit down. 'I want a drink.'

'I'll get you one. What do you—'

'No, don't. I said I *wanted* a drink, not that I'm going to have one.'

She stared gloomily at the wall-sized expanse of darkness on the other side of the almost empty room. Something circular and penumbral, darker than the interstellar night, cut an arc out of the dusting of unwinking stars. 'What's that?'

'Brown dwarf. Uncataloged, it's about half a light year away. I've got the window accumulating a decent visible light image of it right now.'

'Oh, okay.' Rachel leaned back against the wall. The designers had tricked out the promenade deck in a self-conscious parody of the age of steam. From the holystoned oak planking of the floor to the retro-Victoriana of the furniture, it could have been a slice out of some nuclear-powered liner from the distant planet-bound past, a snapshot of the *Titanic* perhaps, a time populated by women in bonnets and ballooning skirts, men in backward baseball caps and plus-fours, zeppelins and jumbos circling overhead. But it wasn't big enough to be convincing, and instead of a view across the sea, there was just a screen the size of a wall and her husband wearing a utility kilt with pockets stuffed with gadgets he never went anywhere without.

'How bad was it?' he asked quietly.

'Bad?' She shrugged. 'On a scale of one to ten, with the New Republic an eight or nine, this is about an eleven. A chunk of it is die-before-disclosing stuff, but I guess there's no harm in letting you in on the public side. Which is bad enough.' She shook her head. 'What time is it?'

'Mm, about 1500, shipboard. There was some announcement about setting the clocks forward tonight, as well.'

'Okay.' She tapped her fingertips idly on the lacquered side table. 'I think I *will* take you up on that drink, as long as there's some sober-up available just in case.'

'Umph.' Martin twisted one of his rings. 'Pitcher of iced margaritas on the promenade deck, please.' He watched her closely. 'Is my ex-employer involved?'

'Hmm. I don't think so.' Rachel touched his shoulder. 'You haven't heard anything, have you?'

'I'm on the beach, I think.' His cheek twitched. 'And between contracts, so there's no conflict of interests.'

'Good,' she said, taking his free hand, '*good*.'

'You don't sound happy.'

'That's because—' She shook her head. 'Why the *hell* are people so stupid?'

'Stupid? What do you mean?' He lifted her hand slightly, inspecting the back of her wrist intently.

'People.' It came out as a curse. 'Like that asshole in Geneva. Turns out there was a, a—' She swallowed, and before she could continue the dumb waiter beside the table dinged for attention. 'And that bitch in Ents. I set a search going, by the way. Pulled some strings. I should have all the dirt on her when we get home.' She turned to open the dumb waiter and found there was a tray inside. 'That was fast.' She removed two glasses, passing one to Martin.

'Where was I? Yes, stupid, wanton, destructive assholes. About five years ago, that supernova out near the Septagon stars, a system called Moscow. Turns out it wasn't a natural event at all. Someone iron-bombed the star. That's a causality-violation device, and about as illegal as they come – also apparently unstable to build and hazardous as hell. I'd like to know why it didn't attract a certain local deity's attention. Anyway, the Moscow republic had a modest deterrent fleet in their Oort cloud, far enough out to just about survive the blast, and they were in the middle of a trade dispute. So they launched, and now we're trying to talk their diplomatic staff into calling off a strike on a planet with nearly a billion inhabitants who we are pretty damn sure had nothing to do with the war crime.'

'Sounds bad.' She watched him raise his glass, a guarded expression on his face.

'The headache is, the place they launched on – New Dresden – isn't squeaky clean. They had a series of really bloody civil wars over the past century or so, and what they're left with may be stable but isn't necessarily happy. Meanwhile, Moscow – damn!' She put the glass down. 'Worlds with a single planetary government aren't *meant* to be peaceful and open and into civil rights! When I see a planet with just one government, I look for the mass graves. It's some kind of natural law or something – world governments grow out of the barrel of a gun.'

'Um. You mean, the good guys are getting ready to commit genocide? And the bad guys are asking you in to talk them out of it? Is that the picture?'

'No.' She took a quick pull of her ice-cold margarita. 'If that was all it was, I think I could cope with it. Just another talk-down, after all. No, there's something much worse going on in here. A real stinking shitty mess. But George wants to keep a lid on it for the time being, so I can't dump it on your shoulder.'

'So.' One of the most soothing things about Martin was that he could tell when not to push her. This was one of those times: instead of shoving, he stretched his arm along the back of the sofa, offering her a shoulder. After a moment, she leaned against him.

'Thanks.'

'It's all right.' He waited while she shifted to a more comfortable position. 'What are we going to do, then? When we arrive? Dresden, did you say?'

'Well.' She considered her words carefully. 'I'm on the Ents budget listed as a cultural attaché. So I'm going to do some cultural attaché things. There's a memorial ceremony to attend, meetings, probably the usual bunch of diplomatic parties to organize. Luckily Dresden's relatively developed, socially and industrially, not like New Prague.' She pulled a face. 'You're probably going to have the wonderful, unmissable, once-in-a-lifetime chance to be my diplomatic wife for a few weeks. Once-in-a-lifetime's all you'll take before you flee screaming back to a shipyard, I promise you.'

'Ten ecus says you're wrong.' He hugged her.

'And fifty says you won't make it. Sucker.' She kissed him, then pulled back to arm's length, smiling. Then her smile slipped. 'I've got some other stuff to do,' she said quietly, 'and maybe a side trip. But I can't talk about it.'

'Can't, or don't want to?'

'Can't.' She emptied her glass and put it down. 'It's the other I told you about. Sorry.'

'I'm not pushing,' he said slyly. 'I just want to know everything you get up to when I'm not around!' He continued in a more serious tone of voice: 'Promise me if it's anything like, uh, last week, you'll try to let me know in advance?'

'I—' She nodded. 'I'll try,' she said softly. 'If it's remotely possible.' Which was entirely true, and she hated herself for it – he meant well, and the idea that he might think she was lying to him stung her – but there were things she wasn't at liberty to talk about, just as there were topics Martin wouldn't raise within earshot of her coworkers. Serious, frightening, things. And if she didn't cooperate with Cho's covert agenda, she'd be gambling with other people's lives. Because, when she thought about it, she couldn't see any sane alternative to what George was proposing to do.

Flashback, one hour earlier

'Here's the Honorable Maurice Pendelton, ambassador of the Republic of Moscow to the court of Ayse Bayar, Empress of al-Turku.'

George Cho stood up and fiddled with a control ring. The wall behind him flickered to a view of an office – ornately paneled in wood, gas-lit and velvet-draped, richly carpeted and dominated by a ponderous desk bearing an antique workstation. There was something else on the desk; for a moment Rachel couldn't quite work out what she was looking at, then she realized that it was a man, slumped across the green leather blotter. A timer counted down seconds in the top left corner of the display. In his back—

'Murder?' asked Jane, tight-lipped. Rachel hadn't seen much of her since the events back on New Prague, when Jane had uncomplainingly shouldered the burden of Rachel's research work inside the diplomatic compound. She wondered idly how Jane would cope with a field assignment if she couldn't even figure out a scene like this for herself.

'The inquisitor's report was very clear about the fact that his arms weren't long enough for him to stab himself in the back – at least, not with a sword,' Tranh said drily. 'Especially not with enough force to nail the torso to the tabletop. Proximate cause of death was a severed dorsal aorta and damage to the pericardium – he bled out and died within seconds, but most of the mess is behind the desk.'

George fidgeted with his rings and the camera viewpoint slewed dizzyingly around the room. The scene behind the ambassador's desk was a mess. Blood had gouted from the wound in his back and splattered across his chair, pooling in viscid puddles beneath his desk. Footprints congealed in the rich carpet, an obscene trail leading toward the door.

'I take it this is important to our mission,' said Rachel. 'Do we have a full crime scene report? Was the killer apprehended?'

'No and no,' Cho said with gloomy satisfaction. 'The Office of the Vizier of Morning took control of the investigation outside the embassy, and while the Turku authorities have been polite and helpful to us, they have declined to give us full details of the killing, other than this diorama shot. Note, if you will, the theatrical red nose and bushy moustache a party or parties unknown applied to the Ambassador's face – after he was dead, according to the Vizier's Office. Oh, in case you were wondering, the killer wasn't apprehended. For the sake of face the Vizier's Office rounded up a couple of petty thieves, forced them to confess, then beheaded them in front of the public newsfeeds, but our confidential sources assure us that the real investigation is still continuing. Which brings me to incident number two.'

Another wall-sized photograph of chaos. This time it was a roadside disaster – the wreckage of a large vehicle, obviously some sort of luxury people mover, lay scattered across a road, uniformed emergency crews and rescue vehicles all around it. Blue sheets covered misshapen mounds to either side. Much of the debris was scorched; some of it was still smoking.

'This was an embassy limousine, taking her excellency Simonette Black to a conference on resettlement policy for refugee populations in Bonn, the capital of the Frisian Foundation, a confederation of independent states on Eiger's World. Which, unlike al-Turku, is a Deutsch McWorld with no real history of political violence other than a couple of wars fought over oil fields and states' rights a century or two ago.'

George pointed at some bushes to one side of the road, and the screen obligingly zoomed. Something gleamed: '*That* is a reflector post for an infrared beam. If we look at the source' – the viewpoint flipped dizzyingly into the sky then back down, 180 degrees away from the post – 'we find *this*.' A green box, with a round hole in its front, above a complex optical sight and some kind of rubber mat. The box, too, looked scorched. 'I'm told that's a disposable anti-armor missile launcher, hypervelocity, with a two-stage penetrator jet designed to punch through ceramic armor or high-Tesla fields. The poor people in the limousine – Black, her wife, their driver, the chargé d'immigration, and two bodyguards – didn't stand a chance. It was stolen from an army depot one week before the incident. It was armed by remote control and rigged to fire when the beam was interrupted. I'm told that the plastic object underneath the missile launcher is an, ah, whoopee cushion. A rubber bladder that emits a flatulent sound when sat upon.'

Rachel looked down at her pad. To her surprise, she realized she'd begun to doodle on it with her stylus in ink transfer mode. Pictures of mushroom clouds and Mach waves knocking over groundscrapers and arcologies. She glanced up. 'Once is happenstance, twice is coincidence,' she said. 'Any more?'

George's shoulders fell. He looked very old for a moment, even though Rachel knew he was seven years her junior. 'Yes,' he said. Another diorama filled the wall. 'I've been saving this until last. This is the Honorable Maureen Davis, ambassador to the United Nations of Earth in Geneva.' Gail looked away, visibly upset, and Rachel wondered distantly if she was going to cry. Violent death didn't just strip the victims of their dignity, it insulted the survivors. And it was a personal insult to Rachel. *We were supposed to protect her!* An attack on a visiting diplomat reflected on the honor of the nation or coalition that played host to them. And this—

'Did we let this happen on our watch?' she demanded angrily. '*After* knowing that two other ambassadors had died in questionable circumstances?' She closed the dossier in front of her and flattened it against the table, pressing until her knuckles turned white.

'No.' George took a deep breath. 'She was the first to die – just the last for us to be aware of. At first we penciled it in as a simple murder – horrible, but not special. Unlike the other two incidents we have a complete crime scene breakdown and we're pursuing the murderer with every resource at our disposal. We are' – he took another breath – 'appalled and outraged that this has happened. But more than that, we're very much afraid that it's going to happen again. Tranh, could you explain?'

Tranh stood up again and began to recite in a flat monotone that suggested that he, too, was trying to hold down the lid on his outrage. 'Ambassador Davis was discovered in the state you see by a housekeeper maintenance contractor who called to deal with a fault alert by the house cleaning 'bot. The amah was confused by, well, a conflict between its recognizer for human beings and its garbage collection monitor. That doesn't happen very often these days, but Ambassador Davis had an antique that still had a heuristic support contract in force. Embassy security admitted the maintenance contractor and immediately discovered the ambassador in this state. They immediately requested our assistance – unlike their counterparts on Turku.' His voice quivered with outrage as he added, 'The killer used a bungee cord for a ligature.'

Foul play? That's one way of putting it, Rachel observed. Ambassadors did not, as a rule, hang themselves in the stairwell of their own residences using rubberized ropes.

Nor did they do so after pinioning their hands behind them, not to mention fracturing the backs of their skulls on mysteriously missing blunt objects.

'Ah yes, she shot herself three times in the back of the head and jumped out of the sixth floor window *just* to make us look bad,' she muttered, drawing a wide-eyed look of confusion from Gail. 'When did this happen relative to the others? In the empire time defined by the Moscow embassy causal channels, if you've got the figures. That might tell us something.'

'The order was' – George flipped pages in a separate file – 'Ambassador Davis at datum zero, followed by Simonette Black at T plus fourteen days, six hours, three minutes. Then Ambassador Pendelton thirty-four days, nineteen hours and fifty-two minutes later.' He gazed at Rachel tiredly. 'Any other questions?'

'Yes.' She leaned back in her chair, tapping her stylus on the cover of her briefing file. 'Are Turku and the, uh, Frisian Foundation coordinating their investigations? Are they even *aware* of the other assassinations?'

'No and no.' George inclined his head slightly. 'You have more question. Let's hear them, and your reasoning.'

'All right.' Rachel sat up straight and looked at Gail. 'You might not want to hear this.'

'I can take it.' She looked back, angry and bewildered. 'I don't have to like it.'

'Okay.' Rachel tapped the file in front of her. 'As the man said, once is happenstance, twice might be coincidence, but three times is enemy action. We have a very nasty situation evolving, in which there exists a dwindling pool of assets – ambassadors – such that if the total drops below three, 800 million people will die. From an initial nine survivors, three have been murdered in the past three months. I assume the rest are under heavy guard—'

'Wherever possible,' George murmured.

'—But we basically have a crisis on our hands. Someone has figured out how to kill 800 million birds with just six stones. Leaving aside the killer's evident penchant for cruel practical jokes, we know absolutely nothing about who they are and what motivates them. In fact, what we appear to know may actually be deliberate deception. And we're the only people who are treating these assassinations as part of a big picture, rather than isolated killings.'

'That's essentially correct,' said Tranh. 'There are other investigative measures we are taking, but' – he shrugged, looking unhappy – 'it takes time.'

'Well then.' Rachel licked her lips, which had become unpleasantly dry. 'As I see it, our ideal outcome is to convince them to issue the abort code to the bombers immediately, before any more of them die. But right now they'll probably view any such request with extreme suspicion – the murders could be seen as a conspiracy to force them to issue the code. Or we could prove to them that the New Dresdeners didn't do the dirty deed and show them who did – if we have any idea.'

She nodded when Cho shook his head. 'was afraid of that. The other option is to stake out a goa, wait for the assassins to show up, and try to trace them back to their masters. But we have a mess of motives at work here. Someone seems to want to ensure that the Muscovite weapons destroy New Dresden, and I've got to ask, why? Who could possibly benefit from wiping out one – or maybe even two – planets?' She glanced around the table.

'That's essentially where we've got to,' George said heavily, 'except for the final part.'

'Explain.' She leaned forward attentively.

'We don't have time to stake them all out. Given the current attrition rate, we've got to face the risk of losing

four more ambassadors in the next month. We haven't caught a single assassin, so we don't know who's doing it. So tell me what you deduce from that fact.'

'That we're in the shit,' Rachel said in a low monotone. She leaned forward tensely. 'Let's look at this as a crime in progress. If we shelve the means and opportunity questions, who's got a motive? Who could possibly gain by arranging for Moscow to bomb the crap out of Dresden in thirty-five years' time?'

She held up a hand and began counting off fingers. 'One: a third party who hates Dresden. I think we can take that as a non sequitur; nobody is ever crazy enough to want to exterminate an entire planet. At least, nobody who's that crazy ever gets their hands on the means to do it.' *Well, virtually nobody*, she reminded herself, flashing back a week. *Idi would have done it – if he'd had an R-bomb. But he didn't. So . . .* 'Two: a faction among the Muscovite exiles who really, really hates Dresden – enough to commit murder, murder of their own people, just to make sure. Three: someone who wants to strike a negotiating position of some kind. It could be blackmail, for example, and the ransom note hasn't arrived yet. Four: it's a continent smasher. Could be a *really* nasty bunch of folks have decided to make sure it goes home, as a prelude to a, uh, rescue and reconstruction mission of a rather permanent nature.'

'You're saying it could be some other government that wants to take advantage of the situation?' Gail looked aghast.

'That's realpolitik for you.' Rachel shrugged. 'I'm not saying it is, but . . . do we have any candidates?' She raised an eyebrow at Tranh.

'Possibly.' He frowned. 'Among the neighbors . . . I can't see the New Republic doing that, can you?'

Rachel shook her head. 'They're out for the count.'

'Then, hmm. Forget Turku, forget Malacia, forget Septagon. None of them have an expansionist government except Septagon, and they're not interested in anything with a primary that masses more than point zero five of Sol or comes with inhabitable planets. There's Newpeace, but they're still in a mess from the civil war. And Eiger isn't likely. Tonto, that's another of those weird semiclosed dictatorships. They might have an angle on it. But it's not anything obvious, is it?'

Rachel frowned. 'There seem to be a couple of dictatorships in this sector, aren't there? Funny: they aren't normally stable enough to last . . .'

'There's some kind of weird political ideology, calling themselves the ReMastered. Tonto went ReMastered forty or fifty years ago,' offered Jane. 'Don't know much about them: they're not nice people.' She shivered. 'Why do you ask?'

Rachel's frown deepened. 'If you can dig anything up I'd appreciate hearing it. George, you're holding something back, aren't you?'

The ambassador sat up slightly, then nodded. 'Yes, I am.' He glanced round the table.

'You probably figured out why I wanted you; it's because none of you had any conceivable link either to Moscow or New Dresden. Which, incidentally, is where we're en route to. It so happens that Ambassador Elspeth Morrow is in residence in Sarajevo, and Harrison Baxter, former trade minister of the Muscovite government – and the highest surviving government officer, he's also on the code schedule – is there, too. He was sent just before the incident, to attempt to resolve the trade dispute. I strongly suspect that they're the next logical target, being a two-for-one hit. Our cover story – for everyone outside this room – is that we're here to discuss the R-bomb situation with Morrow and Baxter.

'The real task in hand is somewhat different. It's to keep them alive and if possible capture one of the killers and backtrack to their masters. Which is where you come in, Rachel. Tranh, your job is to brief the embassy guard and the Dresdener Interior Ministry special security police and act as external security liaison. Gail, you and I are going to talk directly to the Minister and the Ambassador and impress the urgency of the situation upon them. You handle protocol, I'll handle diplomacy. Pritkin, you're our switchboard and front office. Jane, I need you on back office, coordinating any intel we get from home about the circumstances of the murders. Rachel, you've got a nasty, suspicious mind. I want you to try and set up a trap for the killers – assuming they surface. And I've, well, got a little surprise.'

'Surprise,' she mimicked. 'Uh-huh. One of *those* surprises?'

'Those?' echoed Jane.

'Those.' Rachel grimaced. 'Spill it, George.'

Cho took a deep breath. 'For you, I've got a covert job in mind. You're about the same size and build as Ambassador Morrow. You fill in the dotted line.'

'Oh. Oh no.' Rachel shook her head. 'You can't do this to me!'

'Oh yes?' Tranh's smile wasn't entirely friendly. 'What was that you were saying earlier about wanting to nail the culprits?'

'Um.' She nodded like a puppet with a blown feedback circuit. '*If* you're right about there being a hit planned.'

'I think we're right.' George nodded. 'Because there's another datum I haven't given you.'

'Oh yeah?'

'In addition to a time series on the murders, we ran a spatial map and a full shipping traffic analysis. It turns out that there are about three starships that called at each location a day or so before the hit, then moved on afterward. They're busy places, mostly. Anyway, one of those ships is a freighter, and none of the crew went down from orbit at any port on its cycle. Another is – well, if you want to accuse the Malacian Navy of trying to start a war with three of their neighbors by whacking diplomats, *you* draw their attention to the suspicious maneuvers of one of their cruisers. Whose flight plan for the current goodwill tour was finalized nearly a year before Ambassador Black arrived on Eiger's World. Which leaves just one suspect.'

'Stop winding me up, George. Just tell it straight.'

George looked at her, his expression one of wounded dignity. 'My, my! Very well, then. It's the WhiteStar liner *Romanov*, outbound from Earth on a year-long tour circuit. It was in orbit around Eiger's World when Ambassador Black was murdered. It was in orbit around Turku when Pendelton was murdered. And while it wasn't parked over Kilimanjaro when Ambassador Davis was murdered, the smoking gun is that it arrived a day later, then departed. That was the zero incident. The arrival times line up. It is in principle possible that an assassin joined the *Romanov* after killing Ambassador Davis, then traveled to Turku and Eiger's World to repeat the task.'

Rachel knotted her fingers together. 'Tell me it isn't calling at New Dresden next?'

'It's not. It's en route to Septagon Four – but first port of call after that is New Dresden, sure enough. We should get there a couple of weeks ahead of it. And that's basically why I wanted you on board. We'll show up as a special diplomatic team tasked with demonstrating that the Dresdener governments' hands are clean. You will be attached to our team – that's your cover story – but your real job will be to set up a trap in which you body double for Ambassador

Morrow, a week before our killer turns up. And when they try to take you out, we'll have them. And then' — his expression was fierce — 'let's hope we can get to the bottom of this before the assassins murder 800 million people.'

spy vs spy

Wednesday was so busy working on a better way of expressing her rage that she didn't notice when the walls around her recliner softened and flowed, containerizing her in a lozenge of dark foam and dropping her through the floor of the terminal into the cargo mesh of an intrasystem freighter bound for Centris Noctis. '*Stupid* brainless unplanned intelligence, no, stupid brainless unplanned stupid – *what*?'

Her itinerary cleared its throat again: 'Please hold on tight! Departure in three hundred seconds! Departure in—'

'I heard you the first time, fuckmonster.' Anger was better than the gaping hole in her life, the absolute bitter despair she was trying so hard to ignore. The walls, flowing past and re-forming into the shape of a compact hexagonal cabin, did nothing to soothe her. 'How long am I in transit?'

'Eep! Don't hurt me! TransVirtual TravelWays welcomes all passengers to the transit shuttle *Hieronymus B.*, departing Centris Magna hab four port authority bay sixteen for

Centris Noctis hab eleven port authority bay sixty-two in four minutes and thirty seconds. Please familiarize yourself with our flight profile and safety briefing. After a few seconds of free fall, we will be under continuous acceleration at one-tenth of gee standard for eight hours, dropping to—'

Wednesday shut it out, nodding along vaguely and watching the blurred images in the wall through a thin haze of angry tears with her arms wrapped around her legs. *Fuckmonsters,* she thought vacantly. *Following me, vaccing out the apartment, Mom, Dad, Jerm—* The concrete horrors of the vision rubbed it all in, forcing it home. People chasing her, Herman admitting a mistake, unimaginable. Her credit balance when she'd checked it, *This has got to be a mistake:* there was enough money to buy a house, a good-sized cubic in an upmarket swing zone, never mind a ticket out of town on the next shuttle. 'Give you a job.' *Yeah, but how much use is it?* She'd give it all back in an instant to have the past day to run again with a different outcome. Just to be able to have that chat with Dad.

'How long?' she asked through her misery.

'Total transit time to Centris Noctis, currently six point one million kilometers distant, is sixteen hours and forty-one minutes. We hope you enjoy your flight and choose TransVirtual TravelWays again!'

The itinerary froze, motionless. Wednesday sighed. 'Sixteen *hours?*' *I should have caught the high-delta service,* she realized. Not that she was used to flying anywhere at all, but this would take almost a day. 'What shipboard facilities are available? Am I stuck in here for the whole trip?'

'Passengers are invited to remain in their seats for the duration of path injection maneuvering. Your seat is equipped to protect you from the consequences of local vertical variances. Eep! Please do not damage company assets willfully as these items are chargeable to your account.

When the "thrust" light is extinguished you may release your safety belt and walk around the ship. You are on A deck. B deck, C deck, and D deck are the other passenger decks on this flight. F deck provides a choice of entertainment arcades and the food court—'

'Enough.' Wednesday's stomach lurched; she looked up in time to see the stylized thrust light in the ceiling flash urgently. Loops of safety webbing crawled out from the sides of her chair, wrapping around her securely as the gravity failed. 'Oh, shit. Uh, how many other people are on this flight?'

'The manifest for this flight shows a total of forty-six passengers! You are one of five lucky Sybarite-class travelers! Below you in space, comfort, privacy, and our estimate are six Comfort class business passengers! The remainder are making use of our Basic-class package in common—'

'Shut up.' Wednesday squeezed her eyes shut tiredly. 'I'm trying to think. I *should* be thinking.' Memories of lessons, way back in her early teens when Herman had first tempted her with strange adventure games. *Playing at spy versus spy?* She wouldn't put anything beyond him: clearly Herman wasn't simply a pet invisible friend, and equally clearly he had fingers in a lot of pies. All that stuff about evasion and tailing, how to locate surveillance nets and make use of blind spots, how to break relational integrity by finding camera overlaps and spoofing just one of them so the system interpolated an error . . . *Wear the black hat. I'm chasing me, Wednesday. Just killed* – her train of thought faltered for a moment, teetering on the edge – *and now I'm after her. Who, how, where, what?* 'Can you stop listening until I call your name, ticket?'

'Madam is now in full privacy! All speech commands will be ignored until you unlock your suite. Call for "Wendigo" when you want to discontinue privacy.'

'Uh-huh.' She glanced at the itinerary; it curled up, gripping the end of her recliner, and mimed mammalian sleep. 'Hmm. At least two bad guys. If I'm lucky they think I was in the apartment when they, when they—' *Don't think about that.* 'If not, what will they do? Worst case: they're covering the transit ferries so there's one aboard right now. Or they've got friends waiting for me at the other end. I can't evade that. But if they're limited to following me, then, then . . .'

She sighed. *Shit.* The prospect of spending nearly seventeen hours trapped in the recliner was already beginning to seem like hell. There was a quiet chime, and the thrust light went out. 'Oh.' It seemed to be taunting her. 'Maybe they didn't cover the port. Maybe.' She stared at it for another minute, then reached for the quick release on her safety belts and picked up her itinerary, stuffing it into a jacket pocket. 'Wendigo. Open the door. There's a manual outside? Okay, close the door and go back to full privacy mode as soon as I've gone.'

Outside the door of her room she found herself in a narrow circular corridor, with cabin doors spaced around the circumference and a twisting circular staircase leading down to the other decks. The ship hummed quietly beneath her as she took the steps six at a time, floating effortlessly down. The two lower passenger decks looked like open-plan seating, rows of recliners bolted side by side. As she passed she saw that most of them were empty. *Business must be down*, she decided.

The food court turned out to be a cramped circle of tables in the middle of a ring of food fabs programmed for different cuisines, a belt of arms waiting overhead to take orders. Wednesday found a small table at the edge and tapped it for the menu. She was just beginning to figure out her way around it when somebody sat down opposite her.

'Hi.' She looked up, startled. He smiled shyly at her. *Wow!* Two meters tall, he had blue eyes, blond hair that looked so real it had to be a family heirloom – tied back in a ponytail – diamond earrings, not too much muscle or makeup, skin like – 'I couldn't help noticing you. Are you traveling alone?'

'Maybe not.' She found herself smiling right back. 'I'm Wednesday.'

'Leo. May I . . .?'

'Sure.' She watched him sit down, graceful in the low-gee environment. 'I was about to do lunch. Are you hungry?'

'I could be.' *Beat.* He grinned. 'Food, too.'

Oh. Wednesday watched him, beginning to have second thoughts about the idea of a full stomach. He was gorgeous, and he was focused right at her. *Where were* you *at Sammy's party?* 'Where are you traveling?' she asked aloud.

'Oh, I'm on vacation. Going to stay with my uncle.' He shrugged. 'Can I interest you in a drink?'

'What, you want to get me drunk and drag me off to my cabin?' She tapped on the tabletop for a bowl of miso soup and a hand roll. 'Hmm. What kind of drink did you have in mind?'

'Something exquisite and bubbly, I guess. To fit in with the company.' He leaned forward, close enough for her to inhale the faint scent of his skin: 'If you're interested?'

'I think so.' She waited a second, then leaned back, watching him with narrowed eyes. 'Are you going to order anything?'

'Mm-hmm.' She watched him as he scrolled the table-top, jabbing at the wine submenu and ordering a plate of spiced noodles – *coordinated* and *confident,* she thought – and a bottle of something that was not only exquisite and bubbly, but also expensive. 'Do you often go to stay with your uncle?' she asked, feeling idiotic, a conversational casualty in progress. 'I don't mean to pry or anything—'

'Not really.' The waitron was back, bearing a bottle with an intricate pressure-relief cork and a pair of fluted glasses. He took them and raised an eyebrow at her. 'It's not like there are more than two flights a day between Magna and Noctis, is it?' He poured carefully, and handed her a nearly full glass. 'To your very good . . . taste?'

Wednesday took a gulp of sparkling wine to hide her turmoil. Everything about Leo was right, and he was an eminently eligible choice for a friendly fuck to while away the journey – except that he was *too* right. Too polished, too witty, too includable. He was the sort of fashion accessory the 'in' crowd always had on display. Why pick on her for an evening's dalliance? She glanced around. There was a double handful of other passengers in the food hall, mostly in groups, but there were one or two singles of indeterminate age: well, maybe he was telling the truth. 'To my very good luck – in meeting you,' she said, and knocked back the rest of her glass. 'I was really afraid today was going to be a dead loss.'

The food arrived, and Wednesday managed to drink her soup without taking her eyes off him. Lust confused her. *What is it about him?* she wondered. 'Are you traveling in Comfort or Syb?' she asked.

'Cattle class.' He frowned momentarily. 'All I get is a seat, a curtain, and a boring neck massage. Why?'

'Oh, nothing,' she said innocently. *My place or yours?* was a no-brainer. In fact—

Her earlobe began to vibrate.

' 'Scuse me a moment.' She tapped the table for privacy, then yet more privacy: everything around her went distant and fuzzy, like being inside a velvet-lined black hole. 'Yeah?' she demanded.

'Wednesday?' He sounded hesitant.

'Who – wait a minute. My phone was switched off!'

'You said if I was serious I should find your links myself?'

Well not exactly, but – She crossed her legs, uneasy. 'Yeah, you did, didn't you? Look, I'm going to be away for a while. You were lucky to get me without a twenty-second lag. I won't be back for months. Is there anything we need to say?'

'Uh, yes.' Blow sounded hesitant at the end of the bit-stream. 'I, uh, I wanted to apologize for being too talky last night. Uh, I guess if you don't want to see me—'

'No, it's not that.' Wednesday frowned minutely. Outside her cone of silence she could see Leo watching her intently; she moved instinctively to cover her mouth with the palm of her hand as she spoke. 'I really am going on a voyage right now. I know I didn't want to get downheavy last night, but that was just the way it was then. If you want to look me up when I get back, that would be great. But I'm off-station already, so there's no chance to meet up first.'

'Are you in some kind of trouble?' he asked.

'No, I – yes. Shit! Yes, I'm in trouble.' She caught Leo's gaze, rolled her eyes at him, lying with her face. He winked at her, and she forced a grin. The warmth in her belly turned to ice. *My rings. These are Herman's rings. The untraceable ones.* 'Who told you?'

'This, uh, guy I sometimes work for, he called me up just now and told me you were in bad trouble and needed a friend. Is there anything I can do to help?'

Leo was pulling a face at her: Wednesday pulled a face right back. 'I think you just did, just by calling. Listen, are *you* in trouble? Has anyone been round to talk to you? Cops?'

'Yes.' His voice tended to break out into a croak when he was worried. 'Said they just wanted to clear something up. Asked if I'd seen you. I said "no".'

She relaxed slightly. 'Your invisible friend, is he called Herman?'

A second's silence. 'You know Herman?'

'Listen to him,' she hissed, rolling her eyes some more and shrugging through the sound screen at Leo. 'There's something bad going on. I'm being followed. Just stay out of this, all right?'

'Okay.' He paused. 'I want to ask you lots of questions sometime. Are you coming back?'

'I hope so.' Leo was looking bored. 'Listen, I've got to go. Problem to deal with. Thanks for talking – I've got your callback. Bye.'

'I – uh. Bye.'

'Privacy off.' She grinned at Leo.

'Who was that?' he asked, curiously.

'Old friend,' she said carelessly. 'Didn't know I was leaving.'

'Well, isn't that a shame?' He pointed at her place setting. 'Your soup's cold.'

'Oh well.' She shrugged, then stood up, her heart beating fast. It wasn't arousal anymore, though. At least, it wasn't sexual arousal. Her palms were cold and her stomach threatening to twist itself into knots. 'Where are you staying on Noctis?' she asked. 'I was thinking, maybe I could come visit you?'

'Uh, I don't know. My uncle, he's got some pretty weird ideas,' he said edgily. 'How about we try your cabin? I've always wanted to see how the other half live.'

Shit. He knew which class she was in. *Careless of him* – or he was overconfident. 'Okay,' she said lightly, smiling as he took her wrist and pulled her toward him. Another sniff of that enticing man-scent, something about his skin that made her want to slip her arm under his shirt and inhale. *That's something specific for your vomeronasal organ, something to go straight to your hypothalamus and get you wet, isn't it?* Her senses seemed to sharpen as she leaned against him. 'Come on,' she breathed in his ear, wondering how on earth she was going to get out of this mess. Her heart was pounding, and it *felt* like lust, or terror, or both. She was actually leaning against him, knees weak with something. A *neurotoxin?* she wondered, but no – that would be much too public if he was what she thought he might be. Probably just pheromone receptor blockers. 'Come on.'

On the staircase he paused for a moment and pulled her close. 'Let me carry you?' he whispered in her ear. She nodded, dizzy with tension, and he picked her up, her head resting close to his ear as he climbed the stairs two steps at a time. A deck, the ring of Syb-class capsules. 'Where's your—'

'Hold on, put me down, I'll find it.' She smiled at him and leaned close. The corridor lights were dim, most of the other passengers snoozing their way through the flight. He smelled of fresh sweat and something musky, treacherously intoxicating. Herman had taught her a term for this: *Venus trap.* She grabbed him and pressed her lips against his in a kiss that he returned enthusiastically. Hips bumped. 'Shit, not here.' She tugged him along the corridor, nerves on fire. 'Here.' She tapped the door panel. 'I need the rest room. You go on inside and make yourself at home. I won't be long.'

'Really?' he asked, stepping inside her room.

'Yeah.' She leaned close, nibbled him delicately on the neck. 'I won't be a minute.' Heart pounding, she stepped back and hit the door close button. Then she tapped the panel next to it, the privacy lock. Her heart was trying to climb out through her rib cage: 'Did I *really* just do that?' she asked herself 'Wendigo. Suite, can you hear me?'

'Greetings, passenger Strowger! I can hear you.' Its voice was tinny, coming to her through the external control plate.

'Please lock my suite door. Do not unlock the door until one hour after arrival. I want to sleep in. Divert all incoming calls, cancel outgoing routing. Maximum sound damping. Return to full privacy mode and add voiceprint authentication to keyword.'

The simpleminded suite agent swallowed it. 'Warning! Privacy may be overridden by authorized crew members in event of accident or medical emergency—'

'How many crew does this flight carry?' Her stomach lurched, icy cold soup sloshing.

'This is an unattended flight.'

'Keep it that way. Now shut up and don't talk to anyone.'

There was a tentative knocking from inside the cabin, almost inaudible through the smart foam. Then a faint bump as if something massive had bounced off the inside of the door. Wednesday pouted at it, then headed for the staircase, a wistful urge to run back and apologize still fighting it out with her common sense. Sex on legs, packaged just for her? *Where were you during Sammy's party?* 'Vacc'ing out Mom'n'Dad,' she muttered to herself, half-blind with anger and loss as she hunted round C deck for an empty seat to sleep in. 'Unless he's the best friendly fuck I've ever dropped by mistake . . .' She carried on arguing with herself for a long time before she dozed off, and by the time she was awake again the ferry had passed turnover and was nearly ready to dock.

'Okay. I'm here. What do I do now?'

Noctis concourse wasn't built with fail-safe operation in

mind. It was a product of the ebullient Septagonese economic miracle, so optimistic that nothing could possibly go wrong. Gravity thereabouts was a variable, vectored in whichever direction the architects had willed it. There were jungles on the walls, sand dunes on the ceiling, moebius walkways snaking through them for maximum visual impact.

Wednesday hurried along a strip locked to a steady half gee, trailing behind a flickering lightbug. She passed occasional clumps of other long-distance travelers – a mix of emigrants, merchants taking the long caravanserai, *wanderjahr* youth on the Grand Tour – and a variety of variously enticing and annoying shops disguised as environmental features. Butterflies the size of dinner plates flapped slowly past overhead, their wings flickering with historical docudramas. A small toroidal rain cloud spun slowly over a bright crimson nest of muddy-rooted mangroves, small lightning discharges clicking across its inner hole. Wednesday glanced past it, through a chink in the artistic foliage that led into a sudden perspective shift; stars glinted through diamond windows over a kilometer away. It was very Septagon, life defying vacuum, and for a moment she was dizzy with homesickness and the infinitely deep pool of depression that waited just beneath the thin ice of her self-control. *If we hadn't come here, Mom and Dad would still be alive.* If. If.

'Follow the lightbug to your connection with the liner *Romanov.* Once you reach the *Romanov*'s dock you should go aboard and remain in your stateroom until departure. Which is due in under six hours. I can cover for you for some time, but if you venture around the terminal, it is possible that a police agent will spot you and place you under volitional arrest. I believe there is a high probability that no charges will be brought, but you would miss the departure, and there is a high risk that the individuals pursuing you would locate you and make another attempt on your life. At the very least, they would be able to regain their lock on you. Good work with the suite, by the way.'

'But what do I *do?*' she demanded nervously, stepping around a gaggle of flightless birds that had decided to roost in the middle of the footpath.

'Once you are on the liner and it is under way, they cannot reinforce their surveillance. I believe they are stretched thin, covering the orbitals around Centris Delta. There may be one or more aboard the ship, but you should be able to avoid them. Use the funds in your account to buy essentials aboard the ship; keep yourself alert. The next port of call is New Dresden, and I expect by that time to have fully identified your pursuers.'

'Wait – you mean you *don't know* who they are? What *is* this?' Her voice rose.

'I believe them to be a faction of a group calling themselves the ReMastered. Whether they are an official faction, or a rogue splinter group, is unknown at this time. They may even be using the ReMastered as a cover: they've concealed their trail very effectively. If you go along with my suggestions, you will force them to expose themselves. Do you understand? I will have help waiting for you at New Dresden.'

'You mean this ship is going to New Dresden? I—' She found herself talking into silence. 'Shit. ReMastered.' Whoever they were, at least she had a name, now. A name for something to hate.

The loop path branched, and her lightbug darted off to one side. Wednesday followed it tiredly. It was past midnight by her local time, and she badly needed something to keep her going. Here, the concourse took a turn for the more conventional. The vegetation thinned out, replaced by

tiled blood diamond panes the size of her feet. Large structures bumped up from the floor and walls, freight lifts and
baggage handlers and stairwells leading down into the
docking tunnels that led out to the berthed starships. Some
ships maintained their own gravity, didn't they?
Wednesday wasn't sure what to expect of this one – wasn't
it from Old Earth? She vaguely remembered lectures about
the place, docutours and ecodramas. It had all sounded con-
fusingly complicated and backward, and she'd been trying
to keep Priz the Axe from cracking her tablet instead of listening to the professora. Was Earth a high-level kind of
place, or backward like home had been?

The lightbug paused in front of her, then went dark.
'Welcome to embarkation point four,' piped her itinerary,
somewhat muffled from inside a jacket pocket. 'Please have
your itinerary, identification documents, and skinprint
ready for inspection!' The bug lit up again, darting back
and forth between Wednesday and a powered walkway
leading to the level below the concourse.

'Okay.' Wednesday unsealed her pocket. 'Uh, identification. Hmm.' She fumbled with her rings for a moment.
'Herman,' she hissed, 'do these rings authenticate me?'

Click. 'Default identity, Victoria Strowger. Message from
owner: Have fun with these, and remember to check the
files I've stored in them under your alias.' *Clunk.*

She blinked, bemused. 'O-kay . . .'

Down below the wild efflorescences of the port concourse she found herself in a cool, well-lit departure hall
fronting a boarding tunnel. A redheaded woman in some
kind of ornate blue-and-gold uniform – *How quaint!* she
thought – stood by the entrance. 'Your papers, please?'

'Uh, Vicky Strowger.' She held up her itinerary. 'Have I
come to the right place?'

The woman glanced aside at some kind of internal list.

'Yes, we've been expecting you.' She smiled with professional ease. 'I see you've got a companiotronic guide. Would you like me to update it for shipboard use?'

'Sure.' Wednesday handed the furry blue nuisance over to the woman. 'If you don't mind me asking, who are you and what happens next?'

'Good questions,' the woman said distractedly, stroking the back of the guide's skull while it spasmed in a fit of downloading. 'I'm Elena, from the purser's office. If you have any questions later, feel free to ask room service to put you through to me. We're not scheduled to depart for another five and a half hours, but most passengers are already aboard, which is why – Ah, hello! Mr. Hobson? You're earlier than usual, sir. If you'd care to wait one second – Here you are, Victoria. If you'd like to go through into the elevator it will take you straight to the accommodation level you're on. Do you have any luggage?' She raised an eyebrow at Wednesday's small shake of the head. 'All right. You're in Sybarite-class row four, Corridor C. There's a fab you can use for the basics in your room, and a range of boutiques two levels down and one corridor across from you if you want to shop for extras later. Anything else you need to know, feel free to ask for me. Bye!' She was already turning to deal with the unusually early Mr. Hobson as Wednesday slid the talking travel guide back into its pocket. She shook her head: *Too much, too fast.* So Earth had fabs? Then it wasn't a backwater like New Dresden – or home – and she wasn't going to have to camp out in a refugee cell for a week. Maybe the journey would turn out all right, especially if Herman had given her his usual thorough map of the service facilities . . .

interlude: 2

The darkened tool storage pod hanging from the aircon stack at the top of ring J normally smelled of packing foam and damp. Now it stank of silicone lube grease and fear.

A quiet voice recited a list of sins. 'Let me recap. You hired ordinary goons who tracked the kid as far as a dead zone, but they lost her inside a derelict housing module. She was on her way to a fucking party, but nobody thought to trace her friends, find out where it was, and go there. Meanwhile, your other proxies liquidated her family, thus losing all possible links to the primary target and simultaneously warning her that her life was in danger. So tell me, Franz, *how* does a nineteen-year-old refugee manage to outsmart a pair of even remotely professional gangsters? And why did her skin traces show up all over the *inside* of the emergency lock leading into the depressurized cell?'

Pause. 'Uh, would you believe, shit happens?' A longer pause. 'The goons were tracking her via her interface rings. It's my fault for not anticipating that she had evasion training; I expected it to be a straightforward track and tag. When she took off—'

U. Portia Hoechst sighed. 'Give me some light in here, Jamil.'

The interior of the service pod lit up.

'Are you going to kill me now?' asked Franz. He looked mildly apprehensive, as if steeling himself for an unpleasant dental procedure. He didn't have much of an alternative. Portia's bodyguard Marx had done a thorough job of trussing him to a couple of anchor beams.

'That depends.' Portia tapped the end of her stylus against her front teeth thoughtfully as she stared at him. She narrowed her eyes. 'There has been a culture of unacceptable slackness in this organization.'

Franz opened his mouth as if about to say something, then shut it again, slowly. A bead of sweat jiggled on his forehead, just below the hairline. It was growing visibly bigger, as she watched, held in place by surface tension, unable to run away in the milligee environment.

'What did you do next?' she asked, almost kindly.

'Well, I concluded she'd run. Either to the authorities for protection or somewhere outside the hab. So I sent Burr, Samow, and Kerguelen off to grab seats on the next departing ferry shuttles to other habs, with orders to do a full cap routine on her if she showed up, and I took myself and Erica down to the local cop shop to puppetize our way into their holding tank in case she turned out to have stayed home. As we only had the one puppetry kit in the entire system . . .' His voice trailed off.

'What other resources did you have? You only covered three shuttle flights with one finger on each. Isn't that a bit thin?' Her voice was almost gentle.

'I was fully committed.' Franz sounded tense. 'I only have six residents here, including me! That isn't even enough to maintain a twenty-four-by-seven tail on a single individual, much less conduct a full penetration or cleanup. Why do you think I had to use paid muscle instead of properly programmed puppets? I've been requesting additional backup for months, but all that came down the line were orders to make better use of my resources and a 10 percent budget cut. 'Then your group . . .' He trailed off.

'Your requests. Were they at least acknowledged?'

'Yes.' He watched her warily, unsure where this chain of inquiry was leading. She watched him watching her, speculating. Franz was the resident in Centris, a station chief left over from U. Vannevar Scott's operation, and therefore, automatically suspect. But he was also the only station chief in this entire system, the complex of orbital habs circling in the accretion belt around the brown dwarf at the heart of Septagon B. It was sheer luck that he'd even been able to move his team onto the right hab in the first place. If he was telling the truth, hung out to dry with six staff to pin down three hundred million people scattered through nearly five hundred orbital habitats and countless smaller stations and ships, he'd clearly been starved of support. While U. Scott had been pouring funds into his central security groups, snooping on his rivals within the Directorate.

Portia stared at him. 'I will investigate this, you know.'

Franz watched her unflinchingly, not even sparing a glance for Marx. Marx was the one who'd pith him if it came to it, or even kill him, simply wasting his memories, leaving everything that he was to drain into nothingness.

'Has your crew reported back about the loose end?'

Now his expression broke: irritation, even a spark of outright rebellion. 'I'd be able to tell you if you'd unwrap me and give me a chance to find out,' he said waspishly. 'Or ask Erica. Assuming you haven't already decided she's a broken tool and discarded her.'

Portia reached a decision. The practicalities of it were risky, but then so was life. 'Release him,' she told Jamil.

'Is this wise?' Marx grunted, keeping his eyes focused dead center on Franz's forehead. 'We could repurpose him—'

'I prefer my subordinates to have free will.' Her smile vanished abruptly. 'Do you have a problem with that?'

'Just looking out for your safety, boss.'

'I'm quite sure that U. Franz Bergman will remember whose purpose he serves now that External Environmental Control Four has been, ah, absorbed by Group Six.'

Jamil produced a knife from somewhere and began slicing away at the tape fastening Franz's arms to the support bars.

Franz's eyes widened. 'Did you say *absorbed*? What happened to Control Four?'

'U. Vannevar Scott has been an extremely naughty boy,' Portia trilled. 'So naughty that Overdepartmentsecretary Blumlein saw fit to take all his toys away.' Slight emphasis on the *all*, a raised eyebrow, a pouting lip. 'You're on the gray list.' Gray, as opposed to black, whose status was *pith and reclaim with extreme prejudice.* 'It's not very big, but you're on it. Who knows? If you work hard, you may even stay there.'

Franz slumped slightly, floating free of the anchor beams, nervously apprehensive. 'What do you want me to do?' he asked. 'Nobody told us anything about—' He swallowed.

'Indeed.' Portia nodded at Jamil, big and solidly muscled. 'You and Jamil are going to go and do the rounds. You're going to give me a sitrep, and Jamil is going to sit on your shoulder and see how you go about it. Think of it as an entrance exam.' She recognized his unspoken question. 'You and your people, both.'

'I'm, uh, very grateful—'

'Don't be.' The brilliant smile was back. 'I want to know what's going on out there in the wild. You've got two kiloseconds to find out. And believe me, until I decide to pass you, dying will seem like the easy option.'

By the time he got back to the pod, Franz was truly frightened. As if the mess he'd been holding together for the past nine months wasn't bad enough, having the DepSec from hell descend on him with bodyguards and a full-dress away team was worse. Luckily Erica was with him, a calming influence. But the news—

He glanced over his shoulder at her. She stared back at him, trying to look unaffected. A competent deputy station chief, following her boss's lead. Jamil followed them both, imperturbable, threatening. 'I'll handle this,' he reassured her.

'I understand.' He wanted to reach out and grab her hand, but he didn't dare. Not in front of Jamil. She looked rattled enough as it was. Maybe it was because she'd figured out where they stood for herself, but he couldn't be sure.

The DepSec was waiting for him like a spider at the center of her web, black and shiny and carnivorous when she smiled, disturbingly red lips parting to reveal perfect teeth. Sea-green eyes as cold as death watched him. Behind her, the bodyguard waited. 'You made it with fifty seconds to spare!' She glanced at Erica. 'So, you're U. Erica Blofeld?'

Franz noticed Erica nodding out of the corner of his eye. He could *smell* the DepSec, the warm mind-fuzzing sense of family coming off her in waves. He could feel Erica's nervousness. 'Ye-es. Boss.'

'Let her speak for herself,' Hoechst said gently. 'You can speak, can't you?' she added.

'Yes.' Erica cleared her throat. 'Yes, uh. Boss? Nobody told us anything.'

'Jamil. Did U. Franz Bergman tell U. Erica Blofeld anything substantive about the change of management structure?'

'No, boss.'

'Good.' Hoechst focused on the woman. 'What's the situation, Erica? Tell me.'

'I—' She shrugged uncomfortably. 'Burr and Samow drew a blank. Kerguelen messaged to say he'd found the target, in transit to Noctis hab in a first-class berth. Last he sent, he was closing on her to lay a honeypot and do a field-expedient pickup. Since then I've heard nothing. He last called in about eleven hours ago, and they should be arriving at Noctis real soon, but he's missed three checkpoints, and while I can think of several reasons for doing so, none of them are good.' She watched Hoechst closely, eyes flickering back and forth between her face and her hands.

'Well, that is convenient.' Hoechst's expression was bland. 'Did it occur to any of you that the target of this action might be trained in evasion and self-defense?'

Franz tried to answer. 'We didn't—'

'Shut up! That was a rhetorical question.' Hoechst looked past him at the doorway. 'You've told me what I needed to know, and I thank you,' she said graciously, nodding to Erica. 'Jamil, give U. Erica Blofeld coffee *now*.'

Franz kicked off the floor, hit the ceiling and rolled, intending to bounce off it and take Jamil in the gut. Desperation triggered his boost reflexes, narrowing focus until the world was a gray-walled tunnel. But Jamil had already brought up something like a silvery hand-sized Christmas tree, and he stabbed it toward the back of Erica's head. Erica's eyes bulged. She spasmed, beginning to turn as blood gouted—

Something hit Franz hard, in the small of his back.

*

'Can you hear me?'

'I think he's playing moppet, boss.'

Not exactly. There was a searing pain in his back, and his head felt as if he had the worst hangover in human space. In fact, he felt sick. But that wasn't the worst part of it. The worst part of it was that he was conscious again, which meant that he was still alive, which meant . . .

'Listen to me, Franz. Your station deputy was on the black list. She reported to U. Scott's Countersubversion Department. I will ensure that her reclaimed state vector is dispatched to the Propagators with all due decency, and leave judgment of her soul up to the unborn god. But you *will* open your eyes within thirty seconds, or you'll join her. Do you understand?'

He opened his eyes. The twilight was painfully bright. A quivering black sphere of uncoagulated blood floated past, wobbling slowly in the direction of one of the extractor vents. Despair hit him like a velvet club.

'We were—' He paused, carefully, searched for an acceptable word, unsure why it was so important to do so now that his real life was over before it had even begun. His throat was dry. 'Close.' *Close*, that was the word. It brought it all home, while revealing nothing.

'If you value your intimacy so highly, you're welcome to join her,' hell's handmaiden told him half-seriously. She moved across the room in front of him, a blur before his eyes. He had to struggle to focus. 'The ReMastered race doesn't need moral weaklings. Or were you naive enough to think you were *in love?*'

'I'm—' *angry,* he realized. 'I feel ill. Dysfunctional.' He was angrier than he'd ever been before – angry in his helplessness. He hadn't been angry when her bodyguard had stunned him and he'd awakened strapped to a set of beams; just frightened and apprehensive beyond all reason. But now, with the thought that he might survive, there was room for anger. *Erica's dead.* It shouldn't have meant that much to him, but they'd been living outside the Directorate for too long. They'd been a little reckless, adopting feral ways, naive native sentimentality. And now, naive native pain and loss.

'You're angry,' Hoechst said soothingly. 'It's a perfectly understandable human reaction. Something you thought was yours has just been taken away from you. I don't blame you for it, and if you want to yell at me later, you're welcome to. But right now Blumlein himself has given us a very important task, and if you get in my way, I'll have to crush you. Nothing personal. And just in case it hasn't sunk in, your friend was a *countersub* agent. Reporting directly to U. Scott's Office of Internal Inquiries. Programmed to execute you at the first sign of disloyalty to Scott.' Franz found himself nodding, unconsciously agreeing; but all the time he was full of the scent of her skin, the memory of her laughter, their secret shared sin of commission, out here beyond the Directorate, where love wasn't a state of war and hate wasn't politics.

She wouldn't have given me away, he thought. *Not ever.* Because she'd told him all about her second job within a day of their first frantic assignation, holed up in a hotel, hungry to the point of starvation for intimacy. It had been their dirty little secret, a shared furtive fantasy about eloping, defecting, lighting out for the event horizon. Either Hoechst – in her capacity as death's angel – knew far less than she thought she did about the cell she was taking over, or the Directorate was rotten to the core anyway, and the unborn god a sick fantasy.

But you couldn't ever let yourself dream such thoughts when you were around other ReMastered, not if you wanted to live. So Franz bundled up his scream of loss and pain, and shoved it down a long way, deep down where he could curl up around it later and lick the suppurating wound – and forced himself to nod vigorously.

'I'll be all right soon,' he said meekly: 'It was just a shock.' If he let them realize how deeply he and Erica had been involved . . .

'That's good,' Hoechst said reassuringly. His nostrils flared, but he gave nothing away. Marx floated behind her like a lethal shadow, holding a spinal leech casually in one hand.

'What do you want me to do now?' he asked hoarsely.

'I want you to rest up and recover. We're going on a journey, soon as we gather up the rest of your cell.'

'A journey—'

'New Dresden, via yacht.' She pulled a face. 'Some yacht – it's an old Heidegger-class frigate with its weapons systems ripped out and replaced with stores compartments and bunks. We've got about eight days to get there ahead of your runaway, who is traveling master class on a liner. When we get there, we're going to rescue the situation, nail down all the loose ends, and stop the avalanche U. Vannevar Scott set in motion. Got that?'

'I—' He flexed his left hand; a stabbing pain in his wrist made him gasp. 'I think I damaged something.'

'That's all right.' She grinned at him with easy cama-raderie: 'You're going to damage lots more things before this is over . . .'

It took an entire week for Portia to get round to raping him. For Franz, most of the time passed in a blur as he worked like an automaton; he was too busy rounding up his remaining agents to notice the cool, speculative looks she was sending his way.

It happened after Hoechst dealt with Kerguelen.

Missing his target might have been excusable if he hadn't already been on the gray list, and debatable even in spite of it, but he'd compounded the error by alerting the girl. She'd locked him in her own Syb-class cabin, turning the tables. Hoechst was incandescent with fury when she found out, and even Franz had felt an answering twinge of indignation through his haze of loss.

Portia collected Kerguelen from Noctis herself, ordering a diversion that cost the *DD-517* almost a day's headway while it stooged around pretending to be a luxury yacht. She wore a watered silk gown of blue and violet to the police station where the unfortunate Kerguelen was being held, along with a blond wig and a king's ransom in precious stones; she had the mannerisms and giggle down to perfection for her role as the second wife of a rich ship-owning magnate from al-Turku. Franz and Marx and Samow marched behind her stiffly, wearing the archaic uniforms and pained air of superiority of her household retainers. The show ended about five milliseconds after they got the anxiously grateful Ker across the boarding tube threshold and behind a 'lock door. Then she was at his throat.

'*Bastard!*' she hissed, wrist muscles standing out like steel bands as she choked him. It was a deadly insult among the ReMastered, but nobody was interested in Ker's reply. Marx and Samow held his arms as he bucked and kicked against the bulkhead while she crushed his larynx. When he stopped moving, Hoechst looked round their small circle, sparing Franz such a malice-filled glare that he shuddered, sensing how close his own neck was to those strong hands, but then she relaxed slightly and nodded at him. 'He showed me up,' she said coolly. 'Worse, he made the Directorate look foolish. You also.'

'I understand,' he said woodenly, and that seemed to satisfy her.

'Samow, see that his neural map is reclaimed, then ditch the remains. Marx, give my compliments to the pilot and tell her it's time to execute Plan Coyote. U. Bergman, come with me.' She turned and stalked toward the lift up to the crew decks. Franz followed her, his mind blank. Kerguelen had worked for him for three years, a happy-go-lucky youngster on his first out-of-system assignment. He was prone to living it up, but not self-consciously sloppy, and there seemed to be a serious ideological commitment underlying his actions. His self-evident belief in the cause, in the unborn god and the destiny of the ReMastered, had sometimes left Franz feeling like a hollow fraud.

Kerguelen had lived life as large as he was allowed to, as if he were working in the early days of a better universe. To see him broken and discarded rubbed home Franz's own inadequacy. So he didn't protest, but followed Hoechst, wafting in her trail of rustling silks and expensive floral triterpenoids and volatile oils. The faint smell of old-fashioned powder cosmetics stung his nose.

The DepSec's suite was larger than the cubbyhole Franz was bunking in. It held a pair of chairs, a rolltop desk, and a separate folding bed. Perhaps it had once been the friggatenführer's quarters, back when the yacht had been a warship. Hoechst shut the door and waved him to a seat, but remained standing and busied herself with something at her table. He couldn't take his eyes off her. She was beautiful, in a feral, ex-Directorate sort of way, but also frightening. Intimidating. A predator, beautiful but deadly and incapable of behaving any other way. She eased her wig off and placed it on the desk, then ran her fingertips through her close-cropped pale hair. 'You look as if you need a drink.'

She was offering him a glass, he realized through a cloud of befuddlement. He accepted it instantly, his instinct for self-preservation kicking in. 'Thank you.' She poured herself another from a cut-crystal decanter, some kind of amber fluid that stank of alcohol and ashes. 'Is this an imported whisky?'

She curled her lower lip thoughtfully, then replaced the decanter stopper and sat down on the chair opposite him. 'Yes.' She smoothed her gown over her knees and looked momentarily abashed, as if she couldn't remember how she came to be there, a fairy-tale princess aboard a warship of the ReMastered race. 'You should try it.'

He raised his glass, then paused, trying to remember the formula: 'To your very good health.' He silently appended a less flattering toast.

She raised her glass back to him. 'And yours.' Her cheek twitched. 'If that's your idea of a toast to my health, I can't imagine what my painful death would warrant.'

Her words struck home. 'Boss, I—'

'Silence.' She watched him over the rim of her glass, green eyes narrowed. Sweat-spiked black hair, high cheekbones, full red lips, narrow waist: a warrior's body held in a sheath of silk that had taken master couturiers a month to stitch. She had the inhumanly symmetrical features that only a first-line clade could afford to buy for the alpha instances of their phenotype. 'I brought you here because I think we may have gotten off on the wrong foot when we were first introduced.'

Franz sat frozen in his chair, the glass of scotch – worth a small fortune, for it had been imported across more than two hundred light years – clutched in his right hand. 'I'm not sure I understand you.'

'I think you do.' Hoechst watched him, unblinking except for the occasional flicker of her nictitating membranes. 'I've been following your profile. You would be surprised how much information on their subjects even the privacy fetishists of Septagon manage to collect. Our target refugee, for instance. I think I've got a handle on her – she made the mistake of talking to some friends after her unfortunate run-in with that waste of air, and I think I know where she's bound for. But she's not the only one.'

Now it comes, he realized, the muscles in his neck tensing involuntarily. *She's going to – what?* If she wanted him dead, she could have executed him along with Ker.

She kept her eyes on him, avaricious for information: 'You were "in love" with U. Erica Blofeld, weren't you?'

A stab of unreasoning anger provoked him to speak frankly: 'I'd rather not talk about it. You've got what you want, haven't you? My undivided attention and the liquidation of an elite countersub agent from Scott's personal cadre. Isn't that enough?'

'Perhaps not.' Her cheek muscles tensed, pulling the sides of her mouth up into something that resembled a smile but didn't touch her eyes. 'You've been in Septagon space for too long, Franz. In a way it's not your fault. It could happen to anyone, spending too long on their own without backup and indoctrination, forming their own little schismatic reality, wondering if perhaps the Directorate was really the only way of doing things, wondering if you could possibly ignore it and pretend it would go away. Isn't that it? You don't need to admit anything, by the way, this isn't an inquisition. I'm not going to feed you to the Propagators. But you can express yourself freely here. I don't mind. You have my permission to shout at me. Remember what I said earlier?'

'You . . .' His fingers tightened on the glass. For a despairing moment he thought about smashing it and going for her throat, before the reality of his situation struck home. 'So what? Nothing I can say matters. You wouldn't believe my denials.'

'Well then!' She smiled, and it filled him with anger, because her expression was so genuine – she looked joyously happy, and grief and envy said that *nobody* should be allowed to look that way, ever again – when Erica was dead. And even though he knew it was just his glands speaking, that this, too, would pass, it goaded him. 'I have a problem,' she said, continuing as if nothing was wrong. She rubbed her right knee through the sheer fabric of her gown. 'We're about to go and close down some loose ends. If we succeed, the sky is the limit. Not only will everybody in this unit be rehabilitated, but I will be – well, promotion is not the most of it.' She leaned toward him, confidingly. 'At the higher levels, Franz, things are a little different. Unforgivable disciplinary errors become understandable personality flaws. The Propagators become tools with which the garden is teased into a pleasing shape: servants, not masters. Quite possibly, expedient termination orders become reversible.'

He licked his lips. 'Reversible?'

'I haven't sent U. Blofeld's state vector to the Propagators yet,' she said softly, as if the very thought was new to her. 'We don't have a Propagator with us, so I bear responsibility for life records and a memory diamond that is to be turned over to them only at the end of our mission. And I retained tissue samples.'

Thoughtfully: 'The sole complete upload image of her brain currently exists right here aboard this ship. And they need not end up with the Propagators, if a suitable alternative presents itself. What I do with them is still open. I'm short on personnel here – you were right about your mission being grossly underresourced. U. Scott was systematically overreporting his manifest, filtering people off your team for missions elsewhere, and maintaining two sets of books. I didn't bring enough support staff along, and

I'm even shorter on people who understand the feral humans out here. I need someone who can act as my right hand while Bayreuth is holding things down back home.'

She leaned toward him confidingly and took his left hand in hers: 'If we succeed, I can give her back to you, Franz. There's a medical replicator in the medical suite aboard the CG-52. My support ship. It's expensive and against normal operational procedure, but they can clone her a new body and download her into it. You can have her back again if that's what you want. As long as you're willing to do some things for me.'

'Things?' Franz felt himself leaning toward her, drawn by the terrible force of her will and by the abominable hope she dangled in front of him. *Bring Erica back? In return for . . . what?* His stomach churned with hope and dread.

'They're not the sort of jobs I can give an ordinary subordinate. They're jobs that only someone who's lived among feral humans for several years can do.'

'What jobs?'

She pulled his hand close, placing it palm down on her thigh. 'You fell in love, didn't you? That's still supposed to be possible for us, but I've never heard of two ReMastered who did it to each other at the same time. So you'll have a better grasp of how to use the phenomenon to manipulate ferals than anyone else here.' She smelled of floral extracts, and something else: the musk of power, sebaceous glands expressing pheromones that were only switched on in alpha ReMastered.

It was exciting and frightening and made him angry. He dropped his glass and pulled back, away from her. 'I don't want—'

She was on her feet, then leaning over him. 'I don't care what you want,' she said coolly. 'Unless it's U. Erica. In which case you'll do as I say with a shit-eating grin for the next three months, won't you?'

He stared at her breasts. Under the thin layers of silk he could see her nipples, aureoles flushed and crinkled with dominance. The dizzying smell was getting to him. His own traitorous hope prevented him from resisting. 'Love is a grossly underrated tool within the Directorate, Franz. You're going to teach me how to use it.'

'How—'

'Hush.' She pulled up the skirts of her gown, bunched them around her waist, and sat down on his lap. He couldn't get away, much less force himself not to respond to her dominance pheromones. He grew stiff and felt his face flush as she unbuttoned his comic-opera jacket and rubbed her breasts against him. 'I want you to teach me about love. It's going to take a few sessions, but that's all right – we've got time for a first lesson right now. How did you do it with her? Did she start it, or did you, or was it something else?' She began to work at the buttons of his trousers. 'If you want to see her again, you'll show me what you did for her . . .'

hold the front page

The Times of London – *thundering the news since 1785! Now brought to you by Frank the Nose, sponsored by Thurn und Taxis Arbeitsgemeinschaft, Melting Clock Interstellar Scheduling Specialists PLC, Bank Muamalat al-Failaka, Capek Robotica Universuum, and The First Universal Church of Kermit.*

LEADER

Let's talk some more about the Moscow disaster and its inevitable fallout – this time from the point of view of the people at ground zero, staring down the flight path of the oncoming bullets. These people are edgy and unhappy, and you should be, too – because what's sauce for the goose is sauce for the gander, and if we allow this slow-motion atrocity to set a precedent, we might be the next bird on the block.

New Dresden is not a McWorld: it's a shitty little flea hole populated by pathologically suspicious Serbs, bumptiously snobbish Saxons, three different flavors

of Balkan refugee, and an entire bestiary of psycho-
pathic nationalist loons. The planetary national sport
is the grudge match, at which they are undisputed
past masters. I say 'past masters' for a reason – they're
not as bad as they used to be. The planet has been
unified for the past ninety years, since the survivors
finished merrily slaughtering everyone else, formed a
federation, had a nifty little planetary-scale nuclear
war, formed another federation, and buried the
hatchet (in one another's backs).

For most of the past forty years, New Dresden has
been ruled by a sinister lunatic, Colonel-General
Palacky, chairman of PORC, the Planetary
Organization of Revolutionary Councils. Most of
Palacky's policies were dictated by his astrologers,
including his now-notorious abolition of the currency
and its replacement with bills divisible by 9, his
lucky number. Palacky was a raving egomaniac; he
renamed the month of January after himself and fixed
the rest of the calendar, too, except for November and
December (his mother-in-law got August, for some
reason). However, toward the end, he became a
recluse, seldom venturing beyond the high iron gates
of the presidential palace. There he presided over an
endless party, providing fire-eaters, wrestlers, tribal
dancers, drag queens, and prostitutes for his guests,
while dwarfs balancing silver platters loaded with
cocaine on their heads patrolled the corridors to
ensure all his protégés had a good time. Needless to
say, the palace gates were topped with the decaying
skulls of those army officers and PORC delegates who
disagreed with the Colonel-General over such fundamental policy issues as the need to feed the people.

The inevitable revolution – which finally came

four years ago, in the wake of the Moscow scandal —
saw Palacky thrown from his own executive
ornithopter and installed a more pragmatic junta of
bickering, but not entirely insane, PORC appar-
atchiks. Thus proving some point about it being bad
form for any one PORCer to hog the entire trough.

Anyway, that's the dark picture. On the bright
side, they're not as remorselessly reactionary as
Gouranga, as totalitarian and oppressive as Newpeace,
as boringly bucolic as Moscow used to be, as intoler-
antly Islamic as Al-Wahab, or . . . you get the picture.
A planet is a big place, and even the excesses of the
PORC junta can't really damage the economy too
badly. Given a couple of decades of civilization and a
few war crimes tribunals, New Dresden will be well
on the way to being the sort of place that rational
tourists don't automatically cross off their itineraries
with a shudder.

In fact, as long as you don't question the political
wisdom of a system with sixteen secret police forces,
thirty-seven ministries with their own militias, four
representative assemblies (three of which are run on
single-party-state lines by *different* single parties and
all of which have veto power over one another), and
above all, as long as you *don't mention the civil war*,
New Dresden can be a welcoming place for visitors.
Just as long as your purpose in visiting is to buy the
pretty rustic souvenirs and quaint quantum nanocom-
puters, ooh and aah at the wonderful reconstructed
ethnic villages in Chtoborrh Province, and drink the
fine laagered ales in the alpine coaching houses, you
can't go wrong.

Life isn't that bad for the ordinary people, as near
as I can tell. I couldn't get close enough to be sure,

because to do that I'd have to spend twenty years as a deep-cover mole. I wasn't exaggerating the national suspicion toward strangers. It's a survival trait on New Dresden; they've been breeding for paranoia for centuries. But from outside, the standard of living is clearly rising and looks pretty damned good compared to a clusterfuck like the New Republic.

These people have got automobiles – real fuel-cell-powered people movers, no messing around with boilers or exploding piston motors – and they've got music-swapping networks and cosmetic surgery and package holidays on the moons and seven different styles of imported extraplanetary fusion cuisine. Wealthy people have less time and energy for shooting each other to bits, so mostly the grudges fester on in the form of elaborate social snubs rather than breaking out in revolutions. And there are only 800 million people, so they've got a lot of potential if they can break the violent cycle of the past two and a half centuries.

And there *are* signs of peace breaking out. These days the secret police spend most of their energy spying on each other. They leave the civilians alone and drink in the same bars at the weekend. There are actually homegrown independent journalists there these days. Who knows? Any day now the place might be civilized . . .

. . . Except that three faceless bureaucrats are about to murder everyone.

I'm talking, of course, about whichever of the surviving Muscovite diplomats put their fingers to the trigger and push simultaneously. As opposed to the two of them who *could*, if they had the bravery to concede that the game is not worth the candle, issue a reprieve to this promising planet of nearly a billion people who are, when you get right down to it, not that much different from the former citizenry of Moscow.

Intestinal fortitude, and the lack thereof. If you're going to appoint yourself supreme judge in a death penalty case, you should damn well make sure that you're prepared to pass judgment and live with the consequences. And I don't believe these cunts have got what it takes.

Which is why I'm on my way to New Dresden. I'm going to corner Ambassador Elspeth Morrow and Trade Minister Harrison Baxter and put the question to them — exactly why are they willing to execute 800 million people, in the absence of any evidence that they're responsible for the crime of which they are accused?

Watch this space.

Ends (*Times* Leader)

Frank stretched his arms toward the ceiling of the breakfast room and yawned tremendously. He had slept in, and had a mild hangover. Still, it was better than being hagridden by memories of the incident in the bar the night before. For which he was grateful.

The breakfast lounge was like the other dining rooms — only slightly smaller, with a permanent heated buffet and no bar or cabaret stage against the opposite wall. That late in the morning it was almost empty. Frank helped himself to a plate, loaded it down with hash browns and paprika-poached eggs, added a side order of hot blueberry bagels fresh from the fabricator, and hunted around for a free table. The sole steward on duty wasted no time in offering him a coffeepot, and as he dug into his food Frank tried to kick his tired brain cells into confronting the new day's agenda.

Item: Transfer point with Septagon Centris Noctis. Passengers departing and boarding. Hmm. Worth staking out the bulletin boards in case? Next item: See to transmitting latest updates. Spool incoming news, read and inwardly digest. Then . . . fuck it, eat first. He poured a measured dose of cream into his breakfast coffee and stirred it. *Wonder if anything's happened since the last jump?*

It was the perpetual dilemma of the interstellar special correspondent – if you stayed in one place, you never got to see anything happen up close and personal, but you could stay plugged into the network of causal channels that spread news in empire time. If you traveled around, you were incommunicado from the instant the ship made its first jump until the moment it entered the light cone of the destination. But what the channels paid Frank for was his insights into strange cultures and foreign politics. You couldn't get those by staying at home; so every new port of call triggered a mad scramble for information, to be digested into editorials and opinion pieces and essays during the subsequent flight, and spat out at the net next time the ship arrived in a system with bandwidth to the outside universe.

Frank yawned and poured himself another cup of coffee. He'd had too little sleep, too much rum and whisky, and faced a day's work to catch up on preparation for the liner's arrival at New Dresden. Septagon was so connected and so well covered that there was no real point going ashore there: it was a major data exporter. But New Dresden was off the beaten track, and directly in jeopardy as a result of the slow-motion disaster unfolding from Moscow system. When he got there he faced four days of complete insanity, starting with a descent on the first available priority pod and ending with a last-minute dash back to the docking tunnel, during which he had to file copy written en route, gather material for two weeks' worth of features, and do anything else that needed attending to. He'd checked the timetables: he figured he could make the trip with two and a quarter hours to spare. Okay, make that three and a half days of buzzing around like a demented journalistic blue-bottle, released on a ticket of leave in the middle of a promising field of diplomatic bullshit – it was a good thing that New Dresden wasn't uptight about pharmaceuticals, because by the time Frank was back in his stateroom he'd be ready for the biggest methamphetamine crash in jour-nalistic history. Which was precisely what you deserved if you tried to cover four continents, eight cities, three diplo-matic receptions, and six interviews in three days, but *c'est la vie.*

Stomach filled and coffee flask emptied, Frank pushed back from the table and stood up. 'When do we push back?' he asked the air casually.

'Departure is scheduled in just under two thousand sec-onds,' the ship replied softly, beaming its words directly into his ears. 'Transition to onboard curved-space generator will be synchronized with the station, and there will be no freefall lockdown. Acceleration to jump point will take a further 192,000 seconds approximately, and bandwidth access to Septagon switching will be maintained until that time. Do you have further requests?'

'No thank you,' Frank replied, slightly spooked by the way the ship's expertise had anticipated his line of ques-tioning. *Damn thing must be plugged in to the Eschaton,* he thought nervously. There were limits to what anyone sane would contemplate doing by way of artificial intelligence experiments – the slight ethical issue that a functioning AI would have a strong legal claim to personhood tended to put a brake on the more reckless researchers, even if the

Eschaton's existence didn't hold a gun to their heads – but sometimes Frank wondered about the emergent smarts exhibited by big rule-driven systems like the ship's passenger assistance liaison. Somehow it didn't seem quite right for a machine he'd never met to be anticipating his state of mind.

He strolled distractedly around the promenade deck on C level, barely conscious of his surroundings. C deck by day shift was a different place to the darkened night-time corridors. Elegant plate-diamond windows to either side displayed boutiques, shops, beauty salons, and body sculptors. Whole trees, cunningly constrained in recessed tubs, grew at intervals in the corridor, their branches meshing overhead. Below them, tiny maintenance 'bots harvested browning leaves before they could fall and disturb the plush carpet.

The corridor wasn't empty, but passengers were thin on the ground – mostly they were still coming through the docking tube from Noctis orbital, the WhiteStar open port in Septagon system. Here went a young couple, perhaps rich honeymooners from Eiger's World strolling arm in arm with the total inattention of the truly in love. There went a stooped old man with lank hair, a facial tic that kept one cheek jumping, and the remains of breakfast matted in his beard, heading toward a discreet opium den with a dull look of anticipation in his eyes. A gamine figure in black stopped dead and gaped into the window of a very expensive jewelry studio as Frank stepped around her – him, it – and slid to one side to avoid a purposefully striding steward. The ship was a shopping mall, designed to milk idle rich travelers of their surplus money. Frank, being neither idle nor rich, focused on threading a path around the occasional windowshoppers.

The promenade deck stretched in a two-hundred-meter

loop around the central atrium of the ship's passenger decks, an indoor waterfall and the huge sculptured stair-cases rising through it like glass-dressed fantasies. Halfway around it, Frank came to a gap in the shop fronts and a radial passage that led to a circular lounge, carpeted in red and paneled in improbably large sheets of ivory scrimshaw, with a stepped pit in the middle. It was almost empty, just a few morning folk sipping cups of coffee and staring into the inner space of their head-ups. Frank headed for a deca-dent-looking sofa, a concoction of goosedown cushions in cloned human leather covers, soft enough to swallow him and luxurious as a lover's touch. He sprawled across it and unpocketed his keyboard, expanded it to full size, and donned his shades. 'Right. Priorities,' he muttered to him-self, trying to dismiss yet more intrusive memories from the night before at the caress of the leather. *Whom do I mail first, the embassy or the UN consulate? Hmm . . .*

He was half an hour into his morning correspondence when someone touched his left shoulder.

'Hey!' He tried to sit up, failed, flailed his arms for a moment, and managed to get a grip on the leading edge of the sofa.

'Are you Frank the Nose?' asked a female voice.

Frank pulled his shades right off, rather than dialing them back to transparency. 'What the f— eh, what are you talking about?' he spluttered, reaching for his left shoulder with his left hand. It was the young woman he'd seen in the corridor. He couldn't help noticing the pallor of her skin and the fact that every item of her costume was black. She was cute, in a tubercular kind of way. *Elfin, that's the word*, he noted.

'I'm sorry to disturb you, it's, like, I was told you were a warblogger?'

Frank spent a moment massaging his forehead as, briefly,

a number of responses flitted through his head.

'Who wants to know?' he finally asked, surprising himself with his mildness. *Click.* Physically young – either genuinely young, or just rejuved. Pale, dark hair currently a mess, high cheekbones on clear-skinned face, female. *Click.* Alone. *Click.* Asking for Frank the Nose by name. *Click.* Is there a story here? *Click.* Get the story . . .

'A friend said I should get in touch with you,' said the kid. 'You're the journalist who's looking into the – the end of Moscow?'

'What if I am?' Frank asked. She looked tense, worried about something. But what?

'I was born there,' she mumbled. 'I grew up on Old Newfie, uh, portal station eleven. We were evacuated after – in time—'

'Have a seat.' Frank gestured at the other side of the sofa, trying to keep his face still. She flopped down in a heap of knees and elbows and impossibly long limbs. *So what's she doing* here? 'You said something about a friend?' he asked. 'What's your name?'

'You can call me Wednesday,' she said nervously. 'Uh, there are people' – she glanced over her shoulder as if she expected assassins to come swarming out of the walls – 'No, uh, no! That's not where to begin. Why can't I get this right?' She ended on a note of plaintive despair, as if she was about to start tugging her hair.

Frank leaned back, watching her but trying to give her some space to decompress in. She was tired and edgy. There was something indefinable about her, the insecurity of the exile. He'd seen it before. *She's from Moscow!* This could be good. If true, she'd make excellent local color for his dispatches – the personal angle, the woman in exile, a viewpoint to segue into for a situation report and editorial frame. Then he felt a stab of concern. *What's she doing here, looking for me? Is she in trouble?* 'Why did you want to talk to me?' he asked gently. 'And what are you doing here?'

She looked around again. 'I – shit!' Her face fell. 'I, uh, I have to give a message to you.'

'A message.' Frank had an itchy feeling in the palms of his hands. The lead item walking in off the street to spill his or her guts into the ear of a waiting reporter, the exclusive waiting to happen, was a legend in the trade. It so rarely happened, vastly outnumbered by hoaxers and time-wasters, but when it did – *Let's not get ahead of the game*, he told himself sternly. He watched her eyes and she stared right back. 'Begin with the beginning,' he suggested. 'Who's your message from? And who's it for?'

She huddled in the corner of the sofa as if it was the only stable place in her universe. 'It's, um, going to sound crazy. But I shouldn't be here. On this ship, I mean. I mean, I've *got* to be here, because if I stayed behind I wouldn't be safe. But I'm not *supposed* to be here, if you see what I mean.'

'Not supposed – do you have a ticket?' he asked. His brow wrinkled.

'Yes.' She managed a faint flicker of what might have been an impish grin if she hadn't been so close to exhaustion. 'Thanks to Herman.'

'Uh-huh.' *Is she a crazy?* Frank wondered. *This could be trouble* . . . He pushed the thought aside.

'The – information – I've got for you is that if you visit Old New – sorry, portal station eleven, and go down to cylinder four, kilo deck, segment green, and look in the public facility there you'll find a corpse with his head down the toilet. And, uh, behind the counter of the police station in cylinder six, segment orange, there's a leather attaché case with handwritten orders in, like, real ink on paper, saying that whoever the orders are for is to wipe all the customs records, trash the immigration tracking and control system – but bring a single copy home – and if necessary, kill anyone who looks like they're going to notice what's going on. Fat chance, as the customs and immigration cops were pulled out six months earlier, but the man in the toilet was in uniform—' She swallowed.

Frank realized that his fingers were digging into the arm of the sofa so tightly that the soft leather was threatening to rip. 'Customs records?' he said mildly. 'Who told you to tell me this?' he asked. 'Your friend?'

'Herman,' she said, deadpan. 'My fairy godfather. Okay, my rich uncle then.'

'Hmm.' He gave her a long, cool stare. *Is she a crazy?* 'This message—'

'Ah, shit.' She waved a hand in front of her face. 'I'm no good at lying,' she said guiltily. 'Listen, I need your help. Herman said you'd know what to do. They're, uh, he said the same people, the ones who killed the cop – he's down as missing in the evacuation, nobody wanted to go back for him – are looking for anyone who might be a witness. They tried—' she took a deep breath. 'No, *someone* tried to mug me a few days ago. Or worse. I got away. They're looking for me because the shipboard security came back onto the station and found me and I'm one of the only loose ends, and now they're not panicking over the evacuation they're trying to tie everything up . . .' She subsided in confusion.

'Oh.' *Oh very good, Frank,* he told himself sarcastically. *How very articulate of you!* He shook his head. 'Let me get this straight. You're not alone. You ran across something on your station before the evacuation, right before it. Something you think is important. Now someone's trying to kill you, you think, so you hopped aboard this ship. Is that substantially correct?'

She nodded violently. 'Yeah.'

Okay. Heads she's a kook, tails she's tripped over something very smelly indeed. What should I do? Put that way, it was fairly obvious: run some background checks, try to prove she was a kook before accepting anything at face value. But she didn't *look* crazy. What she looked like was a tired, shaky young woman who'd been booted out of her life by forces beyond her control. Frank shuffled against the cushions, struggling to sit up. 'Do you have any idea who the, uh, killers might be?'

'Well.' She looked uncertain. 'The ship that took us off was from Dresden. And the case with the orders was in the Captain's luggage store.'

'It was— ' Frank stared at her. 'How did you get to see it then?'

'I guess you could say I broke in.' She screwed her face into something that might have been meant to look like an embarrassed smile.

'You—' Frank stared some more. 'I think you'd better tell me all about it,' he said quietly. 'By the way, the public spaces here are all monitored, all the time. But the state-rooms are private. If you're going to say anything that might incriminate you, we ought to go somewhere that isn't being recorded. Do you have a room?'

'Uh, I guess so.' She looked at him uncertainly. 'My ticket says I do, but I didn't choose it. And I've only just come aboard.' She glanced at the doorway self-consciously. 'I haven't even bought any stuff yet. I was in a real hurry.'

'Okay, we'll go wherever your ticket says. If you don't mind, I'd like to record an interview and check some facts out. Then—' A thought struck him. 'Do you have any money?' he asked.

'I don't know.' She looked even more uncertain. 'My friend wired me some, I think.'

'You think?'

'There are too many zeroes.' Her eyes were wide.

'Hmm. Well, if that's a problem, I'll see what I can sort out for you. WhiteStar likes to soak you for extras, but at least on board this ship you won't want for complimentary scented Egyptian cotton towels and luxury pedicure kits. And if we're—' He paused. 'Where did your friend buy you a ticket to?' he asked.

'Some place called, uh, Newpeace?'

Shit! An icy calm descended on Frank. 'Well, I think we might just have to see about extending it a bit farther. All the way to Earth itself, and maybe back home afterward.'

'Why?'

'Newpeace isn't somewhere I'd want to send my worst enemy. It's run by scum who call themselves the ReMastered.'

'Oh no!'

Suddenly she was on her feet, looking alarmed. Frank blinked in surprise. 'What have you heard about them?' he demanded.

'Herman said it was probably the ReMastered who killed my—' She choked up, her shoulders shaking.

'Let's go to my room,' Frank said quietly, his pulse roaring in his ears. 'We can talk about it there.'

sybarite class

She'd gone to ground in the morning lounge on A deck, finding a niche between a potted coconut palm and a baby grand piano the color of stressed titanium. Eyes swiveling, refugee instincts humming. This wasn't anything like the trash hauler she'd been on, years ago. Everything around her screamed *luxury!* at high volume. *What am I meant to do here? If anyone finds me—* She had a ticket. Nobody was going to haul her off to the nearest airlock and make her walk home. Still, just being there felt profoundly wrong, and then there was whatever had happened to her family. Just trying not to think about it was a draining experience.

'Okay, Herman, what have you got me into?' she muttered angrily. A twist of her storage ring got her into the files he'd left her. They were copious, but at least he'd left an introduction.

'As soon as you're on board, search for Frank the Nose and tell him about the items you left aboard Old Newfie.

Do so before the ship departs. That will give him time to file a news report, after which your pursuers will be unable to achieve their goal of concealing the existence of the items by killing you. Let me emphasize this: Until you publicize the existence of the sealed orders and the body, your life is in danger. Once you have done so, they can gain nothing by killing you and may only lend credence to your story. And here's a second point. Don't assume that all ReMastered are automatically members of the group hunting you. They're riddled with factions, and whoever is after you may even be using them as a cover. Don't assume *anything*.

'Once you have broken the story, remain aboard the liner. Enjoy the facilities. You are traveling in Sybarite class with a personal allowance suitable to an heiress of independent means. Consider this to be part payment for your earlier work on my behalf. If you become bored by the formal passenger facilities – the shops, the bars and dining rooms, the dances and other social events – feel free to use the attached technical schemata to discreetly explore the service and maintenance spaces of the liner. If anyone asks you, your cover story is that you are a rich, idle, bored heiress. The Moscow trust has paid up a dividend big enough that your parents have agreed to you undertaking a grand tour as a prelude to your coming out. Here's a hint: I don't mind if you're no good at spending money like water, but please find time to become bored. There will be an exam later.

'The next stop on your itinerary is New Dresden, for a four-and-a-half-day layover. The previous New Dresdener government is believed by many people to be responsible for the destruction of your home world. As you probably realize by now, that is untrue. Your layover coincides with the annual remembrance ceremony at the Muscovite embassy in the capital, Sarajevo. I would appreciate it if you would attend the ceremony. You might want to buy some-thing more formal to wear before doing so.

'I will provide further instructions for you on arrival in New Dresden orbit. To recap: Find Frank the Nose and tell him about your adventure on Old Newfie. Doing so will ensure that you have an uneventful voyage. Feel free to explore the ship. On arrival, attend the remembrance cere-mony at the embassy. *Bon voyage!*'

She shook her head in bafflement, but still began to do as he suggested. The ship hadn't even departed yet, and re-sidual nerves kept Wednesday looking over her shoulder as the big guy took her straight to an elevator, tastefully hidden behind a trompe l'oeil painting on one wall. *What if Leo or whatever he's called followed me aboard?* But something about the hulking journalist made her feel safe: he looked like he could walk through walls, but he was mild enough toward her, clearly aware that his appearance tended to intimidate and trying not to look threatening.

The elevator car was narrow and sparse, polished metal with a button-laden control panel. 'It's a crew car,' he explained, finger-pecking at the panel. 'Sven showed me how to use them. They don't just go up and down, they go – aha!' The car lurched sideways, began to ascend, then twirled back on its route for a while before coming to a halt. The doors opened on a dimly lit corridor that reminded Wednesday of a hotel her parents had once taken her and Jerm to, a couple of years ago. 'Here we are.'

Frank's stateroom reinforced the sense of being in a hotel suite – a rumpled, used one pervaded by a horrible, inde-finable stink, as if something had died there. She wrinkled her nose as he closed the door and ambled over to the writ-ing desk, feeling a momentary unease. It passed as he bent down and pulled out a compact multimedia recording deck and positioned it on the table. 'Sit down,' he invited. 'Make yourself at home.' He smiled alarmingly. 'This is a recording cut. We'll do this once, then I'll mail it right back to Joe – she's my researcher and desk ed, back home – immediately. Joe can edit it into shape for a release. The sooner it hits the blog, the better. Comfortable? Okay. Let's start. Would you tell me your name? It'll go better if you look straight at the pickup . . .'

Almost an hour later, Wednesday was growing hoarse. On top of that, she was bone-tired and bored with repeating herself, not to say upset. While Frank was surprisingly gentle and understanding, having to relive the horror of those minutes in the corridor outside her home was disturbing, dredging up tears she'd thought she had under control. She'd managed to snatch a couple of hours of uneasy sleep in her stolen cattle-class seats aboard the ferry, but then she'd had the stress of finding her way to the ship and tracking down Frank. 'I need something to drink,' she said. 'And—'

'I said I'd buy you breakfast, didn't I? I'm sorry, I got carried away.' Frank sounded apologetic – and something else. He hauled out a pad and pointed it at her. 'Pick anything on the menu – anything you like. Listen, that was a great interview.' He frowned at the door. 'Scum, like I said.' Judging from his thunderous expression there ought to be a huge blackened hole in the wall. 'Now, I'm going to put a cover on that interview and push it out right away as unsubstantiated rumor. I mean, you really don't want to leave this sitting around, do you? The sooner we get some physical corroboration, the better, though that might take a while. But the sooner this is out, the sooner the scum who killed your family are going to learn that trying to shut you up was a mistake.' He was positively glowering.

'You said you knew something about the – the ReMastered?' she asked diffidently.

'I, I—' He closed his mouth and shook his head angrily, like a bear pestered by hornets. Then he sighed. 'Yes, I know something about the ReMastered,' he admitted. 'Much more than I want to. I'm just surprised they're snooping around Septagon.' He looked thoughtful. 'Checking out your story about the station is going to cost real money. Need to charter a ship if I have to go poking around a hot station behind a supernova shock front. But the rest's easy enough. You want to order up some food and make yourself at home in here?'

'Mmph.' Wednesday finger-shopped listlessly for agedashi tofu and tuna-skin hand rolls and sing chow noodles and a luminous green smart drink that promised to banish fatigue. 'Food. I remember that.'

'Chill out.' Frank unpacked a battered-looking pocket keyboard of antique design and began typing like a machine gun. 'When you're ready, give it to me and I'll put the order on my tab.'

'Do you think I'm in danger?' she asked, her voice catching.

He looked her in the eye, and for the first time she realized that he looked worried. Fear didn't belong on that face, atop a gorilla of a man. It was just plain wrong. 'Listen, the sooner this is on the net, the better for both of us,' he said. 'So if you don't mind—' He went back to hammering the keyboard.

'Sure.' Wednesday sighed. She finished her menu selections and shoved the pad back at his side of the desk. 'Journalists. Feh!' She spread her fingers out, admiring the rings on her left hand. Smart rings, untraceable fake rings, rings that claimed she was a rich bitch and came with sealed orders. *What's it really like to be rich?* she wondered.

The Times of London – *thundering the news since 1785! Now brought to you by Frank the Nose, sponsored by Thurn und Taxis Arbeitsgemeinschaft, DisneyMob Amusements, NPO Mikoyan-Gurevitch Spaceyards, Motorola Banking al-Failaka, Glossolalia Translatronics, and The First Universal Church of Kermit.*

EXCLUSIVE: Skullduggery in Septagon, Murderers in Moscow

The *Times* has obtained an exclusive interview with a young survivor of the destroyed Moscow system that suggests agents of an external power have something to hide – *after* the holocaust.

Wednesday Shadowmist (not her real name), 19, is a citizen of the former planetary republic of Moscow. She and her family survived the induced nova that destroyed their home world because they lived on Portal Station Eleven, Old Newfie, a refueling and transfer station nearly a light year from the star. They were evacuated aboard a starship belonging to a Dresdener merchant agency and resettled in one of the Septagonese orbitals. For their safety, the *Times* is not disclosing which one.

Immediately prior to the evacuation, Wednesday returned to the portal station for her own reasons. While there, she discovered a body, believed to be that of Customs Officer Gareth Smaile, who was listed as 'missing' after the evacuation. Officer Smaile is confirmed as having been one of the individuals responsible for maintaining immigration records for persons entering and leaving Moscow system via the portal station, before the holocaust. When Wednesday found him he appeared to have been murdered – a unique event on a small colony that averaged one violent crime every five years.

Abandoned by the body were written instructions to parties unknown requesting that all customs records relating to immigration be wiped prior to evacuation, save for a single copy that was to be returned to the author of the letter.

Taking this report at face value, someone wants to cover up the fact that they quietly entered or departed Moscow system through Portal Station Eleven shortly before the catastrophe. Whoever they were, they had an agent or agents aboard the Dresdener starship *Long March* when it called at Old Newfie to evacuate the survivors – an agent who was willing to commit murder.

If this is a hoax, it's a violent one. [Newshound: Trace police blotter report CM-6/9/312-04-23-19-24A, double murder.] Two hit men were sent after our informant; she evaded them, unlike the rest of her family, who woke up dead two days ago. Someone maliciously bypassed the gas-conditioning inlet to their home and disabled the alarms. Police crime investigation officer Robin Gough characterized the murder as an 'extremely professional' hit, and says she's looking for two men [Newshound: Trace police arrest warrant W/CM-6/9/312-B4] wanted for murder. Here's a hint: Septagon police are efficient enough that if they haven't been found within half an hour, they're not going to be found at all because they're not on the station anymore.

The Times is not yet certain about what's going on, but it appears to be a particularly nasty game of spy-versus-spy. The implication – that there is an attempt in progress to cover up the true story of the destruction of Moscow – appears compelling, and we will continue to investigate it. In the meantime, we are releasing this raw and uncooked interview in order to render pointless further attempts to maintain the cover by murdering the surviving witnesses.

The *Times* has this message for the culprits, whoever they are: The truth will out!

Ends (*Times* Editorial)

Cymbals chimed: the floor gave a faint lurch, almost imperceptible, barely sufficient to rattle the china in the dining lounges as the huge liner cut over to onboard gravity. Junior Flight Lieutenant Steffi Grace shook her head. 'That's not very good.'

'It's within tolerances, but only just,' agreed her boss, Flying Officer Max Fromm. He pointed at the big status board in front of her. 'Want to tell me why?'

'Hmm. Kernel balance looks good. We've stabilized nicely, and the mass distribution is spot on – no problems there. Um. I don't see anything on board. But the station . . .' She paused, then brought up a map of the ambient gravity polarization field. 'Oh. We picked up a little torque from the station's generators when we tripped out. Is that what you're after?'

'No, but it'll do.' Fromm nodded. 'Remember that. These big new platforms the Septs are building kick back.' He brought back the original systems map. 'Now, you're going to talk me through the first stage of our departure, aren't you?'

Steffi nodded, and began to take him through the series of steps that the Captain and her bridge crew would be running upstairs as they maneuvered the huge liner clear of the Noctis docking tree. Down here in the live training room things weren't as tense; just another session in the simulator, shadowing the bridge team. The training room was cramped, crammed with console emulators and with space for only a couple of people to crowd inside. In an emergency it could double as a replacement bridge – but it would have to be a truly desperate emergency to take out the flight deck, five levels down inside the hull.

'Okay, now she's pumping up the C-head ring. That's, um, five giga-Teslas? That's way more than she needs to maintain a steady one-gee field. Is she planning on buffering some really heavy shocks? Attitude control – we're steady. No thermal roll to speak of, not out here in Septagon B, so she's put just enough spin on the outer hull to hold us steady as we back out at five meters per second. That's going to take, uh, two minutes until we're clear far enough to begin a slow pitch up toward the departure corridor. Am I right?'

'So far so good.' Max leaned back in his chair. 'I hate these stations,' he said conversationally. 'It's not as if there's much other traffic – we've got nearly a thousand seconds to clear the approaches – but it's so damn crowded here it's like threading a needle with a mooring cable.'

'One wrong nudge—'

'Yeah.' The *Romanov* was a huge beast. Beehive shaped, it was three hundred meters in diameter at its fattest and nearly five hundred meters long. The enormously massive singularity lurking inside its drive kernel supplied it with power and let it twist space-time into knots, but was absolutely no use for close-range maneuvering; and the hot thrusters it could use for altitude control would strip the skin off a hab if the Captain lit her up within a couple of kilometers. That left only the cold thrusters and gyrodynes for maintaining altitude during departure – but they had about as much effect as a team of ants trying to kick a dead whale down a beach. 'One-sixty seconds to burner ignition, and we can crank up to departure speed, a hundred meters per second. Then just under an hour and a half to make it out to fifty kilometers and another blip on the burners to take us up to a thousand meters per second at half a gee. Another two hundred kilometers out, then we begin kernel spin-up. I haven't looked at the flight plan for this run, but if she does her usual, once the kernel is up and running the Captain will crank us up to twenty gees and hold for about twelve hours. And she won't mess around. That's why she ran up the bulkhead rings now, when she's got spare power to pump into them.' He stretched his arms out overhead, almost touching the damage control board. 'Seen one departure, seen 'em all. Until the next time.'

'Right.' Steffi pushed back her chair. 'Do we have time for a coffee before the burn sequence?'

'I don't see why not.'

Steffi stood up and squeezed past Max's chair, trailing a hand across his shoulder in passing. He pretended not to notice, but she caught the ghost of his smile reflected in the screens as she turned toward the door. Two or three weeks of stealing time together didn't make for a serious relationship in her estimate, but it beat sleeping alone on her first long cruise, and Max was more considerate than she'd expected. Not that she was incapable of coping. WhiteStar didn't employ child labor, and she'd joined up at thirty-two, with her first career under her: she'd known exactly what she was letting herself in for. If anyone had accused him of taking advantage of her, she'd have taken a pointy stick to them. But so far discretion had paid off, and Steffi had no complaints.

There was a vending machine near the facilities pod down the gray-painted crew corridor. She punched for two glasses of iced latte, thought about some biscuits, and decided against it. Bridge crew, even trainee bridge crew, dined with the upper-class passengers on a rota, and Max was up for dinner at the end of his shift in a couple of hours. It wouldn't do to spoil his appetite. She was about to head back to the auxiliary control center when she spotted a stranger in the corridor outside — probably a passenger, judging by his lack of ID. 'Can I help you?' she asked, sizing him up. He was tall, blond, male, blandly handsome, and built like an army recruiting poster. *Not at all like Max*, a little voice in the back of her head said critically.

'Yah, yes. I was told the, ah, training bridge was on this level?' He had a strange accent, not hard to understand but slightly stilted. 'I was told it was possible to visit it?'

'Yes, it is.' She nodded. 'But I'm afraid you'll have to make an appointment if you want to look around. It's in use throughout the voyage, and right now it's the backup control center — in case there's a problem with the main bridge. Are you wanting a tour?' He nodded. 'In that case' — she steered him toward the nearest door back into passenger country — 'can I suggest you take it up with your liaison officer after dinner? He or she will be able to take your details and arrange something for you tomorrow or the day after. I've got to get back to work now, so if you'll excuse me . . .'

She gently pushed him back toward the passenger section, waiting until he finished nodding and the door closed. Then she breathed a sigh of relief and ducked back through the closest door into wonderland. Max raised an eyebrow at her. 'She's begun pushback,' he said. 'What kept you?'

'The passengers are wandering.' She passed him an iced coffee. 'I had to herd one out of the corridor just now.'

'Happens every voyage. You lock a couple of thousand bored monkeys in a tin can, and you've got to expect one or two to go exploring. They'll stop poking around eventually, when they realize everything interesting is sealed off. Just remember to keep your cabin door locked whether you're in or out.'

'Hah. I'll do that.' She raised her glass. 'Here's to a quiet life . . .'

'Wow!' Wednesday looked around the room, her eyes wide. *It's bigger than my bedroom back home. It's bigger than our entire apartment!* A pang of loss bit her. She shoved it aside hastily.

She stood in the middle of an ocean of deep-pile carpet the color of clotted cream and looked about. The room was so wide that the ceiling seemed low, even though it was out of reach. A couple of sofas and an occasional table huddled at one end as if they were lonely. One wall looked like raw, undressed stonework; there was a door in it, with a curved, pointy bit at the top, opening onto a boudoir like something out of a medieval fantasy, all rich wooden paneling and tapestries. A huge four-poster bed completed the impression, but the medievalism was only skin-deep. The next door along led to a bathroom with a tub almost as large as the bed recessed into the white-tiled floor.

'If you need anything, please call the purser's office,' the steward told her. 'Someone will be on hand to help you at all hours. Your trip itinerary should be able to tell you how all the suite utilities work, including the fabber in the closet over there.' (The closet lurking behind another open gothic archway looked to be about the size of a small factory.) 'Do you need anything else right now?' he asked.

'Uh, no.' She looked around. 'I mean, yeah, I have to go buy some odds and ends. But, uh, not right now.'

'By your leave.' He turned and left, smiling oddly, and the door to the corridor – no, the promenade deck, they called it – closed behind her.

'Wow!' she repeated. Then she glanced at the door. 'Door, lock yourself.' There was a discreet *clack* from the frame. 'Wow!'

Wednesday ambled over to the nearest sofa and flopped down in it, then unfastened her boots. 'Ouch.' More than a day of wearing them had left her feet feeling like raw meat: she curled her toes in the carpet for almost a minute with her eyes closed, writhing slightly and panting. 'Oh, that is so good!' After another minute, other senses began to intrude. 'Hmm.'

She walked toward the bathroom, leaving a trail of discarded clothing behind her. By the time she reached it she was naked. 'Shower, shower, where are you?' she called. It turned out that the shower was in a separate cubicle from the toilet, the bathroom proper, and the— 'A full-body hair remover?' She boggled slightly. What would you want to remove all your hair for? Legs or armpits or pubes she could see, but eyebrows?

'Manicure and pedicure facilities are available on D deck,' recited a recording, just grainy enough not to make her wonder if a real person was in the room with her. 'A range of basic clothing is available from the apartment fab. Fitted and designer items are available from the tailors on F deck. See the panel beside the sink for additional makeover and service options.'

'Urk.' Wednesday backed toward the shower cubicle, pulled a face, and sniffed one armpit. 'Eew!' *First things first. What did Herman say? You're a rich, idle, bored heiress: play the part.*

She showered thoroughly, staying under the spray nozzles until her skin felt as if it was going to come off. She washed her hair thoroughly, trying to get the grit and desperation of the past week off her body. The all-body depilator she gave a wide berth – the consequences of an accident with the controls could be too embarrassing for words – but the mirror wall by the sink had a full skin programmer that could talk to her chromatophores, so she spent an absorbing half hour reprogramming her makeup: night-dark eyeliner, blue lips, dead white skin, and glossy black hair. *If anyone asks, I'm in mourning*, she thought, and a sudden stab of agonizing guilt made it less than a lie.

She hatched from the bathroom an hour and a half later, naked as the day she was born. The lounge seemed enormous, cold, and empty. Worse, she couldn't imagine putting on her old clothes. So she wandered over to the closet and looked inside. 'Is there a clothing menu for this thing?' she asked.

A lightbug led her to the fabber, a large boxy extrusion from the wall of a walk-in wardrobe she hadn't suspected. 'Please select options. Materials and energy will be billed to your room service total.'

'Oh.' Five minutes scrolling through patterns convinced her of one thing: whoever'd programmed the fab's design library hadn't done so with her in mind. Eventually she settled for some basic underwear, a pair of black trousers and a long-sleeved top that wasn't too offensive, and rubber-soled socks for her feet. The fab hummed and burped up a load of hot, fresh clothing a minute later, still smelling faintly of solvents. Wednesday pulled them on immediately. *Bet the shops are more expensive but have better stuff*, she thought cynically.

An hour spent poking around the shops on F deck convinced her that she was right. The names were unfamiliar, but the attitude of the staff – and the items in the displays – said it all. They were priced to satisfy exactly the sort of rich bitch Herman had suggested she play, but as far as Wednesday was concerned they were a dead loss: the target audience was too old, even if they were well preserved. The ultrafemme gowns and dresses had icky semiotics, the shops for people from cultures with sumptuary laws and dress codes were too weird, the everyday stuff was too formal — *What would I want to do with that, wear it to a business meeting?* she thought, fingering one exquisitely tailored jacket — and there was nothing flaky or uplevel to catch her imagination. No fun.

In the end, she bought a lacy white trouser-skirt combination to wear to dinner, and left it at that. The horrible truth was beginning to dawn on her: *I've got an enormous suite to myself, but nothing to* do! *And I'm here for a* week! *With no toys.* Wednesday didn't have anyone to share the voyage with unless she felt like pestering Frank, and she wasn't sure how he'd respond. He *looked* young, but it was hard to tell. *And he's got a job to do. And there's no news.* Not while the ship was engaged in a series of causality-violating jumps, lock-stitching space time to its drive kernel. *And the shops are crap.* She glanced across the diamond-walled atrium in growing disbelief. *And I bet the other Sybarite-class passengers are all boring assholes, diplomats, and rich old business queens and all.* Clearly, very few people her age traveled this way.

I'm already bored! And there are still three hours to go before dinner!

'Feeding time at the zoo,' Max muttered darkly. 'Wonder who they're feeding?'

'The social director, with any luck. Stuffed and basted.' Steffi kept a straight face, staring right ahead as they headed into the dining room. 'Stupid custom.'

'Now, *now.*' Max nodded politely to a plumply padded dowager whose thirty-year physique belied the fact that her formal business suit was at least a century out of fashion. 'Good evening, Mrs. Borozovski! How are you tonight?'

'I'm fine, Mr. Fromm!' She bobbed slightly, as if she'd already been hitting the martinis. 'And who's your little friend? A new squirt, or am I very mistaken?'

'Ahem. Allow me to introduce Junior Flight Lieutenant Stephanie Grace, our newest flight operations officer. If I may beg your pardon, it's considered bad form to refer to trainees as squirts, outside of the training academy; and in any case, Lieutenant Grace has graduate degrees in relativistic dynamics and engineering.'

'Oh, I'm so sorry!' To her credit, the dowager flushed slightly.

'It's perfectly all right.' Steffi forced a smile and breathed a sigh of relief when Max peeled off to steer Mrs. Borozovski toward a table. *No, I don't mind being patronized by rich drones one little bit, Mrs. Borozovski. Now, where's the table I'm supposed to ride herd on?*

It was a completely spurious ritual, from Steffi's viewpoint. All the business class and higher suites were fully self-catering. There was no damn *need* to have a central galley and serve up a restricted menu and waste the valuable time of human chefs, not to mention the line officers who were required to turn up wearing mess uniforms and act like dinner party hosts. On the other hand, as Commodore Martindale had put it back at staff college, the difference between a steerage passenger flying in cold sleep and a Sybarite-class passenger flying in a luxury apartment was about two thousand ecus per day of transit time – and the experience. Any peasant could afford to travel cold, but to balance the books and make for a healthy profit required cosseting the rich idiots and honeymooning couples, to which end any passenger line worthy of the name devoted considerable ingenuity. Up to and including providing etiquette training for engineers, tailored dress uniforms for desk-pushers, and anything else that might help turn a boring voyage into a uniquely memorable experience for the upper crust. Which *especially* meant sparing no expense over the first night and subsequent weekly banquets. *At least they're not as bad as the house apes Sven puts up with*, she thought mordantly. *If I had his end of this job, I swear I'd go nuts . . .*

At least the honeymooning couples mostly stuck to ordering from room service or the food fabs in their rooms. Which left her sitting at the head of a table of twelve extremely lucrative passengers – think of it as twenty-four thousand ecus a day in value added to the bottom line – smiling, nodding politely, introducing them to one another, answering their inane questions, and passing the port.

Steffi made her way to her table, guided by a discreet pipper on the cuff of her brocade jacket. A handful of passengers had already arrived, but they knew enough to stand up as she arrived. 'Please, be seated,' she said, smiling easily as her chair slid out and retracted its arms for her. She nodded to the passengers, and one or two of them nodded back or even said 'hello.' Or something. She wasn't so sure about the sullen-looking girl in the deliberately slashed black lace top and hair that looked as if she'd stuck her fingers in a power socket, but the three hail-fellow-well-met types in the similar green shirts, two blond men and a straw-haired woman, all looked as if they were about to jump up and salute her. The fat probably-a-merchant-banker and her anorexic beanpole of a male companion just ignored her – probably offended that she wasn't at least a commander – and the withered old actuary from Turku didn't seem to notice her, but that was par for the course. *Senile old cretin*, Steffi thought, writing him off. Anyone that rich who wouldn't stump up the cash for a telomere reset and AGE purge when their hair was turning white was not worth paying attention to. The middle-aged lady cellist from Nippon looked friendly enough, but a bit confused – her translator wasn't keeping up with the conversation – and that just left a honeymooning couple who had predictably elected to call room service instead.

'I'm Junior Flight Lieutenant Steffi Grace, and, on behalf of WhiteStar Lines, I'd like to welcome you to our table for the first night banquet en route to New Dresden. If you'd like to examine the menu, I'm sure your stewards will be with you shortly. In the meantime, I'd like to particularly recommend the—' she glanced at her cuff — 'Venusian Cabernet Sauvignon blanc to accompany the salmon entrées.' Imported at vast expense from the diamond-domed vineyards of Ishtar Planitia, the better to stroke the egos of the twenty-four-thousand-ecu diners.

Things went all right through the entrées, and Steffi made sure to knock back her antidrunk cap with the first mouthful of wine. It *was* an okay vintage, if you could get past the fact that it was wine, and – stripped of the ability to get drunk on it – wine was just sour grape juice. 'Can I ask where you're from?' she asked the square-jawed blonde as she filled her glass. 'I've seen you around, I think, but we haven't spoken before.'

'I am Mathilde, of clade Todt, division Sixt. These are my clade-mates Peter and Hans,' said the woman, waving one beefy hand to take in the strapping young men to either side of her. *Are they young?* wondered Steffi: they looked awfully self-assured and well coordinated. Normally you didn't see that sort of instinctive grace in anyone who was less than sixty, not without martial arts practice. Most people eventually picked up that kind of economical motion if their bodies didn't nose-dive into senescence by middle age, before they had time to mature, but this looked like the product of hard training, if not anabolic steroids. 'We are traveling to Newpeace, as a youth enlightenment and learning mission.' She smiled superciliously. 'That is, we are to learn about the other worlds that have discovered the benefits of ReMastery and spread harmony among them.'

'Uh-huh. And what *is* it, to be ReMastered, if you don't mind my asking? Is it some sort of club?' Steffi prodded. They were, after all, paying her wages. Curiosity about her employers was a powerful instinct.

'It is everything,' Mathilde said gushingly. She caught herself. 'It is a way of life.' Slightly shy and bashful now, as if she had let too much slip: 'It is very fulfilling.'

'Yes, but—' Steffi felt her forehead wrinkling with concentration. *Why do I feel as if I'm being looked down on?* she wondered. *Never mind.* 'And you?' she asked the kid with the black hair. If she *was* a kid; she was about the same build as Steffi, after all.

'Oh, don't mind me, I'll just sit in this corner and drink myself into a new liver. I'm sure the trust fund will pay.' The last sentence came out in a monotone as she caught Steffi's eye, and Steffi realized: *Something's wrong here.*

'We try to take our drinking easy, at least until after the meal,' she said lightly. 'What was your name again?'

'Wednesday,' the girl – *Young woman? Dangerous drunk?* – said quietly. 'That's what they call me. Victoria Strowger on your passenger list. That's what my ID calls me.'

'Whichever you prefer,' Steffi said warily.

The starters arrived, delicately poached small medallions of salmon served under a white sauce, and Steffi managed to get fat Fiona the merchant banker rolling on a paean to the merits of virtual-rate currency triangulation versus more indirect, causality-conserving means of converting funds between worlds separated by a gulf of light years. She was somewhat relieved to find that a lecture on the credit control implications of time travel was sufficient to hold the rapt if slightly incomprehending attention of the three youth leaders from clade Todt, whatever that was. Wednesday, meanwhile, plowed into her third glass of wine with a grim determination that reminded Steffi of some of the much older and more grizzled travelers she'd met – not actual alcoholics, but people possessed by a demon that badly wanted them to wake up with a hangover on the morrow, a demon that demanded an exorcism by the most painful terms available short of self-mutilation. Getting drunk this soon in a voyage, before the boredom began to bite, wasn't a healthy sign. And as for her dress sense, even though Steffi was no follower of style, she could see that Wednesday was relying on a talent for improvisation that must have been labeled 'not needed on voyage.'

The shit refrained from hitting the fan until dessert was served. Steffi had made the tactical mistake of asking Mathilde again just what being ReMastered could do for her – *Is it a religion? Or a political theory?* she'd been wondering ever since the *very fulfilling* crack – and Mathilde decided to deliver a lecture. 'Being ReMastered would give you a new perspective on life,' Mathilde explained earnestly to the entire table. Even Peter and Hans nodded appreciatively. 'It is a way of life that ensures all our actions are directed toward the greatest good. We are not, however, slaves: there is none of the submissiveness of the decadent and degenerate Dar al-Islam. We are fresh and free and strong and joyfully bend our shoulders to the great work out of common cause, with the aim of building a bright future in which all humans will be free to maximize their potential, free of the shadow of the antihuman Eschaton, and free of the chains of superstitious unscientific thinking.'

Wednesday, who until then had been rolling the stem of her empty wineglass between her fingers – Steffi had discreetly scaled back on the frequency of top-ups after her fourth – put her glass down on the table. She licked a fingertip, and began slowly rubbing it around the lip of the glass.

'The clades of the ReMastered are organized among divisions, and their members work together. We rear our children in the best way, with all the devotion and attention to detail that a creche can deliver, and we find useful and meaningful work for them as soon as they are old enough to need purpose and direction. We teach morality – not the morality of the weak, but the morality of the strong – and we raise them to be healthy; the best phenotypes go back into the pool to generate the next harvest, but we don't simply leave that to brute nature. As intelligent beings we are above random chance.' *Whir, whir* went Wednesday's finger. 'We want strong, healthy, intelligent workers, not degenerate secondhanders and drones—'

Mathilde stopped talking, apparently oblivious to the glassy-eyed and slightly horrified stares she was receiving from the merchant banker and the actuary, and glared at Wednesday. 'Stop doing that,' she snapped.

'Tell me what happens to the people you *don't* need,' Wednesday said in a threatening monotone, 'then I'll stop.'

'We do not do anything—' Mathilde caught herself, took a deep breath, and looked down her nose at Wednesday. 'Occasionally a planetary government petitions us for admission. Then we send advisers to help them work out how best to deal with their criminal elements and decadent factions. *Will* you stop doing that, child? It is disruptive. I would go further and say it was typical of your indolence if I didn't believe this was merely an aberration on your part.' She smiled, baring even, gleaming teeth that gave the lie to her veiled jab.

Wednesday smiled right back and kept rubbing the rim of the glass. The Japanese lady cellist chose that moment to join in with her own fingertip, smiling and nodding at her in linguistically challenged camaraderie. Steffi glanced at Mathilde. If looks could kill, Wednesday would be a smoking hole in the bulkhead. 'If you don't take over worlds,' Wednesday said, slurring slightly, 'how's it that people *want* to join you? 'Mean t'say, I've only heard a bit about the concentration camps, an' obviously he's gotta grudge, but you'd think the summary executions and forced labor'd make joining the ReMastered 'bout as popular as rabies.' She bared her teeth at Steffi, in a flicker of amusement that vanished as fast as it had come. *Hum, hum, hum* went the fingertip.

'There are no concentration camps,' Mathilde said icily. 'Our enemies spread lies' – her look took in the whole length of the table, as if no one was above suspicion – 'and obviously some fools fall for them.' She lingered over Wednesday. 'But repeating such slanders—'

'Wanna meet an in – an, uh, ex-inmate?' Wednesday cocked her head on one side. *She's drunk as a skunk,* Steffi realized with a cold feeling in her overfull stomach. *Damn, how'd she get so shit-faced? She's handling it well, but—* The last thing she needed was Mathilde going for Wednesday's throat over the cheeseboard. Not if she wanted to keep the other Syb-class passengers happy. 'Got least one of 'em aboard this ship. Call *him* a liar, why don'tcha.'

'I think that's quite enough.' Steffi forced herself to smile. 'Time to change the subject, if you don't mind,' she added, with a warning glance at Wednesday. But the kid couldn't seem to take the hint, even when it was delivered by sledgehammer.

'I've had more than enough,' Wednesday slurred, sitting up straight but staying focused on Mathilde. *They're like a pair of cats, squaring off*, Steffi realized, wondering if she was going to have to break up a fight. Except that Mathilde didn't look remotely drunk, and Wednesday looked as if she was too drunk to care that the ReMastered woman was built like a gorilla, with muscles where most people had opinions. 'I'm *sick* of this bullshit. Here we all are, sitting round' – she waved a hand vaguely at the rest of the dining room, then blinked in surprise – 'sitting round the table when down in steerage refugee kids are, are . . .'

Steffi was out of her chair almost before she realized she'd come to a decision. Wednesday's back was tense as steel when she wrapped one arm around her shoulders. 'Come on,' she said gently. 'Come with me. You're right, you don't need to be here. Leave everything to me, I'll get it sorted out. Stand up?' For a moment she was sure it wouldn't work, but a second later Wednesday pushed herself upright. She would have been swaying but for Steffi's supporting arm. 'Come on, come with me. You're doing fine.' She steered Wednesday round toward the nearest door, barely noticing the ReMastered woman's stonehard glare drilling into her – or was it Wednesday? 'Come on.' To the gold braid on her left cuff: 'Table six – someone cover for me, please. Taking a distressed guest back to her room.'

They were barely past the doorway when Wednesday tried to break away. Steffi grabbed her. 'No! 'M going to— ' *Oh shit!* Steffi repositioned her grip and hustled Wednesday toward the potted palm she'd taken a tentative lurch toward. But once she was head-down over the plant pot Wednesday proved she was made of stern stuff, drawing deep gulping breaths and slowly getting her stomach under control.

'Table six. Is anyone there?' Steffi mumbled into her cuff. 'I've got a situation here. Who's covering?'

A voice in her earbud: ''Lo, Steffi. I've asked Max to cover for you. Are you going to be long?'

Steffi looked at the young woman, leaning on the rim of the plant pot, and winced. 'Think I'm going to miss the tail end.'

'Okay, check. Banquet control over and out.'

She straightened up in time to see Wednesday doing likewise, leaning against the wall with her eyes shut. 'Come on. What's your room?' She prodded her guest list, still handily loaded in her cuff. 'Let's get you back there.'

Wednesday shambled along passively if somewhat disjointedly, like a puppet with too-loose strings. 'Lying bitch,' she mumbled quietly as Steffi rolled her into the nearest lift. 'Lying. Through her teeth.'

'You're not used to drinking this much, are you?' Steffi ventured. *Wow, you're going to have a mammoth hangover, antidrunk or not!*

'Not . . . not alcohol. Didn't wanna be there. But couldn't stay 'lone.'

Heads she's maudlin, tails she's depressed. Want to bet she wants someone to talk to? Steffi punched up A deck and Wednesday's cylinder, and concentrated on keeping her upright as they passed through fluctuating tidal zones between the electrograv rings embedded in the hull. 'Any reason why not?' she asked casually.

'Mom and Dad and Jerm – lying *bitch*!' It was almost a snarl. I *was right*, Steffi realized unhappily: *Got her away just in time.* 'Couldn't stay 'lone,' Wednesday added for emphasis.

'What happened?' Steffi asked quietly as the elevator slowed then began to move sideways.

'They're dead an' I'm not.' The kid's face was a picture of misery. '*Fucking* ReMastered liar!'

'They're dead? Who, your family?'

Wednesday made a sound halfway between a sob and a snort. 'Who'dya think?'

The elevator stopped moving. Doors sighed open onto a corridor, opposite a blandly anonymous stateroom door. Steffi blipped it with her control override and it swung open. Wednesday knew which way to stagger. For a moment Steffi considered leaving her – then sighed and followed her in. 'Your parents are dead? Is that why you don't want to be alone?'

Wednesday turned to face her, cheeks streaked with tears. Weirdly, her heavy makeup didn't run. *Chromatophores, built into her skin?* 'Been two days,' she said, swaying. 'Since they were murdered.'

'Murdered—'

'By. By the. By—' Then her stomach caught up with her and Wednesday headed for the bathroom in something midway between a controlled fall and a sprint. Steffi waited outside, listening to her throw up, lost in thought. *Murdered? Well, well, how interesting . . .*

It was 0300 hours, day-shift cycle, shortly before the starship made its first jump from point A to point A' across a couple of parsecs of flat space-time.

The comforter was a crumpled mass, spilled halfway across the floor. The ceiling was dialed down to shades of red and black, tunnels of warm dark light washing across the room.

Wednesday rubbed her forehead tiredly. The analgesics and rat's liver pills had taken care of most of the symptoms, and the liter or two of water she'd methodically chugged down had begun to combat the dehydration, but the rest of it – the shame and embarrassment and angst – wouldn't succumb so easily to chemical prophylaxis.

'I'm an ass,' she muttered to herself, slouching to her feet. She headed back to the bathroom again, for the third time in an hour. '*Stupid.* And ugly, and a little bit dumb on the side.' She looked at the bathtub speculatively. 'Guess I could always drown myself. Or cut my wrists. Or something.' *Let the fuckers win.* She blinked at the mirror-wall on the other side of the room. 'I'm an embarrassment.' The figure in the mirror stared right back, a dark-eyed tragic waif with a rat's nest of black hair and lips the color of a drowned woman's. Breasts and hips slim, waist slimmer, arms and legs *too long*. She stood up and stared at herself. Her mind wandered, seeking solace a few nights back. *What did Blow see in me?* she wondered. *No way to find out now. Should have asked him when I had the chance . . .* She was alone here, more isolated than she'd ever been. 'I'm a waste of vacuum.'

On her way back into the bedroom she spotted a blinking light on the writing desk. For want of anything better to do she wandered over. It was something to do with the blotter. 'What's this?' she asked aloud: 'Ship, what does this light mean?'

'You have voice mail,' the ship replied soothingly. 'Voice calls are spooled to mail while guests sleep unless an override is in force. Do you want to review your messages?'

Wednesday nodded, then snorted at her own idiocy. 'Yeah. I guess.'

Message received, thirty-six minutes ago. From: Frank Johnson. 'Hi, Wednesday? Guess you're asleep. Should have checked the time − I keep weird hours. Listen, the story went out okay. Sorry I missed supper, but those social things don't work for me real well. Ping me if you feel like hitting one of the bars sometime. Bye.'

'Huh. Ship, is Frank Johnson still awake?' she asked.

'Frank Johnson is awake and accepting calls,' the liaison network replied.

'Oh, oh.' Suddenly it mattered to her very much that someone else was awake and keeping crazy hours. 'Voice call to Frank Johnson.'

There was a brief pause, then a chime. 'Hello?' He sounded surprised.

'Frank?'

'Hello, Wednesday. What's up?'

'Oh, nothing,' she said tiredly. 'Just, I couldn't sleep. Bad thoughts. You mentioned a bar. Is it, like, too late for you?'

A pause. 'No, not too late. You want to meet up now?'

Her turn to pause. 'Yeah. If you want.'

'Well, we could meet at—'

'Can you come round here?' she asked impulsively. 'I don't want to go out on my own.'

'Uh-huh.' He sounded amused. 'Okay, I'll be round in about ten minutes.'

She cut the call. '*Gods and pests!*' She looked around at the discarded clothes, suddenly realizing that she was naked and what it must look like. 'Damn! damn!' She bounced to her feet and grabbed her leggings and top. She paused for a moment, then wrapped the sarong around her waist, dialed her jacket to a many-layered lacy thing, threw the other stuff in the closet for sorting out later, and ran back to the bathroom to dial the lights up. 'My *hair!*' It was a mess. 'Well, what the fuck. I'm not planning on dragging him into bed, am I?' She stuck her tongue out at the mirror, then went to work on the wet bar in the corner of the main room.

When he arrived Frank was carrying a bag. He put it down on the carpet as he looked around, bemused. 'You said your friends were paying, but this is ridiculous,' he rumbled.

'It is, isn't it?' She looked up at him, challenging.

He grinned, then stifled a yawn. 'I guess so.' He nudged the bag with his foot. 'You said you didn't want to go out so I bought some stuff along just in case—' Suddenly he looked awkward.

'That's okay.' She took his arm and dragged him over to the huge floppy sofa that filled one side of the main room. 'What you got in there?'

He pulled out a bottle. 'Sambuca. From Bolivar. And, let's see, a genuine single malt from Speyside. That's on Old Earth, you know. And here's a disgusting chocolate liqueur from somewhere about which the less said the better. Got any glasses?'

'Yep.' She walked over to the bar and came back with glasses and a jug of ice. She sat down cross-legged at the other side of the sofa and poured a glassful of chocolate liqueur for herself, pretending not to notice Frank's mock shudder. 'You weren't at dinner.'

'Those fake formal feast clusterfucks don't do anything for me,' he announced. 'They're there to make the rich passengers think they're getting a valuable service – more valuable than traveling deadhead in steerage, anyway. I guess if you do business or are in shipping, you can make a lot of contacts that way, but in general the kind of people I'd like to talk to over a meal don't travel by liner.' He looked at her sharply. 'Enjoy yourself?'

She nearly took the question at face value, although his tone suggested irony. 'I nearly threw up in a plant pot after making a fool of myself.' She winced. 'She asked for it, though.'

'Who did?' Frank raised his glass: 'Your health.'

'Bottoms up. Poisonous toy bitch kept going on about how great being *ReMastered* was—' She stopped. Frank looked stricken. 'Did I say something wrong?' she asked.

'Was she a blond? Head half-shaved at one side to show off a tattoo?'

Wednesday stared at him through a haze of conflicting emotions. 'Yes,' she said. 'Why?'

He put his glass down, rattling on the tabletop. 'You could have been killed,' he said shakily.

'What do you—' She leaned toward him. 'You said they run Newpeace. Concentration camps, secret police shit. Do you think they're that dangerous here, though?'

'They're dangerous everywhere!' Frank straightened up and picked up his glass, took a hefty mouthful, and coughed for a while. 'Never, *never*, push a ReMastered button. Please? Tell me you won't do it again?'

'I was drunk.' Wednesday flushed. His concern was immediate and clear, cutting through the fog of worry. 'Hey, I'm not crazy.'

'*Not crazy.*' He chuckled edgily. 'Is that why you didn't want to go out on your own?'

'No. Yes.' She peered at him, wondering why she trusted him. *Alone with a gorilla after midnight and* he *wonders if I'm crazy?* 'I don't know. Should I?'

'You should always know why you do things,' Frank said seriously. 'Inviting strange men for a late-night drink, for example.' He picked up the liqueur bottle. 'Want a refill? Or should I fuck off now before we both end up with hangovers tomorrow?'

She pushed her glass toward him. 'Stay,' she said impulsively. 'I feel safer while you're around. Couldn't sleep, anyway.' A faint smile tugged at the corners of her mouth. 'Do *you* think I'm crazy?'

As days passed the boredom subsided somewhat. She'd stayed in her room for the whole of the next day, playing with the ship's extensive games library, but most of the other online players were old hands who had forgotten more about strategy than the entire Magna tournament team. After a while she ventured out, first to see if there really wasn't anything she could find to wear, then to visit a public bar with Frank. Who introduced her to fresh zero-gee farmed seafood and single malts. Then she'd spent some time with Steffi, who had hastily introduced her to her old friend Sven the clown and made her excuses. Sven, it turned out, also knew Frank: it was a small world aboard ship.

'So what's the thing with the face paint about?' she asked Svengali, one late-shift afternoon.

The clown frowned thoughtfully. 'Think caricature. Think parody. Think emphasis on nonverbal communications cues, okay? If this was a virtual, I'd be an avatar with a homunculus-shaped head and body, bright blue nose, and huge kawaii eyes. But it isn't, and I'm not a surgical basket case, so you have to settle for programmable grease. It's amazing what it can do to someone's perception of you – you'd be really surprised.'

'Probably.' Wednesday took a swig from her glass – something fluorescent green, with red bubbles in it, and about the same alcohol concentration as a strong beer – and pointed at his jacket. 'But the double seam—'

'Not going to leave me *any* tricks, are you?' Svengali sighed.

'No,' Wednesday agreed, and the clown pulled a ferocious face. 'You're very good at this,' she said, trying to be conciliatory. 'Does it pay a lot?'

'It pays' – Svengali caught himself – 'hey, that's enough about me. Why don't we talk about you, for a change?'

'Uh-uh, you don't get off the hook that easily.' Wednesday grinned.

'Yeah, well, it gets hard when the audience is old enough to look behind the mirror. *Mutter*—'

'What?'

Svengali reached toward her head fast, then pulled his hand back to reveal a butterfly fluttering white-and-blue wings inside the cage of his fingers: '—hear me better, now? Or, oh dear, did I just disconnect your brain?' He stared at the butterfly thoughtfully, then blew on it, transforming it into a white mouse.

'Wow,' said Wednesday sarcastically. 'That was *really* convincing.'

'Really? Hold out your hand.'

Wednesday held out her hand, slightly reluctantly, and Svengali released the mouse. 'Hey, it's real!' The mouse, terrified, demonstrated precisely how real it was with a highly accurate rendition of poor bladder control. 'Ick. Is that—'

'Yes.' Before she could drop it, Svengali picked it up by its tail and hid it in his cupped hands. When he opened them a moment later, a butterfly fluttered away.

'Wow!' Wednesday did a little double take, then frowned at her hand. 'Uh. 'Scuse me.'

'Take your time,' Svengali said magnanimously, leaning back in his chair as she hastily stood up and vanished toward the nearest restroom. His smile widened. 'Homing override on,' he told the air in front of him. 'Return to base.' The butterfly/mouse 'bot was stowed carefully away in the small case in his pocket long before she returned.

'Are you going to tell me how you did that?'

'Nope.'

'Lawyer!'

'Am not.' Svengali crossed his arms stubbornly. 'Now you tell *me* how you did *that*.'

'What, this?' Her face slowly brightened from turquoise to sky-blue.

'Yeah, that's pretty good.'

'Programmable cosmetic chromatophores.' Her face faded back toward its normal color, except for a touch of ruby on her lips and midnight blue lining on her eyelids. 'I had them installed when we moved to Magna.'

'Uh-huh. Want to take a walk?' asked Svengali, seeing that her glass was nearly empty.

'Hmm.' She stared at him, then grinned again. 'Trying not to let me get too drunk?'

'It's my job to look after passengers, not line the sick-bay's pockets. We can come back for another drink later.'

'Okay.' She was on her feet. 'Where to?'

'Oh, I don't know,' he said carelessly. 'Let's just walk. Have you explored the ship yet?'

Her grin widened. 'That would be telling.'

Gods, but she's sharp, he told himself. *If she's got the stomach for it, she might even make it in* my *field.* 'You're right – this job doesn't pay nearly enough,' he grumbled. 'I'm supposed to keep you all amused, not be the amusement myself. They should have put an upper age limit on the clientele. Big kids, all of you.' They were already out in the corridor, another high-class hotel passage with sound-deadening carpet, expensively carved wooden paneling, and indirect lights shining on brightly meaningless abstract art instal-lations every few meters. 'Nine days. I hate to think what you're like when you're bored.'

'I can keep to myself.' Wednesday pulled her hands back into the long and elaborately embroidered cuffs of her jacket. 'I'm not a child. Well, not everywhere. Legal stan-dards differ.'

'Yes, yes, and if you'd been born in the New Republic you'd be married with three or four children by now, but that doesn't mean you'd be an autonomous adult. I'm not supposed to keep an eye on you, I'm supposed to keep you from getting bored. All part of the service. What do you do with yourself when you want some cheap amusement, may I ask, if that isn't an indelicate question?'

'Oh, lots of things,' she said idly. Raising an eyebrow at him: 'But I don't think you want to know all the details. Something tells me I'm not your type.'

'Well whoop-de-do. How perceptive, sister.' Svengali steered them down a side passage then through a door into a conference suite, then out the far side of the room – which doubled as an emergency airlock — and into another passage. 'More competition for the boys.' He pulled a comical face. 'But seriously. What did you get up to at home when you were bored?'

'I used to be big on elevator surfing. Vacuum tunneling, too. I was into tai chi, but I sort of let it drop. And, oh, I read spy thrillers.' She glanced around. 'We're not in passenger country anymore, are we?'

There were no carpets or works of art, the doors were wider and of bare metal, and the ceiling was a flat, emissive glare. 'Nope. This is one of the service passages.' Svengali was disappointed at her lack of surprise, but he decided to continue anyway. 'They connect all the public spaces. This is a crew lift. They don't run on cables, they're little self-powered pressurized vehicles running in the tunnels, and they can change direction at will. You don't want to try surfing these cars — it's too dangerous. *That*' — he pointed at an unmarked narrow door about half a meter high, sized for a small dwarf — 'is the service door into a passenger suite. They're automatically locked while the room's occupied, but the valet 'bots use them while you're out and about.'

' 'Bots? Like, android amahs?'

'Who do you think made your bed?' Svengali carried on down the passage. 'Human spaces and human furniture are built for roughly human-shaped people. They could put something like an industrial fab in each room, or even make everything out of structured matter, but many people get nervous when they're too near smart stuff, and having mobile valet 'bots on trolleys is cheaper than providing one per room.'

'Uh-huh. So you're telling me that everywhere in the ship is, like, connected to everywhere else? Using old-fashioned doors and passages and ducts?' She was so wide-eyed that he decided it could only be sarcasm.

'If you design so that it'll only work with smart-matter utilities, something dumb will happen. That's the fifteenth corollary of Murphy's Law, or something. This ship is *supposed* to be able to get home with just a human crew, you know. That's partly why people are willing to pay for it.' A side door opened onto a spiral staircase, cobwebby steps of nearly translucent aerogel ascending and descending into a dim blue mist in each direction. 'Up or down, m'lady?'

'Up, first.'

'You realize we're only able to do this because I've got a badge,' Svengali remarked, as they climbed. The kid had long legs and was in good shape. He had to push himself to keep ahead of her.

'I guessed.' She snuffled something that might have been a laugh. 'It's still cool. What are those guts for?'

He followed her finger to the peristaltic pipes in the recess that ran alongside the stairs. 'Probably semisolid waste disposal. They can reconfigure this stairwell into a tunnel if there's a major gravity outage, you know.'

'Isn't that unlikely?'

'Probably.' He carried on climbing for a bit. 'Doesn't it worry you to be climbing a staircase inside what is basically a skyscraper sitting on top of a stasis chamber containing a twenty billion-ton extremal black hole?'

'I assume' – she paused for breath – 'that if anything went wrong with it, it would all be over too fast to worry about.'

'Probably.' He paused. 'That's why most of the crew – not me, I'm with Entertainments and Diversions, I mean the black gang, engineering ops – are along. In case something goes wrong, and they have to improvise.'

'Well, isn't *that* comforting to know.'

More sarcasm from Wednesday. It ran off him like water off a duck's back. 'Here we are.'

'Where?' She gawked past his shoulder at the boringly ordinary-looking door.

'Here.' He smirked. 'The backstage entrance to the live action theater on C deck. Want to see a performance? Or maybe the theater bar?'

'Wow.' She grinned. 'Send in the clowns!'

With a flourish, Svengali passed her a red nose. Then they went inside.

preparing for
ghosts and dogs

Rachel Mansour. Commissioner. UN Standing
Committee on Interstellar Disarmament (Investigative
Branch), walked slowly down the intimidatingly wide steps
in front of the building of the Ministry of Cosmic Harmony.
Behind her, huge marble columns supported a massive
mirror-finished geodesic hemisphere that loomed over the
neighborhood like a giant cyborg turtle. A sea of people
flooded around her across the Plaza of Public Affairs, office
workers and bureaucrats going about their daily work
between the offices in the ministry basements, and the scattered subdepartments and public malls at the other side of
the open space. The Eastern Palace squatted to her right, a
pink-and-white brick mansion that had been converted to a
museum to the Hegemony and the people's revolution that
had overturned it more than a century earlier, here in
Sarajevo, capital of the planetary empire.

She felt light-headed, an effect of coming out into the
chilly open air after her claustrophobic interview with the

subminister in charge of security arrangements for foreign embassies. After twenty-six days aboard the *Gloriana*, everything from the unprocessed air to the color of daylight seemed peculiar. There was perhaps just a small amount of gravitational adjustment, too – and a headspinning load of mild culture shock.

She marched down the steps and out onto the plaza. Vendors selling spiced cocoa drinks, stir-fried octopi, and bootlegged recordings of old public executions tried to attract her attention. She ignored them. *He didn't say no*, she thought, remembering the subminister frowning ear to ear behind his desk: he wasn't very happy. 'You are telling me that our security is inadequate?' he'd challenged her.

'No, I'm telling you that three other diplomatic security corps failed, in series, and two of them were forewarned. Your people *might* be better, but I hope you'll forgive me for not taking it on trust.'

'Go ahead with your scheme, then, if the Muscovites agree. We will of course deny all knowledge if it goes wrong.'

It was a step up from what she'd have gotten a generation ago, but New Dresden wasn't *that* bad. They had learned the enlightened self-interest meme here, and picked up the idea of a loyal opposition. They even elected their government officials, these days, although in this city the Party maintained its hereditary veto. All told, New Dresden was more civilized than many places she could have ended up. Less so than some others – but so what? *As long as they follow their best interests. And don't go haring off into the darkness again, like they did seventy years ago*. Still, maybe it would be for the best if she kept Martin out of the frame. She'd have to text him via the embassy channel. She tugged her jacket tighter across her shoulders, trying to think her way into the mind of the bureaucratic herd in their dark, closely tailored uniforms. But she couldn't fool herself about the subminister's likely report to his bosses.

People didn't always follow their best interests. Human beings were distressingly bad at risk analysis, lousy with hidden motivations and neuroses, anything but the clean rational actors that economists or diplomats wanted so desperately to believe in, and diplomats had to go by capabilities, not intentions. In dealing with the Muscovite diplomats in residence the Party officials must feel as if they were handling a hungry and aroused venomous snake, one that could turn on them and bite at any moment. They'd tolerate George Cho playing his little shell game with Ambassador Morrow for precisely as long as it increased the likelihood of Morrow's issuing the recall code, and not a second longer.

Speaking of whom, the Ambassador – easily identifiable by the two bodyguards – was sitting at a table at the pavement restaurant. Rachel walked round to the kitchen side then marched up to the nearest bodyguard – who was focusing on the square, not on the waiters approaching from the restaurant entrance – and tapped him on the shoulder. 'Rachel Mansour, to see the Honorable Elspeth Morrow.'

The bodyguard jumped. 'Whoa!'

Morrow looked up, her face colorless and her expression bored. 'You're late. George Cho said I should talk to you. Strongly implied that I needed to talk to you. Who *are* you?'

Rachel pulled out a chair and sat down. 'I work for the same people as George. Different department, though. Officially, I'm on protocol. Unofficially, I'll deny everything.' She smiled faintly.

Morrow waved at the chair with poor grace. 'Okay, spook. So, what does George want?'

Rachel leaned back, then glanced at the bodyguard. 'You

know about the, ah, problem that concerns us.' She studied Morrow intently, seeing a slim woman, evidently in her early forties. Moscow hadn't been good at antiaging therapy, but she could easily have been twenty years older. She wore her chestnut hair shoulder-length, and her green eyes seemed haunted by . . . just haunted. There had to be hundreds of millions of ghosts already riding at her shoulder, and the knowledge that she could add to their ranks – *What must that do to her?* Rachel wondered. 'Forgive me for asking, but did you know Maureen Davis, Simonette Black, or Maurice Pendelton well?' she asked.

Morrow nodded. 'Maurice was an old friend,' she said slowly. 'I didn't know Black other than by repute. Maureen . . . we knew each other. But Maurice is the one I feel for.' She leaned forward. 'What do you know about this?' she asked quietly. 'Why did George bring you? You're black ops, aren't you?'

Rachel raised a hand to summon a waiter. 'I'm, um, working with George's team from the other side,' she said quietly. 'George works for a diplomatic solution. Me, it's my job to . . . well, George very urgently wants to ensure that if someone tries to kill you – which we think is a high probability in the next week or so – firstly, we want them to fail, and secondly, they should fail in such a way that we can find out who they are and why they're doing it, *and* roll up not only the point assassin but their entire network.'

'You do assassinations yourself?' Elspeth stared at her as if she'd sprouted a second head. 'I didn't know Earth did—'

'No!' Rachel gave a little self-deprecating laugh. 'Quite the opposite.' The waiter arrived. 'I'll have the mango croquette and roast shoulder of pork, thanks. And a glass of, um, the traditional red bonnet viper tisane?' She spoke without looking up, but from the corner of her vision noticed the bodyguard shadowing the waiter with aggressive vigilance.

She nodded at Morrow. 'The UN, as you can imagine, would very much like to resolve the current impasse between the government of Moscow in Exile and New Dresden. If for no other reason than to avoid the horrible precedent it would create if your vengeance fleet completes its mission. We especially *don't* want to see a situation where a party or parties unknown butcher so many of the remaining Muscovite government-in-exile's senior ranks that the situation becomes irrevocable. We want to know who is trying to engineer this situation, and why.'

Morrow nodded. 'Well, so do I,' she said calmly. 'That's why I have bodyguards.'

Rachel managed a faint smile. 'With all due respect, I'm sure your bodyguard is perfectly adequate for dealing with run-of-the-mill problems. However, in all three cases to date the assassin succeeded in passing through a secured zone and making an unobstructed getaway. This tells us that we're not dealing with an ordinary lunatic – we're dealing with a formidable professional, or even a team. Ordinary guards don't cut it. If I was the killer, you would be dead by now. My briefcase could be loaded with a bomb, your bodyguard could be shot with his own weapon . . . do you see?'

Elspeth nodded reluctantly.

'I'm here to keep you alive,' Rachel said quietly. 'There's a – well, I can't go into our sources. But we think there's probably going to be an attempt on your life between six and ten days from now.'

'Oh.' Morrow shook her head. Oddly, she seemed to relax a trifle, as if the immediacy of the warning, the concreteness of the high jeopardy, gave her something to cling to. 'What do you think you can do if this master assassin wants to kill me?'

The waiter arrived with Rachel's order on a tray. 'Oh, I

can think of half a dozen possibilities,' Rachel said. She smiled tiredly. Then she peered at Elspeth's face closely until the ambassador blinked. 'We'll have to run it past the ship's surgeon, but I think Plan A can be made to work.'

'What? What have you got in mind?'

'Plan A is the shell game.' Rachel put her glass down. 'We're assuming that our unidentified but highly competent assassins are also well informed. If this is the case, they'll probably learn or guess that you've been warned before they set up the hit. So what George would like to do is play a shell game with them. Step zero is to send Dr. Baxter off-planet – somewhere where we're fairly certain there are no assassins. We'd like you to ensure that you've got as few public appearances and important meetings as possible during the window of opportunity.

'And then . . . well, I'm about your height, and the body mass difference can be finessed with padding and loose clothing. The real trick will be getting the face and hair and posture right. We're going to ensure that for your remaining public appearances you have a body double. Bait, in other words. *You* will be hiding in a locked room in a nuclear bunker with a closed-cycle air supply and half an assault division sitting on top of it – or as a guest on board a UN diplomatic yacht, sovereign territory of Earth, with a couple of cruisers from the New Dresden navy keeping an eye on it, if you prefer. It's up to you: they want to keep you alive, too, as long as those missiles are heading in this direction. But I'm going to hang my tail out where someone can try to grab it – not with a long gun, but up close and personal, so we can snatch them.'

Elspeth looked at her with something like awe – or whatever the appropriate expression was for dealing with suicidal idiots. 'How much do they pay you to do this job?' she asked. 'I've heard some foolhardy things in my time, but that's about the craziest—' She shook her head.

'I don't do this for money,' Rachel murmured. *Responsibility. Get it wrong, and nearly a billion people die.* She glanced at the square. 'I was here about ten years ago. Did you ever take the time to go round the museums?'

'Oh, I've been round the Imperial Peace Museum and the People's Palace of the Judiciary,' Elspeth replied. 'Captured it all.' She tapped a broad signet ring and a sapphire spot blinked on it. 'These people have the most remarkable history – more history than a world ought to have, if you ask me.' She fixed Rachel with a contemplative stare. 'Did you know they've had more world wars than Old Earth?'

'I was vaguely aware of that,' Rachel said drily, having crammed three thousand pages of local history on her first journey here, many years earlier. 'How are the museums these days?'

'Big. Oh, this month there's a most extensive display of regional burial costumes, some sort of once-in-a-decade exhibition that's on now.' Slowing even more, Elspeth continued thoughtfully: 'There was a whole gallery explaining the sequence of conquests that enabled the Eastern Empire to defeat their enemies in the south and get a stranglehold on the remaining independent cornucopia-owning fabwerks. Fascinating stuff.'

'Nothing on the mass graves, I take it,' Rachel observed.

'No.' Elspeth shook her head. 'Nor the blank spots on the map of North Transylvania.'

'Ah.' Rachel nodded. 'They haven't gotten around to talking about it yet?'

'Life extension, amnesia extension. It takes longer to admit to the crimes when the criminals are still taking an active role in government.' Elspeth drained her glass, then looked away. 'Why were you there?' she murmured.

'War crimes commission. I'd rather not talk about it, thanks.' Rachel finished her drink. 'I'd better get back to the embassy to start preparations.' She noticed Elspeth's expression. 'I'm sorry, but we've got to get under way as soon as possible. It's going to take time to work up to this. I think I'll skip the museums.'

For a moment she felt agonizingly old: she felt every minute of her age, a length of time no human being could endure without learning to ignore it from moment to moment. She had made a habit of reinventing her life every thirty years, forcing herself to adopt new habits and attitudes and friends, but even so a common core of identity remained; a bright spark of rage against the sort of people who could do the sort of thing that had happened in North Transylvania, less than a century earlier. One of Rachel's most recent peculiarities was that she'd recently found that museums made her feel ill, physically nauseous, with their depictions of horrors and atrocities disguised as history – especially when they were horrors and atrocities that she had lived through. Or worse, their glib evasions and refusals to face the truth.

'I could——' Elspeth shook her head. 'There's more to you than you're letting on.'

Rachel smiled at her sourly. 'Why, thank you very much.' She sniffed. 'I said my job was about bomb disposal. But maybe it'd be more accurate to say I'm in the business of abolishing history.'

'Abolishing history?' The Ambassador frowned. 'That sounds positively revisionist.'

'I mean, abolishing the kinds of events they build places like the Imperial Peace Museum to remember.' She glanced at Elspeth. 'Your call?'

Ambassador Morrow stared at her through half-narrowed eyes. 'I think your ambition is very laudable,' she said slowly. 'And I'd like to hear about your experiences here sometime.' *But not right now. I don't want to lose my lunch*, Rachel projected cynically. 'Meanwhile, why don't you work with Willem here to arrange a follow-on meeting, at our mutual convenience?'

'I'll do that.' Rachel nodded. 'Take care.'

'I shall,' said Morrow, standing up and holding her arms out for her coat. 'You, too,' she said impulsively, then her bodyguards and secretary followed her, the latter watching Rachel mistrustfully as his mistress walked away. They vanished into the crowd, and her main course arrived. Rachel ate it slowly, her thoughts elsewhere. *I wonder what Martin will think?*

'You *can't* be serious!'

She'd rarely seen him so disturbed, and never by something she'd told him: 'Why? What makes you think I'm joking?'

'I—' He was pacing, always a bad sign. 'I don't.' *Ah, a sign of realism.* 'I just don't like it, for extremely large values of *don't* and *like*.' He turned to face her, his back to the wall-screen of the promenade deck: with the almost flat horizon of the planet behind him, it looked as if he was walking on the atmosphere. 'Please, Rachel. Please tell me this isn't as bad as it sounds?'

She took a deep breath. 'Martin, if I wanted to kill myself, do you think I'd go about it this indirectly?'

'No, but I think your sense of responsibility' – he saw where he was going almost before she did, and swerved to avoid the abyss – 'may lead you into working within operational constraints that you don't need to be bound by.' He stopped and took a deep breath. 'Phew. Don't mean to lecture you. It's your specialty, and so on.' Then he looked at her, with worry in his eyes, and she felt herself beginning to melt: 'But are you sure it's safe?'

'Don't you go quoting William Palmer's last words at me,' she threw back at him. 'Of course I'm not sure it's safe!' She folded her arms defensively. 'It's as safe as I can make it, and for sure it's safer than letting some lunatic sign a death warrant for 800 million mostly innocent people. But it's not *safe*-safe. Now if you're through trying to mother me, will you listen while I talk you through the threat tree and tell me if you spot anything that everybody else has missed?'

'The threat tree—' Martin almost went cross-eyed trying to hold the topic in his head. 'Rachel?'

'Oh shit!' She looked at him with mingled affection and exasperation. Two years of being married to him hadn't blunted the former, but she'd been a big girl with her own life before Martin – in his late sixties, despite looking like a mid-twentysomething – had been even a twinkling in his mother's eye. And sometimes she felt like a cradle snatcher. He didn't yet have the chilly detachment that came from having a child die of avoidable old age, embraced by reason of either religious conviction or plain old-fashioned boredom with life. Maybe he never would, and she'd love him no less for it, but at times it made him a mite hard to live with. 'Do you really think that I'd do something rash enough to cost me this?' She took two steps forward and buried her chin in the base of his neck, as his arms automatically wrapped around her.

'I *know* you would, Rache. I know about you and your quixotic campaigns to fix entire fucked-up planets. Remember?'

She whispered in his ear: 'Only because you'd do the same.'

'Yeah, but I was doing it strictly cash on delivery. And for the best possible reason.' Because the nearest thing this crazy universe could provide to a deity had phoned him up one day and asked him how much he'd charge for sabotaging time machines before the lunatics who built them could switch them on and destroy the coherency of history, including the chain of events leading to the creation of the god in question. 'You tend to do it when you get overenthusiastic.'

'No, I tend to do it when I get *angry*,' she replied, and goosed him. He yelped. 'You don't like it when I get angry!'

'No, no, I like you fine.' He gasped. She laughed: she couldn't help herself. A moment later Martin was chuckling, too, leaning on her shoulder for support.

After a while they sobered up. 'I'm not going to let some crazy get close enough to kill me, Martin. I'm just going to wear the face and stand at the back of a room with a couple of tons of concealed security in front of me. I want them to *think* they've got a clean shot at me, not give them the real thing.'

'I've seen too many harebrained schemes like this go wrong.' She let go of him, took a step back to watch his face. 'And it leaves me feeling like a spare wheel. Not' – he glanced over his shoulder – 'that I'm anything else, here.'

'Well, that's what you get for marrying into the diplomatic corps.' She frowned. 'But there's one thing you could do for me. I asked George, and he says it's okay. It's not dangerous—'

'Not dangerous?' He squinted suspiciously. 'That'll be a first for something you cooked up.'

'Shut up. Listen, George thought it would be a good idea if while I'm at the Muscovite embassy running this little honeypot scheme, you took a trip up the beanstalk and had a guided tour of the *Romanov* while she's in dock. Your usual employer built bits of her, and I can get you an intro with the Captain. I just want you to go take a look around, see if you smell anything fishy. We can make it official if you want.'

'The last time you guys wanted me to go take an *unofficial* sniff around a ship I seem to recall we both got shanghaied into a six-month cruise to a war zone,' he said drily.

'That's not the idea this time.' She smiled, then turned away. Mixed memories: Martin had not enjoyed the experience much, and at the time neither had she, but if it hadn't happened, they wouldn't have met, wouldn't have married, wouldn't be together. It was too easy, after the event, to gloss over the dark, frightening aspects of a bad experience inextricably linked to something else that was very good indeed. 'I'm not sure what, if anything, I expect you to find. Probably nothing, but if you can hit on the Captain for a full passenger manifest including stopovers, and ask around if anyone's been behaving oddly. I mean, if there's a passenger in first class who never shows up at dinner because the voices in his head tell him to stay in his cabin and polish the guns . . .'

'Check.' He sighed. 'It's a WhiteStar ship, isn't it?'

'Yes. Why, is that good or bad?'

'Commercial, *very* commercial. I hope you guys have got something on the bottom line to offer the Captain, or he's not going to be too keen on wasting time on someone like me.'

'*She*, Captain Nazma Hussein. And she's not going to yelp too loudly. Why do you think George put you on the payroll? She doesn't need to know you're down as an unpaid intern; just turn up and wave your diplomatic passport at her and act polite but firm. If you get any shit, pass it on to George.' She grinned. 'It's about the only perk of the job.'

'You're going to take care, aren't you?' He stared at her. 'You bet.'

'Okay.' He closed the gap between them, and she wrapped her arms around him. He leaned close to kiss her forehead. 'Let's hope you can get this nailed down so we can go home soon.'

'Oh, I'm sure we will.' She held him tight. 'And I'm not going to take any risks, Martin. I want to live long enough to see that child of ours decanted.'

Three days of frenetic preparation passed like quicksilver running down a rainy gutter, until:

'Four hours ago? First passengers should have hit the terminal when? Very good. Thanks, I'll be ready.' Rachel flipped her phone shut and tried to get her racing pulse back under control. 'It's started,' she called through the open door.

'Come over here. I want to give this a last run-through,' said Tranh.

Rachel walked across the hand-woven rug and paused in the open doorway. 'What kind of way is that to talk to a foreign ambassador?' she asked, forcing herself to stand with her legs slightly apart, the way Elspeth did. Tranh was waiting in the Ambassador's bedroom with Gail and a worried-looking Jane, still busy setting up the mobile communications switch on Morrow's desk. Like Rachel, Gail was dressed for a formal diplomatic reception: unlike Rachel, she wore her own face along with the dark suit and gown of office of a dignitary.

Tranh peered at her intently. 'Hair,' he said.

'Let me look.' Gail approached Rachel, holding a brush as if it were a handgun. 'No, looks all right to me. Hmm.' She reached out and adjusted a stray wisp. 'How does it feel?'

Rachel grimaced. 'Like wearing a rubber mask, how do you think it feels?'

'As long as you can wear it comfortably. No slipping?'

'No. Membrane pumps seem to be fine.' The layered

gunk was threaded with osmotic pumps, able to suck up sweat from down below and exude it through realistic-looking pores.

'Other stuff?'

'Fine.' Rachel turned round slowly. 'Can't bend over too easily. Wish the armor could sweat, too.'

'Your gun's showing,' Tranh said critically. 'When you let the robe fall open – that's better.' Rachel hitched it into place. 'Hmm. Looks okay to me. Wire test.' There were no wires, but an elaborate mix of military-grade intelligent comms to tie the ambush team together.

'Testing, testing.'

Tranh held up a hand. 'Tests out okay. *Can you hear me?*' She winced, and he hastily hit a slider on the communications panel. 'That better?' She nodded.

Glued into a skin-tight mask, wearing somebody else's clothes over body armor and trying to conceal a handgun, Rachel felt anything except better. But at least Martin was out of the picture for the moment – on his way up the planetary beanstalk to poke around the liner docked in geo-synchronous orbit. 'Gail, remind me of the order of battle?'

'The order – oh.' She cleared her throat. 'It's 1730. Doors open, 1800. We're expecting Subminister for Cultural Affairs Ivan Hasek, the usual dozen or so cultural attachés, deputy ambassadors, sixteen assorted business dignitaries, including six locals anxious to resolve reparations lawsuits, three from Septagon, who're concerned about commodity futures in event of a rather unpleasant future shortage of Dresdeners to trade with them, and seven export agents for defunct Muscovite firms. There's Colonel Ghove of the Ministry of Education, Professor-Doctor Franck from the Ministry of Internal Enlightenment, the diva Rhona Geiss, who is apparently due to sing for us, about a billion journalists – four, actually – and a few dozen refugees who live here or are passing through and took up the invitation. Plus the caterers, a quartet of musicians, eight dancers, three entertainers, eleven waiters, a bunch of students on a cultural exchange trip, a video crew making a documentary about what happens to nations after their planet dies, and a partridge in a pear tree. I double-checked the list with Pritkin and the ambassador, and you've got a clear field — no existing acquaintances according to your service log.'

'Delightful.' Rachel winced. 'Horizon is five hours off. Got any rat's liver pills for me?'

Gail produced a strip of tablets with a flourish and a small grin. 'Have one on me.'

'Uck.' Rachel popped the first pill, resigning herself to an evening of sobriety. 'Toilet?'

'Along the hall, door under the main stairs on the left. Cubicles all wired, of course.'

'Guards?'

'Two on the front, two on the back, and two on each landing. They've been briefed. Safeword is—'

'"Ghosts." I got it. And "dogs" for an intruder.'

'Right.' Tranh stood up. 'You happy?'

'As happy as . . .' Rachel gave it some thought: '. . . anyone would be in my shoes. How's Elspeth taking it?'

'I could phone her if you want?'

'No, I don't think so.' Rachel could see it all in her mind's eye. A drably boring safe house on the other side of town, discreetly ringed by a prince's escort of secret policemen. Ambassador Morrow would be trying to relax, with George Cho to keep her company, along with a subminister from the Ministry of External Affairs and her secretary, whatshisname. There was growing tension over Earth's diplomatic corps muscling in on the mess: Earth was a third party with only a vague claim to involvement, thanks to the assassin's choice of transport. The only reason Dresdener spooks weren't handling this was the likely response of the Muscovite diplomatic corps if they dropped the ball. The ticking clock, the slowly rising tension as they waited for the call from the embassy. Anxiety: *What if they're right?* And uncertainty: *What if they're wrong?* And paranoia: *What if these people from Earth are behind it all?* It was enough to sour Rachel's stomach, not a good way to start a long and stressful evening.

She concentrated on her autonomic implants for a while. The Dresdener authorities had a serious bias against personal augmentation and the unregulated use of smart matter: Rachel's ability to override her thalamus, accelerate her reflexes, and see in the dark would go down like a lead balloon if they came to light. But they wouldn't, not unless someone came out of the darkness and tried to kill her. That was only too possible, now they were into the eighty-hour frame between the *Romanov*'s arrival and its clearance for departure from the beanstalk's orbital dock. And she had reason to be nervous. Someone had managed to infiltrate three diplomatic residences, one of them under a state of heightened security, carry out three kills, and get away clean. That implied very good intelligence, or inside help, or both. And if the inside help knew about the substitution . . .

'Time check,' said Tranh. 'The first guests should be' – he glanced at the switch – '*are* arriving now.'

There was a discreet knock at the main door to the outer room. 'I'll check it,' said Gail, walking over. Rachel slid out of sight behind the inner door as Gail held a brief whispered conversation. 'It's Chrystoff,' she said, and Rachel relaxed slightly. Morrow's bodyguard was one of the few people on the whitelist – if *he* was an assassin, they'd lost before they even got started.

'Good,' she said, walking back into the middle of the room. She caught the bodyguard's eye: 'You happy with this?'

'No.' He returned the inspection. 'But, you're — it's uncanny.' He looked tense. 'It's not you that I'm worried about.'

'Indeed.' She nodded soberly. 'I need to go downstairs and greet people. I really don't expect our hypothetical hitter to risk witnesses, so as long as I stay out of view of the outside we should be all right. The fun starts if any of the guests goes out of bounds or when the hitter departs from the script. Ready?'

Chrystoff froze for a moment, then gave a slight nod.

'Then let's get this show on the road.'

showtime

With the ship docked and resupply under way, Steffi was annoyingly busy. In addition to spending some of her off-hours with Wednesday – the kid had problems and needed a shoulder to unload on, but it was remarkably draining to be in the firing line – she was filling in for Max and Evan, running errands between Bridge and Engineering, generally acting as understudy and gofer for the executive team, and minding the shop while her superiors were dealing with the port authorities. If it went on this way, she'd be lucky to get any time on the surface at all – and after three weeks of constant work she needed to get out of the ship for a while very badly indeed. If she didn't do her share on the surface, Svengali would have harsh words for her; of that, she was certain. Which was why Elena's call from the purser's office came as an unwelcome distraction.

'Lieutenant? We have a situation here. I'm on tube four, northside. Can you come up right away?'

Steffi glanced at the two engineering auxiliaries who were hooking up the ship's external service cables – power, so they could strip down the number two generator, and crypto, so they could dump the bulk mail spool. 'I can give you five minutes. That's all. On my way. What's the situation?'

'I can't tell you until you get here.'

'What do you mean, "can't"?' Steffi was already moving toward the nearest crew lift capsule. *Got to sign off the cable hookup, then see Dr. Lewis gets her transport for the new surgery unit . . .*

'It's very irregular.' Elena sounded apologetic. 'I've got an override B-5.'

'A—' Steffi blinked. 'Okay, I'm on my way.' She twitched her rings to a different setting, then told the lift to take her to the lock bay. 'Max? Steffi here. I've got a problem. Do you know something about an override B-5 coming up?'

Max sounded distracted. 'A B-5? No, I haven't heard anything. You can try to field it if it's within your remit. If it goes over your head, get back to me. I'm covering for Chi right now, so I've got my hands full.'

'Uh, okay.' Steffi shook her head. 'B-5, isn't that a *diplomatic* exception?'

'Diplomatic, customs, police, whatever. If they've got a warrant for a passenger, it's the purser's office. If it's to do with shipboard ops, get back to me.'

'Okay. Steffi out.' The elevator slowed, then opened its doors on the passenger country side of docking tube four. This level of the tube – a pressurized cylinder the diameter of a subsonic trash-hauler jet – was a wide corridor, ramping up at the far end into the arrivals processing hall of the station. At the ship end, various lock doors and high-capacity elevators opened off it. Just then, a trickle of passengers were idling on their way portside. Elena and a crewman from the purser's office were waiting by the barrier with a passenger – no, wait, he was on the wrong side, wasn't he?

'Hello, Elena. Sir.' She smiled professionally. 'How can I help you?' She sized him up rapidly: dark hair, nondescript, young-looking with the self-assurance that came with age, wearing sandals, utility kilt, and a shirt in a style that had been everywhere back home. Then he held up a small booklet. With a white cover.

'My name is Martin Springfield,' he said diffidently, 'and I'm attached to the UN special diplomatic mission currently in residence in Sarajevo.' He smiled faintly. '*Nicky* didn't look like this last time I was aboard, I must say.'

'*Nicky?* Excuse me?' Elena was trying to catch her eye, but too late.

'That's what we called her back in the yard. Must have been eight or nine years ago.' Springfield nodded to himself, as if confirming something: 'I'm sorry to have to pull this on you, but I'm here because Ambassador Cho needs some questions answered urgently. Is there somewhere private we can talk?'

'Private—' Steffi's eyes nearly crossed as she tried to reconcile conflicting instincts: *Get this annoying civilian out of the way so I can go back to work;* and *oh shit,* government *stuff! What do I have to do now?* 'Um, yes, I suppose so.' She cast a warning glance at Elena, who shrugged and looked helpless. 'If you'd be so good as to step this way? Can I have a look at that, sir?'

'It's genuine,' Elena volunteered. 'Carte blanche. He's who he says he is. I already checked.'

Steffi forced herself to smile again: 'I'm sure you did, or you wouldn't have called me.' She looked at Martin. 'Follow me.'

As if everything wasn't complicated enough, as she

turned, a small clot of people were coming down the tube —
a couple of staff entertainers, one or two business travelers,
a handful of tired-looking recently thawed steerage cus-
tomers with their shipping trunks, and Wednesday.
Wednesday noticed her at the same time and couldn't leave
well alone. 'Uh, Lieutenant Grace? Are you busy? I just
wanted to say, I'm sorry about the other day—'

'It's all right,' Steffi said tiredly, wondering how she was
going to talk her way out of this. 'Are *you* all right? Going
groundside, I see – do you have anything in mind? Some
sightseeing?'

Wednesday brightened slightly. 'I'm sightseeing, yeah.'
Then she was abruptly sober. 'There's a memorial ceremony
tomorrow at the, the embassy. In the capital. Anyone from
Moscow who's in-system is invited. It landed in my mailbox this morning. Thought I ought to go. It's been five
years, empire time.'

'Well, you go,' Steffi said hastily. 'If you need to talk
when you get back to the ship, feel free to call me – I'm just
a bit snowed under right now.' To her relief Wednesday
nodded, then hurried off to catch up with the flock of
daytrippers. *What did I let myself in for?* she wondered. After
that devastating breakdown on the first night, she'd sat
with Wednesday for a couple of hours while she poured out
her grief. It had left Steffi wanting to strangle someone –
starting with whoever had killed the kid's family, followed
by the kid herself when she realized how much of a time
sink Wednesday could be. But she'd filed a report with the
stewards, disentangled herself carefully, and when she
checked the next day Wednesday seemed to be fine. And she
was spending a lot of time with the troll from B312. They
were resilient at that age. She'd been made of rubber herself,
back when her parents were splitting up; but she didn't
remember collapsing on a total stranger's shoulder and

spilling her soul, or trying to pick a fight over supper. Spoiled, like most rich kids, she figured. Wednesday had probably never had anything to worry about in her life.

Steffi reached the crew elevator and realized with a start that the man from the embassy was still with her. *What is he, the human glueball?* she wondered. 'We can find a corner of the executive planning suite, or maybe a conference room. Or if it's okay with you, I can go check on a couple of jobs I'm meant to be supervising.' *Let's get you out of my hair, huh?*

'If you can check those jobs in person, I'll just tag along and stay out of your way while you're doing it.' Springfield leaned against the side of the lift car. He looked either tired or worried – or both. 'But I'm afraid I'm going to be generating a lot of work for you. Ambassador Cho sent me to poke around here because I'm the nearest thing to a shipping specialist he's got. We have a bit of a needle and haystack problem, I'm afraid. Specifically, we have reason to think that one or more of the long-stay passengers have been using this vessel as a vehicle for serial naughtiness at the last few ports of call.'

The elevator began to slow as it neared the power hookup bay. 'Are we talking about smuggling, sir? Or barratry, or hijacking? Because if not, I don't see what this could possibly have to do with WhiteStar. It's been a remarkably peaceful voyage so far.'

The doors hissed open, and Steffi stepped out. Yuri was leaning against the wall beside the big gray switchbox. 'All hooked up, ma'am. Would you like the tour?'

Steffi nodded. It took her only a minute to confirm that Yuri and Jill – who had hurried off, needed elsewhere – had done a good job. 'Okay, let's test it, turn it on, and sign it off.' She waited while Yuri called down to the engine room and ran through the checklist before tripping in the circuit.

The cabinet-sized switchbox hummed audibly as it came under load, nearly fifty megawatts of electricity surging into it through superconductor cables no fatter than Steffi's thumb. 'Okay, here's my chop.' She signed off on Yuri's pad, then sealed the cabinet.

'Let's go find a conference room,' she told Martin. 'If you still feel you need to check our records . . . ?'

'It's not whether I feel any need, I'm afraid,' he said quietly, then waited for the lift pod doors to close: 'I don't expect you to have any trouble in flight. The person or people we're looking for are more likely to be causing trouble groundside.'

'Trouble? What kind of trouble?'

Springfield looked grim. 'I can't tell you. But it's bad enough to get a full-dress diplomatic mission out here to paper over the cracks. If you want confirmation, wire Victoria McEllwaine in Legal back at WhiteStar head office and ask her what you should do. Meanwhile, I need to go over your entire passenger manifest since the current cruise began. And your temporary staff, for that matter – anyone who's been here for less than six months. I may also need to gain access to staterooms. If you can't authorize a search, point me at someone who can. Finally, I need to make an inspection tour of your engineering spaces and check cargo consignments for certain destinations – any small to medium items that have been drawn out here by passengers, checked in from Earth, Turku, and Eiger's World.'

'Is that all?' Steffi asked disbelievingly. He'd outlined enough work there to keep someone occupied for a week. With passenger churn approaching 40 percent per destination, they'd gone through six or seven thousand embarkations, not to mention the Entertainments staff: they'd shipped an entire chamber orchestra from Rosencrantz to Eiger, never mind the other irregular performers that Ents kept hiring and firing. 'I'd better get you sorted out right away. If you don't mind, I'm going to boot you upstairs to my CO – I'm due off duty in two hours with shore leave tomorrow.'

'Well, I won't keep you – but let's get started. I'm supposed to report back within twenty-four hours. *With* results. And then I may have to call on you to help me arrest someone.'

Meanwhile, Frank was groundside and frustrated. 'Can you explain why they won't see me? I made this appointment forty-three days ago; it's been cleared via the consulate in Tokyo. Is there some kind of problem?'

'Problem.' The man on the small screen cleared his throat. 'You could say that.' He eyed Frank curiously. 'I'm afraid we're in the middle of a staff training drill right now, and Minister Baxter isn't available. Also, all embassy engagements have been scaled back, and I can't find any mention of you in our workgroup diary. Would you like to make a fresh appointment for sometime next week?'

'My ship leaves the day after tomorrow,' he said as calmly as he could manage. 'So next week is right out. Would Minister Baxter be available for a phone interview instead? If security is a concern, there's no need for face-to-face contact.'

'I'll just check.' The screen blanked for a moment, then: 'I'm sorry, sir, but the Minister isn't available at all until next Thursday. Can I help you make any alternative arrangements? For example, by long-range channel?'

'I'll have to check my budget,' Frank admitted. 'I have a limited bandwidth spend. Can I get back to you on that? Would you mind just double-checking that I'm not on your list anywhere? If the Minister's unavailable, would it someone to snatch his window/camera in this crowded place.

'Frank? It's me. I'm here. Where are you?'

'You're—' His eyes crossed with the unexpected mental effort of trying to figure it out, then he hit on the caller's geocache location. 'Eh. What do you want, Wednesday?'

'I've, uh, I've only just got off the ship, but I was wondering, are you busy this evening?' It came out in a rush. 'See, there's this wine-and-cheese reception thingy, and I've been invited to it, says I can bring a guest, and I haven't done one of these things before, but I have been *strongly advised* to go—'

Frank tried not to sigh. 'I've just had an interview fall through. If I can't refill the slot, I guess I might be free, but probably not. Just what kind of do is it?'

'It's some kind of fifth-anniversary dead light get-together, a reunion for any Moscow citizens who're on Dresden. At the embassy, you know? My, uh, friends said you might be interested.'

Frank sat bolt upright, barely noticing the other commuters on the platform, as they began to move toward the doors. 'Wait, that's excellent!' he said excitedly. 'I was wanting to get some local color. Maybe get some interview slots with ordinary people. When is it, you said—' The doors were opening as passengers disembarked: others moved to take their place.

'The Muscovite high consulate in Sarajevo. Tonight at—'

Frank started. The platform was emptying fast, and the train was waiting. 'Whoa! Mail me? Got to catch a train. Bye.' He hung up fast and trotted over to the doors, stepping aboard just as the warning beeper went off.

'Potrobar?' he muttered to himself, glancing around for an empty seat. '*Potrobar?* What the fuck am I going *there* for?' He sighed, and forced himself to sit down as the PA

be possible to arrange a chat with Ambassador Morrow instead?'

'I'm sorry, but the Ambassador's busy, too. As I said, sir, this is about the worst possible week you could have asked for an interview. If you leave things with me, I'll see what I can do, but I'm making no promises.'

Frank put his temporary phone away and stood up tiredly. At times like this he felt as if he was walking blindfolded along a corridor pre-greased and strewn with banana skins by a cosmic jester. *Why now? Why did they have to lose the fucking thing now, of all times?* A quote from Baxter, or even Morrow, admitting that their colleagues were being stalked – that would be explosive. Only they weren't playing ball. The whole thing smelled like a discreet security lockdown: scheduled interviews canceled, public appearances held to carefully controlled zones with vetted guest lists, the bland stench of denial hovering over the rotting corpse of business as usual. Just like one of Mom's dinner parties when she'd been trying to break back into the charmed circle of political movers and fixers who'd dropped her the first time around, after her electoral defeat.

The air was still cool and slightly damp in the park, but the heated benches were dry enough to work on. Frank folded up his mobile office and stood up. The poplars were flowering, and he walked slowly under a ceiling of catkins, bouncing and shedding in the morning breeze. The path merged with two others at one of the bronze war memorials that were heartbreakingly common hereabouts. Frank paused for a minute to scan it with his glasses, capturing the moment forever. Almost a hundred years earlier, at this very spot, an enemy battalion had put up a spirited resistance to the forces of the All-Conquering. Their souls, large and warlike, had gone to Valhalla: the victors had raised the stele not out of magnanimity but with the more subtle intention of magnifying their own prowess. *Nobody likes to boast that they massacred a bunch of terrified, starving, ill-equipped conscripts,* Frank reminded himself. *It's easier to be a hero when your vanquished enemies are giants.* Something he'd have to bring up if he ever got close enough to interview the honorable Elspeth Morrow. 'So how does it feel sentencing to death 140 million children, 90 million crumblies, and another 600-million-odd ordinary folks who were content to mind their own business and don't even know who you are?'

Farther along the path Frank passed a patrolling gardener 'bot. Judging from the smell, it was collecting and fermenting either slugs or waste from the citizens who walked their dogs at dawn. The trees were farther apart on this walk, with park benches between them and fields stretching away beyond. Each bench bore a weathered pewter plaque, stained almost gray by age: *In loving memory of Private Ivar Vincik, by his parents,* or *Gone forever but not forgotten, Artillery Sergeant Georg Legat.* The park wore its history as proudly as a row of medals: from the memorials to the fallen to the white charnel house built from the skulls and femurs of the enemy battalion, used by the groundskeepers to store their lawnmowers.

The trees came to an end, and the path began to descend toward a concrete underpass that slid beneath the road that separated park from town center. If you could call it a town center, these days. First there'd been a small rural village. Then there'd been a battle. Then there'd been another village, which grew into a town before the next battle flattened it. Then the town had been rebuilt and turned into a city, which had been bombed heavily and rebuilt again. Then the Mall that Ate Vondrak had turned into the Arcology that Absorbed Vondrak, all concrete towers and gleaming glassy

Penrose-tiled roof, a groundscraper sprawled acro landscape like a sleeping giant. The place was h contaminated by history, war memorials marking worst pollution hot spots.

It was a quiet day, but there was still some traffic few people about at ground level even that early i morning – a couple out for an early-morning run tog three kids on walksters, an old woman with a huge pack, worn boots, and the wiry look of a hiker poring an archaic moving map display. A convoy of local del vans hummed past on the road deck, nestling behind long-haul tractor like a queue of ducklings. A seagull, prisingly far inland, circled overhead, raucously claiming territory.

'When's the next train to Potrobar?' he asked aloud.

'You have twenty-nine minutes. Options: Make a res vation. Display route to station. Rescan—'

'Reservation and route, please.' The ubiquitous geocon puting network there was crude compared to the varie services on Earth, but it did the job, and did it without inserting animated advertorials, which was a blessing. A light path flickered into view in front of him, strobin toward one of the arcology entrances. Frank followed across the ornamental cobblestones, past a gaggle of flo ing unicyclists and a fountain containing a diuretic-affli Eros.

The train station was on level six, a glazed atrium sliding doors along one side to give access to the pas compartments. Frank was slouched in a seat, pec his keyboard in a desultory manner (trying to cap atmosphere of a chrome-and-concrete station trying to turn a burned lump of charcoal back into thought dispiritedly) when his phone bleeped tion. 'Yeah?' he asked, keeping to voice-only –

system gave a musical chime and the train lifted from the track bed and began to slide toward the tube entrance. 'When's the next train from Potrobar to Sarajevo?' he asked plaintively.

set us up the bomb

Ring ring. 'Hey, what took you so long? I've been waiting for *hours*! I'm going to be late—'

'You are not late. There will be another capsule in less than half an hour, Wednesday. Did you receive my message about the reception?'

'Yes.' Wednesday sighed theatrically. 'I'm on my way there. Will you tell me what this is all about?'

There was a momentary pause. 'In due course.'

Wednesday shook her head. 'In other words, no.' She bent down and buckled up her boots. They looked really fine with the white lacy shalwar trousers she'd bought for dinner and never worn. 'So what's the point of me going there?'

'There is going to be trouble,' said Herman, his voice a distant monotone. 'The conspirators who are currently assassinating Muscovite diplomats—'

'*What?*'

'—Please do not interrupt. Did you think you were the only target?'

'But, but—'

'The chancelleries of a hundred worlds will be shaken by the exposure of this conspiracy, Wednesday. *If* the primary annealing state vector collapses to — excuse me. If the outcome I am betting against myself on comes to pass. I apologize, human languages are poor vehicles for describing temporal paradoxes.'

'You're going to have to try harder if you want to impress. I'm just an airhead party animal, me.'

'Just so.' Pause. 'Attend. Three ambassadors have been murdered. Their deaths coincide with the arrival of this ship in orbit around whichever planet they were on at the time. On this planet, there is an ambassador, and another senior government official. The reasons I brought you here are threefold. Firstly, I am interested in knowing who is killing these diplomats, and why, because I believe it will answer a very important question — who destroyed Moscow.' There was another brief pause. 'Backward chaining from the resolution of that situation, I must have sent a message to my earlier state vector — acting in my capacity as an ex-officio oracle and deity within the light cone — to pick you up at an early age. Your involvement was implicit in the development of this situation, although I don't yet fully understand why, and I believe the reason the faction of the assassins tried to kill you is connected. The information you stumbled across on Old Newfie was more important than I realized at the time. Unfortunately, unless I can arrange transport there for you, it may not be easy to retrieve it.'

'You want to take me back *home*?' It came out as a squeak. Wednesday stood up hastily: 'You didn't say anything about that! Isn't it dangerous? How will we get there—'

'That was the second reason,' Herman continued

implacably. 'My third reason is this: I am a distributed intelligence service, linked by causal channels. I am highly dependent on state coherency that can only be maintained within the light cone – whenever the ship that is the focus of my attention makes an FTL transit, I lose contact. You are my reset switch. You are also my blind spot coverage. If I am inaccessible when critical events occur, you are sufficiently intelligent and resourceful that, if adequately informed, you can act as my proxy aboard ship. Now. Are you ready?'

'Ready for—' Wednesday took a deep breath. 'What *am* I meant to be ready for?' she asked, her voice puzzled and slightly worried. 'Is it going to be dangerous?' She pulled on her jacket (which she had dilated to an ankle-skimming coat, showy but thin and useless against the elements).

'Yes.'

'Oh, how nice.' Wednesday pulled a face. 'Is there anything else?'

'Yes. You should be aware of several things. Firstly, there is another human agent of mine involved in this situation. His name is Martin Springfield. You can trust him implicitly if you meet him. He is acting as my unofficial liaison with another diplomatic element that is investigating the situation – more or less on the same side. Secondly, I owe you an apology.'

'An—' Wednesday stopped dead. 'What's that supposed to mean?' she asked suspiciously.

'I failed to prevent the destruction of your home world. I am worried, Wednesday. Preventing incidents like that is the purpose of my – this component's – existence. A failure to do so suggests a failure of my warning mechanisms. A failure of intelligence on my part suggests that the entities responsible for the destruction of Moscow are far more powerful than previously realized. Or are agencies of such an entity.'

Wednesday leaned against the wall. '*What?* But you're the Eschaton!'

'Not quite. It is true that I am a component of the ensemble intelligence referred to as the Eschaton.' Herman's voice had gone very flat, as if to emphasize the fact that any color in its tone was simply a modulation trick. 'The Eschaton preserves global causality within a realm approximately a thousand parsecs in radius. It does so by recursively transmitting information back in time to itself, which is used to allow it to edit out temporal anomalies. Such temporal paradoxes are an inevitable side effect of permitting faster-than-light travel, or of operating an ensemble intelligence employing timelike logic mechanisms. I receive orders from deep time and execute them knowing that in doing so I ensure that the descendant state vector is going to exist long enough to issue those orders. If I do *not* receive such orders, then it may be that the events are not observable by me. Or my future state vector. This situation may occur if the Eschaton is disrupted or edited out of the future of this time-line. I am advising you, Wednesday, that I *should* have prevented the destruction of Moscow. That I failed to do so raises questions over my future survival.'

'Oh fuck! You're telling me—'

'There appears to be a complex play in progress against me, executed by a party or parties unknown. I revise my previous estimate that the threat was emergent from the ReMastered. Their desire to destroy me is well understood, as are their capabilities, and countermeasures have been in place for some time. This threat emerges from a higher realm. The possibility of a hostile Eschaton-equivalent intelligence existing in the future of this light cone must now be considered. It is possible that a ReMastered faction is being manipulated by such an external entity. My ability to project ahead has therefore been called into question. Fallback logic modules employing neo-Bayesian reasoning suggest that when you return to the ship they will send a team of agents after you, but this is a purely speculative assumption. You must be on your guard at all times. Your job is to draw out the hostile proxies and expose them to me, starting at the embassy memorial ceremony. If you fail, the consequences could be far worse than the destruction of a single planet.'

Click. 'Oh shit.' For a moment she thought she was going to be all right, but then her stomach twisted. She barely made it to the bathroom in time, holding back the dry heaves until she was over the toilet bowl. *Why me? How did I end up in this mess?* she asked the mirror, sniffing and trying to dry her eyes. *It's like some kind of curse!*

Fifty minutes later, it was a shaken but more composed Wednesday who climbed the two steps down from the space elevator capsule into a concrete-and-steel arrivals hall, presented her passport to the immigration official, and staggered blinking into the late-afternoon sunlight on New Dresden.

'Wow,' she said softly.

Her rings vibrated for attention. She sighed. 'Cancel block.'

'Are you feeling less stressed?' asked Herman, as if nothing had happened.

'I think so.'

'Good. Now please pay attention to where we are going. I am adding your destination to the public geotracking system. Follow the green dot.'

'Green dot – okay.' A green dot appeared on the floor, and Wednesday followed it passively, feeling drained and depressed. She'd almost psyched herself into looking forward to the reception, but Herman's news had unhinged her again, bringing her tenuous optimism crashing down. Maybe Frank would be able to cheer her up, but just then she wanted only to go back to her luxury suite and lock the door and get stinking drunk.

It took another three hours of boredom, dozing in the seats of a maglev capsule hurtling at thousands of kilometers per hour through an evacuated tunnel buried deep under oceans and continents, before she arrived in the capital. *Typical, why couldn't they build the beanstalk closer to the main city? Or move the city?* she sniffed to herself. Getting around on a planet seemed to take a very long time, for no obvious reason.

Sarajevo was old, with lots of stone buildings and steel-and-glass skyscrapers. It was badly air-conditioned, with strange eddying breezes and air currents and a really disorienting, upsetting blue-and-white fractal plasma image in place of a decent ceiling. It was also full of strange-looking people in weird clothes moving fast and doing incomprehensible things. She passed three women in fake peasant costume – New Dresden had never been backward enough to have a real peasantry – waving credit terminals. A bunch of people in rainbow-colored luminous plastic gowns rollerbladed past, surrounded by compact remotes buzzing around at ear level. Cars, silent and melted-looking, slunk through the streets. A fellow in grimy ripped technical mountaineering gear, bubble tent folded at his feet, seemed to be offering her an empty ceramic coffee cup. People in glowing glasses gesticulated at invisible interfaces; laser dots all over the place danced ahead of people who needed guidance. It wasn't like Septagon, it was like—

It's like home. If home had been bigger and brasher and more developed, she realized, tenuously making a connection to her memories of their last family visit to Grandma's house.

One thing pricked her attention: it was the lack of difference. She'd been worried at first about going down-well wearing a party costume she'd have been comfortable with back home. 'Don't worry,' Herman told her. 'Moscow and Dresden are both McWorlds – the original colonists had similar backgrounds and aspirations. The culture will feel familiar to you. You can thank media diffusion for that; it will not be like the New Republic, or Turku, or even as different as Septagon.' And indeed, it wasn't. Even the street signs looked the same.

'And we were nearly *at war* with these people?' she asked.

'The usual stupid reasons. Competitive trade advantage, immigration policy, political insecurity, cheap slow transport – cheap enough to facilitate trade, too expensive to facilitate federalization or the other adjustments human nations make to minimize the risk of war. The McWorlds all took something from the dominant terrestrial globalized culture with them when they were settled, but they have diverged since then – in some cases, radically. Do not make the mistake of assuming you can discuss politics or actions of the government safely here.'

'As if I would.' Wednesday followed her green dot round a corner and up a spiraling ramp onto a road-spanning walkway, then into a roofed-over mall. 'Where am I supposed to be meeting Frank?'

'He should be waiting for you. Along this road. There.'

He was sitting on a bench in front of an abstract bronze sculpture, rattling away on his antique keyboard. Killing time. 'Frank, are you okay?'

He looked up at her and pulled a face – a grimace that might have been intended as a smile but succeeded in doing nothing to reassure her. His eyes were red-rimmed and had bags under them, and his clothing looked as if he'd been living in it for a couple of days. 'I, I think so.' He shook his head. 'Brr.' He yawned widely. 'Haven't slept for a long, uh . . .' He trailed off.

Party overload, she thought dispassionately. She reached out and took his hand, tugging. 'Come on!'

Frank lurched to his feet and caught his balance. The keyboard concertinaed away into a pocket. He yawned again. 'Are we in time?'

She blinked, checking her timepiece: 'Sure!' she said brightly. 'What have you been doing?'

'Not sleeping.' Frank shook himself. 'I'm a mess. Mind if I freshen up first?' He looked almost apologetic.

She grinned at him. 'That looks like a public toilet over there.'

'Okay. Two minutes.'

He took nearer to a quarter of an hour, but when he returned he'd had a shower and run his outerwear through a fastcleaner. 'Sorry 'bout that. Do I look better?'

'You look fine,' she said diplomatically. 'At least, you'll pass. Are you going to fall over on me?'

'Nope.' He dry swallowed a capsule and shuddered slightly. 'Not until we get back to the ship.' He tapped the pocket with his keyboard in it. 'Captured enough color for three features, interviewed four midlevel government officials and six random civilians, grabbed about four hours of full-motion. One *last* push and—' This time his smile looked less stressed.

'Okay, let's go.' She took his hand again and led him along the street.

'You know where we're going? The embassy reception hall?'

'Never been there.' She pointed at the floor. 'Got a guide.'

'Oh *good*, tell everyone where we're going,' he muttered.

'I just hope they don't mistake me for a vagrant.'

'An, uh, what? What was that?'

'A vagrant?' He raised an eyebrow at her. 'They don't have them where you come from? Lucky.'

She checked the word in her lexicon. 'I'll tell them you're my guest,' she said, and patted his hand. Having Frank around made her feel safe, like walking through a strange town with a huge and ferocious guard dog – the biological kind – to protect her. Her spirits rose as they neared the embassy.

Embassies were traditionally the public representatives of a nation abroad. As such, they tended to be built with a swagger, gratuitously broad facades and conspicuously gilded flagpoles. The Muscovite embassy was typical of the breed, a big, classically styled limestone-and-marble heap squatting sullenly behind a row of poplar trees, a discreet virtual fence, and a lawn that appeared to have been trimmed with a micrometer gauge and nail scissors. But something about it wasn't quite right. It might have been the flag out front – set to half-mast ever since the dreadful day, years ago, when the diplomatic causal channel went dead – or something more subtle. There was a down-at-heel air to it, of retired gentry keeping up appearances but quietly living beyond their means.

And then there was the security cordon.

'I'm Wed— uh, Victoria Strowger,' Wednesday chattered to the two armed cops as they examined her passport, 'and this is Frank Johnson, my guest, and isn't this exciting?' She clapped her hands as they waved her through the archway of an explosive sniffer. 'I can't believe I've been invited to a real embassy function! Wow, is that the Ambassador? No?'

'You don't have to lay it on quite that thick,' Frank said tiredly, catching up with her a minute later. 'They're not idiots. Pull a stunt like that at a *real* checkpoint, and they'll have you in an interrogation cell before your feet touch the ground.'

'Huh?' She shook her head. 'A real checkpoint? What was that about, then?'

'What it was about was telling everybody that there are guards about. There are all sorts of real defenses all around us, and barely out of view. Dogs, drones, all sorts of sur-veillance crap. Guess I was right – this stinks of a high-alert panic.'

'Oh.' She leaned closer to him as she glanced around. There was a large marquee dome behind one wing of the embassy, lights strung between trees – and a handful of adults, one or two of them in elaborate finery but most of them simply wearing office garb, wandering around clutch-ing glasses of fizzy wine. 'Are we in danger?' *From what Herman said—*

'I don't think so. At least, I hope not.'

There were tables in the dome, attentive catering staff and bottles of wine and battalions of glasses waiting to be filled, a spread of canapés and hand rolls and other bite-sized snacks laid out for the guests. A clump of bored-looking visitors clutched their obligatory glass and disposable platter, and in one or two cases a sad-looking handheld flag. The first time Wednesday saw a flag she had to look away, unsure whether to laugh or cry. Patriotism had never been a huge Muscovite virtue, and to see the way the fat woman in the red pants held on to her flag as if it were a life preserver made Wednesday want to slap her and yell *Grow up! It's all over!* Except it also felt like . . . like watching Jerm, aged three, playing with the pewter pot containing Grandpa's ashes. Abuse of the dead, an infection of history. And now, *he* was gone. She looked away, sniffed, and tried to clear the haze in her eyes. She'd never much liked her kid brother anyway, but not having him around to dislike felt *wrong*.

A man and a woman wearing sober outfits that would have been at home in a law office were working the guest crowd in a low-key manner. Wednesday's turn came remarkably fast. 'Hello, I'm pleased you could be here today,' said the woman, fixing Wednesday with a professionally polished smile that was almost as tightly lacquered as her hair. 'I'm Mary-Louise. I don't believe I've had the pleasure of meeting you before?'

'Hi, I'm Wednesday.' She forced a tired smile. Crying earlier had dried out the skin around her eyes. 'I'm just passing through, actually, on board the *Romanov*. Is this a regular event?'

'We host one like it every year to mark the anniversary. Is there one where you live, can I ask?'

'I don't think so,' Wednesday said doubtfully. 'Centris Magna, in Septagon. Quite a lot of us went there from Old Newfie—'

'Station eleven! Is that where you came from?'

'Yes.'

'Oh, very good! I had a cousin there. Listen, here's Subminister Hasek, come to be very cultural with us tonight. We've got food, drink, a media presentation, and Rhona Geiss will be singing – but I've got to see to everyone else. Help yourself to everything, and if you need anything else, Mr. Tranh there will see to you.' She vanished in a flurry of wide sleeves and coattails, leaving Wednesday to watch in bemusement as a corpulent old man the size of a brown bear shambled slowly into the dome, a gleaming, polished woman at either side. One of them reminded Wednesday of Steffi so much that she blinked, overtaken by an urge to say hello to the friendly ship's officer. When she looked again, the moment of recognition passed. A gaggle of teenagers gave ground to the threesome reluctantly as they walked in front of a circle of stewards setting up a table.

Wednesday accepted a glass of wine and cast around for Frank, but he'd wandered off somewhere while the greeters had been working her. *Expect trouble.* Sure, but what kind?

A row of glass doors had been shoved back from the room at one side of the embassy, and a couple of embassy staffers were arranging rows of chairs across the floor, then out onto the manicured lawn. The far wall of the reception room had become a screen, a blue-white-green disc eerily similar to the one Wednesday had seen from orbit as she boarded the orbit-to-surface elevator capsule. It floated in the middle of a sea of stars. *Home*, she thought, dully. She hadn't felt homesick for years, not really, and then it had been for Old Newfie rather than this abstraction of a place she'd been born on — but now she felt a certain dangerous nostalgia begin to bite, and an equal and opposite cynical impulse to sneer at the idea. *What has Moscow ever done for me?* she asked herself. Then memory stabbed at her: her parents, the look on Mayor Pocock's face as they'd hauled down the flag in the hub concourse before the evacuation . . . too many memories. Memories she couldn't escape.

Herman spoke in her earbud: 'Most people come for the readings, remain for the singing of the national anthem, *then* leave and get steaming drunk. You might want to emulate them.'

Twenty minutes and one glass of wine later, Wednesday found a corner seat at one end of the front row. The other visitors were filtering in slowly, nothing like as organized as a funeral party entering a chapel of rest. By all appearances a number of them were already leading her at the drinking.

As the room filled up, and some people spilled onto the

overflow chairs on the lawn, Wednesday felt someone sit in the chair next to her. 'Frank?' She glanced round.

'These are your people?' he said. Something in his expression made her wonder if he had internal ghosts of his own to struggle with. He seemed haunted by something.

'What is it?' she asked.

He shook his head. 'Some other time.' She turned round to face the front. A few stragglers were still filling the seats, but a door had opened to one side of the podium and a dig-nified-looking albeit slightly portly woman – possibly middle-aged, possibly a centenarian, it was difficult to tell – walked up to the stage.

With her chestnut hair tied back with a ribbon, her black embroidered coat buttoned at the waist and cut back above and below, and the diamond-studded chain of office draped across her shoulders, she was exactly what Wednesday had expected the Ambassador to be. She cleared her throat and the sound system caught and exploded her rasping breath across the lawn. 'Welcome,' she said. 'Again, welcome. Today is the fifth anniversary, absolute time stan-dard years, of the death, and exile, of our compatriots. I' – she paused, an unreadable expression on her face – 'I know that, like you, I have difficulty understanding that event. We can't go home, now or ever. The door is shut, all options closed. There is no sense of closure: no body in a coffin, no assailant under arrest and charged with murder.

'But—' She took a deep breath: '*I shall try to be brief.* We are still here, however much we mourn our friends and rela-tives who were engulfed by the holocaust. *We* survive. We bear witness. We go on, and we will rebuild our lives, and we will remember them.

'Someone destroyed our homes. As an agent of the sur-viving caretaker government, I dedicate my life to this task: to bear witness, and to identify the guilty parties, whoever they are and wherever they may be sheltering. They will be held to account, and the accounting will be sufficient to deter anyone else who ever contemplates such monstrous acts in future.'

She paused, head tilted slightly to one side as if she was listening to something – and, as she continued, Wednesday realized, *She is listening to something. Someone is reading her a speech and she's simply echoing it!* Startled, she almost missed the Ambassador's next words: 'We will now pause for a minute in silent contemplation. Those of us who believe in the intervention of higher agencies may wish to pray; those of us who don't may take heart from the fact that we are not alone, and we will make sure that our friends and families did not die in vain.'

Wednesday was disinclined to meditate on much of anything. She looked around surreptitiously, examining fixtures and fittings. The ambassador's girth – *She's not fat, but she's carrying a lot of padding around the waist. And those boxes around the podium . . . and the guy at the back there, and that woman in the dark suit and business glasses . . .* Something smelled wrong. In fact, something smelled *killing zone*, a game Herman had taught her years before. How to spot an ambush. *This is just like a, a trap*, she realized. *But who—*

Wednesday turned back and was watching the Ambassador's eyes as it happened. They widened slightly as somebody a couple of rows behind Wednesday made a nervous noise. Then the Ambassador snapped into motion, sudden as a machine, arms coming up to protect her face as she ducked.

Then:

Why am I lying down? Wednesday wondered fuzzily. *Why?* She could see, but everything was blurry and her ears ached. *I feel sick.* She tried to moan and catch her breath and there was an acrid stink of burning. Abruptly she realized that her right hand was wet and sticky, and she was curled around something bony. Dampness. She tried to lever herself up with her left hand, and the air was full of dust, the lights were out, and thinly, in the distance through the ringing in her ears, she heard screams.

A flicker of light. A moment later, she was clearer. The podium – the woman wasn't there. The boxes to either side had exploded like air bags, blasting heavy shields into the air in front of the Ambassador as she ducked. But behind her, behind them . . . Wednesday sat up and glanced down, realized someone was screaming. There was blood on the back of her hand, blood on her sleeve, blood on the chairs. *A bomb*, she thought fuzzily. Then: *I ought to do something.* People were screaming. A hand and an arm lay in the middle of the aisle next to her, the elbow a grisly red mess. Frank was lying on the floor next to her. The back of his head looked as if it had been sprayed with red paint. As she recognized him, he moved, one arm flailing at the ground in a stunned reflex. The woman who had been seated behind him was still seated, but her head ended in a glutinous stump somewhere between her neck and her nose. *Bomb,* Wednesday realized again, confused but trying to hold on to the thought. More thoughts: *Herman warned me. Frank!*

She leaned over him in panic. 'Frank! Talk to me!' He opened his mouth and tried to say something. She winced, unable to hear him. *Is he dying?* she wondered, feeling lost and anxious. 'Frank!' A dizzy laugh welled up as she tried to remember details from a first-aid course she'd taken years ago – *Is he breathing? Yes. Is he bleeding?* It was hard to tell; there was so much blood everywhere that she couldn't see if it was his. Frank mumbled something at her. He wasn't flailing around. In fact, he seemed to be trying to move. 'Wait, you mustn't—' Frank sat up. He felt around the back of his head and winced, then peered at Wednesday owlishly.

'Dizzy,' he said, and slowly toppled toward her.

Wednesday managed to brace herself with one arm as he fainted. *He must weigh over a hundred kilos*, she realized fuzzily. She looked round, searching for help, but the shout died in her throat. It hadn't been a big bomb – not much more than a grenade – but it had burst in the middle of the audience, ripping half a dozen bodies into bloody pulp, and splashing meat and bone and blood around like evil paint. A man with half his clothes blasted off his body and his upper torso painted red stumbled into the epicenter blindly, arms outstretched as if looking for someone. A woman, sitting in her chair like an incisor seated in a jaw between the empty red holes of pulled teeth, screamed and clutched her shredded arm. Nightmares merged at the edges, bleeding over into daylight, rawhead and bloodybones come out to play. Wednesday licked her lips, tasted bright metal dampness, and whimpered as her stomach tried to eject wine and half-digested canapés.

The next thing she knew, a man in black was standing over her, a gun at the ceiling – looking past her, talking urgently to a floating drone. She tried to shake her head. Something was crushing her. '—an you walk?' he said. '— your friend?'

'Mmf. Try.' She pushed against Frank's deadweight, and Frank tensed and groaned. 'Frank—' The guard was away, bending over another body and suddenly dropping to his knees, frantically pumping at a still chest.

'I'm, I'm—' He blinked, sleepily. 'Wednesday?'

Sit up, she thought fuzzily. 'Are you okay?'

'I think—' He paused. 'My head.' For a miracle, the weight on her shoulder slackened. 'Are you hurt?' he asked her.

'I—' She leaned against him, now. 'Not badly. I think.'

'Can't stay here,' he said faintly. 'The bomb. Before the bomb. Saw you, Sven.'

'Saw who?'

'Jim. Clown.' He looked as if he was fading. Wednesday leaned toward him. 'Sven was here. Wearing a waiter's—' His eyelids fluttered.

'Make sense! What are you *saying*?' she hissed, driven by a sense of urgency she didn't understand. 'What do you mean—'

'Svengali. Back. Performer.' His eyes opened. 'Got to find Sven.'

'Are you telling me you saw him—' Shock brought Wednesday into focus.

'Yes. Yes. Find him. He's . . .' Frank's eyes closed.

Wednesday waved at a passing guard: 'Here!' A head turned. 'My friend, concussion. Help?'

'Oh shit, another—' The guard waved one of her colleagues over. 'Medic!'

Wednesday slid after Frank, torn between a pressing need to see that he was all right and a conviction that she should go look for the clown. Leaving Frank felt *wrong*, like letting go of her only lifeline to stability. Just an hour ago he'd seemed so solid he could anchor her to the universe, but now everything was in flux. She stumbled toward the side door, her head whirling, guts churning. Her right hand stung, a hot, aching pain. *Svengali?* She wondered: *what could he be doing here?* A short passage and another open door brought her weaving and stumbling onto the lawn at the back of the embassy building. Bright light glared down from overhead floods, starkly silhouetting a swarm of cops buzzing around the perimeter like disturbed hornets. *Sven?* she thought.

She stumbled around the side of the building. A woman blocked her way: 'You can't come—'

'My friend!' She gasped, and pushed past. For some reason, no arms restrained her. Bodies were laid out on the grass under the harsh spotlights, some of them unmoving, others with people in paramedic orange frantically working over them. Other people stood or shambled around in a daze, prodded by a couple of enhanced police dogs that seemed to have a better idea of what was going on than any of the humans. Only a couple of minutes had passed, and the noise of sirens was still getting closer, audible over the ringing in her ears.

She found him squatting on the grass, wearing face cake and a red nose spattered with blood, holding his head in his hands. His costume was a clown's parody of a snobbish chef's outfit. 'Sven?' She gasped.

He looked up, eyes red, a trickle of blood running from one nostril. 'Wed-Wed—'

'We've got to go,' she said, trying to think of anything else that wasn't inane. 'We'll miss our, our . . .'

'You go, girl, I'll, I—' He shook his head, looking dizzy. 'Help?'

Was he here to perform? she asked herself. Then: 'You're hurt? Come on, on your feet. Back to the dining room. There's medical triage in there, first aid. Let's get you seen to and pick up Frank and catch a taxi. If we stay here, they'll ask questions till we miss the ship.'

'Ship.' His hands came down. He looked at her eyes cautiously, expression slightly puzzled. 'Came here to, had to, set up? Frank? Hurt? Is he—'

'Deafened and shocked, I think.' She shivered, feeling cold. 'But we can't just—'

'We can. Listen, you're one of my *two* guests, right? And we'll give them a statement but we've got to do that right now, our ship leaves tonight. If you're a guest, they won't grill you like a performer or staff. I hope.'

Svengali tried to stand up, and Wednesday backed off to give him room. 'Must. Just tell the, the medics—' He staggered, and somehow Wednesday caught his left arm and pulled it over her shoulder – and she was walking Svengali drunkenly around toward the front of the embassy as the first ambulance arrived on a whine of electric motors.

grateful dead

'I don't fucking *believe* this!'

Rachel had never, ever, seen George Cho lose his temper before. It was impressive, and would have been frightening if she hadn't had more important things to worry about than her boss flapping around like a headless chicken.

'They missed,' she said with forced detachment. 'Six dead and however many more injured, but they missed. The reactive armor deflected most of the shrapnel straight up, and I hit the floor in time.' She clenched her hands together to keep them from shaking.

'Why weren't the grounds sealed off afterward? Why don't we know who – the cameras—'

'Did you think they would be amateurs?' she asked angrily, pacing past him to look out the window overseeing the lawn. The indoor lights had blown, along with most of the unshielded electronics in the embassy. The EMP pulse had been small, but was sufficient to do for most non-MilSpec equipment on-site. And someone had done a real number on the cameras with a brace of self-adhesive clown-face stickers. 'Murderous clowns, but not amateurs.'

The convoy of ambulances had taken most of the injured to various local clinics, which had activated their major incident plans immediately. Those vehicles that were left were parked, sirens silenced, not in any hurry to remove the bodies until the SOC team had finished mapping the mess left by the bomb and Forensics had taken their sample grams of flesh, and the polite men and women in their long black coats had asked their pointed questions of the catering staff—

'We set them up for a long gun,' Rachel reminded him, shuddering slightly. Remembering the icy feeling in her guts as she'd walked out onstage wearing a bulletproof vest, knowing there was a reactive armor shield in front of her, and a crash cart with resuscitation and stabilization gear waiting behind the door, and an ambulance in back. Knowing that a sniper would have to shoot in through a fixed arc constrained by the windows and the podium at the back of the room, knowing the ballistic radar at the front of the killing zone *should* be able to blow the armor slabs into the path of a bullet-sized guided missile before it could reach her, knowing there were two anti-sniper teams waiting in the hedgerow out front – she'd still been unsure whether each breath would be her last. 'They weren't stupid. Didn't bring a knife to a gunfight. Took an antipersonnel mine instead.'

'And they got away with it again.' George sat down heavily on the edge of the lacquered and jade-inlaid desk, head bowed. 'We should have fucking *known*—'

'Tranh?' called Rachel.

'We leaked,' the researcher said quietly. 'We made it a honeypot, and we attracted the wasps, but probably only one of the passengers from the *Romanov* was involved, and we can't tell which one because they fried the surveillance records and probably exfiltrated among the wounded. For all we know the assassin is among the dead. Worse, if they're from an advanced infrastructure society like Septagon or somewhere with access to brain-mapping gear, the killer could have been any other guest or member of staff they managed to get five minutes alone with. And we couldn't prove a thing. It looks like the only thing left to do is bring down the hammer and stop the ship leaving. Detain everybody. Want me to get on line to Martin? Have him lock it down?'

'Don't do that yet,' said Rachel.

'Yes, do it,' said Cho. He took a deep breath. 'We're going to have to arrest them,' he told Rachel. 'Even if it tips them off. They already know something – must suspect, surely, or else they wouldn't have declined the honeypot—'

'Not necessarily,' Rachel said urgently. 'Listen, if you hold the ship, we'll probably uncover an assassin – a *dead* one, if these people are as ruthless as we think. If we do that, what happens next? I'll tell you what happens next: there's a hiatus, then a different killer starts making the rounds, and this time we'll have broken the traffic analysis chain so we won't know where they are or where they're going next. We need to let them run – but we have to stay in front of them.'

George stood up and paced across the room. 'I can't take the risk. They've grown increasingly reckless, from selective assassination to indiscriminate bombing! What next, a briefcase nuke? Don't you think they're capable of that?'

'They—' Rachel stopped dead. 'They almost certainly are,' she admitted. 'But don't you think that makes it all the more important that we keep track of them and try to take them alive, so we can find out who's behind it?'

'You want to go aboard the ship,' said Tranh.

'I don't see any alternative.' There was a horrible famil-
iarity to the situation; to keep on top of a crisis moving at
FTL speeds, you had to ride the bullet. 'My recommen-
dation is that we let the *Romanov* depart on schedule, but
that I — and any other core team members you see fit to
assign to me — should be on board as passengers, and you
serve your bill of attainder on the Master and tell her
that she's damn well going to do as I say in event of an
emergency.

'Meanwhile, the rest of the team should proceed aboard
the *Gloriana* to the next destination where there's a
Muscovite embassy — I think that'll be Vienna? Or wherever — and set up the next trap. Leaving behind a
diplomatic support group here to keep an eye on Morrow
and Baxter, and anyone off the *Romanov* who's staying on.'
She swallowed. 'While we're under way, I'll liaise with the
ship's crew to try to identify anyone who's acting suspiciously. Before and after the events. Martin may have
spotted something while we were busy down here, but I
haven't had time to check yet. If we can get access to the
onboard monitoring feeds, we might be able to wrap everything up before we arrive at the next port of call.'

'You'll have no backup,' said Cho. 'If they panic and
decide to bury the evidence—'

'I'll be right there to stop them,' Rachel said firmly. She
glanced out the window. 'It won't be the first time. But if
we do it, we have to do it right now. The *Romanov* is due to
depart in less than five hours. I need to be on board with a
sensible cover story and a full intrusion kit. A diplomatic
bag, if possible, with full military cornucopia, just like the
one we used last time.' She pretended not to notice George's
wince. 'And I need to get out of this fucking rubber mask,
and call Martin to tell him to stay aboard the *Romanov*, if
you don't mind.'

'If I—' George shook his head. 'Tranh. How do you evaluate Rachel's proposed course of action?'

'I'm afraid she's right,' Tranh said stiffly. 'But I—' he paused. 'Who do you need?'

'For a job like this?' Rachel shrugged. '*Nobody* is ready for this. I submit that the best cover is no cover. If I go with Martin, we should be overt – a couple of UN diplomats taking low-priority transport between postings, to meet up with the rest of our mission on Newpeace. No cover story at all, in other words – it takes the least effort to set up and it also gives me a clear line of authority back home, reason to talk to the Captain, that sort of thing. I'll—' She looked worried. 'First New Prague, then Newpeace. I heard that name before somewhere, didn't I? Something bad, some atrocity.'

'Newpeace.' George made a curse of it. 'Yes. You don't want to go there without immunity. Even *with* immunity. I'm going to have to send you the internal briefings on the place, Rachel. You don't want to land there.'

'Is it that bad?'

'It's a dictatorship run by the ReMastered,' Tranh said grimly. 'Nasty little local ideology that seems to pop up like a poisonous toadstool in patches. And that fits with a bit of intel our back-office trawl pulled in. We've been grepping the public feeds for any references to Moscow, and we got a high probability hit off of a warblogger who's traveling on the *Romanov*. He's poking around the Moscow business from the other end, making some unsubstantiated but very paranoid suggestions about survivors – not diplomats – being tracked down and murdered. What's *more* interesting is that he's on board the *Romanov* and ReMastered was one of the keyword hits that flagged his column in our trawl. Nothing but innuendo so far, and he's got an axe to grind – I was following up his history when things fell apart here – but they're a local power, and they've been known to meddle in foreign affairs before now.'

'They're also ruthless enough that if they're involved in this mess, I don't want you going anywhere near one of their worlds, with or without diplomatic papers,' George added. 'Look, you've got five hours until departure, and you're going to take at least three to get up the beanstalk and into orbit. Get going. Get ready. I'll get Gianni to open a credit line to the mission for you to use, and you, Tranh, you're going along as Rachel's backup. Make sure to brief her on who these ReMastered are, just in case. Rachel, Martin will travel with you. He knows the ship, so he's your technical adviser. We'll talk by channel once you're under way and damn the expense. Right now I've got this mess to clean up. So don't hang around.' He extended a hand. After a moment, Rachel took it. 'Good luck,' he said. 'I've got a feeling you're going to need it.'

The horror never ended, but after a while you could learn to live with it, Rachel reflected. Or rather, you learned to live *between* it, in the intervals, the white space between the columns of news, the quiet, civilized times that made the job worthwhile. You learned to live in order to make the whitespace bigger, to *reduce* the news, to work toward the end of history, to make the universe safe for peace. And you knew it was a zero-sum game at best and eventually you'd lose, but you were on the right side so that didn't matter. Somebody had to do it. And then—

Scum. There was no other word for it. Fragmentation grenades in the audience at a nondenominational secular-friendly memorial ceremony spelled *scum*. The audience screaming, a child with her hand blown off, a woman with no head. The pale-faced girl in the front row, desperately leaning over her friend, his head bloodied by the—

'Is the payload ready?' she asked mildly.

'One moment.' Pritkin unplugged his diagnostic probe. 'Primed. Stick your finger in here. Shared secret time.'

'Okay.' Rachel extended a hand, wrapped her fingers around the probe and waited for it to bleep, signifying successful quantum key exchange. Pritkin stuck the probe back into the slot in the large traveler's trunk and waited for the light on its base to begin blinking red. Then he ejected it. 'It's all yours. Armed and loaded.' He straightened up and put the probe away.

'Which department is this one billed to?' Rachel asked. 'After the last time . . .'

'Department of Collective Defense.' Pritkin smiled grimly. 'You may find its inventory tree a little alarming.'

'Indeed.' Rachel eyed the trunk appraisingly. 'Full military fabworks?'

'Yup. This little cornucopia can, with a bit of guidance and your authority, generate an entire military-industrial complex. Try not to lose it.'

'Once was an accident, twice would be careless. All right.' She spoke to the trunk. 'Do you recognize me?'

The trunk spoke back, in a flat monotone: 'Authorized officer commanding. You have control.'

'Hey, I like that. Trunk, follow me.' She nodded to Pritkin. 'See you at Newpeace.'

Scum! she thought, her rage controlled for the time being, directed and channeled. *I'm coming for you. And when I find you, you'll be sorry . . .*

The express elevator up the beanstalk gave Rachel time to confront the horrors and try to shove them back into a corner of her mind. Tranh, she noted, was even more quiet and reserved than normal. The elevator car was almost two-thirds full, carrying a good number of crew members and tourists returning to the *Romanov* before it departed; also a sprinkling of quiet, worried-looking Dresdener citizens. While the R-bombs remained decades away, and the recall codes could still be issued, the panic hadn't set in. Only the most paranoid tinfoil-hat wearers would be thinking about emigrating already. But with a population of hundreds of millions, even the lunatic fringe was large enough to populate a medium-sized city, and some of the middle-aged men and small family groups wore the cautious, haunted expression of refugees. They'd probably be checking in to steerage, to sleep away the long jump sequence without spending precious savings. Rachel figured her assassin wouldn't be among them. He or she would want to be awake, to plan the next atrocity and keep a weather eye open for pursuers.

She tilted her seat back as far as it would go and waited for the oppressive shove of acceleration to go away. The car was only pulling two gees, but it was enough to make walking unfeasible and lifting a drinking cup uncomfortably difficult. The glowing blue space elevator cable zipped past beyond the transparent ceiling, an endless string with knots flickering by several times a second – the bulbous shells of the boost coils that coupled the car to its invisible magnetic corridor. *They're up there*, she reminded herself. *Along with a couple of thousand innocent passengers and crew.* Over six hundred people had come down from the *Romanov* while it was docked; nearly four hundred had returned to the ship. Of those, three hundred and fifty had been aboard the ship – and taken their leave on the surfaces of each planet it had visited, including the ones where Muscovite diplomats had been attacked.

Only twenty or so of the passengers had been at the embassy reception, but that didn't mean anything. *If it is a bunch like the ReMastered, there won't be a causal link*, she decided. *They're not fools.* She'd spent the first hour of the journey skimming George's diplomatic backgrounder on known ReMastered black operations and was wondering how the hell she'd failed to hear about them before. *It's a big galaxy, but not that big when you get, what was Rosa's term, bampots like these running amok.* Working to a hunch was risky; it could blind you to who was really pulling your strings – but now she'd seen Tranh's dossier, Rachel had a gut-deep feeling that they were somehow involved. The whole thing had the stench of diplomatic black ops all over it, and these guys were clearly crazy and ruthless enough to be responsible. The only question was *why*.

'Why the fuck didn't you tell us this was a possibility?' she'd asked Tranh, halfway through reading – and then rereading in disbelief – the first page.

He'd shrugged apologetically, squirming under the acceleration load. 'George said to keep it low-key. To avoid prejudicing the investigation.'

'Prejudice, hah.' Rachel had looked away.

Despite her violent aversion to museums, Rachel had an overdeveloped sense of historical contingency. Thanks to the arrival of cheap life-prolongation mods, her generation was one of the first to have lived through enough history to have a bellyful of it. She'd grown up in a throwback religious community that didn't accept any social development postdating the midtwentieth century, and spent her first few adult decades as a troubled but outwardly dutiful surrendered wife. Then she'd hit middle age and jumped the hedge to see the world, the flesh, and the devil for herself. Along the way she'd acquired a powerful conviction that history was a series of accidents – God was either absent or playing a very elaborate practical joke (the Eschaton didn't count, having explicitly denied that it was a deity) – and that the seeds of evil usually germinated in the footprints of people who knew how everybody else ought to behave and felt the need to tell them so. When she'd been born, there had still been people alive who remembered the Cold War, the gray behemoth of ideology slouching toward a nuclear destination. And the ReMastered rang some uneasy bells in the echoing library of her memory. She'd heard of things like this before. *Why hasn't anybody stepped on them yet?* she wondered.

As she considered the question there was a chime. The elevator car slowed, and, for a stomach-churning moment, spun upside down. Acceleration resumed, pressing down on her like a lead-weighted net. 'We will arrive in reception bay three in approximately nineteen minutes,' announced the cabin attendant. 'Slowing to one gee two minutes before arrival, if you need to use the en suite facilities.'

Tranh caught her eye. 'You ready?' He grunted.

'Yes.' Rachel didn't elaborate. Tranh was nervous, and he'd let her know. 'Done reading.' She tapped her secure notepad to demonstrate, and he attempted to nod – unwise and uncomfortable, judging from his grimace. Earlier, Rachel had tried holding the pad up, two-handed, and found it workable, except that her arms tried to go to sleep if she held the position for more than a couple of minutes. For a gadget that could fit in her wallet it felt remarkably like a lead brick. But there was something unhealthily compulsive about reading about the ReMastered. It was like scratching a fleabite until it bled: she didn't want to do it but found herself unable to stop.

Scum, she thought as she read the in-depth report on Newpeace. *How did they get away with it? It's the most brilliant, horrible, thing I've seen in years.* It made the imperial megalomania and straitlaced frigidity of the New Republic seem cozy and forgivable by comparison. *Seminars on history's most onerous tyrannies – so they know which errors of leniency to avoid?*

The planet arrayed above her head was showing a visible disc, gibbous and misty, with a thin rind of atmosphere. *Are they out to conquer this world, too?* she wondered. The ReMastered showed every sign of being aggressively expansionist, convinced their ideology was the one true way. But logistical nightmares and the presence of STL bombers around almost every target world made interstellar power grabs unfeasibly risky. It was as if, during Earth's nineteenth century, every imperialist set on colonizing another land had been forced to resupply by wooden sailing ship across the breadth of the Pacific Ocean, while facing defenders armed with nuclear-tipped missiles.

'So they came from Tonto and executed a classic Maoist-Fischerite insurgency campaign, mediated by zombies with brain implants driven by causal channel from a nest in the same solar system,' she noted beneath a harrowing account of the Peace Enforcement Agency's subversion. Arranging a terrorist insurgency to justify a state clampdown, then providing the tools and trained personnel for the panicking incumbents to deploy, before decapitating them in a coup and consolidating power. 'Hmm.' *And if they grab the levers of power cleanly, before anyone realizes that half their politicians are brain-scooped moppets, they can decommission the STL bombers before they become a threat. Which in turn means . . . Hey, have they actually invented a repeatable strategy for interstellar conquest? And if so, did they come from somewhere else, before Tonto? In which case . . .*

The whole ReMastered project, to destroy the Eschaton and replace it with another god, one with access to the uploaded memories of every human being who'd ever lived – and then to re-create humanity in the image of the new god they intended to serve – sounded so ridiculous on the face of it that it pleaded to be written off as a crackpot religion from the darkness beyond the terrestrial light cone.

But something about it made Rachel's skin crawl. *I've heard of something like this before, somewhere else. But where?*

She was still trying to answer the question when there was a succession of chimes, the elevator capsule spun around once more, and the view was replaced with smooth metal walls inching past at a snail's pace. She had her safety harness unbuckled before the attendant managed to say, 'Welcome to orbital transfer station three.' By the time the doors were open, she was on her feet with her pad stowed in a pocket, ready to collect her luggage from the hold.

The station blurred past her, unnoticed: departure gates, an outgoing customs desk she cleared with an imperious wave of her diplomatic tags, bowing and scraping from functionaries, a luggage trolley to carry her heavy case. Then she reached a docking tunnel that was more like a shopping mall, all carpet and glassed-in side bays exhibiting the blandishments of a hundred luxury stores and hotels. The white-gloved officer from the purser's team at the desk took one look at her passport and priority pass, and tried to usher her through into a VIP lift. She had to make him wait until Tranh caught up.

'Where are we berthed?' she asked.

'Ah, if I can see your – ah, I see.' The Junior Lieutenant blinked through the manifest. 'Ma'am, sir, if you'd like to follow me, you're to be accommodated on Bravo deck, that's executive territory. I show a Queen-class suite reserved for each of you. If you'd just care to wait a moment while I find out if they're ready – this was a very-short-notice booking, I'm terribly sorry – ah, yes. This way. Please?'

'Is Martin Springfield about?' she asked anxiously.

'Springfield? I know of no – oh, him. Yes he is. He's in a meeting with Flying Officer Fromm. Do you want me to page him for you?'

'No, that's fine. We're traveling together. If you could

message him my room details when he comes out of his meeting?'

More corridors, more lifts. Exquisite wood paneling, carved on distant worlds and imported at vast expense for the fitting-out of the liner. Gilded statuary in niches, hand-woven rugs on the floors of the first-class quarters. *So this is what Martin works on for a living?* she wondered. A door gaped wide and two white-uniformed stewards bowed as Rachel tiredly led her luggage inside. 'That will be all for now, thanks,' she said, dismissing them. As the door closed, she looked around. 'Well, that's an improvement over the last time . . .'

Last time Rachel had traveled on a diplomatic passport she'd had a cramped berth in officer territory on a battle-cruiser. This time she probably had more space to herself than the Admiral's suite. She locked the door, bent to unfas-ten her shoes, and stretched her feet in the thick pile carpet. 'I ought to do this more often,' she told the ceiling. Her eyes were threatening to close from exhaustion – she'd been on her feet and alert for danger most of the time since the debacle at the embassy, and it was four in the morning, by Sarajevo local time – but business came first. From her shoulder bag she removed a compact receiver and busied herself quartering the room until she was satisfied that the only wireless traffic she could pick up consisted of legit-imate emanations from room service. She sighed and put the machine down, then raised her phone. 'Voice mail for Martin, copy to Tranh,' she said. 'I'm going to crash out for four hours, then I'm going back on duty. Call me if there are any developments. If not, we'll meet up to discuss our strategy tomorrow after I have time to talk to the Captain. Martin, feel free to come round whenever you get out of your meeting. Over.'

Finally, she checked the door. It was locked. *Good*, she

thought. She walked over to the bed, set a wake-up alarm on her rings, and collapsed, not bothering to undress first. She was asleep almost as soon as her head hit the pillows, and the nightmares, when they came, were as bad as she'd feared.

Lights, sirens, and night. A welter of impressions had closed around Wednesday, threatening to engulf her and cast her adrift on a sea of nightmare fodder. Svengali staggered alongside her, nursing an arm. A paramedic shone a torch in her face. She waved it aside. 'He needs help!' she shouted, holding the clown upright. She sat beside him for an eternity while a paramedic strapped up his arm, ran a terahertz scanner across his skull to check for fractures – someone else was working on her bruised forehead, but it was hard to keep track of things.

An indeterminate time later she was standing up. 'We need to get to the port,' she was explaining in nightmare slow motion to a police officer who didn't seem to understand: 'Our ship leaves in a couple of hours—'

She kept having to repeat herself. Why did she keep having to repeat herself ? Nobody was listening. Lights, sirens. She was sitting down now, and the lights were flashing past and the sirens were overhead . . . *I'm in a police car*, she realized hazily. Sitting between Svengali and Frank. Frank had one arm around her shoulders, sheltering her. But this was wrong. They hadn't done anything wrong, had they? Were they under arrest? *Going to miss the flight—*

'Here you go.' The door opened. Frank clambered out, then held Wednesday's arm, helping her out of the car. 'We're holding the capsule for you – step this way.' And it was true. She felt tears of relief prickling at her eyelids, trying to escape. Leaning on Frank. Svengali behind her, and two more carloads – the police were helping, shunting the off-worlders off-world. The full VIP treatment. *Why?* she wondered vaguely. Then a moment's thought brought it home: *Anything to look helpful to the diplomats . . .*

Wednesday began to function again sixty kilometers above the equator, as the maglev pod began to power up from subsonic cruise to full orbital ascent acceleration.

'How do you feel?' she asked Frank, her voice sounding distant and flat beneath the ringing in her ears.

'Like shit.' He grimaced. His head was bandaged into something that resembled a translucent blue turtle shell and he looked woozy from the painkillers they'd planted on him. 'Told me to go straight to sick-bay.' He looked at her, concerned. 'Did you just say something?'

'No,' she said.

'You'll have to speak up. I'm having difficulty hearing.'

'What happened to Sven?' she asked.

Svengali, who was sitting on Frank's far side, took it on himself to answer. 'Someone tried to kill the Ambassador,' he said slowly. 'The Dresdener government shat a brick. I have no idea why they let us go—'

'No. It was you,' Frank said flatly. 'Because you're Muscovite. Aren't you?'

'Yes.' Wednesday nodded uncertainly. 'Whatever that means . . .'

'So.' Frank nodded tiredly. 'They assumed your guests were, too. As the embassy net was down and all they had to go on were passports issued by wherever the guests lived – you're traveling on Septagon ID, but you're not a citizen yet, right?'

'Oh.' Wednesday shook her head slowly, her neck muscles complaining because of the unaccustomed gee load. '*Oh!* Who could it be?' she asked hesitantly. 'I thought you said whoever was after me—' Her eyes narrowed.

'Who's after you?' Svengali asked, clearly puzzled.

'I was *sure.*' Frank looked frustrated. 'The, the security alert. They canceled my interviews. In fact, that was the only public appearance the Ambassador put in while we were groundside. And did you notice the way she didn't go outside? Didn't even move outside of that podium with the reactive armor? But they left the windows and doors open. And there were cops everywhere on the grounds as soon as that bomb went off. Didn't she look padded—'

'The Ambassador was miming the speech,' said Wednesday.

'What?' Svengali looked surprised. 'What do you mean she was miming?'

'I saw her,' Wednesday said. 'I was right in the front row. It was the way she spoke – and she was wearing an earbud. From where I was sitting I could see it. Wearing body armor, too, I guess. You know what? I think they *expected* something to happen. Only not what did, if you follow me.'

'An assassination attempt. The wrong assassination attempt.' Frank sounded almost dreamy. 'On the wrong target. Not you, Wednesday.' He gave her arm a light squeeze. 'A different assassin. One who didn't play ball. Sven, what were you doing down there?'

'I was hired to do a fucking floor show after dinner!' he snapped tensely. 'What do you think? This isn't a vacation for me, laughing boy.'

'That's okay,' said Frank. He closed his eyes and leaned back in his chair.

'Sorry,' Svengali grumbled.

'This would be for the house you're planning on buying when you retire,' prompted Wednesday, a cold sweat prickling in the small of her back.

'Yeah, that's it,' Svengali agreed, sounding almost grateful.

'I hope you get there,' she said in a small voice.

'I hope they find the fucking assholes who crashed the party,' Frank said, sounding distantly angry. Wednesday stroked his knuckles, soothing him into silence, then leaned against his shoulder.

The rest of the trip back to orbit passed uneventfully.

interlude: 3

Several new passengers had joined the *Romanov* at New Dresden. One of them had taken an imperial suite with the nobs on A deck while the rest were accommodated variously in business- and tourist-class staterooms, but all of them had these things in common: they had booked rooms on the liner at short notice roughly a day after a private yacht, the *Heidegger*, had briefly called at Dresden station, and they were all traveling under false passports.

The luxury suite was not an extravagance, but a necessity. As was the way Lars swept it regularly for transmitters and the various species of insect that might creep into a room aboard a luxury liner that had been booked by an arms merchant from Hut Breasil. Portia wanted the cubic volume for conferencing and a base of operations, and the cover identity excused some of the rather more alarming contents of her personal luggage. Which was why Mathilde, answering the invitation to visit the imperial suite, was startled to find the door being held open for her by an armed bodyguard and the room's occupant seated on a chaise longue in front of an open crate of self-propelled gun launchers.

'U. Mathilde Todt. Come in.' Hoechst inclined her head. 'You look confused,' she said.

'Ah. I was expecting—'

Hoechst beamed at her. 'An austerity regime?' She rose. 'Yes, well, cover identities must be maintained. And why would a rich arms dealer travel in cabbage class?'

Marx let the door close behind the woman. She stepped forward, as if sleepwalking. 'It's been too long.'

Hoechst nodded. 'Consider yourself under direction again.'

Mathilde rubbed her face. 'You're my new control? Out here in person?' A note of gratified surprise crept into her voice.

'Unlike U. Scott, I don't believe in letting things slide,' Hoechst said drily. 'I've been running around for the past two months, tying ligatures around leaks. Now it's your turn. Tell me how it's going.'

'It's—' Mathilde licked her lips – 'I've got everything in place for both the scenarios I was given, the abduction or the other one. Everything except the primary strike team. We've scoped out all the critical points, and the necessary equipment is on board. We had to suborn three baggage loaders and one bellboy to get it in place, but it's done, and they swallowed the cover story – there was no need to get technical with them.' *Getting technical* was a euphemism for sinking a tree of nanoelectrodes into their brain stems and turning them into moppets – meat puppets. What it left behind afterward wasn't much use for anything except uploading and forwarding to the Propagators. 'Peter is my number two in charge of line ops, and Mark is ready with the astrogation side of things. In fact, we're ready to go whenever you give the word.'

'Good.' Hoechst was no longer smiling. 'Now tell me what's gone wrong. I want to know *everything*.'

'With the plan? Nothing's—'

'No, I mean *everything*. Every little thing that might have drawn attention to you.'

'Uh, well, um. We're not used to working undercover or in feral conditions, and I think we made one or two mistakes in the early days. Luckily our ops cover is just about perfect; because they know we're ReMastered, they make allowances for our being odd. It's astonishing how willing they are to believe that we're harmless passengers. Nobody even questioned that we were a youth leadership group! I thought it was absurd—'

Portia cleared her throat pointedly. Mathilde nearly jumped out of her skin. 'Let's get something straight.' Hoechst's gaze drilled into the young task group leader. 'If you've done your job right, you have nothing to fear. If you've made honest but noncritical mistakes, and admit them and help remedy the situation, you have nothing to fear. What you should be afraid of is the consequences of *covering up*. Do I make myself clear? So cut the nervous chatter and tell me. What went wrong? What should I be aware of?'

'Oh.' Mathilde stared at her for a moment as if she'd sprouted a second head. Then her shoulders slumped very slightly. 'Hans made a scene with one of the passengers on our first night aboard ship. We were all in one of the social areas – a bar, I believe they call them – when one of the ferals attempted to poison him with some sort of intoxicant. Nobody hurt, though. There is a small but vociferous group of passengers who appear to dislike us for some reason. But apart from that, not much has happened that I would classify as untoward. Hans I disciplined, and I consider the matter closed. The others—' She shrugged. 'I cannot control what feral humans think of our program. I was uncertain I should even draw it to your attention . . .'

'I understand completely.' Hoechst bent her head over the cargo case, inspecting the boxy black plastic contents within. 'The, ah, excesses of some of our predecessors have cast ReMastery in a very poor light, I'm afraid, and our overall goal of extending its benefits to everyone can only make them more suspicious.' She brooded for a moment. 'I don't intend to aggravate the situation.' She looked up, catching Mathilde's gaze: 'There will be no reports of atrocities or excesses arising from this intervention. One way or another.'

Mathilde smiled slowly.

Wednesday ran through abandoned hab spaces in the high-gee rings of an ancient station. Doorways gaped like empty eye sockets to either side of her; the floor sucked at her heels like molasses, dragging her backward. Something unseen ran behind her, dogging her footsteps like a nightmare – the skitter of claws, the clack of boots. She knew it was sharpening knives for her, but she couldn't remember why – everything behind her was blank. Ahead of her was bad, too. Something hidden, something waiting. The pursuer was catching up, and when it caught her a fountain of red pulp splattered across her face. She was in the entrance to a toilet block on the admin deck, and there was a body and when she tugged at it, saying, 'Come on, Dad,' it looked round and it wasn't her father, blue-faced with asphyxia; it was Sven the clown, and he was *smiling*.

She came awake with a gasp. Her heart felt as if it was about to burst, and the sheets under her were cold and clammy with sweat. Her left arm was numb, trapped under her because she lay on her side and behind—

A grunting snuffle that might have been a snore. She shifted, and he rolled against her back, curled protectively around her. Wednesday closed her eyes and leaned back. *Remember*, she thought dreamily, and shuddered. She could still almost smell the hot metallic taste of blood on her lips, the fecal stink of ruptured intestines. She'd gone to her stateroom and scrubbed for half an hour in the shower, but still felt as if she was soiled by the visceral fallout. Then he'd called, from the sick-bay, checking out. She'd told him she wanted to see him, and he'd come to her. Opened the door and dragged him inside and down onto the floor like animals. His urgency was as strong as hers. She smiled, still sleepy, and shuffled her hips back toward him until she could feel his penis against the small of her back.

'Frank?' she said quietly.

Another mumbled snore. He moved against her in his sleep. He'd been very careful: aware of his physical bulk. Not what she'd expected, but what she'd needed. Afterward, they'd clung together as if they were drowning, and he'd cried. *Is this wise?* she wondered. And then: *Who cares?*

Sleeping, Frank surrounded her. The slow rumble of his breath and the huge bulk of his body made her feel safe, really safe, for the first time since the terrible night of the party. She knew it for a bitter illusion, but it was a good one, and comforting. *I hope he doesn't want to pretend this never happened*, she mused.

An indefinite time later, Wednesday carefully crawled out of bed to go to the bathroom. Almost as soon as she was upright, her earlobe vibrated like an angry bee. 'Hello?' she said angrily, trying to subvocalize. 'What kind of time do you call this?'

'Wednesday.' It was her own voice, weird and hollow-sounding as usual when it came from outside her own head. 'Can you hear me?'

'Yeah. Herman? It's middle of night shift here. I was trying to sleep.'

'Your motion triggered a callback to alert me. The ship you are on has already undocked and is now accelerating toward its primary jump point. Once it jumps, the causal channel I am currently using will decohere, and you will be on your own. Normally the *Romanov*'s flight plan would take it via two hops to New Prague, but a number of new passengers joined the ship at Dresden station, and you can expect a diversion.'

'*A diversion?*' Wednesday yawned, desperately wishing she was awake, or back in bed. She glanced through the door wistfully: Frank was a dark mountain range across the spine of the sleeping platform.

'The ReMastered group aboard your vessel has been exchanging coded communications with the office of an arms dealer from Hut Breasil. The arms dealer and their bodyguards are now aboard the *Romanov*. At the same time, the arms dealer has exchanged message traffic with the office of one Overdepartmentsecretary Blumlein on Newpeace, the de facto chairman of the Planetary Oversight Directorate and maximum leader of the Ministry of State Security. I lack informants on the ground, but I believe the arms dealer is a cover identity for a senior MOSS official who is taking personal control over the mop-up operation arising from their internal conflict over the incident at Moscow.'

'Whoa — stop! What do you mean? What mop-up? MOSS? What internal conflict?' Wednesday clutched her head. 'What's this got to do with me?' I *want to go back to bed!*

Herman kept his tone of voice even and slow, patient as ever. 'I am developing a hypothesis about the destruction of your home, and the motivation behind the assassinations. Moscow system, and New Dresden, lie along the ReMastered race's axis of expansion. Newpeace and Tonto are merely their most recent conquests, and the closest to Earth. They lie close to both Moscow and New Dresden, and those worlds would be logical targets for subversion and conquest. However, the ReMastered are prone to internal rifts and departmental feuding. They can be manipulated by outside influences such as the Eschaton. It is possible that one such department within the Ministry of State Security on Newpeace was induced to exploit their growing influence over domestic political figures in Moscow to use them as a proxy agency in a side project, the development of a causality-violation weapon. Such devices are hazardous not only because the Eschaton intervenes to prevent their deployment later up the time line, but because they tend to be unstable—'

'Later up the *what*? Hey, I thought you *were* the Eschaton! What *is* this?'

'Can a T-helper lymphocyte in a capillary in your little finger claim to be you? Of course I am part of the Eschaton, but I cannot claim to *be* the Eschaton. The Eschaton acquires most of its power by being able to harness causality violation – time travel – for computational purposes. Working causality-violation devices in the hands of others – whether designed as weapons, or as time machines, or as computers – would threaten the stability of its time line. That is why agencies such as I exist – to monitor requests from the oracle to take action that will defend the Eschaton's causal integrity. In the case of Moscow, the most reasonable explanation is that the Muscovite government was experimenting with weapons of temporal disruption and blew their own star up by accident. But there was absolutely no rational explanation for why they might want to develop such weapons, left to their own devices. Which is why evidence of ReMastered infiltration would be most interesting. Especially in conjunction with the silence of the oracle.'

Wednesday was silent for a minute. Then: 'Are you telling me that some asshole in the military destroyed my world *by accident*? Or because the ReMastered asked them to?'

'Not exactly.' A few seconds' silence. Wednesday's emotions churned, aghast and outraged. 'When acquiring a new planet, the ReMastered do not walk in and take everything over at gunpoint. They infiltrate by inducing a crisis and being invited in to calm things down. Their main tool is their expertise in uploading and neural interfaces. While blackmail is often used for indirect leverage, they frequently work by abducting key midlevel officials – pithing them, copying their existing neural architecture, then installing an implant. Sometimes they leave the personality in place, just add an override switch – or they wipe everything and turn the body into a remote-control meat puppet. By using a causal channel to control the body, they can ensure that nobody will be able to tell that it's being run by a ReMastered agent unless it is subjected to a brain scan or forced to make an FTL transit. The ReMastered are patient; frequently they will arrive in a system, take fifty to a hundred low-to-mid-ranking officials, then wait twenty or thirty years until one or more of their moppets is promoted into a position of influence. It is a very slow and labor-intensive process, but far cheaper and safer than attempting an overt war of interstellar conquest.'

'You mean they do this regularly?'

'Not often. They have fewer than twenty worlds, so far.

My models do not predict that they will become a major threat for at least two centuries.'

'Oh.' Wednesday fell silent. 'But none of the diplomats are puppets,' she pointed out. 'They'd have made FTL transfers to get to their embassies. So there's no evidence, is there?'

'There *is* evidence,' Herman pointed out. 'The ReMastered focus on you, and the items you found aboard Old Newfie before its evacuation, suggest that it was used as a point of entry for some years, and that the insurgency group operating in Moscow were careless. The ReMastered focus on assassinating Muscovite diplomats is itself suggestive, although I am not yet certain of their motives. The faction responsible appears to want to force the Muscovite diplomatic corps to send the irrevocable go code to the R-bombers, thus precipitating a political crisis on New Dresden with implications elsewhere. But it is difficult to be sure.'

'But you – you' – Wednesday struggled for words – 'you're part of the Eschaton. Can't you *stop* them? Don't you *want* to stop them?'

'Why do you think I am talking to you?' Her own voice, calm and sympathetic. 'I cannot undo the destruction of Moscow because the accident did not trigger the Eschaton's temporal immune response. Higher agencies are investigating the possibility of a threat to the Eschaton itself. *I* am trying to prevent the ReMastered from achieving their goal of taking New Dresden, or whatever else they want to achieve. I'm also trying to stop them from acquiring the final technical reports from the weapons project on Moscow. And I'm trying to ensure that the diplomatic corps from Earth is alerted to the threat. This is a low-level response by the standards of the Eschaton. The ReMastered belief system requires the destruction of the Eschaton. They are nowhere near acquiring that capability, and have not yet triggered the Eschaton's primary defense reflexes, but if they do . . . you would not wish to live within a thousand light years.'

'Oh.' It came out sounding weak, and Wednesday hated herself for it. 'And what about me? What am I going to do afterward? My family . . .' A huge sense of loss stopped her in her tracks. She glanced at the sleeping figure in the bed and the sense of loss subsided, but only a fraction.

'You are old enough to make up your own mind about your future. And I cannot accept responsibility for events that I was not forewarned about or involved in. But I will ensure that you do not lack money in the short term, while you sort your life out, if you survive the next few days.'

'If?' Wednesday paced over toward the picture wall. 'What do you mean, *if*?'

'The ReMastered group from MOSS is aboard this ship for a reason. Sometime after the next jump I expect them to do something drastic. It might be as crude as an attempt to snatch and puppetize you, but there are too many witnesses aboard this ship to whom you might have spoken. A more sensible approach would be to ensure that this ship never reaches its destination. You should prepare yourself. Learn the crew access spaces and the details I downloaded into your ring. One other thing: three diplomats from Earth's United Nations Organization have joined the ship. You can trust them implicitly. In particular, you can talk to Martin Springfield, who has worked for me in the past. He may be able to help protect you. And one other point. If you get the chance to reacquire the documentary evidence of ReMastered weapons tests in Moscow system, turn it over to the diplomats. That is the one thing you can do that will cause the most damage to the ReMastered.'

'I'll bear it in mind.' Her voice wavered. 'But you said

they're going to break the door down and kidnap me — what am I supposed to do about that?'

'Simple: don't be in your cabin when they come for you.' Herman paused. 'Too much time. I have downloaded some further design patterns into your rings. Keep your jacket by you at all times.'

'My *jacket*?'

'Yes. You never know when you'll need it.' Herman's tone was light. 'Good luck, and goodbye. Oh, and if by some chance the *Romanov* ends up at New Prague, talk to Rachel before you decide to take a day trip to the surface. Otherwise, it might come as a shock . . .'

Click. The call ended. Wednesday cursed quietly for a moment, then noticed a change in the room. She glanced up.

'What was that about?' asked Frank, his expression grave. 'Was someone picking an argument?'

She stared at him, her heart suddenly pounding and her mouth dry. 'My invisible friend—' she began. 'When do we jump?'

'Not for at least a day. Why don't you come here and tell me about it?' He moved to one side of the bed, making a space for her.

'But I—' She stopped, the sense of dread receding somewhat. 'A day?' Long habit and ingrained distrust told her that mentioning Herman to anyone would only get her into trouble. Logic, and something else, told her that concealing him from Frank would be a mistake. 'I'm not supposed to talk about it,' she said. 'And you'll think I'm crazy!'

'No.' He looked at her thoughtfully. 'I don't think you're crazy.' His expression was open and surprisingly vulnerable – which only made him harder for her to read. 'Why don't you start at the beginning?'

She climbed into bed and leaned against him. He put an arm round her shoulders as she took a deep breath. 'When I was ten I had an invisible friend,' she admitted. 'I only discovered he worked for the Eschaton after home blew up . . .'

Martin glanced up as Rachel opened the door to the cramped office cube, off to one side of the executive planning suite. His face was lined and weary. 'You're all right?' he asked.

'Never been better.' Rachel pulled a face, then yawned. 'Damn, need a wake-up dose.' She looked at the table, glanced at the young-looking Lieutenant sitting at the other side of it from Martin. 'Introduce me?'

'Yeah. This is Junior Flight Lieutenant Stephanie Grace. Just back from ground leave. While she's been away I've been working with her boss, Flying Officer Max Fromm. Um, Steffi? This is my wife, Rachel Mansour. Rachel is a cultural attaché with—'

'Not *that* introduction.' Rachel grinned humorlessly as she held up a warrant card. Her head, surrounded by the UN three-W logo on a background of stars. 'Black Chamber. That's Colonel Mansour, Combined Defense Corps, on detached duty with the UN Standing Committee on Interstellar Disarmament. Purely for purposes of pulling rank where appropriate, you understand. I'd rather the passengers and crew outside your chain of command didn't learn of my presence just yet. Do we understand each other?'

The kid – no, she was probably well out of her teens, quite possibly already into her second or third career – looked worried. 'May I ask what you think is going on? Because if it's anything that threatens the ship, the Captain needs to know as a matter of urgency.'

'Hmm.' Rachel paused. 'Until six hours ago, I thought we were looking for a criminal – a serial killer – who was traveling aboard your ship and killing a different victim in every port.' She stopped.

The Lieutenant winced, then met her eyes. 'I hardly think that would normally warrant a Black Chamber investigation, would it, Colonel?'

'It does if the victims are all ambassadors from a planetary government in exile that has launched R-bombs on another planet,' Rachel said quietly. '*That* stays under your hat, Lieutenant: our serial killer is trying to precipitate a war using weapons of mass destruction. I'll brief your Captain myself, but if word of it gets back to me through other channels—'

'Understood.' Steffi looked worried. 'Okay, so that's why your husband' – her eyes flickered toward Martin – 'has been dredging through our transit records for the past six months. But you said there was something else.'

'Uh-huh.' Rachel met her eyes. 'It's a motive thing. I don't think it's a lone serial killer; I think we're up against a professional assassin, or a team of assassins, from an interstellar power. And they're intent on obscuring their tracks. Now they know we're onto them, they could do anything. I hope they won't do anything that threatens the ship, but I can't be sure.' She shrugged uncomfortably.

Steffi looked alarmed. 'Then I must insist you tell the Captain immediately. If there's any question that the, uh, killer might do something aboard her vessel, she's responsible for it. Master and commander and all that. And so far' – her gesture took in the mound of open windows and entity/relationship diagrams in the table-sized screen – 'we're not getting very far. We have about two and a half thousand passengers, and seven hundred crew. We generate over three thousand personnel movements every time we berth, and frankly, the two of us are snowed under. If you've got something solid to tell the skipper, it'll make it easier for me to get you more help.'

'Okay, then let's go see the Captain.' Martin stood up. 'Want me to come along?' he asked.

Rachel took a deep breath. 'Think you can carry on without us for a while? I don't expect it'll take long to fill her in . . .'

'I'll keep at it.' Martin shook his head. 'I'm still working through the tourist-class passengers. I thought it was going to be simple, then Steffi here asked what if a passenger disembarked and checked out, did the job, then took passage under a different name in a different class? It's a real mess.'

'Not totally,' Steffi volunteered. 'We have some biometrics on file. But we're not geared up for police-style trawls through our customer base, and pulling everyone's genome out for inspection would normally take an order from—' She glanced at the ceiling. 'So shall we go visit the skipper?'

Captain Nazma Hussein was not having a good day.

First departure had to be delayed six hours because of some stupid mess downside, delaying a couple of passengers who had diplomatic-grade clout – enough to hold the ship, even though each hour's delay cost thousands. Then there was a problem with mass balance in one of the four ullage tanks that ringed the lower hemisphere of the liner's hull, a flow instability suggesting that a stabilizer baffle had been damaged during the last docking maneuver. She'd managed to get away from the flight deck, leaving Victor in charge of the straightforward departure, only to find a queue headed by the deputy purser waiting in front of her desk for orders and/or ruffled-feather smoothing. And now this . . .

'Run that by me again,' she said, doing her best to

maintain the illusion of impassive alertness that always came hard after a twelve-hour shift. 'Just what do you expect to happen aboard my ship?'

The diplomat looked as tired as she felt. 'One or more of your passengers or short-term crew have been bumping off people at each planetside port of call,' she explained again. 'Now, I've been ordered to make sure it doesn't happen again. Which is all very well, but I've got reason to believe that the killer is acting under orders and may try to cover their tracks by any means at their disposal.'

'Disposal?' Captain Hussein raised one sharply sculpted eyebrow. 'Are you talking about a matter of killing witnesses or passengers? Or actions that might jeopardize the operational safety of my ship?'

The woman – Rachel something-or-other – shrugged. 'I don't know,' she said bluntly. 'I'm sorry I can't reassure you, but I wouldn't put anything past these scum. I was downside yesterday, and we managed to abort their latest hit, but the trap misfired, mostly because they demonstrated a remarkable willingness to kill innocent bystanders. It looks as if they started out trying to keep a low profile, but they're willing to go to any lengths to achieve their goals, and I can't guarantee that they won't do something stupid.'

'Wonderful.' Nazma glanced sideways at her overflowing schedule screen. Numerous blocks winked red, irreconcilable critical path elements, overlapping dependencies that had been thrown out of balance by the late departure. 'Do you know *who* you're looking for? What would you have me do when you find them?' She looked past the diplomat. The trainee kid was doing her best to melt into the wall, clearly hoping she wouldn't dump on her for being the bearer of bad tidings. *Tough, let her worry for a few minutes.* Nazma gave her a grade-three Hard Stare, then looked back at the spook. It hadn't been so many years that she had forgotten what the kid would be feeling, but it wouldn't hurt to make her ponder the responsibilities of a mistress and commander for a while. 'I really hope you're not going to suggest anything like a change of destination.'

'Ah, no.' The woman, to her credit, looked abashed. *Bet that's exactly what you were about to suggest*, Nazma told herself. 'And, um, the safety of your ship is paramount. My main concern is that we identify them so that they can be discreetly arrested when we arrive at the next port of call – or sooner, if there's any sign that they're a threat to anyone else.' Nazma relaxed slightly. *So, you're not totally out of touch with reality, huh?* Then the diplomat spoiled it by continuing: 'The trouble is, you generate so many personnel movements that we've got a pool of about 200 suspects, and only ten days to check them. That's the number who've been downside on all of the planets where an incident occurred – if we're looking for a team, alternating targets, the pool goes up to 460 or so. So I was wondering if we could borrow some more staff – say, from the purser's office – to help clear them.' She forced a tense smile at Nazma.

Give me patience! Captain Hussein glanced back at her display. The red bars weren't getting any shorter, and every additional hour added to the critical path added sixteen thousand to her operating overhead. But the alternative . . . 'Lieutenant Grace.' She watched Steffi straighten her back attentively. 'Please convey my compliments to Commander Lewis, and inform her that she's to provide you with any and all personnel and resources from her division that you deem necessary to requisition for, for Colonel—'

'Mansour,' offered the woman.

'—Colonel Mansour's search. When you have a final suspect list I want to see it before any action is taken. File daily updates with Safety and Security, cc'd to my desk. I also want to know if you *don't* find a murderer aboard my ship, of course.' She nodded at the spook. 'Satisfied?'

Rachel looked surprised. 'More than,' she admitted. This time her smile was genuine. 'Thank you!'

'Don't.' Nazma waved it away. 'I wouldn't be doing my job if I didn't take murderers running around my ship seriously.' She sniffed, nostrils flaring as if at the scent of skullduggery. 'Just as long as you keep it low-key and don't frighten the passengers. Now, I trust you will excuse me, but I have a ship to run.'

He looks like a gorilla, Martin thought apprehensively as he approached the warblogger across the half-empty lounge. The journalist was slouched on a sofa with a smile on his face, one arm around a pale-skinned young woman with a serious blackness habit – black hair, black boots, black leggings, black jacket – and a big baby blue dressing on her left temple. She was leaning against him in a manner that spelled more than casual affection. *Isn't that sweet*, Martin thought cynically. The blogger must have been about two meters tall, but was built so broadly he looked squat, and it wasn't flab. Close-cropped silver-speckled black hair, old-fashioned big horn-rimmed data glasses, and more black leather. The woman was talking to him quietly, occasionally leaning her chin on his shoulder. The gorilla was all ears, grunting agreement from time to time. They were so wrapped up in each other that they didn't seem to have noticed Martin watching them. *Here goes*, he thought, and walked over.

'Hi there,' he said quietly. 'Are you, um, Frank Johnson of the London *Times*?'

The gorilla glanced up at him sharply, one eyebrow rising. The young woman was also staring. Martin barely noticed her, fine-boned alarm and black nail paint. 'Who's asking?' said the big guy.

Martin sat down opposite them, sprawling inelegantly in the sofa's overstuffed grip. 'Name's Springfield. I'm with the UN diplomatic service.' *That's odd*, he realized distantly. Both of them had tensed, focusing on him. *What's up?* 'Are you Frank Johnson? Before I go any further—' He held up his diplomatic passport, and the big guy squinted at it dubiously.

'Yeah,' he rumbled. 'And this isn't a social call, is it?' He rubbed his left arm meditatively and winced slightly, and Martin put two and two together.

'Were you at the Muscovite embassy reception yesterday evening?' he asked. He glanced at the young woman. 'Either of you?' She started, then leaned against the big guy, looking away, feigning boredom.

'I see a diplomatic passport,' Frank said defensively. He stared at Martin. 'And I see some guy asking pointed questions, and I wonder whether the purser's office will confirm if the passport is genuine when I ask them? No offense, but what you're asking could be seen as a violation of journalistic privilege.'

Martin leaned back and watched the man. He didn't *look* stupid: just big, thoughtful, and . . . *Huh. Got to start somewhere, right? And he's not top of the list by a long way.* 'Could be,' he said reflectively. 'But I'm not asking for the random hell of it.'

'Okay. So why don't you tell me what you want to know and why, and I'll tell you if I can answer?'

'Um.' Martin's eyes narrowed. The woman was staring at him with clear fascination. 'If you were at the Moscow embassy in Sarajevo, you probably saw rather a lot of bodies.' The journalist winced. *A palpable hit.* 'Maybe you weren't aware that the same thing also happened before. We have reason to believe that the responsible party' – he paused, watching the implication sink in – 'was probably aboard this ship. Now, I can't compel you to talk to me. But if you know anything at all, and you don't tell me, you're helping whoever blew up all those people to get away with it.' *Holed below the waterline*: the journalist was nodding slightly, unconscious agreement nibbling away at his resolute dedication to the cause of journalistic impartiality. 'I'm trying to put together a picture of what happened that night to aid the investigation, and if you'd like to make a statement, that would be very helpful.' He gave a small shrug. 'I'm not a cop. It's just a case of drafting every warm body who can hold a recorder.'

Frank leaned forward, frowning. 'I'm going to check your passport, if you don't mind,' he said. 'Do you?' He held out a hand. Martin thought for a moment, then reluctantly handed the white-spined tablet over. Beside him the woman leaned over to look at it. Frank glanced at the passport then snapped his fingers for a privacy cone and said something muffled to the ship's passenger liaison network. After a moment he nodded and snapped his fingers again. 'Okay,' he said, and handed the passport back. 'I'll talk to you.'

Martin nodded, his initial apprehension subsiding. Frank was going to be reasonable – and having an experienced journalist's view of affairs would be good. He pulled out a small voice recorder and put it on the low table between them. 'This is an auditing recorder, write-once. Martin Springfield interviewing—'

'Wait. Your name is *Martin* Springfield?' It was the young woman, sitting straight up and staring at him.

'Wednesday—' The big guy started.

'Yeah. I'm Martin Springfield. Why?'

The girl licked her lips. 'Are you a friend of Herman?'

Martin blanked for a moment. *What the fuck?* A myriad of memories churned up all at once, a hollow voice whispering by dead of night over illicit smuggled causal channels. 'I've worked for him,' Martin heard himself admitting as his heart gave a lurch. 'Where did you hear the name?'

'I do stuff for him, too.' She licked her lips.

'Wednesday.' Frank glared at Martin. 'Shit. You don't want to go telling everyone about—'

'It's okay,' said Martin. He raised his recorder. 'Recorder. Command delete. Execute.' He put it down. *What the* fuck *is going on here?* He had a hollow feeling in the pit of his stomach. This couldn't be a coincidence, and if Herman was involved, it meant the whole diplomatic ball of string had just gotten a lot knottier. 'Ship, can you put a privacy cone around this table? Key override red koala greenback.'

'Override acknowledged. Privacy cone in place.' All the sounds from outside the magic circle became faint and muffled.

'What are you doing here?' Wednesday asked, tensing. Martin glanced from her to Frank and back. He frowned; their body language told its own story. 'Back downside—' she swallowed. 'Were they after me?'

'You?' Martin blinked. 'What makes you think you were the target of a bombing?'

'It wouldn't be the first time,' rumbled Frank. He looked at Martin warningly. 'She's a refugee from Moscow, one of the survivors of the peripheral stations. She settled in Septagon, except someone murdered her family, apparently for something she'd taken, or left behind, or something. And they tried to follow her here.'

Martin felt his face freeze, a sudden bolt of excitement stabbing through him. 'Did *Herman* send you here?' he asked her directly.

'Yes.' She crossed her arms defensively. 'I'm beginning to think listening to him is a very bad idea.'

You and me both, Martin agreed silently. 'In my experience Herman never does anything at random. Did he tell you my name?' She nodded. 'Well, then. It looks like Herman believes your problem and my problem are connected — and they're part of something that interests him.' He looked at Frank. 'This isn't news to you. Where do you come in?'

Frank scratched his head, his expression distant. 'Y'know, that's a very good question. I'm roving diplomatic correspondent for the *Times*. This trip I was basically doing a tour of the trouble spots in the Moscow/Dresden crisis. She just walked up and dumped her story in my lap.' He looked sideways at Wednesday.

She shuffled. 'Herman told me to find you,' she said slowly. 'Said that if you broadcast what was going on, the people hunting me would probably lay off.'

'Which is true, up to a point,' Martin murmured, more to himself than to anyone else. 'What else?' he demanded.

Wednesday took a deep breath. 'I grew up on one of Moscow's outlying stations. Just before the evacuation, Herman had me go check something out. I found a, a body. In the Customs section. He'd been murdered. Herman had me hide some documents near there, stuff from the Captain's cabin of the evac ship. I got away with it; nobody noticed that bit.' She shuddered, clearly unhappy about something. 'Then, a couple of weeks ago, someone murdered my family and tried to kill me.' She clung to Frank like a drowning woman to a life raft.

'I don't believe in coincidences,' Martin said slowly, the sweat in the small of his back freezing. *Herman's involved in this.* A dead certainty, and frightening enough that his palms were clammy. Herman was the cover name that an agent – human or otherwise – of the Eschaton had used when it sent him on lucrative errands in the past. *So there's something really serious following her around. Wait till I tell Rachel! She'll shit a brick!* He caught Wednesday's gaze. 'Listen, I'd like you to talk to my wife as soon as possible. She's – you probably saw her on stage. At the embassy.' He swallowed. 'She's the expert in dealing with murderous bampots. Between us we can make sure you're safe. Meanwhile, do you have any idea who's after you? Because if we could narrow it down or confirm it's the same bunch who're after the Muscovite diplomatic corps, it would make things much easier—'

'Sure I do.' Wednesday nodded. 'Herman told me last night. It's a faction of the ReMastered. There's a group of them aboard this ship, traveling to Newpeace. He reckons they're going to do something drastic after the first jump.' She grimaced. 'We were just trying to figure out what to do . . .'

clowning around

Franz was snared.

Some time ago he'd heard a story about wild animals – he wasn't sure what species – which, when snared, would chew a leg off to escape the hunter's trap. It was a comforting myth, but clearly false in his estimate: because when you got down to it, when your own hand was wedged in the steel jaws of a dilemma, you learned to make do with what you'd got.

Hoechst had come up from the depths of the Directorate like a ravening black widow, carrying away Erica and menacing him with the poisoned chalice of her acquisitive desire. His own survival was at stake: I *wasn't expecting that.* But he'd done as she told him, and she hadn't lied. She hadn't bitten his head off and nibbled daintily at the pulsing stump of his neck as she consummated her desire. Even though his trapped conscience hurt as violently as a physical limb. Her luggage included almost fifty grams of memory diamond, loaded with the souls and genomes of everyone in U. Scott's network who'd failed her purge. Each morning he awakened with his heart racing, panting with the knowledge that he was walking along the lip of a seething crater. Knowing that death at her hands would be a purely temporary experience, that he'd awaken with his love and uncounted billions more in the simulation spaces of the unborn god, did not make it easier to bear. For one thing, the unborn god had to be built – and that meant the destruction of the enemy. And for seconds . . .

Falling in love was like losing your religion. They were two sides of a coin that Franz and Erica had flipped some years ago, out among the feral humans. He was no longer sure what he believed. The idea of the unborn god picking over the bones of his human fallibility made his skin crawl. But this was foreshadowed: when the ReMastered finally destroyed the Eschaton and began their monumental task of reimplementation, the deity they'd build in their own image would hardly be a merciful and forgiving one. Perhaps it would be better to die the permanent death than to meet his share in the collective creation, down at the omega point at the end of time. But the more he contemplated it, the more he found that he couldn't quite bring himself to pick one horn of the dilemma – either to chew away the restraining grip of his conscience and flee alone, or to force the black widow to execute him out of sheer disgust.

Which was why, on the evening of the first full day in flight, one hour before the first jump, he was kneeling on the floor of Portia's Sybarite-class stateroom next to Marx, helping him load ammunition into a brace of handheld recoilless gun launchers while Samow and Mathilde armed their little bags of tricks. *We're really going to do this*, he thought disbelievingly, as he stared at a squat cartridge. *She's really going to do it.*

The idea was disorienting. Franz had thought, in his more optimistic – unrealistic – moments that maybe he and Erica could manage the trick: that perhaps they could flee the iron determination of the ReMastered race, escape from history, run and hide and find a distant world, live and work and indulge in the strange perversion called love, die forever and molder to humus, never to rise beneath the baleful gaze of the omniscient end child. But escape was a cruel illusion, like freedom, or love. A cruel illusion intended to temper the steel of the ReMastered.

He snapped the round into the box magazine before him, then picked up another and loaded it on top. It was the size of his thumb, nose gleaming with sensors and tail pocked with the tiny vents of solid-fuel rocket motors. *One shot, one kill*. Every time he pushed another BLAM into the magazine he felt something inside him clench up, thinking of Jamil plunging the propagation bush into the back of Erica's head, turning her into so much more reliable meat to place on the altar of the unborn god for judgment. *Kill them all, god will know his own* meeting *god is dead: we must become the new gods*.

'This one's full,' he said, and passed it to Marx.

'That's enough for this set.' Marx carefully set aside one of the handguns and a linked bundle of magazines. 'Okay, next one. Hurry up, we've only got an hour to get this sorted.'

'I'm hurrying.' Franz's hands flew. 'Nobody's told me what I'm assigned to do during the action.'

'Maybe that's because she hasn't decided if she wants you alive for it.'

Franz tried not to react in any way before Marx's harsh assessment. It was all too possible that it was a test, and any sign of weakness might determine the outcome. 'I obey and I labor for the unborn,' he said mildly, working on the ammunition case. 'Hmm. The power charge on this one is low. How old is this box?' The big guided antipersonnel rounds needed a trickle charge of power while they were on the shelf – the biggest drawback of smart weapons was the maintenance load.

'It's in date. Anyway, we'll be using them soon enough.'

I could defect, he told himself. *All I'd have to do is tell the Captain what's happening*— Except he didn't know who else might be involved. All he knew about was Portia's team, and Mathilde's group. There might be others. *Restart. If I defect*— Erica would be dead forever, or doomed to resurrection beneath the hostile scrutiny of an angry god. Even if he could get his hands on the package of souls Portia was carrying for the Propagators, he had no easy way of instantiating Erica's mind, let alone growing her a new body. That was privileged technology within the Directorate, ruthlessly controlled by the Propagators for their own purposes, and expensive and rare outside it. *And if Hoechst is telling the truth* – there were worse things to be than a DepSec's serf. Much worse.

'Ah, Franz.' A warm voice, behind him. He forced himself to focus on what his hands were doing – pick, load, pick, load. *She doesn't mean anything*, he thought. 'Come with me. I've got a little job for you.'

He found himself standing up almost without willing it, like a sleepwalker. 'I'm ready.'

'Hah! So I see.' Hoechst beckoned toward one of the side doors opening off her suite. 'Over here.'

He followed her over and she opened the door of what he'd taken for a closet. Spot on: it was indeed a closet. With a chair in it, straps dangling from the armrests and front legs.

'What's this?' he asked, heart thudding.

'Got a little job for you.' Hoechst smiled. 'I've been

studying this love phenomenon, and it has some interesting applications.' Her smile slipped. 'It's a pity we can't just work our way through the passengers until we have the girl, then puppetize her and force her to comply.' She shook her head. 'But whoever's behind her almost certainly took precautions. So we'll have to do this the old-fashioned way.'

'The old—' Franz stopped. 'What do you mean?'

Hoechst pulled out a tablet and tapped it. A video loop started cycling, just a couple of seconds showing its target waving at someone off-screen. 'Him.' She pointed at the face. 'I'm giving you Marx and Luna. While everyone else is executing Plan Able, you will go to his cabin and bring him here. Undamaged, to the extent possible. I want a bargaining chip.'

'Hmm.' Franz shrugged. 'Wouldn't it be easier simply to force her?'

'This *is* force, of a kind.' Hoechst grinned at him. 'Don't you recognize it?' The grin vanished. 'She has a history of evading capture, Franz. Kerguelen was not entirely negligent: he was up against experience. I've been reading U. Scott's field files, predigested raw transcripts, not the pap he was content with. She won't dodge *me*.'

'Ah,' Franz said faintly. 'So what do you want me to do with him?'

'Just snatch him and bring him here while I'm dealing with the rest of the ship. If he cooperates, he and the girl can both be allowed to live – that's the truth, not a convenient fiction. Although they and the rest of the passengers will be sent for ReMastering when we arrive at Newpeace.'

'Got it.' Franz frowned. *She's going to ReMaster everyone on the entire ship? Is she planning on making it disappear?* 'Do you want anything else?'

'Yes.' Hoechst leaned close, until he could feel her breath

on his cheek. 'This is job number one for you. I've got another lined up after we dock with station eleven. It's going to be fun!' She patted him on the back. 'Cheer up. Only another three weeks to go, and we'll be home again. Then, if you're good, maybe we can see about giving you back your toy.'

Steffi stifled a yawn as she lowered herself into the chair at the head of the table in the dining room. An overlong shift spent poring over personnel movements with Rachel had left her bleary-eyed and wanting to throttle some of the more willfully persistent tourists. Having to follow that by stealing ten minutes to freshen up, then sitting at the head of a dining table for three or four hours of stroking the oversized egos of the more stupid upper-class passengers, was the kind of icing she didn't need on her cake. *But it's better than being on the outside of the investigation*, she told herself. And maybe she'd get some quality time with Max afterward; he was sitting up on the high table at the other side of the room, lofty but affable, everybody's favorite picture of a senior officer. He'd need to blow off steam, too.

'Mind if I join you?' She looked round. It was Martin, the diplomatic spook's right hand.

'By all means.' She managed a wan smile, keeping up appearances. Down the table, the middle-aged Nipponese woman smiled back at her, evidently mistaking its target, triggering an exchange of polite nods. By which time Martin was sitting to her left and idly scrolling through the menu. She looked around the table. It was half-empty. The troublesome kid was evidently eating in her room. So, come to think of it, were those creepy cultural exchange students from Tonto. *Fucking stupid cover*, she thought. *A blind idiot could see there's more to them than that.* No such luck with the bankers, though.

'How's your day been?' she asked quietly as the stewards collected the empty soup bowls. 'I haven't seen your wife in here – is she working?'

'Probably.' Martin winced and pinched the bridge of his nose. 'She's looking for someone, and she tends to overdo it when she's got her teeth into something. I tell her to take some time off, it'll make her more effective, but . . . I've spent all day interviewing tourists. It's giving me a headache.'

'Did any of them have anything useful to say?' she asked.

'Not for the most part, no.'

Liar, she thought, tensing. *What are you concealing?*

The lighting strips lining the arched sculpture niches along the walls flickered, distracting her.

' 'Scuse me.' Steffi raised her left hand and twisted her interface rings urgently, hunting the command channel. The lights aboard a starship never flickered without a reason – especially not aboard a luxury liner with multiple redundant power circuits. Steffi hadn't felt any vibration, but that didn't mean anything. The ship's curved-space generators were powerful enough to buffer a steady thirty gees of acceleration, and absorb the jolt of any impact unless it was large enough to cause a major structural failure. 'Bridge comm, Grace here. Bridge—' She frowned. 'That's odd.' She glanced across the room at Max. He was standing up, turning to step down off the raised platform of the high table. He caught her eye, jerked his chin toward the main entrance, then strode toward it. Across the room she saw stewards discreetly breaking off their tasks, disappearing in the direction of their emergency stations.

She caught up with Max a couple of meters down the hall. 'Bridge isn't answering.'

'I know.' He opened an unmarked side door. 'Nearest emergency locker is – ah, here.' Yanking the yellow-and-black handle forward, he pulled out the crash drawer and handed her an emergency bag – rebreather hood, gloves, multitool, first-aid 'bots. 'No callback.' He looked thoughtful. 'One moment—'

'Already there.' Steffi had her tablet fully unfolded; she pasted it against the wall and tried to bring up the ship's damage-control schematics. 'Shit, why is it so *slow*? She stabbed at a local diagnostic pane. 'There's no bandwidth! Shipnet is down.'

'We've got lights, air, and gravity.' He looked thoughtful. 'What's out is data. Listen, it may just be a major network crash. Relativistics weren't due to start jump spool-up for half an hour yet, so we're probably okay if we sit tight. You're not trained for this, so I want you to go back to the dining room and keep a lid on the passengers. Relay any orders you hear and keep your ears open and try to stay out of trouble until you're needed. Meanwhile, I'm going to get some stewards together and go find out what's happening. Bridge first, engineering control if the bridge is out . . . Your story for the passengers is that everything is under control, line crew is investigating and there'll be an announcement in due course. Think you can handle it?'

'I'll do my best.'

Steffi headed for the passenger corridor, sparing a glance behind her as he waved a hand at a crewman who'd appeared from one of the service spaces: 'Hey, you! Over here, I've got a job for you right now . . .'

Everything seemed to be under control in the dining room. Steffi did a quick survey. The passengers were still wrapped up in conversation, not yet having noticed anything unusual. *Small mercies* . . . For a moment she considered leaving them in ignorance, but as soon as someone tried to check mail or call a friend they'd realize something was up.

She took a step up onto the platform supporting the high table. 'Excuse me, ladies and gentlemen, may I have your attention, please?'

Curious eyes turned toward her. 'As some of you may have noticed, we've experienced a minor technical anomaly in the past few minutes. I'd like to assure you that the engineering crew are working on it, and there is no danger—'

The lights flickered for a moment, then went out. One or two stifled screams rose from the corners of the room – then the lights came back on. And with them a stranger's voice, amplified, over the passenger liaison circuit, its tone calm and collected: 'We regret to inform you that there has been a minor problem with the propulsion and engineering control center. There is no cause for alarm. Everything is under control, and we will be diverting to a nearby port rather than proceeding directly to New Prague. WhiteStar Line will announce a compensation package for your inconvenience in due course. In the meantime, we would appreciate it if you would return to your cabins and stay there until further notice. When the passenger liaison network is back up, please do not hesitate to use it to contact one of our team. We're here to help you.'

Rachel was looking for Wednesday in the mostly-deserted D deck lounges when the gadget went off under the bridge. The bridge was on E deck. It was separated from D deck by two pressure bulkheads, a structural truss, and an electrograv ring designed to even out tidal surges, so the immediate blast effect was lost on her.

Martin had called her a couple of hours earlier, full visual via an office cam. 'It checks out and it stinks like a month-dead cheese,' he insisted. 'She's a Moscow survivor, someone's been trying to abduct or kill her, she was at the embassy reception when you were – oh, and there's something else.'

His cheek twitched. He was about as agitated as she'd ever seen him get. 'What else?' she demanded, annoyed with herself for going after such a transparent hook.

'She's got a friend called Herman, and he's why she's here.' Martin shut up. She stared at him through the magic mirror in her visual field.

'You're kidding.'

'Nope. *Frank* didn't know any more – but I mean, hit me with the clue bat, right?'

'Oh shit.' She'd had to lean against the wall. 'Did she pass anything else on to you?' She'd gone dizzy for a moment, as things dropped into place. *Herman* was the cover name an agent of the Eschaton had used to contact Martin, paying him to run obscure errands – errands that had emergent side effects that shook the chancelleries of a dozen worlds. *Herman* was only really interested in human beings when they tried to build time machines, violate causality, experiment with forbidden weapons. *Moscow* had died when, entirely without warning, its star had exploded. Which just *didn't happen*, not to G-type dwarf stars in the middle of the main sequence of their life cycles.

'Yes. Maybe it's a coincidence, and then again maybe there's a large pig on final approach to the main docking bay – see the reaction control clusters on each flank? Herman said it was something to do with the ReMastered group aboard this ship and that they're going to pull something after the first jump. Tonight, in other words. Rachel, I am *not* happy. This—'

'Stop. Let's not go there right now.' She shook her head. 'I need to find the girl before whoever's looking for her catches up with us. Send me her details?'

'Sure.' Martin shuffled the rings on his left hand, and her

tablet bleeped, then threw up a picture – young-looking physio, dark hair built up in an outrageous swirl, eye shadow like midnight. 'Hard to miss. You'll probably find her with Frank the journalist; they seem to be personally involved. Oh, she's as young as she looks, too, so go easy on her.'

Rachel frowned pensively. 'Don't worry about me, worry about her. You go and have a word with the Captain – tell her we're expecting some kind of trouble from a group of passengers. If necessary, tell her exactly who – but don't tell her where the warning came from. There might be a leak in the crew. Besides which, if we overreact, we might not have a chance to learn anything . . .'

'Happy hunting.' He'd smiled at her until she cut the call. And that was why she came to be prowling past nine-tenths empty lounges and casually eyeballing the few passengers who were out in public, chatting, drinking, or schmoozing in the overstuffed furniture that seemed to be a WhiteStar trademark. Wednesday seemed to have vanished, along with her new boyfriend, and neither of them were carrying their locater badges. *Damn these privacy freaks, anyway!* Nowhere did she see a skinny girl with spiky hair and a serious luminosity deficiency, or a journalist built like a silverback gorilla.

Two hours after she'd begun, Rachel had combed decks G through D, making a pass around each circle corridor and checking every single public room, and she was getting frustrated. *Where on earth can she have gotten to?* she asked herself. Leaving a message on Wednesday's voice mail didn't seem to have gotten anywhere. It was getting to the point where she had half a mind to raise things with Steffi, see if the crew couldn't do the job more efficiently: if only she could eliminate all the crew from the suspects list—

The luminous ceiling tiles flickered briefly, and the

world filled with multicolored static. A vast silence went off inside her head. Rachel felt herself falling and tried to raise her arms to protect herself. *Vertigo!* She hit the deck bruisingly hard and rolled sideways, her vision flickering. The static was slow to clear, leaving a line of bleeding ghost trails across her retinas. Rachel caught her breath, dizzy with fright, then realized that it wasn't her eyesight: her intraocular displays had crashed and were rebooting. 'Shit!' She glanced around. The skinny guy sitting in the leather sofa next to the upright piano in the Gold Lounge was frowning, rolling his rings around his fingers as if puzzled by something. *Rings* – Rachel twisted her own master ring, spun through diagnostic menus until she came to the critical one. *EMP burst*, said her event log. Kilovolts and microamps per meter: someone had just dumped a huge electromagnetic pulse through the walls. There was a faint tang of ozone in the air. The fast fuses in her MilSpec implants had saved them, but the other passengers—

'Oh *shit!*' She picked herself up and lurched drunkenly into the corridor. 'Get me Martin.' *Service unavailable.* 'Hell and damnation.' *No surprise there. Why no sirens?* She glanced around hastily, looking for an emergency locker – they'd be tastefully concealed aboard a liner, but they'd still be there – *Why no partitions?* The fail-safe doors ought to be descending if something bad had happened. A chilly claw of fear tugged at her. 'Shit, time to get moving . . .'

The small boy in one corner of the lounge was walking toward her. 'Hey, ma'am? My gamescape just flaked on me—'

She cast the kid a sickly smile. 'Not now,' she said, then did a double take: 'Why don't you go to your room and tell your folks about it? They'll be able to help you.' *EMP/crashed implants and amusements/assassin traveling incognito/teen from Moscow being hunted/Eschaton involved/war crimes* — she had a nagging sense that a shoe had just dropped *hard*, an enormous boot with a heel stuffed with plutonium or weaponized anthrax or gray goo or something equally apocalyptic, and she'd misinterpreted it as the sound of one hand clapping. *Something like that*. She broke into a trot, heading for the next radial. *Got to find the damage-control point*, she told herself, *find out what's going on—*

She dodged a couple of confused passengers who seemed to be looking for someone. She spotted an anonymous gray side door into crew country and tried to open it. It refused to recognize her until she got tired of waiting and twisted the black-and-yellow emergency handle: from beyond it she could hear distant, muted sirens. The auxiliary lighting circuit had tripped, and the walls shed a lurid shadowless glow. 'Send to Martin, off-line by best emergency mesh routing,' she subvocalized to her personal assist, mumbling at her rings. 'Martin, if you get this message, we're in deep shit. Something—' she turned a corner, followed signs for the G deck ops center — 'big is going down, and I think we're sitting on the target.' The ops center door was open ahead, a couple of crew just visible in the gloom inside doing something. One of them glanced at her, then stepped forward. 'I think—'

She stopped dead, eyes wide, as the public address system came on: 'We regret to inform you that there has been a minor problem with the propulsion and engineering control center . . .'

The man blocking the doorway was pointing an autonomous rifle at her. Rachel froze as it tracked her, snuffling slightly, its barrel pointing right at her face. 'Who are you and what are you doing here?' he demanded.

'I, uh—' She stopped, heart hammering. 'I was looking for a steward?' she asked, her voice rising in an involuntary squeak. She began to take a step back, then froze as the man tensed. He had blond hair, brown eyes, and pale skin: he was built with the sparse, muscular grace of a dancer or martial artist – *or special forces*, she realized. Even a cursory glance told her she wouldn't stand a chance if he decided to shoot her; the gun was some kind of smart shotgun/grenade launcher hybrid, probably able to fire around corners and see through walls. 'My rings stopped working – What's this about help?' she asked, doing her best to look confused. It wasn't hard.

'There has been a minor accident,' the goon said, sounding very calm but clipping his words: 'Return to your cabin. Everything is under control.' He stopped and stared at her coolly.

'Uh, yeah, under control, I can see that,' Rachel muttered, backing away from him. He made no move to follow her, but simply stood in the doorway watching as she turned and walked back toward passenger country. Her skin crawled as if she could feel the gun watching the small of her back, eager to discharge. When she was far enough away she gave in to the impulse to run – he'd probably expect no less of a frightened passenger. Just as long as he didn't realize how good her night vision was. Good enough to have seen the woman slumped over the workstation in the gloom behind him. Good enough to have seen the other woman working on her back with something that looked disturbingly like a mobile neurosurgery toolkit.

Under control. 'Shit,' she mumbled, fumbling with the door and noticing for the first time that her hands were shaking. *Bad guys in G deck damage-control center, infoweapons in passenger country, what* else *do I need?* The door banged shut behind her. She shook her head. *Hijackers—*

She turned toward the central atrium, meaning to take the old-fashioned staircase back up to her room in search of

Martin. She took a single step forward, and the dark-haired girl ran into her.

The air in the flight deck stank of blood, ozone, and feces. The desks and equipment racks around the room looked as if someone had run them through a scrap metal press; anything that wasn't bolted down had fallen over and shattered, hard, including the bridge officers unlucky enough to be in the room when the gadget had gone off. Bodies bent at strange angles lay beneath broken chairs or lay splayed across the floor, leaking.

Portia wrinkled her nose in distaste. 'This really *won't* do,' she insisted. 'I want this mess cleared up as soon as we've got the surveillance net locked down. I want it to look like we've been in charge all along, not as if we just butchered the flight crew.'

'Boss.' Jamil nodded. He glanced at the front wall-screen, which had ripped away from the bulkhead and slumped into a thin sheet across the floor. 'What about operational capacity?'

'That's a lower priority. We've got the auxiliary bridge, we'll run things from there for now.' She pulled a face. 'On second thoughts, before you tidy up get someone to reclaim anything they can get out of these.' She stared at an officer who lay on the floor, her neck twisted and skull flattened. 'Obviously, I don't expect total uploads.'

'Thirty gees for a hundred milliseconds is about the same as falling off a fifteen-story building,' Marx volunteered.

'So she didn't have a head for heights.' Hoechst's cheek twitched. 'Get going.'

'Yes, boss.' He hurried off to find someone with a neural spike.

As he left, Portia's phone rang. She raised the archaic rubbery box to her head. 'Control, sitrep. Ah . . . yes, that's good. Is he all right? Fully programmed? Excellent, get him in front of a screen as soon as you get into the liaison router, we need to reassure the passengers there's a real officer in charge . . . What's the structural load-out like? How high did the surge . . . all right. Right. Good, I'm glad you told me. Yes, tell Maria to detain any other members of the crew who reach D-con on decks G through C . . . Yes, that's what I meant. I want any line officers who survived identified and segregated immediately. Stash them in the C deck D-con center for now and report back when you've got them all accounted for. Be discreet, but in event of resistance shoot first: the unborn god will know his own . . . Yeah, you, too. Over.' She turned and nodded to Franz. 'Right. Now it's your turn. I take it the girl isn't in her cabin?'

Franz straightened up. 'She's missing. Her tag says she's there, but it looks like she fooled it deliberately and her own implants aren't compatible with these damn Earth-standard systems. One of the ship's junior officers was searching for her – I think she's gone to ground.' He delivered his little speech with an impassive face, although his stomach tensed in anticipation of Hoechst's wrath.

'That's all right,' she said mildly, taking him by surprise. 'What did I tell you to expect earlier? Just keep an eye open for her. Mathilde's crew is configuring the passenger access points to work as a mesh field for celldar, and she'll have the entire ship under surveillance in a few hours. Now, what about the other one?'

'Taken, as per your orders. He'd returned to his room for some reason. Marx took him down with no problems, and we've got him stashed in the closet.'

'Good. When the kid surfaces you can let her know we've got him, and what will happen to him if she doesn't cooperate.' She looked pensive. 'In the meantime,

I want you to go and pay off the clown. Right away.'

'The clown,' Franz repeated. *The clown?* That was okay by him. No ethical dilemmas there, nothing to lose sleep over . . .

'Yes.' She nodded. A muscle in her left cheek jumped. 'Bring me the head of Svengali the clown.'

'I don't have a spike—'

'*No* reclaim,' she said firmly. She gave a delicate shudder of distaste. 'There are some things that even the unborn god should be protected from.'

'But that's final! If you kill him without reclaiming his soul—'

'Franz.' She stared at him coldly.

'Boss.'

She tilted her head to one side. 'Sometimes I think you're too soft for this job,' she said thoughtfully. 'Are you?'

'Boss! No.' He took a deep breath. 'I have been slow to adjust to your management style. I *will* adapt.' *That's right, gnaw your own leg off.*

She nodded slightly. 'See that you do.'

'Yes.'

He knew when he was being dismissed. *Bring me the head of Sven the clown.* Well, if that was what she wanted, he'd do it. But the thought of killing the guy and not offering him the last rite was . . . tasteless? No, worse than that. Taste was a value judgment. This was final, a total extinction. The boss had said: *There are some things the unborn god should be protected from.* Meaning, memories that must never be mapped and archived for posterity lest the machineries of heaven expose the machinations of mortals who might arrive on the unborn god's doorstep exposed to criticism. Shit stank, and the unborn god must be born pure, once the abominably abhuman Eschaton was destroyed.

Franz paused just outside the bridge door and took a

deep breath of pure filtered air that didn't stink of carnage. Samow's localized EMP bomb had blipped a massive current surge through the facilities deck below the bridge, accessed via a storage locker. It had overloaded the superconducting electrograv ring under the bridge, temporarily exposing everything above it — as far as the next deck and the next ring — to the bone-splintering drag of the ship's full thirty gees of acceleration for a fraction of a second. Meanwhile, Jamil and one of the trusted strike team goons had taken the training room, slaved to the bridge systems and doubling as an emergency bridge during the run-up to the ship's first jump. The officer on duty hadn't understood quite what was happening at first; Kurt had pithed and puppetized him, and that was their biometric token sorted.

Now they were about three light years off course, crunching on the second jump of the series of four that the nav team had knocked together for them aboard the *Heidegger*. It was a calculated risk, taking over a liner under way, but so far it had worked well. The window of opportunity for the passengers and crew to do something about them was closing rapidly, and when Mathilde finished installing the ubiquitous surveillance software on the ship's passenger liaison network it would be locked down tighter than a supermax prison.

Portia's planning had placed a platoon of special forces troops aboard the liner even before she arrived with her team of spooks and specialists. All they really needed was to take a bridge room, the drive engineering spaces, a couple of damage-control centers, and central life support. Once they could track everybody's movements through walls and floors, and remotely lock the doors or cut off the air supply if they didn't like what they were seeing, the ship would be theirs. Which left Franz facing a dilemma.

There was no way Hoechst was going to let him run

away. In fact, she'd probably kill him or send him for reimplementation as soon as look at him, once the *Romanov* arrived at Newpeace. It was stupid to expect her to grow a new body for Erica: that was a privilege even Director-level officials were rarely granted. If he could steal the memory diamond containing her reclaimed state vector and genetic map, then find some way to reach a polity where downloading and cloning weren't instruments of state under control of the technotheocracy, he might be able to do something . . . but how likely was that? *She's dead, and I'm fucked*, he told himself coldly. *All I can hope for is to try to convince Portia I'm a willing servant—*

He made his way along the radial corridor, empty of all human traffic (Jordaan's messing with the access permissions had locked almost all the crew out of the service tunnels for the duration of the takeover) and caught a crew elevator up to A deck and Hoechst's command suite. When the door opened for him, one of Mathilde's troops shoved a gun at him. 'What do you want?'

'Got a job to do for the boss.' He stepped inside and the door slid shut behind him. 'Is Mathilde here?'

'No.' The guard lowered his gun, went back to his position next to the door. 'What do you need?'

'I need to use the ubiq tap as soon as everything's installed. That, and I'd like to draw a sidearm and a neural spike. Boss wants a loose end tied off.'

'Uh-huh.' The soldier sounded vaguely amused. 'Ferris will sort you out.'

The main room was a mess. Someone had been digging into the floor, opening up crawl spaces and installing a loom of cables that ran to a compact signal-processing mainframe squatting on the remains of what had once been a very expensive dressing table. Three or four techs were hunched over various connectors or blinking and gesturing at the air, shepherding their mobile code around the ship's passenger liaison net. Another soldier was busy with a ruggedized communications console, very low-tech but entirely independent of the shipboard systems. She looked up as Franz came in. 'What do you want?'

'Crewman' – he consulted his implant – '4365, Svengali Q., no last name, occupation, entertainments specialist, subtype juvenile. I need to know where he is. And I need to draw a gun.'

'Crewman 4365,' she drawled, 'is currently locked in—' she frowned. 'No. He's down on H deck, radial four, orange ring, in the second-class dining area doing . . .' Her brow wrinkled. 'What's a "birthday party"?'

'Never mind. Is he scheduled there for much longer?'

'Yes, but there are other passengers—'

'That's all right.' Franz glanced around. 'Now, about a handgun.'

'Over there. Boss's bedroom, there's a crate by the sleeping platform. Uh-oh, incoming call.' She was back at her console without a second glance.

Portia's bedroom was a mess. Discarded equipment cases were scattered across the floor, the remains of a half-eaten meal cooling on the pillows. Franz found the crate and rummaged in it until he found a carton that contained a machine pistol and a couple of factory-packed magazines loaded with BLAMs. He held the gun to his forehead for long enough for its tiny brain to handshake with his implants, and upload its recent ballistic performance record and a simple aiming network. Franz didn't much like carrying a gun; while he knew how to use one, having to do so in his line of work would usually mean that his cover was blown and his job, if not his life, was over. He rummaged further, and despite Portia's injunction, he took a neural spike. You never knew . . .

He was about to leave the room when he noticed something else. There was a pile of dirty clothing heaped on an open suitcase next to the bed. It looked like stuff the boss had been wearing earlier. He paused, momentarily curious. *Would she?* he wondered. *Is it worth a look?* Well yes, it was . . . probably. He glanced at the half-open door. There was nobody in sight. He knelt and ran his hands around the inside of the case, then the lid. He felt a lump in one side pocket. Cursing himself for his optimism, he unzipped the pouch and pulled out a small box. Then he stopped cursing. 'Wow,' he breathed. He flipped the box open, then hastily closed it again, stood up, and shoved it into one hip pocket, then headed back into the reception room, his pulse pounding with guilty intent.

The box had contained a gemstone the size of his thumb, sitting atop a ceramic block studded with optical ports – the reader/writer head. It was memory diamond, atoms arranged in a lattice of alternating carbon 12 and carbon 13 nuclei: the preferred data storage format for the unborn god's chosen few. Dense and durable, twelve grams was enough to store a thousand neural maps and their associated genome data. This was Hoechst's soul repository, where the upload data from anyone she terminated in the course of service would be stored until they could be archived by the Propagators, against the day when the unborn god would be assembled and draw upon the frozen imprints. Such careless concealment in a piece of nondescript luggage had to be deliberate; probably she'd decided the ship's strong room was too obvious a target. It was a symbol of her authority, of her power of life after death over those who served her. He could expect no mercy if she found him in possession of it. But if he could dig a single stored mind out of it and put it back; he'd be fine. And that was exactly the prospect that had his hands sweating and his heart pounding with pity and fear . . . and hope.

Nobody paid any attention as he slipped back into the dayroom. 'I'm going down to drop in on my target,' he told the comms specialist. 'Got a field phone?'

'Sure.' She tossed him a ruggedized handset. 'Turns back into a pumpkin next jump. Bring it back for a reset.' *Must be a causal channel*, he realized. The untappable instant quantum devices were the tool of choice for communications security — at least between FTL hops.

'Check.' He slipped it into his pocket. 'See you around.'

There was an uproar in the dining room. Steffi stood up. 'Please!' she shouted. 'Please calm down! The situation's under control—'

Predictably, it didn't work. But she had to try: 'Listen! Please sit down. Lieutenant Commander Fromm is investigating this problem. I assure you nothing serious is wrong, but if you would just *sit down* and give us time to sort things out—'

'I'd give up, if I were you,' Martin said quietly. Half the passengers were flocking toward the exits, evidently in a hurry to return to their rooms. The rest were milling around like a herd of frightened sheep, unsure whose lead to follow. 'They're not going to listen. What the hell *is* happening, anyway?'

'I don't—' Steffi caught herself. *Shit! Play dumb, idiot!* 'Max is looking into it. At best, some idiot's played a prank with the liaison network. At worst?' She shrugged.

'Who made the announcement?' Martin asked.

'I don't know.' *But I can guess.* She frowned. 'And no *way* would the skipper divert from our course — for one thing, New Prague is about the closest port of call on our route! For another—' She shrugged. 'It doesn't add up.'

'I'm not going to say the word,' Martin said slowly, 'but I think something has gone very wrong. Something to do with the investigation.'

Steffi's guts turned to ice. Confirmation of her own worst fears: it was a stitchup. 'I couldn't possibly comment. I should be heading to my duty station—' She forced herself to pause for a couple of seconds. 'What would you do if this was your call?'

'It's either a genuine accident, in which case damage control is on top of it or we'd be dead already, or – well, you put it together; the net's down, a stranger is announcing some weird accident and telling passengers to go to their rooms, and we've got a couple of killers loose on board. Frankly, I'd send everyone to their cabins. They're self-contained with emergency oxygen supplies and fabs for basic food, it's where they want to go, they can hole up, and if it *is* a hijacking, it'll give the hijackers a headache. Meanwhile we can find out what's going on and either try to help out or find somewhere to hole up.' The ghost of a smile tugged at his lips, then fell away. 'Seriously. Get them out of here. Dispersal is good.'

'Shit!' She stood up and raised her voice again: '*If* you'd all go straight to your cabins and stay out of the corridors until somebody tells you it's all right, that would help us immensely.'

Almost at once the crush at the exits redoubled as first-class passengers streamed away from their seats. Within a minute the dining room was almost empty. 'Right. Now what?' she asked edgily. If Max was all right, he should have sent a runner by now. So he wasn't, and the shit had presumably hit the fan. Twitching her rings didn't seem to help; she was still locked out of the network.

'Now we go somewhere unexpected. Uh, your rings still not working?' She nodded. 'Right, switch off everything.'

'But—'

'Just *do* it.' Martin reached into a pocket and pulled out a battered-looking leather-bound hardback book. 'PA, global peripheral shutdown. Go to voice-only.' He shook his head, wincing slightly. 'I know it feels weird, but—'

Steffi shrugged uncomfortably, then blinked her way through a series of menus until she found the hard power-down option on her personal area network. 'Are you sure about it?'

'Sure? Who's sure of anything? But if someone's taking over the ship, they're going to view nailing down line officers – even trainees – as a priority. Way I'd plan it, first your comms would go down, then people would simply vanish one by one.' Steffi blinked and nodded, then sent the final command and watched the clock projected in her visual field wink out. Martin stood up. 'Come on.' They followed the last diners out into the main radial heading for the central concourse, but before they'd passed the nearest crossway Martin paused at a side door. 'Can you open this?'

'Sure.' Steffi grasped the handle and twisted. Sensors in the handle recognized her handprint and gave way. 'Not much here but some stores and—'

'First thing to do is to cover up that uniform.' Martin was already through the door. 'Got to get you looking like a steward or a passenger. Don't think they'll be looking for me or Rachel yet.' He pushed open the next door, onto a dizzying spiral of steps broken every six meters by another pressure door. 'Come on, long climb ahead.'

Steffi tensed, wondering if she was going to have to break his neck there and then. 'Why do you—'

'Because you're a line officer, why else? If we're being hijacked, you know how to fly this damn thing; at least you're in the chain of command. I know enough about the drive layout on this tub to spin up the kernel, but if we get control back, we're going to need you to authenticate us to the flight systems and log me in as flight engineer. If I'm wrong, we'll hear about it as soon as the PLN comes back up. So start climbing!'

Steffi relaxed. 'Okay, I'm climbing, I'm climbing.'

too many children

'You—' Rachel swayed on her feet. The girl shook her head violently, looking spooked, and muttered something inaudible. Then she glanced over her shoulder. 'Are you Victoria Strowger?'

Wednesday's head whipped round. 'Who wants to know?'

Her shoulders set, she was clearly on the defensive. 'Calm down,' said Rachel. 'I'm Martin's partner. Listen, the ReMastered are going to be all over us in a couple of minutes if we don't get the hell out of the public spaces. All I want is to ask you a couple of questions. Can we take this up in my suite?'

Wednesday stared at her, eyes narrowing in calculation. 'Okay. What's going on?'

Rachel took a deep breath. 'I think the ship's being hijacked. Do you know where Frank is?'

'I – no.' Wednesday looked shaken. 'He was going to go back to his room to fetch something, he said.'

'Oh dear.' Rachel tried to keep a straight face; the kid looked really worried at her tone of voice. 'Are you coming? We can look him up later.'

'But I need to find him!' There was an edgy note of panic in her voice.

'Believe me, right now he's either completely safe, or he's already a prisoner, and they'll be using him as bait for you.'

'Fuck!' Wednesday looked alarmed.

'Come *on*,' coaxed Rachel. 'Do you want them to find both of you?' A sick sense of dread dogged her: if Martin was right, Wednesday and Frank were romantically entangled. She cringed at the memory of how *she'd* once felt, knowing Martin had been taken. 'Listen, we'll find him later – get to safety first, though, or we won't be able to. Switch your rings off right now, unless you want to be found. I know you're not on the shipboard net, but if they're still emitting, the bad guys may know how to ping them.' Rachel turned toward the main stairwell. It was filling up with people, chattering hordes of passengers coming out to see what was going on, or heading back to their rooms; a handful of harried-looking stewards scurried hither and yon, or tried to answer questions for which they didn't have any answers.

'You know what's going on, don't you?' Rachel concentrated on the stairs, trying to ignore her shaking muscles and the urge to shiver whenever she thought back to what she'd seen in the D-con room. Six flights to go. 'What *is* going on?'

'Shut up and climb.' *Five* flights to go. 'Shit!' They were nearing D deck, and the crowd was thinner – there were fewer staterooms – and there was the first sign of trouble, a man standing in the middle of the landing and blocking the next flight of stairs. His face was half-obscured by a pair of bulky low-tech imaging goggles, like something out of the dawn of the infowar age; but the large-caliber gun he held looked lethally functional.

'You. Stop. Who are you and where are you going?'

Rachel stopped. She could feel Wednesday a step behind her, shivering – about to break and run, if she didn't do something fast. 'I'm Rachel Mansour, this is my daughter Anita. We were just going back to our suite. It's on B deck. What's going on?' She stared at the gun apprehensively, trying to look as if she was surprised to see it. *Ooh, isn't it big!* She steeled herself, prepping her military implants for the inevitable. If he checked the manifest and realized—

'I'm with the shipboard security detail. We've got reason to believe there's a dangerous criminal loose aboard ship.' He stared at them as if memorizing their faces. 'When you get to your rooms, stay there until you hear an announcement that it's safe to leave.' He stepped to one side and waved them on. Rachel took a deep breath and sidled past him, glancing over her shoulder to make sure Wednesday was still there.

After a moment's hesitation the young woman followed her. She had the wit to keep quiet until they were round the next spiral in the staircase. 'Shipboard security my ass. What the fuck was *that* about?'

'Network's down,' murmured Rachel. 'They've probably got a list of names, but they don't know who I am, and I lied about who you are. It'll last about five milliseconds once they get the ship's systems working for them, but we're in the clear for now.'

'Yeah, but who's Anita?'

Rachel paused between steps to catch her breath for a moment. *Three flights to go.* 'Anita's been dead for thirty years,' she said shortly.

'Oh – I didn't know.'

'Leave it.' Rachel resumed climbing. She could feel it in her calves, and she could hear Wednesday breathing hard. 'You get used to letting go and moving on. After a while. Not all of them die.'

'She was, your daughter?'

'Ask me some other time.' *Two flights to go. Save your breath.* She slowed as they came up to the next landing, emergency pressure doors poised like guillotine blades overhead, waiting to cut the spiraling diamond-walled staircase into segments. But there was no checkpoint. *They don't have enough people*, she thought hopefully. *We might get away with this.*

'My suite. Can't go. Back?'

'No.' *One more flight.* 'Not far now.' They paused at the top of the next flight. Wednesday was panting hard. Rachel leaned against the wall, feeling the hot iron ache in her calves and a burning in her lungs. Even militarized muscles didn't enjoy climbing fifty vertical meters of stairs without a break. 'Okay, this way.'

Rachel palmed the door open and waved Wednesday inside. The kid glanced at her for a moment, her expression troubled. 'Is this—'

'Talk inside.' She nodded, and Rachel followed her in. 'Sit down. Got some stuff to do.'

'Stuff?'

Rachel was already leaning over her trunk. 'I want – hmm.' She raised the lid and stuck her finger in the authentication slot, then rapidly scrolled through items on the built-in hard screen. She glanced at Wednesday. 'Come over here. I need to know what size clothing you take.'

'Clothing? Earth measurements? Or Sept—'

'Just stand up. Your name's Anita and you don't exist, but you're down on the passenger list. So we'll just have to make sure you don't look like Victoria Strowger when they get the passenger liaison net back up again, all right?'

'What's going *on*?'

Rachel straightened up as the trunk began to whine, holding a small scanner. 'I was hoping *you* could tell *me*. That jacket's programmable, isn't it? You've made them panic, and they're springing a trap. Can it do any colors other than black? Prematurely, I hope. Quick, they could be calling any minute. Why don't you tell me how you got in this mess—'

There was no knock on the door. It swung open, and two figures leapt inside. But then one of them kicked it shut – and by the time Rachel finished turning around Martin was leaning against the door, his eyes half-shut, breathing deeply.

'Martin—' She glanced sideways as she stood up, knees wobbly with relief. 'I was beginning to think they'd grabbed you.' They met in the vestibule and she hugged him, then looked past his shoulder at the other arrival. 'Aha! Glad you could make it. Martin, which plan were you thinking of using?'

'Plan B,' said Martin. 'We've got that spare ID you put on the manifest.'

'Uh-oh.' Rachel let go of him, turned, and stared at the bathroom door. 'We may have a problem.'

The bathroom door opened. 'Is this what you wanted?' Wednesday asked plaintively. Rachel blinked at her. In the space of ten minutes her hair had turned blond and curly, the stark black eyeliner had vanished, and the black leather jacket with the spiky shoulders had been replaced by a pink dress with layered puffball underskirts. 'My ass looks *huge* in this. I feel like a real idiot!' She noticed Steffi. 'Oh, hi there. This isn't about the other night, is it?'

Steffi sat down hard on the end of the bed. 'Just *what* are you doing here?' she demanded, a hard edge in her voice.

'Um.' Rachel fixed Martin with a steely gaze. 'We seem to have a slight problem. Can't really have two Anitas running around, can we?'

'No—' Martin rubbed his forehead tiredly. 'Shit! What a mess. One false set of ident tags, and two people to hide. Looks like we've got a problem, folks.'

'Can I just wear a flowerpot on my head and pretend I'm a tree? I know the idea is to look different, but this is just plain embarrassing.'

'Somehow I don't think that would fool them for long.' Martin scratched his chin. 'Steffi?'

'Let me think.' She leaned her chin on one fist. 'I feel so useless right now. I should really be trying to link up with the bridge crew or D-com—'

'Your attention, please. This is your acting Captain speaking.' Everyone looked up instinctively at the voice emanating from the emergency comm panel beside the door. 'There has been an accident on the bridge. Captain Hussein has been incapacitated. In her absence I, Lieutenant Commander Fromm, am in charge of this vessel. For your safety and comfort you should remain in your rooms until further notice. Passenger liaison facilities will be reenabled shortly, and if you need anything, your needs will be attended to. In view of the crisis, I have asked for volunteer help. We are lucky to be carrying a group from Tonto, and I have enlisted these people to provide assistance in this critical period. Please comply with any instructions they issue. I will make further announcements when the situation is fully under control.'

'Uh-oh,' said Wednesday.

'He's gone crazy!' Steffi exploded. 'The skipper would never do that, she'd—' Her eyes were wide. 'It's a hijacking, isn't it? But why is Max cooperating?'

'I hate to break it to you,' Martin said gently, 'but that

wasn't Lieutenant Commander Fromm you were listening to. It was his voicebox, but not him talking.'

'What do you mean?' Steffi stared at him, trying to figure out how much he might know.

'The ReMastered have made something of a specialty out of brain mapping and digitization,' said Rachel, her tone dispassionate. 'They can save minds to off-line storage and reincarnate them later – at great expense – by building a new body. But mostly they use the technique to turn living bodies into puppets. Zombies, zimboes with the illusion of self-awareness, whatever.' She clenched her hands together. 'That's how they take planets. They acquire some key government officers, destabilize the place by exploiting local political tensions, declare a state of emergency – using their puppets – and move in.'

Steffi's face was white. *Shit! I have to warn Sven! We've got to get out of here!* 'Max went to the flight deck to find out what was going on! I let him—'

'Don't blame yourself. They've got the bridge, drive engineering control, damage control, sentries on the main stairs, and passengers under lock and key in their rooms. This was a well-planned operation.' Rachel glanced at Wednesday. 'Bet you they're turning over your suite right now. And yours,' she added, looking back at Steffi. 'They made a big mistake, missing you.'

'But I, I—' Steffi stopped. She looked horrified.

'It'll take them time to check on us in here,' Martin said slowly, thinking aloud. 'When they do, we want you well hidden. You're probably the senior line officer on the ship. We'll need you around for your pass codes and retinal print if we're to stand a chance of taking back control.' He glanced at the cupboard. 'Once we arrive where they're diverting us to. *If* we get there without them tagging us in a search. Ever heard of a priest's hole?'

'A what?' Steffi looked dazed. 'What are you talking about? I'm just a trainee flight officer! I don't have clearance—'

Martin walked over to the trunk containing the military fabricator. 'You'll be the ranking line officer on the ship once this is over,' he told her. 'Rache, can you clear everything out of the walk-in? I'm going to need some basic tools, some supports, and a load of paneling to fit. Plus any special toys you can have the fab turn out in less than half an hour that won't show up as weapons on a terahertz scan. Bet you they're working on a ubiquitous surveillance mesh already. Need clothing for you, me, and the kid; it's in the deception and evasion library. Steffi, have you got a rebreather mask? We'll need a couple of buckets, some cushions, something to cover one of the buckets with—'

'Rebreather mask?'

'We've got maybe an hour,' Martin said impatiently. He pointed at Wednesday. 'You're going to be Anita. *You*—' he pointed at Steffi – 'are going to be Anne – Anne Frank. Rachel, run the kid through the Anita background while I get our stowaway stowed. Steffi? You and I are going to build a false back to the wardrobe, and I'm going to wall you in until we get wherever we're going. The name of this phase of the game is hide-and-seek, and the goal is to stay out of custody for now. Once we know which way the wind's blowing we'll see about taking back the ship.'

'If you can hear me, blink twice.'

Blink blink.

'That's good. You're Frank, aren't you? Blink once for yes.'

Blink.

'All right. Now listen carefully. You are in big trouble. You have been kidnapped. The people who are holding you have no intention of releasing you. I'm one of them, but I'm different. In a moment, I'm going to give you back control of your vocal cords so you can talk. They're only going to leave me alone with you for a couple of minutes, and we may not be able to talk again, so it's important that you don't scream or give me any trouble. Otherwise, we're both as good as dead. If you understand, blink once.'

Blink.

'Okay . . . say hello?'

'He – hell – ack.'

'Take your time, your throat's probably a bit sore. Here, try to swallow some of this . . . better?'

'Who'urr ooh?'

'I'm one of your kidnappers. But I'm not entirely happy about it. You're here because you're important to someone we're interested in. A girl called Wednesday. You know her?' *Pause.* 'Come on, *I'm* not the one who wants to get at the contents of her head.' *Pause.* 'All right. Let me explain.

'Wednesday knows . . . something. I'm not sure what. She's somewhere aboard this ship, don't know where, and the other – kidnappers – are trying to find her before we arrive where we're going. When we get there, they're going to use you as a hostage to try to make her tell us everything she knows. Trouble is, once she gives them the – the information, her usefulness will be at an end. Yours, too. You're both witnesses.

'Now, two or three things could happen. They might just shoot you, but I don't rate that as very likely. More probably, you'll end up in a reprocessing camp. Or they'll just pith you and turn you into a meat puppet. None of these options are very good for you, are they?'

'No fucking way.' Pause. 'What do *you* want?'

'I happen not to agree with the others. But if they find out what I really think, they'll kill me – I'm a traitor. So

I need to find a way out that, uh, doesn't give them what they want. So they don't get the, the immigration records. Or the go codes. Or the weapon test reports. In fact, I want them to go out the airlock. And I want to vanish, see? I don't want them to find me, ever again. And I figured you could help me do that. They don't know I'm here, talking to you. Between us we can fool them. They've hijacked this ship, but they haven't done the job properly. If you help me, we can regain control and turn everything over to the surviving ship's officers, and I can disappear and you'll be free.'

'What about Wednesday?'

'Her, too.'

Pause. 'So what do you want me to do?'

'For starters, you can look after this diamond for me.'

The clown died with a grin on his face and a warm gun in his hand.

Franz had tracked him down to H deck, where the comms sergeant had said he was working on a 'birthday party.' Gun in pocket, Franz walked down the stairwell to give himself time to think about how to do the job. It wasn't as if hits were his specialty; on the contrary, you only did wetwork in Septagon if your cover evaporated and you needed to clear out fast. Sparrowfart surveillance was deliberately absent there, but as soon as the body count began rising it would come down like a suffocating cloud. Franz shuddered slightly, thinking about the risks Hoechst's team had run, and checked the schematics in his inner eye one more time. Radial four, orange ring, second-class dining area – there were four entrances, two accessible from passenger country. *Not good*, he decided. Even with the ship under the thumb of the ReMastered, a chase and shoot-out could result in a real mess. It wasn't a good idea to underestimate the clown. He was a slippery customer.

At D deck Franz hit the checkpoint. Strasser stared at him coldly as he came down the stairs. 'What do you want?' he demanded.

'Check with control,' Franz grunted. 'Are you free yet?'

'What for?'

'Got a job. Loose end to take care of. I need to cover three exits—'

'Wait.' Strasser raised his bulky phone. 'Maria? Yeah, it's me. Look, I've got U. Bergman here. He says he's running an errand and he needs backup. Am I— oh. Yes, all right, I'll do that.' He pocketed the phone and frowned. 'What do you want me to do?'

Franz told him.

'Okay. I think that'll work.' Strasser looked thoughtful. 'We're spread thin. Can we get this out of the way fast?'

'Yes, but I'll need two more pairs of hands. Who do you suggest?'

'We can collect Colette and Byrne on the way down. I'll send them round the back while I cover the red ring entrance. I'll message you when we're in position. Sure you want to do it this way?'

Franz took a deep breath. 'I don't want to alarm him. If we scare him, he'll lash out, and there's no way of knowing what he's carrying. Remember, this guy has carried out more hits than we've had hot meals.'

'I doubt it. I'll make sure we're in position in not less than six minutes and not more than fifteen. If he leaves, you want us to abort to Plan B and take him in his berth. That right?'

'Right.' Franz headed for the stairwell. 'Get Colette and Byrne in the loop, and I'll brief them on the way there.'

Eight minutes later Franz was walking through the orange ring corridor, past smoothly curving walls and doors opening onto recreational facilities, public bathrooms, corridors leading to shared dormitories. Second class was sparsely furnished, thin carpet barely damping out the noise of footsteps, none of the hand-carved paneling and sculpture that featured in first and Sybarite.

'Coming up on the entrance now,' Franz murmured. 'I'll blip when I'm ready.' He rang off and held his phone loosely in his left hand. There was a racket coming from up ahead, round the curve, high-pitched voices *shouting*. *What's going on, some kind of riot?* he wondered as he headed for the door.

Turning the corner he witnessed a scene he'd never imagined. It *was* a riot, but none of the rioters were much taller than waist height, and they all seemed to be enjoying themselves hugely: either that or they were souls in torment, judging by the shrieking and squalling. It vaguely resembled a creche from back home, but no conditioner would have tolerated this sort of indiscipline for an instant. About thirty small children were racing around the room, some of them naked, others wearing elaborate costumes. The lights were flashing through different color combinations, and the walls were flicking up one fantasy scene after another − flaming grottoes, desert sands, rain forests. A gaggle of silvery balloons buzzed overhead, ducking almost within fingertip reach, then dodging aside as fast as overloaded motors could shift them. The music was deafening, some kind of rhythmic pounding bass line with voices singing a nonsense refrain.

Franz ducked down and caught the nearest rioter by the hand. 'What's going on?' he demanded. The little girl stared at him wide-eyed, then pulled her hand away and ran off. 'Shit,' he muttered. Then a little savage in a loincloth spotted him and ambled over, shyly, one hand behind his back. 'Hello.'

'Hello!' *Whack.* 'Heeheehee—'

Franz managed to restrain himself from shooting the kid – it might alert the target. 'Fuck!' His head hurt. What had the boy used? A club? He shook his head again.

'Hello. Who are you?'

'I'm—' He paused. The girl leaning over him looked taller – no, that wasn't it. She looked *older*, in some indefinable way. She was no bigger than the other children, but there was something assured and poised about her despite the seven-year-old body, all elbows and knees. 'I'm Franz. Who are you?'

'I'm Jennifer,' the girl said casually. 'This is Barnabas's birthday party, you know. You shouldn't just come barging in here. People will talk. They'll get the wrong idea.'

'Well.' Franz thought for a moment. 'I came here to talk, so that's not a problem. Is Sven the clown about?'

'Yes.' She smirked at him unhelpfully.

'Are you going to tell me where he is?'

'No.' He stood up, ready to loom over her, but she didn't show any sign of intimidation. 'I really don't think you've got his best interests in mind.'

Best interests in mind? What the hell kind of infant is this? 'Isn't he going to be a better judge of that than you?'

To his surprise, she acted as if she was seriously considering the idea. 'Possibly,' she admitted. 'If you stay right there, I'll ask him.' *Pause.* 'Hey, Sven! What you say?'

'I say,' said a voice right behind Franz's ear, 'he's right. Don't move, what-what?' Franz froze, feeling a hard prod in the small of his back. 'That's right. Sound screen *on*. Jen, if you'd be so good as to keep the party running? I'm going to take a little walk with my friend here. Friend, when I stop talking you're going to turn around slowly and start walking. Or I'll have to shoot your balls off. I'm told it hurts.'

Franz turned round slowly. The clown barely came up to his chin. His face was a bizarre plastic mask: gigantic grinning lips, bulbous nose, green spikes of hair. He wore a pink tutu, elaborate mountaineering boots, and held something resembling a makeup compact in his right hand as if it was a gun.

'What's that?' he asked.

'Start walking.' The clown nodded toward the door.

'If I do that, you'll die,' Franz said calmly.

'I will, will I? Then so shall you.' The face behind the plastic grin wasn't smiling, and the makeup compact wasn't wavering. It was probably some kind of low-caliber pistol. 'Who sent you?'

'Your client.' Franz leaned back against the wall and laced his fingers together in front of him to stop his hands shaking.

'*My* client. Can you describe this mysterious client?'

'You were approached on Earth by a man who identified himself as Gordon Black. He contacted you in the usual way and offered you a fee of twenty thousand per target plus expenses and soft money, installments payable with each successive hit, zero for a miss. Black was about my height, dark hair, his cover was an export agent from—'

'Stop. All right. What do you *want*? Seeking me out like this, I assume the deal's off, what-what?'

'That's right.' Franz tried to make himself relax, pretend this was just another informer and cat's-paw like the idiots he'd had to deal with on Magna. It wasn't easy with a bunch of raucous children running around outside their cone of silence and a gun pointing at his guts. He knew Svengali's record; U. Scott hadn't stinted on the expenses when it came to covering his own trail of errors. 'The business in Sarajevo with the trap suggests that the arrangement has no future. Someone's identified the sequence.'

'Yes, well, this wouldn't have happened if you'd taken my original advice about changing ships at Turku,' Svengali said waspishly. 'Traffic analysis is always a problem. Like attempts to sever connections and evade obligations on the part of employers. Did you think I worked alone?'

'No,' Franz said evenly, 'but my boss may take some convincing. "Bring me the head of Svengali the clown," she said. I think you'll agree that's pretty fucking stupid on the face of it, which is why I decided to interpret her orders creatively and have a little chat with you first. Then maybe you can carry your head in to see her while it's still attached to your body.'

'Hmm.' Svengali looked thoughtful, insofar as Franz could see any expression at all under the layers of pseudo-flesh. 'Yes, well I think I'll take you up on the offer, and thank you for making it. The sooner this is sorted out, the better.'

'I'm glad you agree.' Franz straightened up. 'We walk out of here together after I signal my backup. I take it your backup is aboard the ship?'

'Believe whatever you want.' Svengali shrugged. 'Send your signal, pretty boy.'

'Sure.' Franz held up his mobile and squeezed the speed button. *Idiot*, he thought disgustedly. Svengali had screwed up, making the fatal assumption that having a friend aboard to keep watch would be sufficient unto the day. It hadn't occurred to him that they might be unable to deliver any damning evidence for rather a long time if the entire ship disappeared. Or that the ReMastered might not want a professional assassin running around while they were trying to sort everything out. Then he gestured at the door. 'After you?'

'You first.'

'All right.' Franz walked through the door back into the corridor. 'Who was the kid?' he asked curiously.

'Who, Jen? Oh, she's just a Lolita from childcare. Helping out with the party.'

'Party? What ideology are they?' Franz added, sounding puzzled.

'Not ideology, birthday. Don't you have any idea—'

One moment the clown was two paces behind Franz, the small box held loosely in his right hand. The next instant he was flattened against the wall and bringing the gun up to bear on Franz, his lips pulled back with a rictus of hate. Then he twitched violently, a shudder rippling all the way through him from head to toes. He collapsed like a discarded glove puppet.

Franz turned round slowly. 'Took your time,' he said.

'Not really. I had to get into position without alerting him.' Strasser bent over the clown and put his weapon away. 'Come and help me move this before it bleeds out and makes a mess on the carpet.'

Franz joined him. Together they lifted the body. Whatever Strasser had shot him with had turned Svengali's eyes ruby red from burst blood vessels. He felt like a warm sack of meat.

'Let's get him into one of the lifts,' Franz volunteered. 'The boss wants to see his head. I reckon we ought to oblige her.'

Martin was still piling the contents of the walk-in closet up against the newly fitted partition when the passenger liaison net came back up. It made its presence known in several ways – with a flood of ultrawideband radiation, a loud chime, and a human voice broadcast throughout the ship.

'Your attention, please. Passenger liaison is now fully reconstructed and accepting requests. I am Lieutenant Commander Max Fromm, acting Captain. I would like to apologize for the loss of service. Two hours ago, a technical glitch in our drive control circuit exposed the occupants of the flight deck and other engineering spaces to a temporary overgee load. A number of the crew have been incapacitated. As the senior line officer, I have moved control to the auxiliary bridge, and we are diverting to the nearest station with repair facilities. We will arrive there in thirty-two hours and will probably be able to proceed on our scheduled voyage approximately two days later.

'I regret to inform you that it is believed that this incident may not have been accidental. It has been reported that our passenger manifest includes a pair of individuals belonging to a terrorist group identified with revanchist Muscovite nationalism. Crew and deputies drawn from the ReMastered youth leadership cadre aboard this vessel are combing the ship as I speak, and we expect to have the killers in custody shortly. In the meantime, the privacy blocks provided by WhiteStar for your comfort are being temporarily suspended to facilitate the search.

'Please stay in your cabins if at all possible. Please enable your communications nodes at all times. Before leaving your cabins, please contact passenger liaison and let us know why. I will announce the all clear in due course, but your cooperation would be appreciated while the emergency is in effect.'

'Corpsefuckers!' Wednesday stood up and paced over to the main door, like a restless cat. 'What do they—'

'Anita,' Rachel said warningly.

Wednesday sighed. 'Yes, Mom?'

Martin finished shoving the big diplomatic fab trunk up against the panels and turned round. *She's got the exasperated adolescent bit down perfectly*, he noted approvingly. And she'd managed to change her appearance completely. Her hair was a mass of blond ringlets and she'd switched from black leather and tight leggings to a femme dress that rustled when she moved. The bows in her hair made her look about five years younger, but the pout was the same, and with the work Rachel had done on her cheeks and fingerprints – *let's just hope they crashed the liaison system hard enough that they don't pay too much attention to the biometric tags*, he thought grimly. *Because—*

'Sit down, girl. You're making me dizzy.'

'Aw, Mom!' She pulled a face.

Rachel pulled a face right back. 'We need to look like a family,' she'd pointed out half an hour earlier, while Martin was walling Steffi and a three-day supply of consumables into the priest's hole. 'There's a chunk of familial backbiting, and a chunk of consistency, and we want you to look as unlike the Victoria Strowger they're hunting for as possible. Wednesday wears black and is extremely spiky. So you're going to wear pink, and be fluffy and frilly. At least for a while.'

'Three fucking *days*?' Wednesday complained.

'They've crashed the liaison network,' Rachel pointed out, 'and crashed it hard. That's the only edge we've got, because when they bring it up again they'll be able to configure it as celldar – every ultrawideband node in the ship's corridors and staterooms will be acting as a terahertz radar transmitter. With the right software loaded into the nodes they'll be able to see right through your clothing, in the dark, and track you wherever you go to within millimeters. We have to act as if we're under surveillance the whole time once the net comes back up, because if they're remotely competent – and they must be if they've just hijacked a liner with complete surprise – it'll give them total control over the ship and total surveillance over everybody they can see.'

'Except someone hidden at the back of a closet inside a Faraday cage,' Martin murmured as he slotted another panel into place, still stinking of hot plastic and metal from the military fabricator's output hopper.

'Yes, Mom.' Wednesday paced back to the armchair and dropped into it in a sea of lace. 'Do you think they'll—'

The door chimed – then opened without pause. 'Excuse us, sir and ladies.' Three crewmen walked in without waiting, wearing the uniforms and peaked caps of the purser's office. The man in the lead had a neatly trimmed beard and dead eyes. 'I am Lieutenant Commander Fromm and I apologize for the lack of warning. Are you Rachel Mansour? And Martin Springfield?' He spoke like an automaton, voice almost devoid of inflection, and Martin noted a bruise near the hairline on his left temple, almost concealed by his cap.

'And our daughter Anita,' Rachel added smoothly. Wednesday frowned and looked away from the men, scuffing the carpet with her boot soles.

'Anita Mansour-Springfield?'

Fromm looked momentarily blank, but one of the men behind him checked a tablet: 'That's what it says here, sir.'

'Oh.' Fromm still looked vacant. 'Do you know of a Victoria Strowger?' he said stiffly.

'Who?' Rachel looked politely puzzled. 'Is that the terrorist you're looking for?'

'Terr-or-ist.' Fromm nodded stiffly. 'If you see her, report to us immediately. Please.' His eyes looked red, almost bloodshot. Martin peered at him intently. *He isn't blinking!* he realized. 'I must revalidate your diplomatic credentials. Please. Your passports.'

'Martin?' Rachel looked at him. 'Would you fetch Commander Fromm our papers, please?' She remained seated on the chaise longue at the side of the dayroom, a picture of languor.

'All right.' He walked over to the closet, throwing the doors wide, and retrieved the passports from the briefcase on top of the fab without turning on the closet light. *Let them get a glimpse of a cluttered closet with no room for anyone to hide . . .* 'We should like you to withdraw surveillance from this suite,' he added, as he handed the passports over. 'And as soon as she's up to it, I'd like you to convey my best wishes for a speedy recovery and a happy code red to Captain Hussein. I'd like to see her when she's got time, if possible.'

'I am sure Captain Hussein will see you,' Fromm said slowly, and passed the passports to one of the other two officers for a check.

Captain Nazma Hussein is almost certainly dead, Martin realized, the cold hand of fear tickling his guts. *And you should know what a diplomatic code red means.* He forced a smile. 'Are the papers in order?'

'Yes,' the man behind Fromm said curtly. 'We can go now.'

Fromm turned round without a word and marched out the door. The two other men followed him. The one who'd checked their papers paused in the doorway. 'If you hear anything, please call us,' he said curtly. 'We're from the ReMastered race, and we're here to help you.'

The door clicked shut. Wednesday was on her feet almost immediately. 'You fuckmonsters! I'm going to rip your heads off and shit down your necks! I—'

'*Anita!*' Rachel was on her feet, too. She grabbed Wednesday's shoulders swiftly and held her. 'Stay calm.'

Martin walked in front of her and held up an archaic paper notepad and a tiny stub of pencil. TERAHERTZ CELL-DAR SIGNAL IN HERE, he scribbled twitchily in small letters. REZ ONE CM. SOUND TOO. CANT READ XPRESSNS, CAN C GESTRS, SOLID OBJECTS IN POCKETS, GUNS.

'What's—' Wednesday gasped, then leaned her head against Rachel's shoulder. Rachel embraced her. She sobbed, the sound muffled. Rachel stroked the back of her neck slowly. CAPTAIN DEAD. FROMM REMASTERED ZOMBI.

'I'm not sure I believe this,' Rachel said quietly. 'It's awful, isn't it?'

Wednesday nodded wordlessly, tears flowing.

'Looks like they lost the liaison network completely,' Martin observed, looking away. *What set that off?* he wondered. *Her family?* He wanted to be able to speak freely, to tell her that the scum who'd done it weren't going to get away, but he also wondered how true any such reassurance would be. 'On the bright side, they revalidated our passports.' *Including the one in the name of Anita, with Wednesday's face and biometric tags pasted in.* 'Liaison,' he said, raising his voice, 'what's this station we're putting into for repairs?'

The liaison network took a moment to reply. Its voice was slightly flatter than it had been the day before. 'Our repair destination is portal station eleven, Old Newfoundland. This station is not approved for passenger egress. Do you require further assistance?'

'That will be all,' Martin said, his voice hollow.

'Old Newfie?' Wednesday asked incredulously, raising her tear-streaked face from Rachel's shoulder. 'Did you hear that? We're going to *Old Newfie*!'

Thirty-two hours:

They stayed in their suite as instructed, forcing small talk and chitchat to convey the impression of familial claustrophobia. Wednesday milked her role for all it was worth – her adolescent histrionics had a sharp edge of bitterness that made Martin fantasize about strangling her after a while, or at least breaking character sufficiently to give her a good tongue-lashing. But that wasn't on the cards. His book-sized personal assist, loaded with nonstandard signal-processing software, showed him some curious patterns in the ambient broadband signals, worryingly tagged sequential pulse trains.

'I'm bored,' Wednesday said fractiously. 'Can't I go out?'

'You heard what the officer said, dear,' Rachel responded for about the fourth time, face set in a mask of unduly tried patience. 'We're diverting somewhere for repairs, and they want to keep the common spaces clear for access.' Wednesday scribbled furiously on Martin's paper notepad: OLD NEWF LIFE/SUPP DOWN HEAVY RAD. Rachel blinked. 'Why don't you just watch another of those antique movies or something?'

WORRIED ABOUT FRANK.

Martin glanced up from his PA. 'Nothing to gain by worrying, Anita,' he murmured: 'They've got everything under control, and there's nothing we can do to help.'

'Don't want to watch a movie.'

'Sometimes all you can do is try and wait it out,' Rachel said philosophically. 'When events are out of your control, trying to force them your way is counterproductive.'

'That sounds like bullshit to me, Mom.' Wednesday's eyes narrowed.

'Really?' Rachel looked only half-amused. 'Let me give you an example, then, a story about my, uh, friend the bomb disposal specialist. She was called out of a meeting one day because the local police had been brought in to deal with a troublesome artist . . .'

Wednesday sighed theatrically, then settled down to listen attentively. She seemed almost amused, as if she thought Rachel was spinning these stories out of whole cloth, making them up on the spur of the moment. *If only you knew*, thought Martin. Still, she was putting on a good act, especially under the stressful circumstances. He'd known more than a few mature adults who'd have gone to pieces under the pressure of knowing that the ship had been taken by hijackers, and they were the target of the operation. If only . . .

He shut down his PA's netlink and scribbled a note on it, leaving it where she'd spot it when Rachel finished. WHY OLD NEWF? 'Anyway, here's the point: If my friend had tried to rush the crazy, she'd have triggered the bomb's defense perimeter. Instead she just waited for him to open up a loophole. He did it himself, really. That's what I mean by waiting, not forcing. You keep looking at the door. Was there something you were thinking of doing out there?'

'Oh, I just need to stretch my legs,' she said disingenuously. It wasn't as if she hadn't been pacing up and down the floor every half hour as it was. 'Maybe go look at the bridge, if they'll let me in, or see things. I think I left some of my stuff somewhere and I ought to get it back.' She caught his eye and he nodded minutely.

LEFT STUFF OLD NEWF? 'What did you lose?'

'Oh, it was my shoulder bag, you know the leather one with the badge on it? And some paper I was scribbling on. I think it was somewhere near the, um, purser's office. And there was a book in it.'

'We'll see about getting it back later,' Rachel said, glancing up from her tablet. 'Are you sure you didn't leave it in the closet?' she asked.

'Quite sure, Mom,' Wednesday said tightly. B-BLOCK TOILET BY POLICE STATION — GOVMNT BACKUP DISK.

Martin managed not to jump out of his skin. 'It was quite expensive, as I recall.' He raised an eyebrow.

'One of a kind.' Wednesday blinked furiously. 'I want it back before someone else finds it,' she said, forcing a tone of spoiled pique.

Trying to figure it out, whatever it was that Wednesday had stashed near the police station in Old Newfie, was infuriating, but he didn't dare say so openly while they might be under surveillance. The combination of ultrawideband transceivers, reprogrammed liaison network nodes, and speech recognition software had turned the entire ship into a panopticon prison – one where mentioning the wrong words could get a passenger into a world of pain. Martin's head hurt just thinking about it, and he had an idea from her tense, clipped answers to any questions he asked her that Rachel felt the same way.

They made it through a sleepless night (Wednesday staked out the smaller room off to one side of the suite for herself) and a deeply boring breakfast served up by the suite's fab. Everything tasted faintly of plasticizers, and sometime during the night the suite had switched over to its independent air supply and life support – a move that deeply unsettled Martin.

Wednesday was monopolizing the bathroom, trying to coax something more than a thin shower out of the auxiliary water-purification system, when a faint tremor rattled the floor, and the liaison system dinged for attention. Martin looked up instinctively. 'Your attention please. We will be arriving at our emergency repair stop in just over one hour's time. Due to technical circumstances beyond our control, we would appreciate it if all passengers would assemble in the designated evacuation areas prior to docking. This is a precautionary measure, and you will be allowed to return to your cabins after arrival. Please be ready to move in fifteen minutes' time.'

The bathroom door popped open, emitting a trickle of steam and a bedraggled-looking Wednesday: 'What's that about?' she asked anxiously.

'Probably nothing.' Rachel stared at her and blinked rapidly, a code they were evolving for added emphasis – or negation. 'I think they just want us where they can keep an eye on us.'

'Oh, so it's nearly over,' Wednesday said heavily. 'Do you think we should do it?'

'I think we all ought to play our parts, Anita,' Rachel emphasized. 'Might be a good idea to get dressed, too. They might want us to go groundside' – *blink blink* – 'and we ought to be prepared.'

'Oh goody.' Wednesday pulled a face. 'It'll be freezing! I'll wear my coat and trousers.' And she vanished back into the bathroom.

'Think she'll be all right?' Martin asked.

Rachel slowly nodded. 'She's bearing up well so far.' She scribbled hastily on her notepad: COMM CENTER? CAUSAL CHANNELS? R-BOMBS?

'Well, we ought to go and see what they want, shouldn't we?' he asked. 'Let me just get my shoes on.'

backups

'Y'know, it's funny. For years I've had this recurring dream, nightmare, what the fuck. I'd be going about my life just like normal, when suddenly they'd *be* there. In the background, just – running things. Business as usual, same as it ever is. And I'd shit myself and go to the port and buy a ticket to, like, anywhere else. And I'd get on the ship and they'd be there, too, and all the crew would be *them*. And then I'd get to wherever the ship was going, and it would be the same. And they'd be all around me and they'd, they'd . . .'

Frank's subvocalized monologue wavered. It was all he could do just then; after the ReMastered guy with the creepy eyes had told him what he wanted he'd put the block back. His throat and the back of his mouth felt anesthetized, his tongue huge and limp. They'd used much cruder restraints on his arms and legs, and his hands felt cold and hurt from poor circulation. If he hadn't seen worse, been through worse, back in the camps, he'd have been paralyzed with terror. But as things stood, what he felt most strongly was a terrible resignation and a sense of regret.

Wednesday, I should have got you off the ship as fast as possible. Can you forgive me? He kept circling back to the mistakes he'd made, the assumption of mediocrity on the part of her pursuers. Even after the bomb at the embassy reception, he'd told himself she ought to be safe aboard a liner under a neutral flag. And – he'd wanted to stay with her. He liked her; she was a breath of fresh air blown into a life that had lately been one damn editorial rant after another. When she'd asked him to drop in and jumped his bones as soon as he shut the door he could have said 'no' gracefully – if he'd wanted to. Instead, they'd given each other something to think about, and inadvertently signed each other's death warrants.

ReMastered.

Frank was under no illusions about what it meant, an unfamiliar voice announcing an emergency on board, then his stateroom door crashing open, a gun buzzing and clicking in his face. They'd stuck him with a needleful of cold darkness, and he'd woken up in this stultifying cubicle, trussed to a chair and aching, unable to speak. *That* moment of panic had been terrible, though it had passed: he'd thought his heart was going to give out. Then the crazy one had come with a diamond the size of a quail's egg, forced him to dry-swallow a king's ransom in memories and pain.

What are her chances? he wondered, trying to think about something other than his own predicament – which, at a guess, would end with a friendly smile and the wrong end of a cortical spike as their anxiously meticulous executioners raped away his free will and sense of self – by focusing on Wednesday. *If she's with Martin or his partner, they might try to conceal her. Or she could hide out somewhere. She's good at hiding.* She'd hidden a lot from him; he'd only really figured out how lonely she was late in the game, when she'd burrowed her chin into the base of his neck and sobbed silently for ten minutes. (He'd felt like a shit, fearing he'd misread her mind and manipulated her into bed – until she'd taken his cock in her hand and whispered in her ear that she was crying at her own foolishness for waiting so long. And who, in the end, was he to deny her anything she wanted?)

The regret he felt was not for himself; he'd already outlived his allotted time years ago, when the ReMastered spat him out like a squeezed pip to drift through the cosmos and begin another life elsewhere. He wasn't afraid for himself, he realized distantly, because he'd been here already – it wasn't a surprise, just a long-deferred horror. But he felt a simmering anger and bitterness that Wednesday was going to go through that, too, sooner or later, the night of darkness in an improvised condemned cell that would only end when the executioner switched on the lights and laid out her tools.

Hoechst stood at the back of the auxiliary bridge behind Jamil and Friedrich, watching as the husks of the two puppetized bridge officers maneuvered the *Romanov* in toward the darkened, slowly precessing space station. Similar events would be unfolding in the engine control room above the drive kernel containment, where Mathilde was personally directing the engineering crew who had been selected for the privilege of serving the ReMastered. But the engineering spaces didn't have anything like the view that filled the front wall of the cramped secondary flight deck – the gigantic stacked wagon wheels of Old Newfie spinning in stately splendor before the wounded eye socket of eternity, a red-rimmed hollow gouged from the interstellar void by the explosion of Moscow Prime six years ago.

'Impressive, isn't it?' she asked Franz.

'Yes, boss.' He stood beside her, hands clasped behind his back to conceal his nervousness.

'They did it to themselves.' She shook her head slowly, almost disbelievingly. 'With barely any prompting from U. Scott.'

'How hot is it out there?' Franz asked nervously.

'Not too bad.' Friedrich leaned past one of the zombies to examine a console display. 'Looks to be about ten centiGrays per hour – you'd get sick in an hour or two if you went out there in a suit, but it's well within tolerances for the ship's shielding. And the station is probably all right, too, for short stays.'

One of the puppets murmured something to the other, who leaned sideways and began working his way through a stack of thruster-control settings. Jamil had edited their parameters so that they thought they were alone on the bridge. They were completely focused on the docking maneuver.

'It's the most beautiful thing I've ever seen,' Portia murmured, staring at the sheets of violet and red smoke that circled the shock ring of the star's death. 'And the most ugly.' Her hands tightened on the back of the command pilot's seat. With a visible effort she tore her concentration back to the job at hand, and glanced at Franz. 'Is the hostage ready? How about you? Are you clear on what you've got to do?'

'Yes, boss.' Franz nodded, trying not to show any sign of emotion. She smiled at him, a superficially friendly expression that set his teeth on edge. Part of him wanted to punch her in the face, to kick and bite and rip with his own hands until she stopped moving. Another part of him wanted to

cast himself at her feet and plead for forgiveness. 'We con-
fine the passengers in the evacuation stations and dump
the corridors to vacuum. Then I make the girl present herself and bring her to you and the others on the station.
Um, may I ask how we're evacuating?'

'You may.' Portia stared at the screen pensively as the
puppets muttered to each other, scheduled a course adjustment to nudge the multimegaton mass of the liner closer
toward the docking tree at the hub of the enormous station.
Methane tanks drifted huge and bulbous at the other end of
the spindle, rimed with a carbon monoxide frost deposited
by the passing shock wave that had swept over the station
years before.

'Boss?' Franz asked nervously.

'The *Heidegger* will be arriving in a day and a half. We
simply remove the puppets and disable the liner's flight-
control network before we leave. There's enough food
aboard – with the resources on the station – to keep them
alive for a couple of months, by which time we'll be able to
send a cleanup team big enough to process them all. If they
don't cooperate, the cleanup team can use the station for
target practice: nobody will find out for decades. Once
they're processed we can ship them off to one of the core
worlds on the *Romanov* for reprocessing. This is as good a
place to store them as any, don't you think?'

'But the records! If anyone finds them—'

'Relax, they won't. Nobody's been back here in years.
The station's too uneconomical to recommission without a
destination in mind, and too far off the track to be worth
retrieving for scrap. All we have to do is retrieve the stolen
records, send out the signals via the station manager's TAL-
IGENT channel, and configure the *Romanov* as a prison hulk
for a couple of months.'

'What if they—' Franz stopped.

'You were thinking about the missing bridge officer, weren't you?' Hoechst prodded. 'Don't bother. She's a trainee, and she's clearly not up to taking back the ship on her own, wherever she's hiding out. We'll leave you a guard detachment after the *Heidegger* gets here, just to make sure they don't try anything silly.' She smiled, broadly. 'If you can turn your mind to thinking up creative ways to booby-trap the flight deck after we've docked, that would be a good thing.'

Franz glanced at the screen and resisted the urge to rub his palms on his trousers. 'You want me to stay behind, with the prisoners?' he asked.

'Not only that: I want you to oversee their processing.' She stared at him, inspecting his face with minute interest. 'If you do well, I'll take it as a sign that you are worth persisting with. I was impressed by the way you handled the clown, Franz. Keep me satisfied and it will be worth your while. Great rewards come to my willing supporters.' Her smile faded, a sign that she was thinking dark thoughts. 'Now I think it's time you winkled out the girl.'

The evacuation assembly point for B deck was near the rim. A radial corridor ran out from it to an emergency airlock that breached the ship's inner hull. Worried passengers converged on it, some of them carrying bags stuffed with their essentials, others empty-handed. A few scattered stewards, harried and just as worried as the passengers, urged them along. Wednesday trailed after Rachel, holding back just a little. 'What do you think they're doing, Mom?' she asked. *Mom? Who do you think you're kidding?* she asked herself ironically. Every time she used the word she felt a tiny stab of betrayal, although it was unfair to Rachel; the woman from Earth had done far more for her than she'd had any reason to expect.

'I'm not sure.' Rachel looked worried. 'It's possible there's some trouble with the ship's systems, since the incident that injured the bridge crew—' *blink, blink.*

Wednesday nodded and pulled a face, sighed theatrically. *Am I looking bored yet?* She glanced around. There weren't that many passengers: they were mostly first-class travelers, rich business travelers and minor aristocracy from those worlds that had such. *Where's Frank?* she wondered, searching frantically while trying not to be obvious about it. *If I got him into this . . . !*

'Excuse me? Where are we going?' a worried-looking man asked Rachel, plucking at her arm. 'You see, nobody's told us any—'

'Don't worry.' Rachel managed a forced smile. 'We're just going to the evacuation station. It's only a precaution, doesn't mean they're going to evacuate us.'

'Oh good.' Still looking worried, he scampered ahead, leaving them in an island of quiet.

'Nervous?' Martin asked quietly, making Wednesday jump.

'Nervous?' She glared at him angrily. 'If they've hurt—' They rounded the curve of the corridor and passed the red-painted crash doors recessed into the wall and blocking access to the airlock tube. The evacuation station was a circular open space about eight meters across, as crowded and nervous as a diplomatic cocktail party where the Ambassador had just announced his resignation. There was standing room only, and a couple of stressed-looking stewards holding their arms across the entrance to the evacuation airlock just in case some of the more skittish passengers decided to rush it for some reason.

'May I have your attention please?' A tall, blond man with hollows under his eyes called from one side of the room. 'Would you mind clearing the inner pressure doors, please? That's right, if you could move into the room, we can get this over with cleanly.'

Oh, shit! Wednesday tensed and ran her right thumb up the frogging she'd had her pressure-smart jacket grow. She'd dialed it into a turquoise tailcoat; it felt stiff and heavy, and simultaneously thin and vulnerable – stretched to cover more than its pressure limit, it'd be useless in an emergency depressurization. The whole idea of walking into an airlock when the bad guys had taken the ship struck her as the height of idiocy, even wearing her lacy white shalwar trousers over pressure leggings and boots—

But people behind her were pushing forward, and the doors back onto the corridor were dropping slowly down, sealing off her route back to the cabins. 'What's—' she began, but Martin gripped her hand.

'Wait,' he said tensely.

'We have an announcement to make,' the blond man called. 'If I can have *silence*, please – that's better.' He smiled thinly. 'We're about fifteen minutes from docking with the repair station. When we do so, you may be asked to evacuate onto the port ring in good order. We won't know for sure if that will be necessary, or if you can return to your rooms, until after we dock. If you have to evacuate, try to do so in an orderly way – no pushing, give everybody room to move, keep walking once you hit the dockside until you reach the designated assembly area. Remember, this isn't a critical pressure evacuation. There's no risk that you'll end up breathing vacuum, and you don't need to run.'

He looked around the room. There was a brief mutter of comment, but no dissent. 'And now for another matter,' he announced. 'I've got a special message for Victoria Strowger, who I *believe* is in this room somewhere.' Wednesday jerked involuntarily, feeling Martin's fingers dig into her wrist. 'Your friend Frank is down on F deck. He sends his regards.

As a rule we're trying to keep everyone together at their designated evacuation stations, but if you want to see your friend again, you can step forward now, and I'll take you there.' His smile widened. 'This is your only chance, I'm afraid. Once we dock it'll be too late.'

Wednesday glanced between Rachel and Martin frantically. She wanted to scream: *What do I do* now? Martin looked puzzled, but dawning horror was writ large on Rachel's face. The man at the front was still talking, something about evacuation procedures. It was so slickly done, the message, that she half doubted she'd heard it.

'*Go*,' Rachel mouthed at her. A quick scribble on her paper pad: U GOT VALUE – PLAY 4 TIME.

'But—' Wednesday looked back at Martin, who was now clearly worried. *They've got Frank*, she thought frantically. *They've got Frank!* She'd been afraid, walking in there, that it was a trap, but she hadn't realized just what kind it would be.

Rachel was still scribbling. OLD NF == UR HOME GRND. Realization dawned: Wednesday nodded, feeling sick in the pit of her stomach. 'Okay,' she said, and before she could change her mind she began to shove through the crowd of bodies toward the front of the room, where the blackmailer was waiting for her.

'So who the fuck are you?' Wednesday asked belligerently. 'And what do you want?'

The woman in charge of the hijackers smiled indulgently. 'You can call me Portia, my dear. And all I want is a little talk.'

Wednesday sized her up suspiciously. The blond guy stood behind her blocking the doorway, and there were a couple of guards – one of them manning a comms console, the other watching her from behind the leader – but they'd made no move to search her or apply restraints or anything. This Portia woman wasn't what she'd expected, either. She wasn't angry, or evil-tempered, or anything. Nor was she wearing one-piece overalls with built-in pressure seals like the others. In fact, she seemed friendly and slightly indulgent. *I'd be indulgent, too, if everything was going my way,* Wednesday warned herself. 'What do you want?' she demanded. 'And where's Frank?'

'Your friend isn't here.' Portia sniffed. 'He's in a suite on B deck that hasn't, ah, been evacuated.' She flashed Wednesday a grin, baring perfect teeth at her. 'Would you like to talk to him? Just to prove that he's all right? My offer was genuine, by the way, when I said you could see him again. In fact, I'll go further; if you cooperate fully with me, then once our business is over you can have him back, intact.'

'You're a liar. Why should you?' Wednesday regretted the words almost before they were out of her mouth: *Stupid, goading her when she holds all the cards!*

But Portia didn't take it amiss. 'Over the years I've found that a reputation for keeping my word is a valuable tool – it makes negotiating much easier if everybody knows you're trustworthy. You, ah, *don't* know that yet – but if you want to talk to your friend . . . ?'

'Ah—' Wednesday felt a sick tension in her gut. 'Yeah. I'll talk to him.' *Shit! If he's all right* – A second interior voice kicked in, icily cold – *They'll be watching you both for leverage. Make no mistake, she's not doing this just for you.*

'Get the prisoner on the secure terminal,' Portia told the guard at the desk.

Wednesday moved to sit down in the offered chair. The camera's-eye view certainly showed her Frank. Her breath caught; they'd put him in a chair and taped his arms down, and he looked ill. His skin was sallow and dry. He looked up at the camera, bleary-eyed, and started. 'Wednesday, is that you?' he said, his voice rasping.

'It's me.' She clasped her hands behind her back to keep from fidgeting. 'Are you all right?'

He rolled his head sideways, as if trying to see something behind the camera. After a moment he replied, 'No, I'm a bit tied up.' He shook his head. 'They got you, too. Was it me?'

'No,' she lied, guessing what the truth would do to him. Behind the terminal she saw Portia make a little tight smile. *Bitch.*

Reality check. 'What was the last thing I did the night before the, uh, accident?' she asked, hoping desperately that he'd get it wrong, that he was just a machinima avatar, and that she'd been caught but he remained at liberty.

'You made a phone call.' He closed his eyes. 'They kept my throat under block too long,' he added. 'Talking hurts.'

'That's enough,' said Portia. The comms specialist leaned over and killed the connection before Wednesday could protest. 'Satisfied?' she asked.

'Huh.' Wednesday scowled furiously. 'So, you've got us.' She shrugged. 'What do you fucking *want*?'

The blond guy at the back of the room, the smiling blackmailer from the evacuation bay, cleared his throat. 'Boss?'

'Tell her, Franz.' Portia nodded agreeably, but Wednesday noticed that when she spoke to her soldiers her smile peeled away, exposing a frigid chill in her eyes.

'You misplaced something belonging to our, uh, predecessors,' Franz said. He looked uneasy. 'We know you hid it on the station. We want it back. When you return it to us, we have a couple of errands to run, then we'll be leaving.' He raised an eyebrow. 'Boss?'

'Here's the deal,' Portia said easily. 'You take us to the

items you left behind. We'll bring your friend Frank along so you can see him, and those nosy diplomats you were hiding out with. No, we weren't taken in by that business with the passports. Do you think we're stupid? It was easier to leave you hiding out in their cabin; that way you immobilized yourselves, saving us the trouble. But I digress . . . if you give us what we want, we'll leave you on board the station when we go. Our own ship will be arriving here soon. We'll send a rescue and salvage expedition for the liner and everybody aboard it as soon as we're clear. Despite what you're thinking, we're not interested in killing people, wholesale or retail: there's been a change of management at the top, and our job is to clean up after them.'

'Clean up?' Wednesday said skeptically. 'Clean up *what*?'

Portia sighed. 'My predecessor had some rather silly plans to, um, build himself an empire.' She flashed Wednesday that grin again. 'I'm not going to make any excuses. You wouldn't believe them anyway. To cut a long story short, he succeeded in taking over some key members of the strategic operations staff in the Moscow government. His ambitions were bigger than his common sense – he wanted to short-circuit a very long-term project of ours, of the whole of the ReMastered actually, by developing a device that's one of a class known collectively as causality-violation weapons. He also wanted to carve out an empire for himself, as maximum leader – an interstellar empire. It was quite the audacious plan, really. It's a very good thing for all of us that he was no good at the little detail work. *Unfortunately*' – she cleared her throat – 'the weapons lab on Moscow apparently tried to test the gadget prematurely. Something went wrong, spectacularly wrong.'

'You're trying to tell me it was an accident?' Wednesday demanded.

'No.' Portia looked uncomfortable for a moment. 'But

the idiot responsible – the treacherous idiot, I stress – is, ah, dead. As a direct consequence of the event. In fact, it's my job to mop up after him, tidy up the loose ends, and so on. Which includes stopping the R-bombs – I suppose you know about them? – by sending the abort codes. Which were in the bag you took, taken from the station administrator's desk, along with a bunch of other records that are of no use to you but of considerable interest to me, insofar as they'll help me root out the last of his co-conspirators.'

'Oh.' Wednesday thought for a while. 'So you want to clear everything up. Make it all better.'

'Yes.' Portia smiled brilliantly at her. 'Would you like to help us? I stress that to do anything else would amount to complicity in genocide.'

Wednesday straightened up. 'I suppose so,' she muttered with barely concealed ill grace. 'If you promise this will put an end to it all, and nobody will get hurt?'

'You have my word.' Portia nodded gravely. 'Shall we do it?'

Behind her, the one called Franz opened the door.

Darkness, stench, and a faint humming. Over the past two days, Steffi's world had closed in with nightmarish speed. Now it was a rectangle two meters long, two meters high, and one meter wide. She shared it with a plastic bucket full of excrement, a bag of dry food, and a large water bottle. Most of the time she kept the torch switched off to conserve power. She'd spent some time trying to read, and she'd done some isometric exercises – careful to ensure there was no risk of kicking the bucket over – and spent some more time sleeping fitfully. But the boredom was setting in, and when she'd heard the announcement through the wall of her cell telling them to prepare for evacuation it had come as a relief. If the hijackers were off-loading the passengers, it meant there wouldn't be anyone to get in her way when she did what had to be done.

A liner the size of the *Romanov* didn't vibrate, didn't hum, and didn't echo when docking on to a station. In fact, any sound or vibration would be a very bad sign indeed, shock waves overloading the antisound suppressors, jolts maxing out the electrogravitics, supports buckling and bulkheads crumpling. But the closet Steffi had helped Martin build her false wall into adjoined the corridor, and after the muffled sound of a slamming door she'd heard faint footsteps, then nothing. The silence went on for an eternity of minutes, like the loudest noise she'd ever heard.

I'm going to get you, she repeated to herself. *You've taken my ship, rounded up my fellow of officers, and, and* – An echo of an earlier life intruded: *back-stabbing bastards*. She wondered about Max, in the privacy of her head: he wasn't likely to have avoided the hijackers, and they might think they could use him against her. If they even cared, if they knew who she was and what she could do. *Fat chance*. Steffi was grimly certain that nobody knew the truth about her – nobody but Sven, and if her partner and front man had talked, they'd have torn the ship apart to get their hands on her. Svengali knew things about Steffi – and she knew things about him – that would have gotten either of them a one-way trip into the judicial systems of a dozen planets if the other ever cut a deal. But Steffi trusted Svengali completely. They'd worked together for a decade, culminating in this insanely ambitious tour: wet-working their way across the galaxy, two political pest control operatives against an entire government-in-exile. The promised payoff would have been enough to see both of them into comfortable retirement, *if* the back-stabbing scumbags who were paying for the grand slam hadn't panicked and hijacked the ship instead. And now, with the plans wrecked and

Svengali quite possibly out of action, Steffi was seeing red.

After an hour of careful planning, she turned the torch on and put her ear to the closet wall. Nothing. 'Here goes,' she mumbled to herself, picking up the box cutter Martin had left her. The tiles he'd had the fabricator spam out were rigid and hard to cut at first, stiffened by the fine copper wire mesh of the Faraday cage threading through them. She stabbed at one edge, then worked the blade through and began tugging it down from the top of her hideaway.

Grunting with effort, Steffi sawed a slit all the way down one side of the wall, then continued sideways at the bottom. Finally, she squatted and peeled the corner up toward her. Fumbling in the twilight she found her way out blocked by something solid. It brought it all home to her, and suddenly the stinking darkness seemed to close around her head like a fist. Gasping, she shoved as hard as she could, and the obstruction shifted.

A minute later she found the light switch in the closet. *Well, that's done it*, she told herself, heart pounding and stomach fluttering with nervous anticipation. *If they're out there—*

She opened the door. The suite was empty. 'Huh.' She took three steps forward, into the dayroom, reveling in her sudden freedom to move, taking in deep breaths of the clean air – suddenly recognizing for what it was the fetor she'd spent more than a day immersed in. Glancing around, she saw the desk. There was some kind of notepad on it, paper covered with writing in dumb pigment. Frowning, she picked it up and began to read by torchlight.

All passengers moving to evac stations. Arriving Old Newfie/station on Moscow system periphery half/hr. Help? May be evac'ing ship.

   Not trust Lt. Cdr. Fromm. The ReMastered good

at controlling people. Fromm is a puppet. PL is now a ubiq. surveillance net. Query officer by-pass working?

Feel free to use the fabricator in the trunk. It makes good toys, and you've got blanket resource access permissions.

Steffi felt her knees go weak. The thing in the closet was a general purpose fabricator, a cornucopia machine? She forced herself to sit down for a moment and close her eyes. 'Fuck!' she said softly. The possibilities were endless. Then she took a deep breath. **Query officer by-pass working.** If the hijackers were still aboard and had turned the liaison network into a surveillance grid, they would already know about her. But if they *had* evacuated the ship, she might just have a chance, *especially* if they'd left the line crew authorization system in place.

Steffi thrust her left hand into her pocket and pulled out her control rings. Sliding them onto her fingers one by one she mouthed the subvocal commands to start up her interface. *If they're watching, they'll be here any moment*, she told herself. But nothing happened; the timer began to spiral in her visual field, and the twist of a ring told her that she had new mail, but there was no knock on the door.

Slowly, she felt the ghost of a grin rising to her face as she scrolled rapidly through the ship's status reports. In dock, evacuation systems tripped, drive systems tripped, bridge systems shut down, life support on homeostatic standby. 'Thought you'd nailed down all the loose ends, did you? We'll see about that!' She turned back to the closet and leaned over the control panel of the fabricator. 'Give me an index,' she snapped at it. 'Show me guns. All the guns you can make . . .'

messengers

Old Newfie's basic systems had continued to run while the radiation shock front swept over it. Humans might be gone, life support might be dead – algal ponds crashed, macroscopic plants killed, even the cockroaches fried by the kiloGray radiation pulse – but the multimegaton wheel continued to spin endlessly in the frigid void, waiting for an uncertain return.

Wednesday's breath steamed in the darkness of the docking hub. One of Portia's minions had rigged up floodlights around the boarding tube from the liner, and stark shadows cut across the gray floor toward the spin coupling zoner. Dim silhouettes drifted slowly round, rotating between the floor and cathedral-high ceiling over a period of minutes.

'Can you hurry it up a bit?' Portia told her phone. 'We need to be able to see in here.'

'Any moment. We're still looking for the main breaker board.' Jamil and one of the other goons had headed off into the station to look for a backup power supply, wearing low-light goggles and rebreather masks in case they hit a gas trap. Getting the main reactors going would be difficult in the extreme – it would take weeks of painstaking work, checking out the reactor windings, then inching through the laborious task of bootstrapping a fusion cycle – but if they could find a backup fuel cell and light up the docking hub, they'd be able to rig a cable from the *Romanov* to the hub's switchboard, and provide power and heat and air circulation to the administrative sectors. Old Newfie had once supported thousands of inhabitants. With a source of power, it could support them again for weeks or months, even without reseeding the life support and air farms.

'So where did you hide the backup cartridge?' Franz asked Wednesday, deceptively casual.

Wednesday frowned. 'Somewhere in the police station – it was years ago, you know?' She stared at him. Something about the blond guy didn't ring true. He looked excessively tense. 'You'll need power for the lifts in order to reach it.'

'This is no time for games,' he said, glancing at Hoechst, who was listening to her comm. 'You don't want to cross her.'

'Don't I?' Wednesday glanced up at the axial cranes, skeletal gantries looming like lightning-struck trees out of the darkness high above. 'I'd never have guessed.'

Portia nodded and lowered her comm. 'We have lights,' she said, a note of satisfaction in her voice. Moments later, a loud *clack* echoed through the docking hub. The emergency floods came on overhead, casting a faint greenish glow across the floorscape. 'We should have heat and fans in a few minutes,' she added, sounding satisfied. A nod at one of her other minions, a woman with straight hair the color of straw. 'Start moving the passengers aboard, Mathilde, I want the passengers off that ship in ten minutes.'

'You're evacuating it?' Wednesday stared.

'Yes. We seem to be missing a Junior Flight Lieutenant. I don't want her getting any silly ideas about flying off while we're all aboard the station.' Portia smiled thinly. 'I'll admit that if she can hide from a ubiquitous celldar net and shoot her way past the guards who are waiting she might have a chance, but somehow I doubt it.'

'Oh.' Wednesday deflated. She felt her rings vibrate, saw a pop-up notice in her left eye: *new mail.* She tried to conceal her surprise. *(Mail? Here?)* 'Why were you killing our ambassadors?' she asked impulsively.

'Was I?' Hoechst raised an eyebrow. 'Why were you hiding out with a pair of spooks from Earth?'

'Spooks?' Wednesday shook her head in puzzlement. 'They wanted to help, once you *hijacked* the *ship*—'

Portia looked amused. '*Everybody* wants to help,' she said, raising her comm to her mouth. 'You. Whoever I'm speaking to – Jordaan? Yes, it's me. The two diplomats from Earth. And that fucking busybody journalist. We're going to the station administrator's office by way of a little detour along the way. Round up the diplomats and the scribbler. Take a backup and meet us at the station admin office in half an hour. Send Zursch and Anders to the communications room with the key, and have them wait for me there. I'll be along after I've finished with the other errands. Understood? Right. See you there.' She focused on Wednesday. 'It's quite simple.' She took a deep breath. 'I'm here to tidy up a huge mess that was left by my predecessor. If I don't tidy it up, a lot of people are going to die, starting with your friends who I just mentioned, because if I fail to tidy up the mess successfully, *I* will die, and a lot of my *people* will die, and killing your friends will be the easiest way of conveying to you – and them – just how angry that makes me. I don't really want to die, and I'd much rather not have to kill anybody – which is why I'm telling you this, to make sure you know it isn't a fucking game.' She leaned toward Wednesday, her face drawn: 'Have you got the picture yet?'

Wednesday recoiled. 'I, uh . . .' She swallowed. 'Yes.'

'Good.' Something seemed to go out of Hoechst, leaving her empty and tired. 'Everybody thinks they're doing the right thing, kid. All the time. It's about the only rule that explains how fucked-up this universe is.' A wan smile crept across her face. '*Nobody* is a villain in their own head, are they? We all *know* we're doing the right thing, which is why we're in this mess. So why don't you show me where this police post is, and we'll dig our way out of it together?'

'Uh, I, uh . . .' She was shaking, Wednesday realized distantly. Shaking with rage. *You fuckmonster, you killed my parents! And you want me to cooperate?* But it was an impotent fury: confronted with someone like Portia, there wasn't anything she could see that would make things better, no sign of any way out that didn't involve doing what the ReMastered wanted. Which was why they were the ReMastered, of course. *Not villains in their own heads.* 'This way.' *You have mail* blinked in her visual field as she walked across the frost-sparkling metal of the dock toward the empty shadows of the lift shafts. Almost instinctively, she twitched her fingers to accept.

> Hello, Wednesday. This is Herman. If you are read-
> ing this message, you are back on the Old Newfie
> communications net – which was not shut down
> when the station was evacuated. Please reply.

'Are you all right?' asked the one called Franz, reaching for her elbow as she stumbled.

'Just a slip. Icy,' she muttered. She thrust her hands

into her pocket to conceal her finger-twitched response.

I'm here. Where are you? *Send.*

The reply arrived as they waited while Jamil went over one of the lift motors with a circuit tester. It was icy cold in the station: breath clouded the air, sparkling in the twilight overspill from the lights.

'I' am where I always was. My causal channel is still linked into the station network. The station's other comms channels are still operational, including the diplomatic channel U. Hoechst intends to use to send the 'stop' code to the Muscovite R-bombs. Hoechst acquired one of the 'stop' codes from her predecessor, U. Scott. There is another code key in the station administrator's safe in the central control office. Svengali and his partner successfully panicked the surviving Muscovite diplomatic corps. My highest-probability scenario is that Hoechst's objective is to take control of the Muscovite R-bombs under cover of decommissioning them, then to use her ownership of the R-bombs to convince both the Muscovite ambassadors and the Dresdener authorities that the R-bombs are committed to an irrevocable attack. This will lay the foundations for a ReMastered takeover of Dresden. The current junta members will flee, providing promotion avenues for ReMastered proxies and generating public disorder in anticipation of an attack that will never arrive.

The lift motors creaked and hummed, and lights flickered

on inside the car. 'Seems to be working,' said Jamil, poking at the exposed control panel. 'It's got a separate flywheel power supply that I'm spinning up right now. Everybody in. What floor are we looking for?' he asked Wednesday.

'Fourth,' she mumbled.

Expect no mercy from the ReMastered. They will honor any promises they make to the letter, but semantic ambiguities will render them worthless.

Important note U. Franz Bergman is a malcontent. Prior to Hoechst's arrival in Septagon he and his partner were preparing to defect. Hoechst's hold on him is his partner's upload data. An offer of medical reincarnation coupled with the upload record may constitute leverage in his case.

Your old implant conforms to Moscow open systems specifications and is therefore able to receive this message. Unfortunately, owing to a protocol mismatch, I cannot contact other people directly. Please copy and forward this message to: Martin Springfield, Rachel Mansour, Frank Johnson, by way of your Septagon-compliant interface.

The lift squealed to a halt. Wednesday shook herself. 'Where now?' Portia demanded.

'Where?' The doors opened onto darkness. The air was freezing cold, musty, and held a residual fetor, the stench of long-dead things that had mummified in place.

'Can I have some light?'

Behind her, a torch flared into brightness, sweeping long shadows into the corners of the curving passage. Wednesday stepped out of the lift car cautiously, her breath steaming in the freezing air. 'This way.'

Trying to re-create the path she'd taken all those years ago came hard. She walked slowly, fingers twitching furiously as she copied and forwarded the message from Herman. No telling when it would arrive, but the mesh networks and routing algorithms used by implants in the developed worlds would spool the mail until she got within personal network range of someone who could handshake with them – maybe even one of the ReMastered, if they'd had their systems upgraded for work out in the feral worlds.

Frozen carpet creaked beneath her feet. Her pulse sped, and she glanced behind her, half-expecting to hear the clicking clatter of claws. Portia, Jamil, and Franz – an unlikely triptych of scheming evil – kept her moving on. They were near the toilet. 'Here,' she said, her voice small.

'You're not going to—' Franz stopped.

'What is it?' Portia demanded.

'There's a body in there. I think.' Wednesday swallowed.

'Jamil. Check it out.' Jamil pushed past, taking his torch. Portia produced a smaller one, not much more than a glow stick really. A minute of banging about, then he called, 'She's right. I see a – hmm. Freeze-dried, I guess.'

'Explain.' Portia thrust her face at Wednesday.

'He, I, I—' Wednesday shuddered convulsively. 'Like the paper said. I left it two decks down, three segments over,' she added.

'Jamil, we're going,' Portia called. 'You'd better not be wasting our time,' she told Wednesday grimly.

Wednesday led them back to the lift, which groaned and whined as it lowered them two more floors into the guts of the station. The gravity was higher there, but still not as harsh as she recalled; probably there'd been some momentum transfer between the different counterrotating sections, even superconducting magnetic bearings are unable to prevent atmospheric turbulence from bleeding off energy over time. *You have new mail*, Wednesday read, as the lift slowed. 'Come on,' Jamil said, pushing her forward. 'Let's get this over with.'

Message received. We understand. Get word out via hub comms? Any means necessary. – Martin

The gaping door and the darkness within loomed out of the darkness. The seed of a plan popped into Wednesday's head, unbidden. 'I think I hid it in one of the cupboards. Can you give me a torch?' she asked.

'Here.' Portia passed her the light wand.

'Let's see if I remember where . . .' Wednesday ducked into the room, her heart hammering and her hands damp. She'd only get one chance to do this.

Turning, she flashed the torch around overturned desks, open cupboards. *There.* She bent down and picked up a cartridge, crammed it into one pocket – scooped up a second and a third, then straightened up. 'Wrong cupboard,' she called. Where *had* she left it? She looked around, saw a flash of something the color of dried blood – leather. *Ah!* She pulled on it, and the bag slid into view. 'Got it,' she said, stepping back out into the corridor.

'Give it here.' Portia held out her hand.

'Can't you wait until we get back to the hub?' Wednesday stared at her, bravado rising. The leather wallet with the diplomatic seal of the Moscow government on it and the bulge where she'd stashed the data cartridge hung from one hand.

'*Now!*' Portia insisted.

'You promised.' Wednesday tightened her grip on the wallet and stared Portia in the eyes. 'Going to break your word?'

'No.' Hoechst blinked, then relaxed. 'No, I'm not.' She

looked like a woman awakening from a turbulent dream. 'You want to hold it until you see your friends, you go right ahead. I assume it *is* the right wallet? And the data cartridge you took?'

'Yes,' Wednesday said defensively, tightening her grip on it. The three riot cartridges she'd stolen felt huge in her hip pocket, certain to be visible. And while only Jamil had a gun slung in full sight, she had an edgy feeling that all the others were armed. They'd be carrying pistols, if nothing else. What was the old joke? *Never bring a taser to an artillery duel.*

'Then let's go visit the control center.' Portia smiled. 'Of course, if you're wasting my time, you'll have made me kill one of your friends, but you wouldn't do that, would you?'

'Never bring a taser to an artillery duel,' muttered Steffi, glancing between the compact machine pistol (with full terminal guidance for its fin-stabilized bullets, not to mention a terahertz radar sight to allow the user to make aimed shots through thin walls) and the solid-state multispectral laser cannon (with self-stabilizing turret platform and a quantum-nucleonic generator backpack that could boil a liter of water in under ten seconds). Regretfully, she picked the machine pistol, the laser's backpack being too unwieldy for the tight confines of a starship. But there was nothing stopping her from adding some other, less cumbersome toys, was there? After all, none of the spectators at her special one-woman military fashion show would be writing reviews afterward.

After half an hour, Steffi decided she was as ready as she'd ever be. The console by the door said that there was full pressure outside. *Negligent of them*, she thought as she pointed her gun through the door and scanned the corridor.

It looked clear, ghostly gray in the synthetic colors displayed by her eye-patch gunsight. *Right, here goes.*

She moved toward the nearest intersection corridor with crew country, darting forward, then pausing to scan rooms to either side. *Need a DC center console,* she decided. The oppressive silence was a reminder of the constant menace around her. If the hijackers wanted to lock down a ship, they could have depressurized it: that they hadn't meant that they'd be back. Before then, she had to eliminate any guards they'd left behind, erase her presence from their surveillance system, and regain control.

Where are *they?* she asked herself, nerves on edge as she came close to the core staircase and lift utility ducts on this deck. *They're not stupid; they'll have left a guard. They've got the surveillance net, so they must know I'm moving around up here. So where's the ambush going to be?* Smart guards wouldn't risk losing her in a maze of passages and staterooms she knew better than they did. They'd simply lock the staircase doors between pressure zones, and nail her as soon as she conveniently locked herself in a narrow moving box.

Got it. Steffi ducked sideways into a narrow crew corridor and found herself facing the blank doors of a lift shaft. Readying herself, she hit the call button and crouched beside the doors, gun raised to scan. There were two possibilities. Either the lift car would contain an unpleasant surprise, or it would be empty – in which case, they'd be waiting for her wherever she arrived.

The gun showed her an empty cube before the doors opened. She moved instantly, jamming her key ring onto the emergency override pad on the control panel. Steffi clicked her tongue in concentration as she commanded the lift car to lower to motor maintenance position and open the doors. There was space on top of the pressurized car, a platform a meter and a half wide and a meter high, ridged with cables and motor controllers leading to the prime movers at each corner of the box. She scrambled aboard, then hit the button for the training bridge deck. What happened next would depend on how many guards they'd left behind for her. If there were enough to monitor the ship surveillance network as well as lay an ambush for her, she'd already lost, but she was gambling that her cover was still intact. As long as Svengali hadn't talked, she stood a chance, because only a paranoid would take the same precautions over a Junior Flight Lieutenant that they'd need to neutralize a professional assassin . . .

The lift seemed to take forever to climb down the shaft. Steffi crouched in the middle of the roof, curling herself around her gun. Her eye patch showed her a gray rectangle, ghost shadows unfolding below it – the empty body of the lift, descending into a tube of darkness too far away for the surface-piercing gunsights to see. Four decks, three, two – the lift slowed. Steffi changed her angle, aiming past the side of the lift where the doors opened, out into the corridor.

Three targets, range five meters, group shots, gun to automatic. The machine pistol stuttered unevenly and the recoil pushed at her wrists, jets of hot gas belching from the reaction-control ducts around the barrel to center it on each target for precisely four shots. It was all over in a second. Steffi twitched around, hunting movement. Nothing: just three indistinct lumps of gray against a background of rectangles.

She hit the DOWN button again, then opened the doors and glanced incuriously at the bodies. Her forehead wrinkled. There was blood everywhere, leaking from two strength-through-joy types she recognized from the dinner table, and from – 'Max?' she said aloud, then she caught herself with a quiet snarl of fury. *The motherfucking clown who planned* this *is going to pay, with interest.* She checked her gun readouts: nothing was moving, up and down the corridor.

She pushed through a crew-side doorway, oriented herself on a narrow corridor, and headed for the emergency room. Instinct stopped her just short of the corner, dropping to one knee with gun raised. *Company?* she wondered, motionless, trying to scan a comprehensible picture through the corner wall with tiny flicks of her fingertips. *Yes? No?* There was something there, and it moved—

They fired simultaneously. Steffi sensed, and heard, the bullet zip past her head as her own gun went into spasm, squirting the remaining contents of its magazine through the wall in a surge of penetrator rounds. There was a damp sound from just around the corner, then a loud thud. Steffi reloaded mechanically, then made a final check and stepped out into the corridor in front of the emergency bridge, stepping over the body of the guard.

'Bridge systems. Speak to me,' she commanded. 'Are you listening?'

'Authenticating – welcome, Lieutenant Grace.' The bridge door slid open to reveal empty chairs, an air of deceptive normality.

'Conversational interface, please.' Steffi slid the door shut, then dropped into the pilot's chair and turned it to face the door, her gun at the ready. 'Identify all other personnel aboard ship, their locations and identities. If anyone moves toward this deck, let me know. Next, display on screen two all-system upgrades to passenger liaison network since previous departure. List whereabouts of all passengers traveling from and native to Tonto and Newpeace.' The walls began to fill up with information. 'Dump specifics to my stash.' Steffi smiled happily. 'Are all officers authenticated by retinal scan? Good. Who authorized the last PLN reload? Good. Now stand by to record a new job sequence.'

Wednesday had walked over to the desk at the front of the evacuation assembly point as if she didn't have a care in the world. Rachel watched with growing misgivings as she spoke quietly to the fair-haired guy and they left together through the side exit into crew country. Martin leaned close. 'I hope she'll be all right.'

Half an hour later it was their turn. The passengers were growing more restive, talking among themselves in a quiet buzz of nervous anticipation, when a woman ducked through the door. 'Rachel Mansour? Martin Springfield? Please come forward!'

She gripped Martin's hand, squeezing out a message in a private code rusty from disuse: '*Rumbled.*'

'*Ack. Go?*'

'*Yes.*' She pulled him forward, pushing between a yakking family group and a self-important fellow in the robe of an Umbrian merchant banker. 'You want to talk?' she asked, staring at the woman.

'No, I want you both to come with me,' she said casually. 'Someone else wants to talk to you.'

'Then we'll be happy to comply,' Rachel said, forcing a smile. *All this, and not even a briefing beforehand?* For a moment she wished she was back in the claustrophobic tenement off the Place du Molard, waiting for the bomb squad. She tried not to notice Martin, whose nervousness was transparently obvious. 'Where do you want us to go?'

'Follow me.' The woman opened the side door and motioned them through. She had a friend waiting on the other side, a big guy who held his gun openly and watched them with incurious eyes. 'This way.'

She led them up a short staircase and out into a wide

cargo tunnel. The air became increasingly chilly as they walked along it. Rachel shivered. She wasn't dressed for an excursion into a freezer hold. 'Where are we?'

'Keep it for the boss.'

'If you say so.' Rachel tried to keep her voice light, as if this was a mystery excursion managed by the crew to keep bored passengers amused. They turned a corner onto a wider docking tunnel, then up a ramp that led into a vast twilight space. Floods glittered high above as the gravity did an alarmingly abrupt fade, dropping to less than a tenth of normal in the space of a few meters. *We're outside the ship*, she squeezed. Martin nodded. Not for the first time she wished she dared use her implants to text him, but the risk of interception in the absence of a secured quantum channel was too great. *If only I knew how complete their surveillance capability was*, she told herself. *If.* She shivered violently and watched her breath steam before her face. 'Far to go?'

The blond woman motioned her toward a doorway at the far side of the docking hub. Warm light shone from it. 'Shit, it's cold out here,' Martin muttered. They hurried forward without any urging on the part of their guards.

'Stop.' The one with the gun held up a hand as they neared the door. 'Mathilde?'

'Yah.' The blond woman produced a bulky comm and spoke into it. 'Mathilde here. The two – diplomats. Outside control. I'm sending them in.' She turned and glared at Rachel and Martin, waving at the door. 'That way.'

'Where else?' Rachel looked around as she entered the room. It was brightly lit, and a whine from overhead suggested that a local aircon unit was fighting a losing battle against the chill. The man with the gun was behind them, and for a sickening moment as she saw the largely empty room, she wondered if he was meant to kill them and leave their bodies there. Then a door slid open in the wall opposite.

'Go in.' Gun-boy waved them forward. 'It's a lift.'

'Okay, I'm going, I'm going.' Rachel stepped forward. Martin followed her, with Gun-boy trailing to the rear. The doors closed and the lift began to move, sinking toward the high-gee levels of the station. It squealed as it went, long-idle wheels protesting as they clawed along toothed rails that had chilled below normal operating temperatures. They descended in silence, Rachel leaning against Martin in the far corner of the cargo lift from the guard. The guard kept his weapon on them the whole time, seemingly immune to distraction.

The lift juddered to a halt, and its door slid open on a well-lit corridor. There were more fans, humming and grating at overload. The chill was less extreme, and when the guard waved them toward an open door at the other end of the passage, Rachel couldn't see her breath. 'Where are we?' she asked.

'Waiting for the boss. Go right in.' Gun-boy looked bored and annoyed, but not inclined toward immediate violence. Rachel tensed, then nodded and went right in. There was a sign on the open door she read as she passed it: DIRECTOR'S SUITE. *Well, what a surprise*, she thought tiredly, mentally kicking herself for not having seen this coming. Then her implant twitched. She had to suppress a start as she blinked, rapidly: *new mail* here, *of all places? How* . . .

She read it quickly, almost trancing out – almost missing the deep pile carpet, the withered brown trees in their pots to either side of the big wood-topped desk, and the door leading into the inner office. Then *more* mail came in – this time, a reply from Martin. She glanced at him sharply, then turned round to stare at Gun-boy. The goon leaned against the wall just inside the doorway. 'Who is this boss of yours?' she asked. 'Do we have to wait long?'

'You wait until she gets here.' The fan in the office rattled slightly, pumping tepid air in to dilute the chill. A thin layer of dust covered the desk, the visitor's chairs, an empty watercooler.

'Mind if I sit down?' asked Martin.

'Be my guest.' Gun-boy raised an ironic eyebrow, and Martin sat down hastily before he changed his mind. Rachel stepped sideways in front of him, and he slipped an arm protectively around her waist, under the hem of her jacket.

'Can you tell us anything?' Rachel asked quietly as Martin slipped something into her waistband. 'Like what this is all about?'

'No.'

'Okay.' Rachel sighed. 'If that's how you want it.' She sat down on the chair to Martin's right and leaned against him, putting her left arm behind his shoulder. *So they're not monitoring the station protocols for traffic yet*, she thought, hungry for hope. *If they were, that mail from Wednesday would have set them off.* She let her arm drop behind Martin's back, then twisted her wrist round and fumbled with the object in her waistband until it went up her sleeve to mate with its companion.

Click. She felt, rather than heard, the noise. The gadget made handshake with her implants, and a countdown timer appeared in her vision: the number of seconds it would take for the gel-phase fuel cell to power up and the gadget to begin assembling itself. She'd seldom felt so naked in her life. If they'd extended the surface-piercing radar surveillance network from the ship into this room seven shades of alarm would be going off right now, and Gun-boy would put a bullet through her face long before the gadget was ready. Otherwise—

A creaking whine from the corridor announced the arrival of another lift car. A few seconds later Mathilde appeared, this time leading Frank. Frank was in a bad way, his skin ashen and his hands taped together in front of him. He looked around, eyes unreadable, wearing the same clothes he'd been in when Martin had interviewed him. They were the worse for wear. 'Sit,' Mathilde told him, pointing to the chair next to Rachel. She produced a box cutter: 'Hold out your hands. We've got the girl. Piss us off, and you'll never see her again.'

Frank cleared his throat. 'I understand,' he grunted, rubbing his wrists. He glared at her resentfully. 'What now?'

'You wait.' Mathilde took a step back to stand beside Gun-boy.

'Lining up all your targets, huh?'

She cast Martin a very ugly look. 'Wait for the boss. She won't be long now.'

'You're Frank, aren't you? What happened?' Rachel whispered to him.

Frank grunted, and rubbed at his wrists again. 'Got me early. In my room. You're his partner?' He jerked his chin at Martin. 'Thought I was the only one at first. Where are we?'

'Old Newfie. Wednesday's station. Listen, we hid her but they – had you. She went with them.'

'Shit!' He met her eyes with an expression of terrible resignation. 'You know what this means.'

Rachel gave a slight nod in the direction of the guards. 'Don't say it.'

'You can say anything you like,' Mathilde called, grinning maliciously at him. 'We have complete freedom of speech – anything you want to say we will listen to.'

'Fuck you!' Frank glared at her.

'Shut up.' Gun-boy pointed his machine pistol at Frank. For a tense moment Rachel was sure he would say something. The seconds stretched out into an infinitely long moment as Frank and the guard stared – then Frank slumped back in his chair.

"Sokay. I can let go.' Frank glanced at her and yawned, his jaw muscles crackling. 'I'm used to it – was used to it.' He rubbed his hands together, making small circling movements. Rachel tried not to show any sign of having noticed his frantic control gestures. *Someone's got a backlog of e-mail,* she guessed, *or itchy fingers.*

They sat in silence for a couple of minutes, then a buzzing noise from along the corridor announced the imminent arrival of yet another self-propelled lift car. Rachel looked round automatically.

The doors opened. Many footsteps, moving toward the office in the curious broken rhythm of fractional gee. First in was a skinny, edgy-looking man; then a woman of a certain age, her eyes cold and her expression satisfied. Then Wednesday, walking in front of a guy with long hair in a ponytail, holding a boxy urban combat weapon. Her expression was ugly when she saw Frank looking like a morning-after wreck.

'Rachel Mansour, from the UN, I presume?' The woman walked behind the station manager's desk, turned the chair round, and sat down in it. 'I'm very pleased to meet you.' She smiled as she reached into an outer pocket and placed a compact pistol on the desk in front of her, its barrel pointed at Rachel. 'I see you've already met our young runaway. That will make things much simpler. Just one more person to come, then I think we'll begin.'

irrevocable

They'd untaped his hands; leaning back, ignoring the guard, Frank had twitched his rings, switching his optic implants and ear pickups to record promiscuously. There was no point missing anything, even his own execution.

BING. He'd jumped a little when the mail flag came up; something from Wednesday. But the guard hadn't noticed. None of them noticed. Just typical ReMastered foot soldiers, obedient and lethal. He read the message and felt his palms go damp. He was glad he was sitting down. *So now Wednesday's invisible friend is sending me e-mail? But he's got to use her as a relay because she's the only one of us with a setup compatible with this station? Shit.*

Frank reflected bleakly on the need for bandwidth. *If there's some way to get that report out, wherever we are . . . we can't all just vanish, can we?* But the truth was anything but reassuring. Liners *did* vanish from time to time, and if this was the hijacking it appeared to be – bearing all the slick signs of ReMastered covert ops, the sly subversion of emergency reflexes – then there was no way word would ever get out.

BING. More mail from Wednesday had arrived, broadcast to him and Rachel and Martin – what? Some sort of code attachment, a new interface protocol for his implant to talk to the station's ether. He tried to keep his face impassive as he mentally crossed his fingers and loaded the untrusted executable.

Then the newcomers arrived. Frank stared at them, his world narrowed suddenly to a single panicky choice, a flashback going back decades. He took it all in, Wednesday sullen between two guards, the woman in front holding the leather satchel, smiling at him. He remembered the bright sunlight on the rooftop of the Demosthenes Hotel, the acrid smell of propane stoves and dog shit wafting on the breeze across downtown Samara. Alice turning toward the parapet with a camera drone in her hands. The woman, again. Blond destruction on the day it rained bullets, the day when everything changed.

Frank blinked up at her. 'Oh holy shitting fucking Christ, it's *you*—'

'Increasing my little piggie count, this time.' Her smile broadened, turning ugly at the edges. 'We really must stop bumping into each other like this, mustn't we?'

'Shit, shit, shit—' Frank felt nauseous. The hot smell of Alice's blood was in his nose; the roar and screams of the crowd as the bullets began spattering into them. 'You were in Samara. On Newpeace. Who *are* you?' He barely noticed Wednesday's jolt of surprise from the other side of the room as he focused in on the woman's face.

'I'm U. Portia Hoechst, DepartmentSecretariat of Division Four of the Department of External Environmental Control, planetary dominion of Newpeace. The "U" is short for ubermensch, or ubermadchen, take your pick.' Her smile was as wide as a shark's gape. 'At this point in the proceedings I'm supposed to gloatingly tell you my evil plans before I kill you. Then, if you believe the movies, a steel-jawed hero is supposed to erupt through the walls and teach me the error of my ways with extreme prejudice.'

She snorted. 'Except there aren't any steel-jawed heroes within sixteen light years of this station.' A hint of mirth in her eyes. 'Not even that Third Lieutenant you've got squirreled away, at least not once the guards are through with her.' Frank felt his nails digging into the palms of his hands; his vision went gray and pixilated for a few seconds, and his heart pounded before he realized that it was the firmware patch from Wednesday loading on his implant's virtual machine, combined with a raw, primal rage.

'Why are you telling us this?' Rachel asked quietly.

'Because I like a fucking audience!' Hoechst sat up. 'And it's going to be over soon, anyway.' She stopped smiling. 'Oh, about the "let me tell you everything before I kill you" bit: I'm not going to kill you. You might wish I *had*, but I'm not. As soon as I've got this station on auxiliary internal power and disabled external communications, all the passengers and crew are coming aboard. It won't be much fun, but you'll be able to last for the couple of months it takes for a rescue ship to reach you. Even you, Frank.' A flicker of a smile. 'No reeducation camps here. You're getting the VIP treatment.'

Frank stayed quiet, his guts tense. *Fuck, we're still on the net!* he realized. The station's causal channels were still working. This packet from Herman, whoever he was, was a protocol converter – with gathering disbelief Frank realized that he wasn't cut off anymore. He could send mail. Or even pipe his raw recording feed straight to Eric, back home, there to do whatever he could with the posthumous spool. *Take it like you give it, you fuckers!* he thought triumphantly.

His hands folded together against the cold, nobody saw him twisting his rings, setting up the narrowcast stream to his inbox on Earth. *I am a camera!*

Steffi watched the rerun of Svengali's execution in grainy monochrome, tracking it through the labyrinthine maze of the surveillance system take spooled by the ship's memory as the bridge systems hummed around her, rewinding the vessel's software model of itself back to the state it had been in before the ReMastered lobotomized it.

She'd thought she was angry when the double-crossing clients ran amok, angry when she'd spent long hours crouched in a dark closet space with the softshoe shuffle of guards outside the door. But she hadn't been angry at all. Not in comparison to her current state of mind. Livid with rage just barely began to describe it.

She'd worked with Sven for just short of a decade. In many ways they'd been closer than a married couple – herself the pretty face up front and visible, and he the fixer in the background, oiling the gears and reeling in the contracts. He'd found her when she was a teen punk, heading for rehab or a one-way trip to the exile colonies, seen through the rust and grime to the hard metal beneath, and polished it to a brilliant shine. In the early years she'd adored him, back before she matured enough to see him as he really was – theirs hadn't been a sexual relationship (beyond an early exploratory fumbling), but it was a partnership based on need, and mutual respect, and blood. And now, just as they'd been on the edge of their greatest coup—

'I'm going to find you, and you're going to wish you'd committed suicide first,' she told the face frozen to the screen. 'And then—' her eyebrows furrowed – 'I'm going to . . .' *Going to do what?*

Steffi leaned back her chair and closed her eyes, forcing the tight ball of rage back into the recesses of her skull, out of the way until it was needed. *Where do I stand?* She had the key to their bank accounts, if she needed it. And she had a couple of other keys, picked up here or there. She'd been in an office in Turku and a roadside rest stop on Eiger's World, and a house on Earth, too, all in the past six months. Sven had done his homework before taking on the job, explained the alarming consequences of success to her and the importance of finding the keys. There'd been no point rummaging by the roadside, but she had *two* of them in her pocket, now, keys to the gates of hell itself. That had to count for something, didn't it? And if the dim-witted UN diplomats didn't know who she was, then all that left was the ReMastered.

If I can take them out of the picture, I can become *Lieutenant Steffi Grace, and nobody will know any different,* she realized. *Or I can try for the third key, and access to a Muscovite diplomatic channel.* She began to smile, her lips pulling back from her teeth in an expression very close to a feral snarl. *See how they like it when I derail their plans.* She sat up and leaned toward the pilot console. 'Bridge systems, get me the full station package on our current port. Display dockside schematics on window four. Do you have access to the loading bay external cameras? Do you have access to the station communications network? Good. Record new job sequence, activation key *rosebud*.'

'You're going to maroon us,' Wednesday said flatly. She took a stride toward the desk, but a tense motion with a gun barrel stopped her sharply. She turned to stare at Frank, wringing her hands together. Frank raised an eyebrow at her. *What can I do about it?* he thought, his stomach turning over. *Why couldn't you have stayed hidden?*

'I'm not going to leave you alone for long.' Hoechst shrugged. 'My own ship's heading for home with a message too secret to trust to certain, shall we say, monitored channels. While it's gone I need to take the *Romanov* on a little errand. I'm mopping up after my predecessor – one U. Vannevar Scott – who got a little bit too big for his boots.' That flickering smile. Almost without willing it Frank found himself staring at Wednesday. She looked as scared as he felt, her face drained and pale, but resolute, the condemned facing the scaffold. He forced himself to look back at Hoechst. The blinking status display in his left eye told its own story: every word that hit his ears was stripped down to its constituent bits, entangled with a qubit interface somewhere in the magical weirdness of a causal channel, the other end of which would pipe the data into Eric's inbox. *Let's see how topical we can make this news, shall we,* he thought at Hoechst, feeling the fear slowly turn to a warm glow of triumphant accomplishment. *J'accuse!*

'Scott decided to carve out his own little Directorate,' Hoechst continued, oblivious to the true size of her potential audience. 'First, he needed a lever. That lever was going to be a bucolic backwater called Moscow. He got funding and clearance to operate on Moscow by offering the Directorate a new way of developing weapons forbidden by the Enemy – you call it the Eschaton – like temporal ablators. Moscow was going to be his weapons proving ground, a backwater nobody would expect to be going after causality-violation devices. *Actually* he wanted to be dictator of a whole bunch of planets, and Moscow was going to be his tool of conquest – also his insurance against the wrath of the High Directorate. But he got sloppy. He puppetized half the Muscovite military high command – an administrative backwater on that planet, nobody paid much attention to them – and thoroughly subverted the interstellar deterrent group. But then he decided to accelerate the weapons test program he'd promised the Directorate and use them himself instead of the original clumsy R-bomb plan.'

Wednesday stared at her. 'You're telling me the nova was a fucked-up weapons test?'

'Well, sure. In fact, it was an *unauthorized* fuck up.' Hoechst looked pensive. She reached into her jacket pocket and pulled out a small key, placing it very carefully in the middle of the desk in front of her. 'We all make mistakes. In Scott's case, it was his last; he'd gotten sloppy, and the – my boss – cleared me to take him down and rectify the situation. That was before we drained him and discovered certain unpleasant facts about his treason. *That cartridge'* – she held out a hand toward Wednesday – 'is one of the loose ends. Immigration records of Scott's agents moving in and out of Moscow. And details of the weapons project and the test schedule. Nothing we want to leave lying around. It's a *severe* political embarrassment.'

'There's more, isn't there?' Frank asked, fascinated.

'Well, no shit!' Hoechst looked at him curiously, as if wondering why he was so interested in the abstract issues, rather than the proximate fate of his own skin. 'There's a flight of four R-bombs coming.' She frowned. 'The cover story is that they're aimed at New Dresden. And that's what the Muscovite diplomats think.'

'What did he—'

'Shut the fuck up!' Hoechst frowned. She tapped one finger on the key. 'They're supposed to be running on New Dresden. That's the official target ops plan that was on file, isn't it? That's what the Muscovite diplomats think. And they're next to invisible when they're under way. Except our fucking asshole Ubermensch Vannevar Scott was too cute by half. While he was puppetizing the Muscovite Defense Ministry, the *first* group he hit was the deterrence operations staff, including the flight crew of one of the bombers – the one that isn't responding to messages. He was planning his defection at least ten years before Moscow went bang: one of those fucking bombers is running on *Newpeace*, our new regional capital, which is about as distant from Moscow as New Dresden.

'Not many ReMastered know this,' she added drily, 'and my boss wants to keep it that way.'

Frank sat up straight. 'Are you telling us the business with New Dresden, the ambassadors—'

'*I* haven't been bumping off foreign diplomats.' She shook her head vehemently. 'That was Scott's plan. I told you he was sloppy, didn't I? When things went wrong, when Moscow Prime exploded, he took steps to sweep the dirt under the rug. He paid an extremely accomplished assassin, the one you called Svengali.' For a moment she looked extremely tired. 'Which is presumably what brought you aboard the *Romanov*,' she murmured in Rachel's direction. Rachel stared at her, face impassive. 'Svengali won't be bothering us anymore, needless to say.'

'You want me to believe that this was all *one man's* rogue operation?' Rachel asked, her voice low and controlled.

'Pretty much.' For a moment Hoechst looked terribly old. 'Don't underestimate him: U. Scott was one of the highest-ranking officials in, ah, External State Security. The foreign espionage service, in other words. And he was planning a coup. He was going to take Moscow and use the R-bombs to hold the entire Directorate at bay, and he was going to leverage his takeover of Moscow to destabilize New Dresden, via the trade war. He was already infiltrating the Dresden Foreign Ministry – without authorization. If he succeeded, he'd have had two planets, the beginnings of his own pocket interstellar empire.' She looked at Frank, meeting his eyes. 'I know what you think of us. Regardless of that, whatever you think of our ideology, we are not insane, and we are not suicidal. One of the goals of the ReMastered Directorate is to render interstellar warfare not merely unthinkable, but impossible. Scott had to go.'

She sounds as if she's trying to convince herself, Frank realized with a sinking feeling. This was *not* what he'd wanted to hear from her. He'd expected venomously triumphant self-justification, perhaps, or a gloating confession. *Not this!* he thought despairingly. *If Eric decides to run this, it'll be about the best piece of pro-ReMastered press they could ask for!* The pot of gold at the end of Frank's starbow had just turned out to be a chamber pot full of shit – and despite what he'd said earlier about journalistic ethics being a crock, he couldn't see any obvious holes in her argument. Even releasing the prisoners in Hoechst's stolen memory diamond – expensive as such a process would be – would probably not reverse its effect by much.

She took a deep breath and continued her confession: 'Luckily, Scott pushed too hard, and the wheels came off. There are a couple of thousand Ubers on Newpeace, not to mention the ordinary humans, who would perhaps be of some concern to you. We're spread terribly thin; if we have to evacuate that planet, we'd lose half a century's hard work. There's no way we could possibly convince all the Muscovite ambassadors to agree to cancel the R-bomb attack if they knew the truth. Doesn't that mean something to you?'

Frank nodded, dazed. He looked around, taking in other shocked expressions. The tension in the ReMastered soldiers. The twitchy look on the blond guy standing against the wall next to Wednesday said it all. She'd laid out the dictator's new suit in front of them, and it was threadbare: they were clearly shocked by Hoechst's revelations. The spook from the revolution on Newpeace all those years ago, the gray eminence at the center of a web of interstellar assassination and intrigue, turned out to be a fixer who was desperately trying to *save* a planet from the posthumous legacy of a genocidal megalomaniac—

'It takes two to send the cancel code. I've got one of them – right here.' She tapped the key again. There's a causal channel connected to the TALIGENT offense control network: they abandoned it when they evacuated the station, but it wasn't disconnected. I had Zursch and Anders collect the station manager's key and take it there already. Hardware authentication, you see, all you need are the tokens. You don't disconnect causal channels without good reason; they're too expensive to set up in the first place.

'You have no idea how much it cost us to get our hands on this key – we had to extract it from the Ambassador to Newpeace. You don't need to concern yourselves with how. The station manager's was easier – silly fool actually left it in his office safe.' She shrugged. 'There's a diplomatic channel here, down in the communications center. One that s linked into the military TALIGENT network.

BING. New mail. *Not now,* Frank thought irritably, blinking it open before him. From: Wednesday. GOT 2 GO. SORRY. *Huh?* He glanced at her. 'What—'

'You'll be wanting that cartridge, I suppose,' Wednesday said, her expression sullen. 'What happens to us then?'

'I destroy it in front of you.' Hoechst nodded at Frank. 'You're here to witness this.' A flicker of a grin. 'Same as last time, without the unpleasant after-effects. Which were not of my choosing, I should add.' Her gaze fell on Rachel next. 'I then send the cancel codes to the R-bombs, using the station manager's console, and take the *Romanov* to go pick up the crews and destroy the evidence. *You* get to wait here in the cold and try to keep everybody on the station alive until the rescue ship from Tonto arrives. After that—' She shook her head. 'Not my department.'

'Diplomatic immunity,' Rachel said in a voice as dry as bone.

'Are you going to get picky? If it means a couple of hundred million innocent people die as a result?' Hoechst stared at her through narrowed eyes. 'Thought not.'

'May I see the key?' Wednesday walked closer to the desk.

'Sure.' Hoechst held it up, twirling it slowly between forefinger and thumb, evidently enjoying the gesture. 'Now, Wednesday child, if you'd be so good as to hand me the cartridge—'

The lights flickered.

Hoechst froze. 'Mathilde,' she said thoughtfully, 'it occurs to me that we haven't heard from Joanna, or Stepan and Roman for that matter. I want you to take every available body – not you, Franz, you're staying here – and deal with that missing Third Lieutenant. Then find out what happened to Joanna and her boys. Nothing good, I expect.'

'Yes, boss.' Mathilde headed for the door immediately, looking annoyed. She tagged Gun-boy on the way through. 'C'mon, hunting time.'

The lights flickered again. 'What do you suppose she's doing?' asked Frank.

Steffi whistled as she walked, hastily, toward the docking tunnel. A head-up clock counted down in front of her left eye: *eighty-two, eighty-one, eighty* . . . She broke into a trot as the count headed for the final minute.

Big passenger-carrying spaceships were not designed to undock from big, high-population space stations by accident, or indeed anything short of a carefully choreographed and scheduled departure, overseen by the port authorities and the ship's bridge crew. Fail-safe clamps pressurized by the atmosphere aboard both craft held the *Romanov*'s docking level against the hull of Old Newfie's lifesystem, thousands of tons of force that could only be released by a controlled depressurization of the clamp rings. But Old Newfie had been reconfigured for undocking without port command authority before the final evacuation, and Steffi had usurped control over the *Romanov*'s life circuit as final officer on board. She'd given the bridge system a program to execute it, and she didn't want to be around when the watchdog timer counted down to zero and set it off.

The main boarding ramp was in sight, a tunnel rising up to the loading deck of the station, huge station pressure doors visible to either side as looming shadows. Steffi ducked into a side door and trotted up the maintenance path alongside the main ramp, gray walls closing in bare centimeters to either side of her shoulders. *Forty-seven, forty-six . . .* And she was facing the emergency airlock, a domed door set in a solid bulkhead beside the main tunnel. She spun the manual override wheel and stepped into the rotating chamber, cranked it round – basic hand cranks were provided in case of a power failure – and tumbled out into the shadows alongside the big station doors.

Too close, she thought, pulling her night-vision goggles down. The twilit dock was a maze of shadows and eerily glowing heat patches. A huge slug trail of luminosity led away from the tunnel, toward a door leading to the main customs post – waste heat from the passengers whom the ReMastered had taken aboard the station, probably. But there was nobody in sight. *Careless*, Steffi thought, and she darted away from the airlock toward the towering wall of one of the station spokes, determined and ready to execute the second stage of her plan.

Something thumped her left arm exactly like a blow

from a careless passerby, just as her threat indicator lit up and her eye patch outlined a door that had just opened. Steffi reacted instinctively, her little machine pistol chattering to itself. The bullet paths curved weirdly in the Coriolis force, spiraling toward the target as the rounds overcorrected for the changing centrifugal effect: another bullet whispered through the air where her head had been a fraction of a second earlier, then her attacker collapsed. Steffi ran as fast as she could for the tower, but something was wrong. She felt as if she weighed too much, and when she tried to reach for a reload her left arm flopped around, not working properly.

'Shit.' She crouched in the doorway, heart pounding, panting for breath in the freezing air. *Now* the pain started, coming in waves that almost made her faint. Her left hand felt sticky. She put down her gun and fumbled, one-handed, for one of the gel trauma packs she'd had the cornucopia spit out for her. 'It's only a flesh wound,' she told herself through chattering teeth. 'It's only—'

The gel pack went in and for a moment everything was gray and grainy. Then the pain didn't so much subside as begin to regularize, not driving her to the brink of unconsciousness, becoming possible to manage. Steffi leaned back against the wall and panted, then picked up her gun. *If I stay here, they'll see my heat trace,* she realized. *And besides . . .*

Two, one, zero: the countdown stopped. A noise like a million steam kettles boiling as one came from the vicinity of the docking doors. Steffi winced as her eardrums pulsed once, twice – then with a huge crashing boom the doors slammed down into the space the *Romanov*'s tunnel had just pulled away from.

Got you, you bastards! she thought, although exhaustion and pain sapped the realization of all pleasure. *Now let's see how accurate that floor plan is.*

Hoechst looked uncertain for a moment, as a faint vibration traveled through the deck. 'The passengers are all in the customs hall,' she said, glancing at Franz. 'Why don't you go—'

Frank, distracted, glanced sideways at Wednesday. He sat up. 'What are you—'

Wednesday pulled a plastic cylinder out of her pocket and held it toward Hoechst. 'Share and enjoy.' There was a note of anger in her voice, and something else, something like triumph that made Frank dive for the floor, covering his eyes as she tossed the cylinder at the desk—

There was a brilliant flash of blue and a loud bang.

Wednesday was already halfway to the door as a hot, damp wave pummeled across the top of Frank's head. It solidified almost instantly, aerogel foam congealing in a hazy fine mesh of fog with glass-sharp knife edges. Someone inside the fogbank was coughing and gargling. The remaining guard dived into it, desperately trying to batter and scoop his way through to Hoechst, choking in the misty sponge created by the riot bomb.

Frank rolled over on his back, taking in a confused kaleidoscope of impressions. *Someone* zipped past his face in a blur of motion. A buzzing rattle set his teeth on edge. Vague shadows at the limits of vision turned and fell. There was a scream, sharply cut off, a gurgling sound from the fogbank, a painfully loud bang from a riot gun discharging through a doorway, and more blue foam drifting into the room, blocking the door, congealing in sticky, spiky lumps.

He finished rolling, gasping for breath. *I'm still alive?* he wondered, dully. 'Wednesday!' he called.

'Save it.' That was Martin. A groaning sound came from the floor.

'You. Frank. Help me.' That was Rachel's voice, panting, gasping. *What's wrong?* he wondered. He sat up, momentarily chagrined not to have seen the fight, expecting a soldier's gun in his face at any moment.

'We've *got* to get her out of there!' Rachel was half-inside the riot foam fogbank, hacking at it with a plastic-bladed knife she'd assembled from the stiffened lapels of her jacket by some kind of sartorial black magic. 'Unless it's set to melt, she's going to suffocate!'

The remaining ReMastered guard lay on the floor, splayed out as if a compact tornado had zapped him with a UV optical taser. The edgy one, the traitor, sat very still, watching everything alertly. For some reason he seemed very calm. 'You,' Frank gasped. 'Help.'

'No.' He cocked his head on one side, eyes bright, and very deliberately crossed his arms. 'Let her choke.'

'What? I don't understand—'

Frank bent over one of the guards, searching his belt for some kind of knife, anything to help Rachel with. Martin seemed stunned, shaking his head like a punch-drunk fighter. The semiconscious man at Frank's feet stirred. Frank did a double take and changed tasks, rolling the man over. 'Anyone got some tape?'

'I have.' The guy who'd given Frank the diamond sounded drained by the effort of talking. He stood up slowly, paused when Rachel looked round at him, then slowly knelt and pulled a roll of utility tape from one pocket. He yanked the guard's arms round and taped his wrists together behind his back, then repeated the job on his ankles and moved on. 'I'd really be happier if you'd leave Portia to die,' he added slowly, raising his voice and looking at Rachel as she panted, digging large lumps of bluish glassy foam loose from the mound. 'She's killed more people than you can imagine.'

'But if I leave her, what does that make *me*?' Rachel gasped between attacks.

'She's—' Frank stopped as Rachel straightened up, shaking her head. He looked past her; she'd dug as far as the edge of the desk, far enough to see that the blue-tinted foam was turning red.

'What the fuck do we do now?'

'We—' the blond guy stopped. 'Portia lies,' he said conversationally. 'She lies instinctively. I don't know whether she was telling the truth or not, but that girl got away with, with the evidence. The smoking gun. I don't know what she thinks she's doing, but if she gets the evidence to the communications room where the secure hotline terminal to the R-bombers is located – or if *you* do – she could destroy a planet. She's got the key. Right now we've got a problem in the shape of about twelve other ReMastered soldiers, mostly standing guard over the passengers, but at least two of them will be on the *Romanov*'s emergency bridge. Unless Portia was right and that missing officer—' He stopped.

'What is it?' Frank leaned toward him: 'Tell me, dammit!'

'Portia sent the other key to the comms room. Wednesday's on her way – she's not a fool, she's got something in mind – and Portia as good as told her that she'd ordered her family killed.' For a moment the blond man looked as if someone had walked over his grave. 'What's she going to do now?'

'Oh shit.' Martin was struggling to his feet, lurching drunkenly. 'We have to get to the comms room. Franz, can you talk your way past whoever's guarding it?'

'I can try.' The blond guy – Franz – stared at him. 'Can I rely on you to support my petition for diplomatic asylum if I do? And to help me obtain a body for one of the involuntary uploads in the memory diamond he's carrying?' He nodded at Frank.

'You want to – *okay*, yes. I think I can swing asylum for you. You won't have to worry about the ReMastered on Earth. They won't be looking our way for a very long time to come.' Rachel stood up, still panting, red-faced and looking as if she'd run a marathon. 'Military boost,' she said, managing to force a smile as Frank focused on her. 'I just hope the comms center systems are shut down right now—'

'Involuntary?' Frank interrupted. 'Would they be a suitable witness for, um, excesses committed by *her*?' He cracked his knuckles.

'I think so,' Franz said, almost absentmindedly. 'The comms center must still be running, no? For the evacuation.' He examined the mound of blue foam that blocked the exit Wednesday had taken. 'Telemetry during undocking, availability for ships coming to visit in the future – like the *Romanov* – that sort of thing.'

'Do we know where it *is*?' Frank asked.

'As far as I know, our only expert on the layout of this station is currently running away from us carrying one of the two keys it will take to kill everyone on Newpeace.' Franz carefully placed a hand on top of a foamy stalagmite and tugged, then winced: his palm was red when he pulled it away. 'I suggest we try to figure out a way to go round.'

'Mail her,' Frank suggested to Rachel.

She paused, thoughtful. 'Not yet. But she sideloaded us the local comms protocol stack—'

He twitched his rings. 'Yeah, there's an online map. Follow the yellow brick road.' He looked worried. 'I hope she's all right.'

The station's communication center was a broad, semi-circular space a couple of decks below the station manager's office. Two horseshoe-shaped desks provided a workspace for three chairs each; one-half of the wall was occupied by a systems diagram depicting the mesh of long-distance band-width bearers that constituted the Moscow system's intrasystem network of causal channels. 'Intrasystem' was a bit of an understatement – Old Newfie and some of the other stations were actually light years outside the system's Oort cloud, and the network also showed those interstellar channels that reached out across the gulf of parsecs to neighboring worlds – and the control center was hardly the core of the comms system. Most of the real action took place in a sealed server room full of silent equipment racks on the floor below. But human management demanded a hierarchy of control, and from this nerve center commands could be issued to send flash messages across interstellar space, queries to the home world, even directives to the TALIGENT defense hotline network.

The flat wall opposite the curved systems map was a solid slab of diamond-reinforced glass, triple-glazed against the chilly vacuum. It looked out from one wall of a spoke, gazing toward infinity. The void wheeled around it outside, a baleful red-and-violet smoke ring covering half the sky.

The room had been left in good order when the station was evacuated. Dark as a desert night and chilly as a freezer, the dust had slowly settled in a thin layer across the work-stations and procedure folders. Years passed as the smoke ring whirled larger, blowing toward the window. Then the humans returned. First came two soldiers, quiet and sub-dued in the face of the staring void: then a small death, remorseless and fast.

Lying outstretched in the duct above the room, looking down through the air recirculation grille, Wednesday explored her third and final cartridge by touch. It wasn't like the two riot foam grenades, and this was a headache: there was someone down there, and she looked vaguely familiar. It was hard to tell through the grille—

Fuckmonsters! Family killers. She remembered Jerm taunting her, Dad looking worried – he did a lot of that – Indica stern and slightly withdrawn from reality, her distant willowy mother. Love and rage, sorrow and a sense of loss. She looked down through the grille, saw the woman sitting back to back in the nearer horseshoe. *They're ReMastered.* She'd heard quite enough about them from Frank to know what they were about. Portia and her mocking grin. Wednesday's teeth ground with hatred, hot tears of rage prickling at the sides of her eyes. *Oh, you're going to regret this!*

She risked a peek of light from her rings, illuminating the scored casing on this cartridge. The activation button had a dial setting with numbers on it, and there was no half-open end. *Is it a banger?* she wondered. It seemed unlikely, on the face of it – grenades on a space station were a crazy idea – but you couldn't rule anything out. So she dialed her jacket to shrink-fit, pulled the hood over her face, and sealed it to the leggings she wore under her trousers. *E-mail:* Herman, what the fuck is this? *Attach image: Send.* Her fingers were trembling with cold. *Come on, reply . . .*

BING. This is a type-20 impact-fused grenade. Stun radius: five meters. Lethal radius: two meters. EMP minimized, tissue ablation maximized. *Attachment: operations manual.* What are you doing with it?

E-mail: Herman, I'm going to make them pay for Mom, Dad, and Jerm. *Send.*

The woman looked up at her, and Wednesday froze. 'You'd better come down right now,' Steffi called up to her. The gun muzzle was a black emptiness, pointing right at her face. 'No messing.'

'Shit,' Wednesday mumbled under her breath. Louder, 'That you, Steffi?'

'Fuck. Hello, wunderkind.' The gun muzzle didn't move. 'I said come down here right now. That's an order.'

'I'm coming.' Something told her that the grenade wouldn't be much use. Wednesday bunched her legs up and kicked hard, twice. The grille fell away. Wednesday lowered herself feet-first through the hole, then dropped; in the lowgee environment it seemed to take forever to reach the floor. 'What were you going to do if I didn't, shoot me?'

'Yes,' said Steffi. Her eyes were hollow: she looked as if she hadn't slept for days. And her voice was curiously flat, lacking all sign of emotion.

Wednesday shrugged uneasily and held her hands out. 'Look,' she said, 'I brought one of the keys along.'

'A key.' Steffi motioned her toward the unoccupied chair. 'How useful,' she murmured. 'Do you know what it's a key to?'

'Yeah.' Wednesday grinned angrily. 'It's a key to the Moscow defense communications network.'

BING. *Mail from Herman:* Wednesday, danger, listen to Rachel.

Huh. Her eyes tracked to the console they'd been nearest. There were a number of authentication key slots in it, and it was much more primitive-looking, even crude, than the others. 'I think that's it.'

'Good guess.' Steffi kept the gun on her. 'Put your key in the slot.'

'Huh?'

'I said, put your key in the slot. Or I'll do it for you, over your dead body.'

'Okay, okay, no need to get nasty.' Wednesday leaned sideways and clicked the key she'd swiped from Hoechst's desk into the slot. She shivered. ' 'Scuse me,' she said, and zipped her jacket up, then tugged the gloves over her hands. 'Cold in here, isn't it?'

'What do you think the code keys do?' Steffi asked mildly.

'Huh? They tell the bombers to commit to an attack or to cancel it, of course.' Wednesday shook her head. 'We've just been through all this. The head ReMastered woman—' She stopped, fright and revulsion working on her together.

'Carry on,' said Steffi. She sounded tired, and Wednesday stared at her, seeing for the first time the nasty smear of goop all over her left arm.

'They've been lying,' Wednesday said flatly. 'That's what this is all about. The R-bombs aren't all heading for New Dresden, some are heading for a ReMastered world. The ReMastered who took the ship were trying to stop that.'

'How interesting.' A flicker of pain crossed Steffi's face as she turned her left hand over and opened it to reveal two keys. 'Take these and insert them into slots four and eight on the same console.'

'What?' Wednesday stared at them in disbelief.

'Do it!' snapped Steffi. The gun barrel twitched at her impatiently.

'I'm doing it.' Wednesday stood up and leaned over Steffi carefully, taking the first key, moving slowly so as not to alarm her. She slid it into one of the slots Steffi had named. A diode lit up next to it, and suddenly the screen board below the keys flickered on. 'Holy shit!'

'You can say that again.' A ghost of a smile flickered around Steffi's lips. 'Do you like the ReMastered, Wednesday?'

'Fuck!' She turned her head away and spat at the ice-cold deck. 'You know better than that.'

BING. *Mail from Rachel:* Wednesday, what's going on?

'Well and good. Now do the same with the second key.'

'Okay.' Wednesday took the key and slid it into the remaining empty slot, her heart pounding with tension.

She stared at it for a moment that dragged on. *This is it,* she thought. Suddenly possibilities seemed to open up around her, endless vistas of the possible. Horizons of power. She'd been powerless for so long it seemed almost like the natural state of existence. She turned round and glanced at Steffi, old and tired. The gun didn't seem too significant anymore. 'Would you like to tell me what you're planning?' she asked.

'What do you think?' Steffi asked. 'They killed Sven, kid. Sven was my partner.' A flicker of fury crossed her face. 'I'm not going to let them get away with that. Undocked the ship, to stop them escaping. Shot my way past the guards. Now they've got to come to me.' She looked at the console, and her gaze lingered on the keys and their glowing authentication lights. 'So sit down and shut up.'

Wednesday sat, staring at Steffi. The gun didn't move away from her. Doubts began to gnaw at the edges of her certainty. *What does she want?* Wednesday wondered. *Three keys, that's enough to send an irrevocable go code, isn't it?*

'What are you going to do?' asked Wednesday.

'What does it look like?' Steffi put her gun down carefully on the desk beside her, next to something boxy. She picked it up.

'I don't know,' Wednesday said cautiously. 'What do you want?'

'Revenge. An audience.' Steffi's cheek twitched. 'Something puerile like that.'

Wednesday shook her head. 'I don't understand.'

'Well, you can answer a question.' Steffi held the box close to her and Wednesday saw that it was some kind of pocket data tablet, its surface glowing with virtual buttons. 'How did you get here? Did *they* send you? Did she think giving me an extra key was a good idea?'

'I don't understand what you mean.' Wednesday stared at her. 'I ran away from them. The boss woman, Hurst or whatever she's called – she had me and Frank and the diplomats in the station mayor's office when something happened. She sent half her guards off to look for you and I, I—' She realized she was breathing too fast, but she couldn't stop. There were flashing lights at the corners of her vision. BING. *Mail from* – Wednesday killed her message interface. 'She forced me to give her the papers. But it was in the police station, and last time I was there I ransacked the arms locker, so I grabbed a riot bomb and when she told me to give her the papers I grabbed the key and dropped a foam ball in front of her.' She finished in a breathless gabble, watching Steffi's face.

'Oh, very good!' Steffi grinned humorlessly. 'So you just happened to be running down here with a key to the defense network?'

'Yes,' Wednesday said simply.

'And one of those bombers is running on one of *their* worlds.' Steffi shook her head. 'Idiots!' she murmured. There was a musical chime from the console next to her. 'Ah, about time.' She raised her voice as she tapped a button. 'Yes, who am I speaking to?'

'It's Rachel,' said Wednesday.

'Steffi, is that you?' Rachel said simultaneously over the conference circuit.

'Yes, it's me.' Steffi closed her eyes but kept her hand on the gadget.

'You got rid of the ship, didn't you? Why did you do that?'

'Oh, it won't go far. *They* were planning on using it: undocking was the easiest way to stop them. As it is, you've got bandwidth here – you can call for help and someone will come and pick you up. And the other passengers.'

'She has keys,' Wednesday called, motivated by an impulse halfway between guilt and malice. 'They're in the console now.'

'You little—' Steffi stopped, glared at her. 'Yes, I've got three keys,' she told the speakerphone. 'They're all locked and loaded into the TALIGENT terminal.' She relaxed slightly. 'Are you listening?'

'Yes,' Rachel said tensely.

'Good. Just so we understand each other.'

'How's Wednesday?' asked Rachel.

Steffi nodded to her. 'I'm fine,' she called. 'Just a bit, uh, confused. Are you calling on behalf of the corpsefucker?'

Rachel sounded weary. 'She's dead, Wednesday. You can't breathe riot foam. You let her have it right in the face.' For an instant Wednesday felt nothing but exultation. Then a moment later she wondered: *What's happening to me?*

'That's very good,' Steffi said approvingly.

'She had it coming,' Wednesday mumbled.

'Yes, I daresay she did,' Rachel replied – clearly the open mike was very sensitive. 'That's why I'm calling. It looks like we won. The ReMastered can't get to the ship, Hoechst is dead, half of them are missing, the rest are doing what U. Franz tells them – and he wants to defect. You've got the keys, *Frank* is right now filing an exclusive report that blows the lid off their operations in Moscow and New Dresden, and it's all over.' She paused for a moment. 'So why have you locked yourselves in?'

Wednesday glanced at Steffi in surprise.

'Because you're going to do exactly what I tell you to do,' Steffi said, her tone deceptively casual. Her face was wan, but she hung on to the box in her right hand. 'I've got perimeter surveillance systems on all surfaces in here. The TALIGENT terminal is armed and on the same subnet as this tablet. Wednesday can tell you I'm not bluffing.' She swallowed. 'Fun things you can do with a tablet.' Her hand tightened on it. 'If I take my thumb *off* this screen, it'll send a message to the terminal. I think you can guess what it will say.'

Wednesday stared at her. 'It sends an irrevocable go code? How did you figure out how to do that?'

Steffi sighed. 'How did I get the keys in the first place?' She shook her head. 'You shouldn't have gone to that embassy reception, kid. You could have been hurt.'

Rachel cleared her throat. 'Hoechst was certain Svengali was the assassin. And she had his paymaster's records.'

'What made you think Sven worked alone?' Steffi winked at Wednesday, a horribly knowing look that made her try to burrow into her chair to avoid it. She felt unclean.

'You set off that bomb—'

'No, that was someone else,' Steffi said thoughtfully. 'One of Hoechst's little surprises. I think she was trying to kill me. I just nailed a couple of others in the comfort of their own diplomatic residences. And relieved them of certain items from their personal safes, by way of insurance.' She held up the tablet: 'Which brings me to the subject at hand.' She looked at Wednesday. 'Can either of you give me a good reason *not* to transmit the irrevocable go code?'

Wednesday licked her lips. 'They killed my parents and brother. They destroyed my home, in case you hadn't noticed. They did – *things* – to Frank. And you want me to tell you not to kill 'em all?'

Steffi looked amused. 'Out of the mouths of babes,' she called in the direction of the mike. 'What's your offer, Rachel?'

'Let me get back to you in a minute.' Rachel sounded very tense. 'You're not helping, Wednesday: remember, only one of the R-bombs is heading for a ReMastered world. The rest are still running on New Dresden. Think about that before you open your mouth again.'

'I'll give you five minutes to talk to your boss,' said Steffi. 'You might consider my pecuniary motives while you're at it.' Then she flicked a switch on the console next to her and raised an eyebrow at Wednesday. 'Do you *really* want me to kill everyone on two planets?' she asked.

'I'm not sure.' Wednesday looked out of the picture window pensively. A huge whorl of violet-red gas, spokes of blue running radially through it, drifted across a black velvet backdrop iced with the unblinking pinpricks of a million stars. *Frank is alive,* she thought. *Hoechst is dead, though. Will they prosecute me? I could claim self-defense against hijackers.* The celestial smoke ring swung slowly past outside, a brilliant graveyard marker that would last a million years or more. *And* Frank *hates them, too.* But then she thought about New Dresden and the people she'd passed through like a ghost that had outlived the destruction of her planet. Jostling kids in a perfectly ordinary city. Blue skies and tall buildings. 'I think I'm too insignificant to make that kind of decision,' she said slowly. 'I don't know who could.' She shivered as a thought struck her. 'I'm glad the murderer's dead. But to blame everyone behind them, their whole civilization . . .'

She stopped as she saw a shadow of a frown cross Steffi's face, and forced herself to shrug, miming disinterest. Suddenly her heart was pounding and her palms sweating. She slowly stood up and, when Steffi said nothing, walked toward one side of the window. As she did so, she waited for the solar nebula to vanish from the view, leaving nothing but a scattering of stars across the blackness. Then she twisted a control tab in one jacket pocket. It stiffened around her, waistband tightening and sealing against her pressure leggings under the lacy trousers. *Black against a black background,* she thought, taking deep breaths. She ran a hand through her hair and surreptitiously popped the seal that held her hood closed inside the collar of her jacket. Then she turned to face Steffi. 'What do you want?' she asked as casually as she could manage.

Steffi chuckled, a deeply ugly sound. 'I *want* about, oh, 50 million in bearer bonds, a yacht with independent jump capability, and some hostages to see me out of the immediate vicinity – oh, and that bitch's head on a trophy plaque. Along with the guy who killed Sven. *He* won't be coming back. What the hell did you think, kid? We were in this for the good of our souls?' She sat up. 'You still listening in, Rachel?'

Martin replied. 'She's trying to find someone to talk to on Earth,' he said diffidently. 'They've got to authenticate her before she can tell them what the situation is—'

'Bullshit!' Steffi snorted. 'I'll give you one hour, no more. At the end of an hour, if you aren't making the right noises, you can kiss Dresden and Newpeace goodbye. If the answer's yes, I'll tell you who to deposit the bonds with and we can discuss the next step, namely transport. The TALIGENT terminal stays with me – it's a causal channel, you know it'll decohere at the first jump, but until then you'll know where I am.' She looked thoughtful. 'As a first step, though, you can bring me Hoechst's head, and the head of the scumbag who killed Sven. *Not* attached to their bodies. I know that doesn't sound like your idea of fun, but I want to be sure they're dead.'

Wednesday stared at her in disgust. *Is this what it comes down to?* she wondered. *Is this what you get if you stop worrying you might be a monster?* She glanced behind her at the window, nervously. *I thought I knew you.* Then over at the side of the room. *Comms, reactivate,* she told her implant.

BING. Wednesday, please respond? It was Rachel.

I'm listening. Who *is* Steffi, really?

The reply took a few seconds to come. Wednesday leaned

against the wall beside the window, experimenting with the fabric texturing controls at the back of her jacket, seeing just how sticky she could make it go without losing its structural integrity. There was some setting called 'gecko's feet' that seemed pretty strong . . .

Near as I can tell, she's an alias for Miranda Katachurian. Citizen, Novy Kurdistan, last seen eleven years ago with a criminal record as long as your arm. Wanted for questioning in connection with armed robbery charges, then vanished.

'Steffi,' Wednesday asked hesitantly, 'what did you do it for?'

BING. Wednesday? Are you all right? Do you need help? Frank.

'For?' Steffi looked puzzled for a moment. Then her expression cleared. 'We did it for the money, kid.'

LBR: LUV U, she replied to Frank, then glanced at Rachel's last message as she answered Steffi.

'And you're, uh, going to send the irrevocable go code to the R-bombers if you don't get what you want?'

Steffi grinned. 'You're learning.' Wednesday nodded, hastily composing a final reply.

'And doesn't it strike you that there's something *wrong* about that?'

'Why should it?' Steffi stared at her. 'The universe doesn't owe me a living, and you can't eat ideals, kid. It's time you grew up and got over your history.'

Case closed, sent Wednesday. 'I guess you're right,' she said, leaning back against the wall as hard as she could and dialing the stickiness up to max. Then she brought up her right hand and threw underhand at Steffi. 'Here, catch!' With her left hand she yanked hard on her collar, pulling the hood up and over her head and triggering the jacket's blowout reflex. Then she waited to die.

The noise was so loud that it felt like a punch in the

stomach and a slap on the ears, leaving her head ringing. A fraction of a second later there was a second noise, a gigantic *whoosh,* like a dinosaur sneezing. Leviathan tried to tear her from the wall with his tentacles; she could feel her arms and legs flailing in the tornado gale. Something hit her so hard she tried to scream, sending a white-hot nail of pain up her right ankle. Her ears hurt with a deep dull ache that made her want to stick knife blades into them to scratch out the source of the pain. Then the noise began to die away as the station's pressure baffles slammed shut around the rupture, her helmet seal secured itself and inflated in a blast of canned air from the jacket vesicles, and her vision began to clear.

Wednesday gasped and tried to move, then remembered to unglue the back of her jacket. The room was a mess. There was no sign of Steffi, or the two chairs at the console, or half the racks that had cluttered the place up. An explosion of snow: they'd kept essential manuals on hard copy, and the blast and subsequent decompression had shredded and strewn the bound papers everywhere. But the window—

Wednesday looked out past shattered glass knives, out at a gulf of 40 trillion kilometers of memories and cold. Eyelids of unblinking red and green stared back at her from around an iron pupil, the graveyard of a shattered star. With an effort of will she tore her gaze away and walked carefully across the wreckage until she found the TALIGENT terminal, lying on its side, still held to the deck by a rat's nest of cables. She bent over and carefully pulled the keys out. Then she walked over to the window and deliberately threw one of them out into the abyss. The others she pocketed – after all, the diplomats from Earth would be needing them.

As the last key disappeared, a mail window from Rachel

popped up. Urgent! Wednesday, please respond! Are you hurt? Do you need help?

Wednesday ignored it and went in search of the emergency airlock kit instead. She didn't have time to answer mail: it would probably take her most of her remaining oxygen supply to get the airlock set up so she could safely reenter the land of the living beyond the pressure bulkhead. She had to prioritize, just like Herman had shown her all those years ago, alone in the cold darkness beyond the stars.

Her friends would be waiting for her on the other side of the wall: Martin who'd helped her to hide, and Rachel who'd shown her what to do without knowing it, and Frank, who meant more to her than she was sure was sensible. They would still be there when she'd worked out what she meant to do. And they'd be there to help her when she said goodbye to home for the final time and turned her back on the iron sunrise.

epilogue: home front

Home. It was getting to be a strange place, as alien as a hotel room on a distant planet. Rachel walked into the hall and dropped her shoulder bag, blinking tiredly: it was still three in the morning by the shipboard time of the *Gloriana* even though it was two in the afternoon there in Geneva, and the cumulative effects of switching from the hundred-kilosecond diplomatic clock back to a terrestrial time zone was going to give her bad jet lag.

Behind her, Martin yawned hugely. 'How's it look?' he asked.

'It's all there.' She ran a finger along the sideboard tiredly. Something buzzed in the next room, a household dust precipitator in need of a new filter or a robot scavenger with a damaged knee. 'Place hasn't burned down while we've been away.' She stared with distaste at the bulletin board on the wall, flashing red with notices of overdue bills. 'Really got to get a proper housing agent who understands three-month trips at short notice. Last time I was away this long they sent the polis round to break down the door in case I'd died or something.'

'You're not dead.' Martin yawned again and let the front door swing shut. 'I'm not dead. I just feel that way . . .'

Three months away from home had built up an enormous backlog of maintenance tasks, and Rachel couldn't face them just then. 'Listen. I'm going to have a shower, then go to bed,' she said. 'You want to stay up and order some food in, be my guest. Or check the bills. But it can wait until tomorrow. Right?'

'You have a point.' Martin shrugged and leaned the big suitcase against the wall next to a hideously ugly wooden statue of the prophet Yusuf Smith that Rachel had picked up in a casbah somewhere in Morocco a few years earlier. 'I was going to message Wednesday, see how she and Frank are doing, but – bed first.'

'Yeah.' Rachel stumbled up the steps to the mezzanine, dropping her sandals and clothes as she went, and gratefully registered that the house automatics had changed the sheets and freshened the comforter. 'Home sweet home, safe at last.' After weeks of tension and the paranoid days at the mercy of the ReMastered, it seemed almost too good to be true.

She returned to consciousness slowly, half-aware of a pounding headache and a nauseated stomach, in conjunction with sore leg muscles and crumpled bedding and a thick, warm sense of exhaustion that pervaded her body as if she'd been drugged. *Someday they'll develop a drug for jet lag that really works,* she thought fuzzily before another thought intruded. Where was Martin?

'Ow!' she moaned, opening her eyes.

Martin was sitting up in bed watching her, concerned. 'You awake? I've been checking the mail, and we've got a problem.'

'Shit!' Rachel came to full consciousness in an instant, exhausted but painfully aware that she'd screwed up. 'What is it?'

'Something about a meeting you're meant to be in later today. Like, in an hour's time. I nearly missed it – it's directed to the household, flagged as low priority. What could it be?'

'Shit! It's a stitch-up. Who is it?'

Martin blinked at the screen on the wardrobe door. 'Something to do with the Entertainments and Culture Pecuniary Oversight Committee?' he asked, looking puzzled.

'Double shit!' A horrible sense of *déjà vu* gripped her as she tried to sit up. 'What time is it?'

'It's two in the afternoon.' Martin yawned. 'Let me forward it to you.'

Rachel read fast. 'Departmental audit,' she said tersely. 'I'm going to have to get into headquarters, in a hurry.'

Martin blinked. 'I thought you'd taken care of that nonsense.'

'Me? I've been away. Thought you might have noticed.' She frowned. 'Leaving the fox in charge of the henhouse, it would seem. I wonder if my sources have found anything out about her . . .'

Bleary-eyed and tired, she spawned a couple of search agents to filter her mail – both the public accounts and a couple of carefully anonymized private ones.

'Looks like the asshole in Ents is acting up. Since I missed some kind of audit investigation six weeks ago, she managed to file a default reprimand against me. She's gotten wind I'm back in town and is moving to file criminal malfeasance charges, embezzling or misuse of funds, or something equally spurious. She's running a board of inquiry right now. If I don't get there—'

'I'll call you a pod.' Martin was already out of bed. 'Any idea what she's got against you?'

'I don't know—' Rachel froze. The search had stopped, highlighting something new and alarming. 'Oops! Head office are pissed.'

'Head office?'

'Black Chamber, not Entertainments and Culture. They don't want her digging.' Rachel began to smile. '"Stop her," they say. They don't say how.'

'Take care,' said Martin, a flicker of concern on his face. 'You don't want to overreact.'

'Overreact?' She raised an eyebrow. 'The bitch tried to get me slung out on my ass, she tried to obstruct a UXB operation, and she's trying to file criminal charges against me, and I'm overreacting?' She paused over the arms locker at the back of the closet. 'No, *that* would be overreacting. Don't want to get blood in the carpet.'

He stared at her. 'Did I just hear what I think I heard? You're going to take her down?'

'Yeah. Although I don't think I'll need to use violence. That would be unsubtle, and I swore off unsubtle, oh, about thirty seconds ago.' Rachel peeled a transdermal patch onto the inside of her left elbow. Her gaze turned to the open case by the bedroom door, full of items she'd acquired over the course of the cruise on the *Romanov*. Gradually she began to smile. 'I've got to make a couple of calls. This should be fun . . .'

The UN headquarters campus hadn't changed visibly in Rachel's absence – the same neoclassical glass-and-steel sky-scraper, looming over old Geneva's stone arteries and quaint domes, the same big statues of founders Otto von Bismarck and Tim Berners-Lee sitting out front in the plaza. Rachel headed into the lobby, looking around tensely. There was a civil cop standing by the ornate reception throne, talking to the human greeter there. Rachel nodded in their direction then moved on toward the antique elevator bank, feeling reassured. *I wonder how George is doing?* she asked herself as the doors slid open. *Handling the aftermath of the New Moscow cleanup. Big headache, that.*

The dossier on Madam Chairman that had been sitting in her mailbox – as per her back-channel requests, pulling in favors while she was away – was rather interesting, albeit increasingly worrying when she thought about the implications. Rising star, come out of nowhere, promoted rapidly, rivals recanting or resigning in disgrace or meeting with disaster: it was all a bit carnivorous for the normally laid-back UN, and to have a desk monster like that aiming squarely at her raised all sorts of nasty questions. Especially when you started asking where she'd gotten the money to buy that big house on the lakeshore . . .

The dossier wasn't the only thing Rachel found in her inbox when she ran a search. Formal notice of a disciplinary tribunal, filed that morning with a hearing scheduled for early afternoon, was not exactly the sort of thing she expected to find mixed in with the bills – not when it could have been sent direct to her phone and flagged as a priority item. She paused outside the committee room, composing her face in a careful smile, then opened the door.

'—Has shown no sign of compliance with the designated administrative orders in spite of disciplinary notices delivered four months, three months, and most recently two days ago—' The speaker paused. 'Yes?'

Rachel smiled. 'Hello, Gilda.' Madam Chairwoman sat up straight and stared at her. Two yes-men to either side, and a secretary-recorder, and some gray-faced executive from accounts who'd been invited to witness all followed suit. 'Sorry I'm late, but if you wanted to get my attention, you really ought to have mailed me direct rather than disguising the summons as a laundry bill.'

'Hello, *Rachel*.' Madam Chairman smiled coldly. 'We were just discussing your negligent attitude to departmental procedures. So good of you to furnish us with a further example.'

'Really?' Rachel shut the door carefully, then turned back to face the room.

'You're Mansour, eh?' began the accountant. 'We've been hearing about you for weeks.' He tapped his tablet portentously. 'Nothing good. What have you got to say?'

'Me? Oh, not much.' Rachel grinned. 'But *she's* got a lot of explaining to do.'

'I don't think so.' Madam Chairman was tight-lipped with irritation. 'We were just discussing your suspension pending a full investigation of your accounting irregularities—'

Rachel opened her hand. 'Accounting irregularities cut both ways,' she said casually.

'I—' Madam Chairman stopped dead. 'Is this some sort of joke?' she demanded.

Rachel shook her head. 'No joke,' she said easily. She glanced at the yesmen. 'You really don't want to get involved in this. It's going to be messy.'

'I'm not sure I understand.' Gray-face glanced between her and Madam Chairman. 'What are you talking about?'

Rachel pointed a finger at him and polled her phone. 'Ah, Dr. Pullman. My apologies. I take it she didn't tell you who I work for?'

'Who you—' Gray-face, Pullman, looked confused for a moment. 'What do you mean?'

'I'm Black Chamber. On the books via Ents purely for diplomatic cover and petty cash, which raises the question of why Gilda here thinks it's her job to go sniffing around my work assignments as if she's responsible for them.'

'Ah.' Pullman nodded thoughtfully. *Good poker face,* Rachel thought. Then he crossed his arms defensively. 'That's interesting.'

The yes-men were beginning to shuffle uneasily. 'Look, I really don't think this is germane to the matter of your time-keeping,' one of them began.

'Oh, but it is,' Rachel said smoothly. She pointed at Madam Chairman. 'Because you're not supposed to be digging into Black Chamber discretionary funding arrangements. I'm afraid I'm going to have to have you arrested.'

'What?' Madam Chairman looked tense. 'You can't do that! You aren't attached to any recognized security service!'

'Oh, but I am.' Rachel's smile widened. She raised one hand and checked her phone. 'By the way, do you know something? You shouldn't have tried digging so obviously. That wasn't very clever, Gilda. It made people question your bona fides. You're not the only person who can pick holes in an expense account, and I'm sure your colleagues will be very interested to know where you got the money to buy that big dacha outside Sevastopol. It's funny where the trail leads. Not that there's any expectation of exclusivity of service in your employment contract, Gilda, but we really don't expect you to be diverting contingency funds intended for the Black Chamber into your own pocket.'

'What *is* this nonsense?' Gilda demanded. She lurched to her feet, clearly upset. 'You're trying to distract attention from your own misdeeds! This is transparent blackmail—'

Rachel twisted one of her rings. The door behind her opened, and the cop from the lobby came in. 'That's her,' Rachel said, pointing at Madam Chairman. 'She's all yours.'

'You can't!' Gilda backed toward the window. 'You've got no grounds!'

'Yes I have.' The cop flipped her visor up and stared at her tiredly. 'Ye'll be Gilda Morgenstern? I'm Inspector Rosa MacDougal. On February 4 of this year you was in a meeting with Rachel Mansour, here. You tried to stop her leaving, didn't you? Aye, that wisnae so canny, was it? Her on her way to a UXB call-out an' all, did it not occur to ye that it's a statutory offense to obstruct a bomb disposal officer in the course of her duties? Or d'ye deny it was you what did that?'

Yes-man number two was looking at his boss in veiled horror. 'Gilda, was it really—

'Take her in and book her,' said Rachel, shaking her head. 'I'll deal with the other stuff later.' She looked at the auditor, Pullman. 'You don't want to get involved in this.'

'Bitch!' Madam Chairman walked around the conference table, all rustling silk and hissing vitriol. 'I had you—'

'Now stop right there,' Inspector MacDougal warned.

Rachel glanced at the inspector, barely registering the angry bureaucrat raising a hand, the protests from the yes-man to her left, as she blinked at an unexpected thought. *Lining her pockets diverting Black Chamber funds, gathering intel about our field activities, big dacha near Sevastopol, works in Ents and Culture—* Something wasn't right here, and there was more to it than simple embezzlement.

She tensed as Madam Chairman pointed a shaking finger at her. 'Fraud!' she snapped. 'I know your kind! Leeching funds from the diplomatic corps to prop up your corrupt schemes, then claiming you're a defender of the public interest. You're just another blood-sucking pawn of the Eschaton! And I can prove—'

Oh shit, Rachel thought, and she went *quick*, reached out through air like molasses to grab Rosa's shoulder and tug her sharply away from the bureaucrat, vision graying at the edges as her implants kicked in. I *know where I've heard that line before, and recently—*

'Hey!' Inspector MacDougal protested as she stumbled backward. On the other side of the table Pullman was beginning to rise, a startled expression on his face as Gilda, her face contorted with rage, raised her other hand, an iridescent metallic bulb protruding between her fingers. She lunged toward Rachel, holding the device at arm's length.

Off-balance, Rachel tried to turn away, but even with boosted reflexes there was a limit to what she could achieve without leverage. She scrabbled for the table edge on her way down toward the floor, feet unable to gain traction as she watched Madam Chairman, Gilda, a bureaucrat possessed, thrust the ReMastered implement toward her.

The first shot surprised Rachel almost as much as her attacker. Gilda jerked backward, eyes widening in confusion as a spray of red erupted behind her. Another shot, and Rachel hit the floor, rebounded in time to see MacDougal's sidearm pointed at the woman. *This is so bad*, Rachel realized with a gut-deep stab of horror as time snapped back into focus, and she thumped painfully against the table legs. *If they're here . . .*

'Oh dear,' said Pullman, his face ashen. 'Was that really necessary?'

'Yes,' MacDougal huffed emphatically. She lowered her gun. 'You. There's a monitor on this room, isn't there? I'm taking the log. I want it forwarded to LJ control immediately under seal of evidence.' She glanced down at her gun's muzzle recorder, breathing deeply. 'Along with the take from this thing.'

'You killed her!' Minion Number One sat bolt upright, an expression of horror stealing over him. 'She won't be able to—' He stopped.

'Upload them all, the unborn god will know its own,' Rachel said grimly, pulling herself to her feet. 'Did you ever hear her say that?'

'No—' Minion Number One was staring at Minion Number Two, who hadn't moved since Gilda stood up. A fine thread of drool descended from the side of the man's mouth. 'What's wrong? What have you done to Alex?'

'Aye, what's going on?' Rosa demanded. 'What *is* that thing?' She gestured at the neural spike, which had rolled half under the table. Rachel glanced at it, then looked at the inspector. The cop was putting a good face on things, but her hands were shaky and her posture tense.

'Some of the shit I work with followed me home.' She laced her fingers together and began dialing her rings hastily. She frowned at Rosa, then glanced around the other committee members. 'We're all in this together. Let's just hope that she was an isolated case.'

'An isolated case of *what*?' asked MacDougal.

'You'll want to check her genetic profile against a murder, Maureen Davis, diplomatic corps, about six months ago.' Rachel realized she was breathing heavily. 'Also anyone who's visited her house in the past year. Colleagues, friends, whoever. Her type uses proxies.'

'And what type would those be?' Rosa stared at her through narrowed eyes.

'ReMastered.' Rachel twisted her rings. 'George? Okay, message.' She waited for the voice mail intro to finish. 'I have a suspect in the murder of Maureen Davis, Muscovite embassy.' She paused. 'They're here. A cell. Infiltrating us.' A frown wrinkled her forehead. 'Probably the rogue faction, but I'm not sure.' She glanced at MacDougal. 'Can you find out if she ever attended a function with a woman name of Steffi Grace, aka Miranda Katachurian? In the past year or so?'

'You're saying this is related to a murder case?' asked MacDougal, as the door opened for Building Security, and a buzzing swarm of concern erupted into the room.

'More than one,' Rachel said grimly. 'And they're still happening.' *What's going to become of us?* she wondered dully and, just for a moment, longed for the clear-cut certainties of a madman with a home brew nuclear device. But something told her that this one wouldn't go away at the sting of a police wasp: indeed, it was only just beginning.

And outside the office – still hundreds of light years away – the Iron Sunrise continued to expand in its silent and deadly splendor, bearing down upon an Earth shrouded in comforting darkness.

ACCELERANDO

Charles Stross

The year is some time between 2010 and 2015. The recession has ended, but populations are ageing and the rate of tech change is accelerating dizzyingly. Manfred makes his living from spreading ideas around, putting people in touch with one another and leaving a spray of technologies in his wake.

Although he lives at the cutting edge of intelligence amplification technology, even Manfred can take on too much. And when his pet robot cat picks up some interesting information from the SETI data, his world – and the world of his descendants – is turned on its head.

Charles Stross's most ambitious novel to date, *Accelerando* is a multi-generational saga following a brilliant clan of 21st-century posthumans.

NEWTON'S WAKE

Ken MacLeod

The Hard Rapture took Earth's best minds away. Now the rest are about to find out where they went . . .

Centuries ago, space settlers and soldiers fled to the stars from the sentient AI war machines that engulfed Earth. They colonised Eurydice, a planet whose rocks contain traces of its own war machines — some of which still guard a vast, enigmatic artefact on a remote tundra.

When an expedition raids this strange artefact, the Eurydiceans discover that they weren't the last survivors of humanity after all. Their leisured lifestyle is about to be disrupted by new arrivals for whom Eurydice is a prize worth fighting over.

And the long-dormant war machines are awakening . . .

THE RISEN EMPIRE

Scott Westerfeld

The undead Emperor has ruled the Eighty Worlds for sixteen hundred years. His is the power to grant immortality to those he deems worthy, creating an elite class known as the Risen. Along with his sister, the eternally young Child Empress, his power within the empire has been absolute. Until now.

The empire's great enemies, the Rix, hold the Child Empress hostage. Charged with her rescue is Captain Laurent Zai. But when Imperial politics are involved the stakes are unimaginably high, and Zai may yet find the Rix the least of his problems. On the homeworld, Zai's lover, Senator Nara Oxham, must prosecute the war against the Rix while holding the inhuman impulses of the Risen councillors in check. If she fails at either task, millions will die.

And at the centre of everything is the Emperor's great lie: a revelation so shattering that he is willing to sanction the death of entire worlds to keep it secret . . .

THE SUNBORN

Gregory Benford

The first manned mission to Mars has been a resounding success, and excitement grows as more new discoveries are made. However, one phenomenon continues to defy rational explanation – the 'marsmat' – a complex anaerobic life-form found in the planet's honeycomb of tunnels.

This raises questions about the nature and meaning of life itself which will lead the curious and the driven to Pluto and beyond, to the cold void at the fringes of the solar system.